# Death's Arbiter

## The Afterlife of Kye Dodson, Book One

Stone Keye

Dragon Tech Media

Dragon Tech Media
Saint Gabriel, LA

Cover Design by Logan Keys
ISBN: 978-1-7348585-1-8
First Edition: July 2021

# DEDICATION

I want to thank my critique group for the honest feedback, the support, and laughter they have given while writing this book. Thank you Lisa, Galand, Vicki, Ryann, Skip, and Mike!

To my parents, who always supported me. I'm sure they are reading my work in Heaven.

## OTHER BOOKS BY STONE KEYE

The Modern Warlock, The Lion and the Hidden Master, Book One
The Modern Warlock, New Friends and Hidden Spies, Book Two
The Modern Warlock, The Dragon and The Lost King, Book Three

Looking for more information? Visit www.StoneKeyeBooks.net to get the latest information on of my books.

# Chapter One

I frowned as I reviewed Lester's text message: *Please meet me at my office, 12th floor of the La Tille building. 9 am if you can get your ass up that early.* For him to reach out to me was unusual.

Lester doesn't approve of my methods or me, as a matter of fact. He's a very by-the-book kind of guy, while I have no problem crossing the line occasionally. For the record, I cross the line to make sure justice is served. It just doesn't help my argument when I also benefit from doing so.

I figure if I am going to break a few rules in the name of justice, I should get something in return.

I tried calling Lester's cell, but he didn't answer, which wasn't a good sign. I really don't feel like getting involved with anything Lester's working on, but I'm not in the best graces with my boss, and hopefully, this will make him happy.

I entered the elevator and hit twelve. Two suits entered after me and hit fifteen.

"Hey, don't you work for Global Arbitration?" one asked, eyeing my floor selection. His suit screamed corporate desk jockey, and he probably was looking for his next career move.

I hate these interactions but have been advised to be more 'congenial.' I hoped my boss was watching. I needed the brownie points.

During my fiftieth annual job review, my boss clearly was not happy with me. "Your latest interactions with mortals came off like an assassin scoping his next kill. You need to work at communicating in a way that isn't seen as menacing or at least not like a sociopath."

1

He was right, of course. I like to pretend it was because I am the proverbial badass. Considering the number of celestials and other things I have killed, it wouldn't be a stretch to think so. The truth is that every kill was in self-defense, and their deaths still give me nightmares.

The real reason I can't deal with mortals is that I've been doing this job for so long, I have almost forgotten what it was like to be mortal. Spending time with reapers, demons, angels, and all sorts of beings changes you. Not in a good way.

I pulled my thoughts back to the corporate suits. "Yes, but not at this office. Just visiting today." I hoped that would put an end to the conversation. I flashed a smile to try and seal the deal. Unfortunately, it only invited more discussion. I gotta come up with some better lines.

"What do you guys do? I looked you up but not much of a presence on the web," the other asked.

"Oh, you know, the usual. We arbitrate souls, human lives, money, power, and stuff like that." I added a smirk to make it sound funny. I smiled. My response is pretty good, and I stored it away for future use.

The two suits laughed. "Yeah, I know what you mean. Don't we all," the first one replied.

I eyed him for a moment, but it must have been too long because the man's face turned pale. I tried to break the tension by adding a laugh. It sounded a bit maniacal, and the other suit lost his smile. Luckily, our fun chat was interrupted when the elevator stopped on my floor.

Knowing the type that Lester hires, I expected to be greeted by an overly efficient receptionist when the doors open. Instead, I walked into an empty reception area. In my line of work, this was never a good sign.

The two suits peered out. "No one home. Don't you guys have any staff?"

The receptionist's desk was empty, the hallway was clear, and it was deathly quiet. I walked a small circle to scout the area. Just when I thought all was clear, I spotted a blood-soaked chair behind the desk.

Well, there went my day.

I needed to get rid of these guys before the fun started. "Staff celebration party down the hall, we all just got bonuses," I said and walked back to the elevator. "Sorry guys, security rules say you have to leave." I stood in front of the elevator until it began to close. Both guys tried to push their business cards into my hand. As the doors closed, one yelled out, "Call me!"

The smart thing to do would be to high-tail it out of there and call for backup from a safe distance. Since I'm a glutton for punishment, I pulled

Kitten out and prepared myself. Kitten's dual blades, each growing to the size of a dagger, heated up.

*It's about time I get to kill something,* Kitten purred.

*Please, just once, I would like for things to end without bloodshed,* I pleaded.

"Anyone there?" I called and received only an echo in reply. A few seconds later, an office light clicked on at the end of the hall. I shook my head. Do they really believe I was going to fall for that trick?

I gripped Kitten tight, and she's red-hot. The skin on my hand began to sizzle as her handle continued to warm, but I felt no pain. Her blades grew several inches to give me a little more protection. Kitten was ready, and she was purring. I put my sunglasses on in anticipation. These guys were acting like amateurs, and I could almost predict what would happen next.

I moved down the hall and lazily swung Kitten to warm myself up. I sensed two celestials, and I'm surprised. One is an angel, the other a demon. As a rule, demons and angels usually don't work together, but they always seem to make an exception for me.

For amateurs, they're carrying some powerful weapons. In response, Kitten's blades grew to the size of swords. I've never been a boy scout, but I do believe in being prepared.

As I neared the end of the hall, the first one stepped out from the end office and unfurled his wings. He released his divine light, hoping to blind me. Even with my specially-equipped sunglasses, I had to squint. Kitten was desperate to kill, and I let her take control.

Kitten roared at the exact moment I released my full arbiter power. The combined blast hit Heaven's angel. He took a step back, and a bit of doubt came over him—too late, sunshine.

As expected, his demon partner burst through a side door and took a swing with a massive sword. He's considerably faster than expected for a demon, and I barely blocked the attack with one of Kitten's blades, almost getting knocked over. Kitten usually cuts through most swords, and my assessment of the amateurs seems to be misguided. Kitten's anger rose as I did a quick spin. My opponent matched my move and tried to bring up his sword, overcorrecting in doing so. I used Kitten to push his blade away and then swung to chop off his head. He ducked but left himself wide open, so I cut his sword arm off at the elbow.

The demon let out a horrific scream as I grabbed the severed arm, his hand still clutched his sword, and I threw it at the angel rushing toward me. He covered the distance in a flash and realized too late what I threw. Heaven's angels hate getting blood on their wings, especially demon blood. The angel almost did a backflip to avoid the arm. But in doing so, he missed the fact that the arm was still attached to a sword. The blade then landed a nasty gash on his chest. As he looked down at his wound, it gave me a chance to use Kitten to remove his sword hand. He let out a squeal and dropped to the floor to grab his severed body part.

"Okay, guys, now that you're both unarmed..." I never got to finish my joke as the kneeling demon attempted to take my leg off with a knife. I kicked my legs out but not in time to keep him from cutting through my pants and slicing open my leg.

Damn, these guys were fast. I tried not to scream as I landed on top of him. The demon grunted as one of Kitten's blades sliced into his demonic heart.

The fight wasn't over as I rolled out of the way of a wild swing by the remaining attacker. Despite missing a hand and spraying blood everywhere, he was moving even faster. He used his remaining hand to swing the sword, with his severed hand still attached. The scene would have been comical if I hadn't been fighting for my life. I barely countered the next swing in time, then rolled to get up.

We circled the dead demon while my opponent spurted blood everywhere. I gave him a full arbiter blast to make sure he knew who he was dealing with. His wild-eyed look told me he was too far gone on something to comprehend anything other than killing me. He lunged forward but slipped in the pool of blood and fell, face first, in front of me. I rammed Kitten's blade through his heart before he could recover.

I stepped back as Kitten shrank to the size of a small pen. She purred, enjoying her kills. "You owe me now," I said. The only response I received was a slightly deeper purring.

I took several deep breaths. My leg throbbed from the cut, and all I wanted was to sit down. I needed to do something about my leg, but the floor is a literal sea of black and white angel and demon blood. I hobbled over and grabbed a chair from an office. Collapsing into it, I evaluated the cut on my leg.

"Shit!" I said to no one in particular.

It didn't look good. My leg was still bleeding, which was weird. An arbiter's body is designed to heal most injuries in seconds. It must be one badass weapon to prevent it from healing. Luckily, all arbiters were required to carry wound cream as a backup. I stifled a curse as I spread it across the cut. The raw edges of the cut began to close, but blood continued to ooze. That should not be happening.

This was bad, even for me. Cursing myself for not letting the reapers take care of this, I pulled out my phone. I hit Jeremiah's number on my not-so-favorite list. He quickly answered.

"Mr. Dodson, I am assuming this is not a social call," Jeremiah said in a slow, formal tone. He's a good guy but can be a royal ass to work with.

"An angel and a demon jumped me, and they paid the price," I replied between deep breaths. The pain in my leg flared despite the wound cream doing its thing.

"For you, that is unusual only because you don't have a current case. Please tell me you didn't go looking for trouble." Concern crept into Jeremiah's voice.

"Nope. I was supposed to meet another arbiter. Instead, I got angels from both sides of the fence teaming up to kill me."

"That is concerning, but why do I get the feeling that there is more to the story?" His voice grew strained as he fought to remain calm.

"Well, first, both were as fast as me. Second, I'm still bleeding even after applying your cream, and third," I paused for a dramatic effect. "Kitten's blades didn't cut through their weapons."

The line went quiet, and I could almost hear Jeremiah swearing up a storm. I had just told him that one of the most dangerous weapons in existence just met its match.

"Don't touch anything, including the weapons, and I will send a team. You need to come here now and report to Death."

"Wait, the rules say the weapons belong to me if..." I began.

"I know what the blooming rules say. I wrote them. You will get the weapons later. For now, get out of there."

"I would, but things just got a whole lot messier." In the office across the way, I spotted a body lying in a pool of blood. Based upon the suit, I'm pretty sure it was Lester. I gimped over to investigate further and found half of whom I assumed was his secretary, next to him. I turned the corpse over and barely recognized Lester, but what's left of his face looked like him. I checked his arm, and the tattoo he was so proud of was there.

It was him. He was worked over pretty well before he died, and his body was a bloody mess. I almost puked at the carnage. For some reason, I can see demon or angel gore all day, but the first sight of arbiter or human blood and guts, and I lose it. After a second, I got myself under control.

"I just found what's left of Lester and his secretary." This was bad. Killing an employee of Death usually led to a lot of trouble. Killing two meant a whole lot of crap was about to happen, and I'll be in the middle of it.

"Kye, get out now!" Jeremiah yelled and hung up.

I'm not a fool, well, not a complete fool, so I hobbled my way to the elevator. With a sweep of my hand, the blood disappeared from my suit, and it's now repaired. Getting in the elevator, I gave a quick thanks for finding it empty. I waved my hand to blackout the security cameras and made sure I had a direct shot to the first floor. As I exited the lobby, I sensed a large group of Death's agents, including a slew of reapers, headed my way. I climbed into my car and stomped the pedal to put as much distance between me and that place.

"Shit!" I yelled and pounded the steering wheel. Why couldn't things go easy for me for once? I should be upset about Lester's death, but I couldn't honestly say I was. He was a numbers guy: cases closed, quality of documentation, and the rest of the stuff I couldn't care less about. Ultimately, Lester's efforts cumulated in him being promoted to management. Lester had been ecstatic about outranking me and threw it in my face every chance he got.

Then Death promoted me to Special Cases, which meant I out-ranked Lester. Something Lester never got over. I could have easily thrown my newfound weight around and messed with him for eternity. I had to admit. It was tempting. Trying to be the bigger man, I ignored him and hoped he would just enjoy his work and forget about me. Instead, that ticked him off even more. He would have loved to get me demoted, but he knew to leave me alone since Death promoted me.

I stopped by my house long enough to shower and change. When meeting Death, it is always best to dress appropriately. I'm not sure why, but it is one of only a few rules I always followed.

An hour later, I pulled my car into a parking spot that didn't exist ten seconds earlier. Sometimes working for Death had its privileges.

No one noticed my arrival in front of a glaringly over-architected skyscraper. It was designed to look like a scythe that legend says Death carried. He does own one, but for show only. He likes the image, but the scythe was a human interpretation. Where it came from, only Death knows.

I hobbled past the parking cop handing out tickets. He smiled and gave a quick wave. I never get tickets, another perk of the job.

I entered the building and walked through the elaborate security system installed to detect weapons and hacking devices. While my boss occupies the top five floors, several tech companies leased the rest. My weapons wouldn't trip their systems even though they made the average assault rifle look like a cap gun.

Everyone else walked on, but I was detoured by a security guard whose head looked like a rock with spikes. Jeremiah created these things to improve security and continued to tinker with them. He initially called them "Rocks" but everyone, including the Rocks, complained. To prevent a rebellion, Jeremiah told the guards they could name themselves. After two years of fighting and killing each other over potential names, they gave up and called themselves Rocks. They still hate my boss for it.

I killed a couple of these things a long time ago when they failed to recognize that I worked for Death. I hoped they didn't remember. His grip on my arm indicated he did.

"I know you. Didn't I kill your sister?" The growl I received told me I had hit the mark. I put my hand on Kitten and waited. He wasn't going to get the chance to kill me.

Jeremiah interrupted our fun and ordered the security guard to return to his post. The guard wasn't thrilled about being dismissed like an errant child, but he knew to keep his mouth shut and his attitude in line. Jeremiah was as dangerous as they come. He wouldn't think twice about slicing an arrogant employee in half.

My new guide was dressed as if he just stepped out of a fashion magazine. He looked in great shape for someone as old as time.

"Would it hurt you to leave your weapons in your car? No one would dare harm you here or even steal anything from your car," he said as he guided me past a contingent of security guards, each giving me a nasty look.

His comment reminded me of when I first got this job. Gabriel, yes, that Gabriel, asked me, "You're employed by Death and have the backing of God and Satan. Why would you need to carry weapons?"

Two hours later, one of Gabriel's assistants tried to kill me. That was my first lesson in never trusting someone in power. I have stopped counting the number of times I have heard 'Don't worry, you're safe here,' then someone tried to kill me.

I quickly learned a few other bits of wisdom, such as Heaven's angels don't lie. They just omit essential details like killing an arbiter wasn't considered a sin. Don't get me wrong, Satan's angels lie, but that's expected from demons. By the way, Satan hates the term demons. Why? I don't know, but I don't have the guts to ask her.

Oh, yes, Satan is a woman and very good at her job. God is male, at least, that is what I have heard. His voice sounds male, but who knows. He's the ultimate trickster, so I'm careful with my assumptions about him.

"Tell that to the two that just tried to kill me," I countered. Jeremiah smirked but said nothing. "So, how is Death's right-hand man doing today?" I asked, knowing it would get a rise out of him.

Jeremiah curled his lip. "I am Mr. Wilson's head of security, not his right-hand anything, and I was fine until your call." He gave me a once-over, then smiled. "It's good to see you in one piece. But you are late and still limping."

Jeremiah reached down and grabbed my aching leg. There was a brief flash and a bolt of pain as the cut healed. He took a couple of deep breaths and glared at my leg. He had to use way too much power to fix a superficial injury. This day kept getting weirder.

"Thanks."

"Just part of the service. Please take elevator two. Mr. Wilson is concerned about your incident and will be happy to hear you are well. I will let him know you are coming."

I headed to the elevator bank and stopped. "The weapons due me?"

"Mr. Wilson has them," Jeremiah turned away, and elevator two opened.

Despite the large group waiting for an elevator, I was the only one that got in. There were no buttons to push, so I simply waited for the doors to close and the elevator to start our journey. It will take a few minutes. I don't know why it takes so long, but I have learned that when dealing with Death, it's best not to ask questions. There are quite a few angels and demons that would do anything for any information about Death.

I've been working for Death for over a hundred years. As it turns out, Death's not a bad employer. Despite the myths, he's not an angel. He's an independent deity that sits between Heaven and Hell. He used to be the one who decided who died and when. But God gave man 'Free will,' and man used it to create some pretty damn good machines of war. These days Death takes some souls, but humans handle the killing most of the time. This made his reapers' job easier, but they don't like it. Killing is the highlight of a reaper's day. Now they simply guide souls to their final destination, and they are bored as, well, Hell.

God and Satan can save someone from dying or kill a target, but they don't bother. So many souls are coming through their doors that they don't want to add to the workload.

The elevator stopped, and the doors opened. I saw no one and carefully stepped out of the elevator with my hands in plain sight. When dealing with Death, it was always best to be careful. During my last case, I broke a few too many rules, and Death was not happy. Usually, his unhappiness manifests itself in some pretty brutal punishments.

My bones ached at the thought.

# Chapter Two

I stepped out of the elevator into a large office with a beautiful view of Los Angeles. I could see the entire city and a few extras, such as Mount Everest. It wasn't really there, but my boss likes to add the illusion. The view did nothing to help my sense of impending doom. To be summoned to meet with Death, or Mr. Wilson as he prefers, was usually not a good sign.

"Kye! Great to see you safe and sound. Drink?" Death said, appearing out of nowhere. I almost leaped back into the elevator. I tried to calm my nerves and let out the breath I unconsciously held. He was smiling, maybe no broken bones today.

Mr. Wilson motioned for me to follow him to the bar. He looked like Santa Claus, including the beard and belly. Every time I meet him, he looks different, but his aura was unmistakable.

"A bourbon would be great. You're looking good, been working out, Mr. Wilson?" I asked and faked a poke to his gut. Touching Mr. Wilson was a no-no.

He laughed and rubbed his stomach. "Please, I told you to call me Carl. I see you brought along the sword of retribution."

A woman moved out of the shadows near a corner of the room. She was almost my height, sandy-blonde hair with fair skin, attractive but not supermodel attractive. She looked younger than me, but for those who worked for Carl, age was irrelevant. She could be two hundred years old and still look younger than me. I noted the gray eyes, a sure sign of an employee of Death.

She reached for her sword, and I went for Kitten. With a flick of Death's hand, we stopped. I don't move a muscle. Carl may be smiling, but with a simple thought, he could transform me into a pile of dust. Carl dropped his hand, and we released our weapons.

"Kitten's my security blanket and the main reason I haven't been cut in half by rogue angels."

The unknown woman shook her head and headed toward me. "Why do you insist on calling a holy relic 'Kitten'? I think it's disrespectful to something as divine as that weapon."

Her catlike approach was my first clue that she was well trained.

"Where are my manners? Kye, this is Jean Kilford. Ms. Kilford, this is Kye Dodson. Jean has almost completed her training under Jeremiah. She's part of his security detail."

Security detail translated meant assassin, strong arm, and the department that deals with any of Death's trickier issues. That meant she was deadly and probably a little unhinged. Kitten purred in approval.

I gave her a slight bow of respect. "I call her that because the disgrace of being killed by a weapon called 'Kitten' irritates my opponents," I said, getting a laugh from Death. "Plus, she likes the name, and I'm not sure I have the guts to try and give her another. She can be quite fickle, not to mention deadly."

I could tell Kilford disapproved, but she said nothing.

"I agree with Kye. Even I would be wary of getting on the sword's bad side. If she wants to be called Kitten, so be it. Since the sword chose him as its bearer, we have no say. He's also correct when he stated that he is alive because of her powers. But I fear even a weapon as powerful as her may not be enough for your next case." Carl took a sip of his drink. "Can you tell me anything about why they killed Lester and attacked you?"

"They said nothing to me," I ran through the entire attack. "I gave them both a chance to surrender, but they were determined to kill me or die. The wild-eyed look I got from them probably means they were high on something, but I don't know what. I have to admit that I have never seen two angels so bent on killing me, not to mention as fast. My best guess was they were juiced by a very powerful entity."

The look on Jean's face told me she didn't recognize the term 'juiced', which surprised me. I was about to ask her about it but then noticed that Carl had gone quiet and just stared at a wall. I've never seen him like this, and it was a bit scary. Death can be very unpredictable, and I wondered if something was about to happen. I mentally prepared for some sort of punishment for failing to get more information.

"And that brings us to the reason why you are here, Ms. Kilford," Carl said, breaking the silence and startling me.

"Jean, may I call you Jean?" It wasn't really a question, few are stupid enough to say no to Death. "Kye is an arbiter. In fact, he's my favorite arbiter. He's worked for me for over a hundred years, which is a record. Kye's survived this long thanks to the sword, and because he refuses to play by the rules that Jeremiah keeps setting down," Carl said, chuckling to himself.

"Sorry, I only know a little about what arbiters do," Jean said, another surprise for me.

This is basic knowledge to those who work for Death. Why hadn't Jeremiah informed her of this?

"Ah, I wasn't sure how much you knew. Kye, would you do the honors?" Death asked. His poker face was impossible to read. The fact that he wasn't surprised by her statement also worried me. This was turning into one of the weirdest days ever. Considering I work for Death, that's quite a statement.

"My pleasure. As you probably know, Heaven and Hell are always on the brink of war, ready to annihilate each other at a moment's notice. Each is building an army of souls. Consequently, they're always recruiting the best souls for their side, even to the point of turning a blind eye to a recruit's background. So, Heaven sometimes overlooks a murderer or rapist to recruit someone who may aid their side. Hell, on the other hand, may overlook years of pious service to get their warrior."

"I am aware of this," Jean said, but I was not sure she was.

"When someone dies, ninety-nine-point nine percent of the time, the two sides work it out who gets the soul. But there are those few, the ones that both sides want badly. They're the business of Death's Arbiters. My job is to figure out why the two sides want a particular soul and then offer my recommendation of who receives the soul to Mr. Wilson. He makes the final decision. Which puts me smack-dab in the middle of two of the most powerful forces anywhere, short of Carl," I said and gave my boss a respectful nod. His smile meant I scored a point. I'm not the greatest at brown-nosing, having been told this several times by Carl and Jeremiah.

"And with the more valuable prizes, the two sides are willing to do anything to win," Jean added.

"Yes, you get it. Hence the reason the attempt on Kye's life today," Carl replied. "Kye has been steadfastly even-handed when dealing with the two sides. He takes the not-so-occasional bribe that I turn a blind eye to," he gave me a knowing smile. "But he always balances things. My guess is that both sides would prefer a less seasoned arbiter for the case I'm about to assign him."

"Kye, as for the case. It's a big one, and you're going to need backup," Carl said. He took a sip of his bourbon and then sat in a chair that just appeared.

"I've never needed backup before, and today wasn't the first time someone has tried to kill me. I don't mind having someone tag along to watch my back, but her?" I asked and nodded toward the assassin. The last part was more to take a dig at Kilford. I was sure she was as dangerous as they come, but it doesn't mean I can't have a little fun.

"Yes, her," he chuckled, then lost his smile. "Your prize's name is Joshua Arbol, and he is obviously highly sought after. Both Lyzark and Eizan, and their teams, are personally monitoring him."

I spewed my bourbon. "As in, they're both on Earth?" I desperately hoped he said no.

"Yes, and the teams are only a short distance from each other," Carl confirmed in an ominous tone.

I internally swore up a storm. This wasn't good by any standard. Lyzark was Satan's right-hand lieutenant. Eizan was the guy that does God's dirty work. Both have nasty tempers, and a battle between them would wipe out most of Los Angeles before Carl could do anything about it.

Carl's right. I'll need backup—lots of it.

"Then I hope you're good," I said to Jean.

She ignored my comment. "Kye works for you. Why would anyone risk provoking you?"

"Normally, my protection would be enough to keep most angels from directly trying to kill you two, but even I have immutable protocols. Lyzark and Eizan are considerably higher in the chain than either of you. If one of them kills you, I can rightfully wipe out their teams, but I couldn't touch them. Based upon what's going on, losing their team would only be a minor irritation to either of them."

I was a little puckered. Being killed by either one of those superpowers meant that I don't come back ever. No Heaven or Hell, I just cease to exist. I died once. I don't want to do it again.

Carl poured himself another bourbon. I downed the rest of mine, and he poured me another. I gripped the glass with both hands to stop the shaking. I always knew there would be an assignment that would kill me. I just didn't think it would have come so soon.

"However, I am permitted to level the playing field," Carl said as he waved his hand.

I took a breath, and I waited for the pain that comes from dealing with Death.

Kitten heated up, and I fought the urge to grab her. Whatever Carl was doing would probably be a mixed blessing but getting in Death's way when he was working was usually a bad idea. The glow and the heat faded, and I relaxed. Kilford's wide-eyed look made me believe she experienced something similar.

"I have augmented your weapons and your abilities to level the playing field if you are forced to fight. Try not to kill too many angels this time, Kye," Carl said and gave me a look of amusement.

"And how many angels and demons have you killed, Mr. Dodson?" Kilford asked, enjoying our banter.

"There are quite a few angels on both sides which are listed as 'missing.' No one asks questions about them, as the answers to those questions may make some uncomfortable. A warning for you, Ms. Kilford," she gave me a look like I was about to die. "In case you ever meet Satan, never call her followers demons. She feels that if God can call his agents angels, so can she. It's one thing that will set her on a murderous tirade."

"Thanks for the warning. I'll try to remember," Kilford replied, relaxing before addressing Death. "If this case is that special, maybe an arbiter that plays it a bit safer might be a better candidate?"

I have to give her credit. She had guts. To second guess Death is always a dangerous gamble.

Death turned to her, and I waited to see if he answered or just killed her. On an average day, he would kill anyone for second-guessing him. Today had been so far from normal, I wasn't surprised when he didn't.

"Ms. Kilford," Carl began, "Yes, Kye pushes the envelope, so to speak, but he has prevented celestial war for the last hundred years. A good trade, I think."

Carl stared at Jean. "Kye is the arbiter I want on this case. Do you have an issue with that?"

Kilford's expression told me she wanted to say something more but saw that she had no chance of winning. "No issues. I welcome a chance to work with Mr. Dodson."

Death smiled, but it unnerved me. I felt like a plate of food, and Death was a starving man. "Good, now that we have that settled, we can get back to what I was doing. I have super-charged your weapons and given you a few extra powers. Your weapons are now strong enough to do serious damage to any angel you may encounter. Although I do believe that if either Lyzark or Eizan want to kill you, I don't think you will have time to use your weapons."

"Unless you give me the ability to travel," I said with great hope. Most angels have some form of wings to fly but usually use the power in them to travel anywhere they want with only a thought. Death had never given me, or any arbiter, that power. We can pop back and forth to Heaven and Hell or back to our offices in Death's domain. But when on Earth, I have to travel just like any mortal. I've had to travel via plane, car, or sometimes hitched a ride with an angel. It's a bit like riding a bike to school when your friends were now driving themselves.

"Being able to get out of their way could help keep me alive. Carl, it will make a big difference." I rested my hand on his arm to help press my argument and instantly regretted it. Death is overly sensitive, and being pushed by Kilford and me was too much. Plus, as I said, touching was a no-no.

"Okay," he said and flicked his wrist. Immediately, Kilford and I flew in opposite directions. We each conveniently found a wall to slam into.

At this point, my day couldn't get any worse.

# Chapter Three

My bones cracked, then broke, and I stifled a scream at the wave of pain that I was almost accustomed to. Because I'm an Arbiter, my body should heal itself, but that doesn't happen. It was clear that Carl wanted to drive home the lesson that getting pushy with him was not a good idea.

"I already gave you that power, next time, be more patient," Carl growled with no smile and a look that could literally kill. He's very close to switching into his full Death persona, so I kept my mouth shut. The room turned dark and cold. From the edges of the darkness, I sensed things waiting, wanting. Kilford took a couple of deep breaths but said nothing. She's scared, which was good. I'm scared shitless. When it comes to making someone pay for their transgressions, neither Heaven nor Hell come close to what Death can dream up.

After a minute, my bones knit themselves back together, and I stand uneasily, avoiding eye contact. "Thank you for the gift. I will not abuse it."

"Thank you for everything you have done, Carl," Kilford added quickly.

I flinched when Carl suddenly smiled. "In that case, why don't you try them out?"

I glanced at Jean, eyebrows raised, but she looked as confused as I was.

"Oh, let me help you," Death said with a snap of his fingers.

I almost jumped out of my skin when a pair of wings sprouted out of my back. I gazed at them in amazement, then folded my wings around me to touch them. The feathers were gray, silky smooth, and soft to the touch. The very tips of my wings were black, and I brush one across my face. It reminded me of my mother's caress. I expanded my wings to their full length and almost knocked over a bottle on the bar ten feet away.

Carl beamed at us like a proud parent. "Careful now. You need to get used to them."

I felt like a kid just given the best Christmas present ever.

Jean wrapped her wings around herself and spun, laughing and giggling. Her wings were also gray but with no black tips. Her look of pure joy was intoxicating.

"You know the rules about when and where you can use wings. I would suggest that when you are on Earth, you use the magic in them to get where you need to go."

I desperately wanted to try out my new wings. But, I knew well enough that I would lose them if I broke the rules.

Jean halted her spin. "Carl, thank you. These are amazing." Before I could stop her, she hugged Death and engulfed him with her wings.

I expected Carl to go ballistic, but instead, he looked confused. Then, to my surprise, he wrapped his arms around her and returned the hug. I was speechless. This is the first time I have seen anyone touch Carl and not pay for it. I shook my head—this day had indeed become the weirdest of my existence. I would not be surprised if a unicorn ran across the room and farted.

Jean released Carl as tears rolled down her face. His eyes were watery, and I made sure not to notice. He quickly dabbed his eyes and checked to make sure I wasn't looking. I was busily examining my wings and hoped he bought it.

Carl glanced at me. "One last thing—the weapons due you from the battle. I took the liberty of having them cleaned."

A table appeared with the two swords from the attack. I furled my wings, and they disappeared. Very handy.

I walked to the table about to say thank you but stopped short. Looking at the blades, they were perfect, too perfect. Kitten didn't cut through them, but she did leave some marks. The lengths of the sword were slightly off, and the pommels were different. I could only believe these are not the weapons from this morning. Death and I have always been completely honest with each other. He has never lied to me before. Arguing with him would only cause more broken bones, and I took a different approach.

I turned back toward Death and bit my lip. I stared at the ground until I was ready, then looked up and locked eyes with Carl. "Thank you. I appreciate everything you have done for me," I then glanced at the swords.

Carl raised an eyebrow, then examined the weapons. A look of surprise came over him for a second, then he recovered. I could see him thinking something through, then walked over and shook my hand. I almost screamed when he touched me, but it was just a handshake. If arbiters could have heart attacks, I would be on my third today.

"Kye, I am sorry for the deception. It was not intentional. These will fetch you more than the real ones would have."

This was odd. Did Carl not know that these aren't the same weapons?

We locked eyes. "I will trust your judgment."

"What about Lester's killers? Someone armed them pretty well," I asked, trying to change the subject.

"I will leave it to you to take care of whoever gave them their weapons," Carl replied. "Now, let's have lunch."

That Carl wasn't upset about the demise of two of his employees was another red flag. Any other time he would be declaring war and calculating how many he needed to kill. I filed the information for later.

Lunch was excellent and the best food I've ever eaten. At least ten thousand calories, but you don't worry about weight gain when you're on Death's payroll.

We finish dessert, and I hoped for an after-lunch drink from Carl's fantastic wine collection, but no such luck.

Carl stood. "You two have to get going, and I have things to do."

We both offered our thanks, and Carl was gone.

"So, do you have a plan?" Jean asked.

"Yes, I want to go see for myself that the two most powerful celestial beings and their teams are actually on Earth and what they are doing," I said.

"Then?"

"Then," I pause for a dramatic flair, "we go to my favorite club."

With a snap of my fingers, we're gone.

# Chapter Four

I watched as Kye and Jean disappeared. I only pretended to have something else to do. I know Kye all too well. If we opened one bottle of wine from my reserve, we would be at it for days. The man can drink like no other. Knowing Jeremiah's training, Jean could give Kye a run for his money. Plus, since I am Death, I had to add a dramatic flair.

"He's a good soul for an arbiter. In retrospect, I should have sent him to Heaven. He would have fit in well there," I murmured, forgetting I had company.

"I'm sorry, sir, I didn't hear what you said," the reaper standing next to me replied.

"Nothing for you to worry about. Now about the weapons that you said you recovered. They were obviously not the ones used in the attack, and I looked like a fool in front of my employees. I want to know who is to blame."

Everything went black except for a light on me and the nervous reaper.

Reapers are one of the most feared creatures anywhere. Even God was disturbed when I created them. Served him right for the whole 'free will' BS we have to put up with now.

Reapers typically aren't fearful of anything, but this one was afraid, very afraid.

"Sir, we arrived right after he left. I picked up the weapons personally. I felt the battle in them. I don't know how this happened," the reaper replied in a trembling voice.

Making me unhappy was something few want to do, not even a reaper. I darkened the area, and my pets wanted to come out of the shadows and play. The reaper felt them and was now frantically looking around.

"Get me the original weapons, or you know what will happen," I said quietly, but the threat was clear.

The reaper turned and disappeared to rejoin his flock. There's the snapping of a whip, then the reaper ordered, "Find me those weapons!"

# Chapter Five

I snapped my fingers and used my newfound power to travel. I'll have to send Carl a bottle of something to thank him. Jean and I appeared under a freeway overpass, not precisely what I hoped for. I preferred assignments that took me to five-star hotels or the beach. To be honest, it rarely happened, but a guy can dream.

I took a few deep breaths to make the world stop spinning. This new power was going to take a little while to get used to.

Surveying our surroundings, I found we were in a less affluent suburb of Los Angeles. Its main tenants—the homeless, gangs, and cops. Not where I would expect to find a superstar wanted by both Heaven and Hell.

Jean looked around in disdain. My guess was she spent her training in one of Jeremiah's immaculately clean facilities. The trash and the smell would be something she would not have experienced.

I checked the Arbiter app on my phone. It displayed a map with the prized soul in the middle marked by a blue pin. Many of my Arbiter brethren don't like technology, but I love it. I bought Lester a phone hoping to make amends. He threw it into the pits of Hell. Some demon retrieved it and was currently using it. Sexting with her was a whole new ball game.

I found the map littered with red and white pins. Heaven's agents were marked with white pins and Hell's in red. There was more celestial power here than in the rest of the world, and no one on Earth knew. I supposed calling the pope was out of the question. Pretty sure he wouldn't take my call. That's a story for another day.

"Now that's weird," I said, trying to figure out what I was looking at.

"What is it?"

"This is where the prize is, and this is where the two groups are," I pointed to them for Jean. "But both groups are at least two blocks from the prize. Normally, they would have spies directly observing the soul. Something's up."

21

"Then why don't we go take a look," she said and walked off in the direction my app indicated the target should be.

I followed, but after ten feet, she bounced off an invisible wall.

"I think I found out why." Jean rubbed her nose then explored the invisible border with her hands.

"If working for Jeremiah doesn't pan out, you could always become a mime," I joked, thinking it was a good one. The look I received told me otherwise.

I turned my attention to the barrier. "I haven't seen something like this in a long time." I waved my hand, and the barrier became visible. I studied the swirling colors. "This is designed to keep angels out. Luckily, we're not angels."

"Then, why did I block me?"

"While it is designed to keep angels out, it also works on many non-mortals. Take my hand," I said, and she frowned. "If I was getting frisky, I would be trying to hold something much more interesting than your hand. If you want to get past this thing, then hold my hand and follow my lead."

She sighed then reluctantly grabbed my hand.

Using Kitten to enhance my power, I used my energy to create a shield that allowed us to pass through the barrier. As an Arbiter, there are very few places I'm not allowed to go. I could do this by myself, but Kitten was still amped up from her kills. Forcing her to use some of her energy would help calm her down.

It felt like we were swimming through thick gel, but we got through and headed toward our objective.

After a city block, we approached a set of makeshift tents, shelters, and lean-tos that the local homeless have cobbled together. Among the tents stood my prize, handing out food and goods to others.

As we approached, he stopped and stared at us. Those around him wandered off as if they suddenly remembered an important appointment somewhere else.

This day just kept getting worse. I raised my hands to show him we meant no harm. Clearly, he didn't get the message because he sent an energy blast flying at us, and we dove out of the way. Jean pulled a throwing knife.

"No, we can't use weapons against him. We can only protect ourselves, at least for now," I warned as I brought up my shield, powered by Kitten, and stepped out into the open with Jean behind me.

The next blast bounced off my shield. A bit jarring, but nothing I couldn't handle.

"Joshua, we just want to talk!" I yelled.

"I want nothing from Heaven or Hell!"

"How the heck does he know about Heaven and Hell?" I whispered to Jean.

"No clue."

"We need to talk about that later." I turned my attention back to Joshua. "I represent a third-party."

"A third-party? Who?"

Jean stepped out from behind me with her own shield.

"Can we do this in a little quieter space? I promise I won't try anything. I just need some information."

I thought I was losing him when his eyes locked on Jean. "Do, uh, I know you?"

Before she could respond, he disappeared. My app showed he was a few hundred yards away behind some boxes, and I decided to leave him be. I stared at his new location on the map. Something about it was strange, but I wasn't sure what. I glanced at him to let him know I saw him, then walked away.

Jean didn't move. "We're just leaving?"

I nodded. "I feel like I am a few steps behind everyone else. I need information, and I know just the place to get it. Also, we might have a little fun."

I snapped my fingers, and we traveled to one of my most favorite places on Earth.

## Chapter Six

e appeared outside the 'House of Angels', a seedy but well-respected LA club that catered to mortals and non-mortals. The front entrance was for mortals, which led to a rather lovely strip club. The back entrance was where the real fun began.

I made my way around the back with Jean trailing me. From a distance, the place looked like the back of a typical warehouse—boxes thrown to the side, trash, etc. The scene changed when we passed through an invisible barrier, and it was as if we just opened a magical present. The place outshined any Vegas club. Lights everywhere, water fountains performing tricks that could only be done with the help of magic. As we passed a fountain, the water formed into a giant dragon complete with flames, then disappeared.

Jean was in awe of the whole thing. A performer approached, carrying a bottle and a lighter. He took a swig from the bottle and held up the lighter. Anywhere else, you would see the guy spew flames—big deal. The performer sprayed the liquid, flicked his lighter, and flames flew out to form an image of Jean and me. The image floated off into the air, and I threw the guy a coin. We spent a few more minutes enjoying the acts. There is nothing like this anywhere else on Earth. It amazes me every time.

We approached the back door to the club, and my least favorite bouncer was waiting. He was seven-feet-tall and over three hundred pounds and positioned in the doorway. He looked human, but he was not, and I didn't care.

"What do you want here?" he asked, trying to play tough.

"I'm here for some entertainment and information. My membership is paid, and unless you want a repeat of our last encounter, I suggest you stand aside." I didn't even try to hide my desire to gut the pig.

Very few people invoke the kind of hatred I hold for him. I have seen some of the vile and depraved things he has done, and if it wouldn't cause a major uproar with the club's owner, I would kill him on the spot. The last time I was here, I found him beating a Fallen because he wasn't happy with her service. She was a mess by the time I intervened. I had broken about half of his bones when Fre-Fre stopped my fun. Why Fre-Fre keeps him, he won't say. But in exchange for a free membership to the club, I promised not to kill him.

I put my hand on Kitten. "Just give me a reason, any reason, to kill you."

He stepped aside, and we walked past. "Good doggie, she's with me."

As Jean stepped through the doorway, he put his hand on her shoulder. "If you ever want a real man…" he began but was interrupted as the assassin sidled up to him.

He's smiled as he foolishly thought she was coming on to him. He squealed when she grabbed him by the balls. Before he could defend himself, she used her other hand to grab him by the neck and hoist him up over her head with super-human strength. If it wasn't clear she was a non-mortal, it was now. I backed away. I'm a little worried that my least favorite bouncer would come bouncing my way.

"I don't need a real man in my bed," Jean yelled.

I cocked an eyebrow at her comment, and her face turned red. "I mean, I do need a man in my bed, but not him."

At this point, I raised my other eyebrow, and my attempt to suppress a laugh failed. Her blush deepened.

"That's not what I meant, Kye. Oh, never mind," she said as she tossed the behemoth to the ground. He bounced and laid moaning on the ground with one hand on his groin and the other on his back.

"Thanks, I like things a little rough," she said, standing over him.

"Oh, I forgot to mention that Jeremiah personally trained her. If you want, maybe he could join you for a threesome," I said gleefully. The bouncer was in a lot of pain, and I tried not to enjoy myself too much. "Maybe someone should get him an ice pack?"

Jean growled. "Can we go?"

With a sweep of my arm, "After you."

We entered a small reception area with four doors. The door on the left was white. The next three were blue, red, and black.

Jean surveyed the doors. "Well, which one?"

"Each door represents a different set of desires." I pointed to the first. "The white one takes you to the best restaurant in the world. Michelin doesn't have enough stars for it. A simple meal costs about a year of my salary. We won't be going there tonight."

"Great, our first date, and I don't get first-class treatment," Jean said with a wink.

I stepped to the blue door. "This leads to a lower-scale restaurant. Still great food, but less attitude and a little more family-friendly. We won't be going there either."

I motioned to the red door. "This is known as 'The Club'. It *was* called 'The Gentleman's Club,' but Satan complained, and it was renamed. If you have the coin, anything you desire can be had. Sadly, we will not be going there tonight."

"I would agree, but my intuition tells me I would prefer it over door number four," Jean said astutely.

I guided her to the black door. "I do believe you are correct." I opened the door, and loud music and flashing lights bombarded us. We entered the largest strip club that I know. At least forty dancers worked various stages. Most are female of various species, including one who was a vampire. On one side, several male strippers have quite the audience. There were a few dancers that I am not sure what species they were, let alone their sex. To the right was a hallway to an area that catered to more exotic tastes. Trolls, werewolves, and several unrecognizable species, looked to be enjoying themselves.

"Is this your way of hazing me?" Jean said with a severe frown. She was avoiding making eye contact with the male stripper trying to get her attention.

"Nope," I said. "My friend Fre-Fre is the owner. Besides having some of the best dancers on the planet, he is also the best source of information about Heaven and Hell."

We headed toward the back where Fre-Fre holds court. Angels, both from Heaven and Hell, along with several other species of magical clientele, pack the club. This place was a neutral site, and causing trouble here could get you killed or worse. The customers police themselves as no one wanted this place shut down. Most of the crowd was drunk and thoroughly enjoying the show.

Jean stopped in front of me and eyed the talent on stage.

"Kye! Are those Fallen angels?" Jean yelled in my ear over the noise.

"Yes. When an angel from either side is cast out, Fre-Fre recruits them for his club."

Jean frowned. "And why would they want to work here?"

"Angels from both sides are not allowed to have relations with mortals. God and Satan have seen to it that if any angel tries to have sex with a mortal, they explode on contact. No pun intended. Which makes mortals a bit of forbidden fruit."

From a distance, a dancer climbed down from a stage and headed toward me. I shook my head—this day kept getting worse.

"Fre-Fre can't get around the rule. Instead, he recruits Fallen angels, which technically aren't covered by the ban. It's a win-win for both sides."

"How so?" Jean asked and eyed the approaching dancer.

"For the Fallen, returning home is an addiction, and they can't resist. If an angel with enough clout is interested, a Fallen will exchange favors for a visit back home and be treated like an angel again. Even if it's for only a little while."

The wayward dancer approached and wrapped her arms and what's left of her wings around me. "Kye, long time no…" she paused, eyeing Jean, "pleasure."

She wore just enough to cover herself, but little was left to the imagination. She's blond-haired, at least today, five-foot-seven, and had a body that I couldn't resist.

Several drunken angels made a fuss that their dancer was ignoring them. I flashed Kitten's blades, and they fell quiet.

"Cassi, I told you to avoid the clubs," I said, with a mixture of anger and disappointment that she was here.

"You can't blame an angel for wanting to go home every once in a while," she said and kissed my neck and pressed her body against me. Fallen angels still have some celestial power, and she was using hers to drive me crazy.

"I'm on a case, but if you leave now, I will take you to Heaven when it is over," I said, my anger rising.

"Mmm, tempting but for how long?"

"Not sure, but at least a few of Mikael's or another top-tier angel's party." I knew that would seal the deal.

She gave me another kiss and adjusted herself against me, and my libido roared to life. If I had my way, we would be doing it on the nearest table. But that would cross a line that even Death couldn't forgive.

"Okay, but if you are lying to me, you will pay," she released me and put out her hand. I gave her a dozen gold coins, and she bounced up and down on her toes, giggling. I clamped my hand around hers and the gold.

I stared directly into her eyes and entered complete Arbiter mode. "You will go straight to my private room. Talk to no one. No drugs, no quid pro quo services, and you don't return here unless it's an emergency. If I get a whiff of you breaking my rules, I will call in every favor owed to me and ban you from Heaven for eternity." The area around me went quiet, and everyone backed away. Arbiters have an aura similar to Heaven's angels, but it's gray and not pleasant. Most of the club was now looking at us, the music blared, but no one moved.

She shuddered. She knows I would do it, and the thought scared her. She broke eye contact, looked down, and nodded. I released her, and she ran off. I relaxed, and everyone around me slowly returned to their partying.

"What was that all about?" Jean asked, watching Cassi run away.

"None of your damn business. Now let's find Fre-Fre," I growled.

My day has put me in a mood, and Fre-Fre was now on my shit list.

# Chapter Seven

W e headed to the back of the club, and one of Fre-Fre's runners hightailed it to warn his master. Kitten has sensed my anger and heated up—she loves a good killing.

"Not now, Kitten. Not now," I murmured. Long-term, I needed Fre-Fre and killing him or his staff, would serve me no good, short of a temporary high.

My assumption that he was at his usual table was correct as I spotted my target. Fre-Fre usually held court here when no big wigs were visiting one of his other clubs. Fre-Fre had always said that this club is where he felt most comfortable, his second home. He created the other three restaurants for the income and the food. He started all four around the same time I became an Arbiter, and neither of us has aged a day. He's no form of an angel that I know of, and he doesn't work for Death. I'm not sure what he is, but to have stayed in business this long means he was smart and probably dangerous.

Fre-Fre stood about six-foot-one, dark skin with an odd grayish tint. Adding his dark blue eyes with gray specks and muscular build, he was a hit with the ladies. Six bodyguards surrounded his table, including two angels. In my current mood, and with Kilford backing me up, they would only keep us busy for a moment.

His runner dashed over and whispered something into Fre-Fre's ear. The owner's smile dimmed, and he called to a man standing nearby, who scrambled over. Fre-Fre whispered something, and the man started to shake his head. Fre-Fre smacked the man, almost knocking him down, then jogged over to greet me, all smiles and happiness. I pulled Kitten, and he eyed it nervously.

"Kye! Honest, I did not know she was here. I have a new manager of talent, and he wasn't aware of the situation," Fre-Fre said nervously and snapped his fingers. When no one moved, two of his guards pushed a now red-faced man toward me. "Meet Spike."

He's short, thin, and has the tell-tale snout-ish face of what I call a wereyote—the coyote version of a werewolf. Like Lycans, they can shift when they want and usually do when scared or angered. Individually, they are only dangerous to the weak and frail. In a pack, they are very dangerous, and I've had to kill a few. They are one of the few species that I would have no issues wiping out. Bullies always send me on a killing spree.

An interesting fact—many of the monsters portrayed in movies were based upon real-life beings. Many of the writers of popular horror and fantasy movies are not human, which makes it pretty easy to write a script about a town overrun by monsters when you have lived it—from the monster's perspective.

I will say, I have never seen a zombie or have known anyone that has. That doesn't mean they don't exist, but considering who I work for, I would think I would know about them by now.

I stepped forward, and Fre-Fre's manager of talent shook like a leaf. His nose darkened as he began his shift to a wereyote, and I shook my head. He stopped his transformation and tried to look me in the eye. "I, I, uh, I'm really sorry! It won't happen again."

I grabbed him by the collar and pressed one of Kitten's blades to his neck. "I'll make you a deal. She shows up again, you put her in my private room with some food, protect her from any visitors, and you let me know. In exchange, I will pay you handsomely—more than he pays you in a year. If you fail me, you will spend eternity wishing you hadn't. Understood?" I growled and stared into his eyes. "Also, if I have found that you mistreated her, in any way, what I will do to you will make Fre-Fre blush."

The man nodded, then fainted.

I released him, and he slumped to the ground. "Good! Now I need a drink and some information." I stepped over the prone man and made myself comfortable at Fre-Fre's table. Kilford grabbed a chair and joined us.

"And why is it that I let you come in here?" Fre-Fre asked with a grin as he resumed his throne.

"One, because you have no one that can stop me. Two, I'm the only thing keeping Jeremiah from closing this place, and three, because deep down, you really like me."

Our host's attention was diverted to Kilford as she smirked at my joke. "And who did you bring with you?" he asked, standing. He took her hand, giving it a polite kiss.

"Sorry, let me make introductions. Fre-Fre, this is Ms. Jean Kilford. Fresh out of training directly under Jeremiah's supervision. She's here to help keep me alive."

Fre-Fre blanched at the Jeremiah reference but quickly recovered himself. "Nice to meet you, Ms. Kilford. May I get you a drink?"

"It is a pleasure to meet you, Mr. Fre-Fre," she said coyly. "I'm guessing you don't serve a decent wine, so rum and coke will have to do."

"Ms. Kilford," he said, putting his hand where his heart should be. I'm pretty sure there wasn't one there. "you wound me." He snapped his fingers, and a cocktail waitress wearing only a G-string hurried over.

"Please get Kye his usual bourbon and two glasses of my personal Cabernet for myself and the lady." The waitress nodded, then rushed over to a bartender who already had the drinks poured. He gave me a knowing nod, and I returned a quick salute. I pay him well to make sure I was well-cared-for when I visited the club.

Our waitress handed out drinks and flashed me a very intense smile. I would have loved to take her up on her implied offer, but with Cassi in the club, I had to pass. Fre-Fre interrupted my ongoing appreciation of our waitress. "I have to believe that you are here on business, Kye? Considering your mood, I would say you have a pretty important case."

"You can say that. Today, two angels, one from each side, teamed up to kill me. Not unusual, but they were not your average angels. They carried some weapons I hadn't seen before," I downed most of my drink, "and they killed an arbiter that I happened to have liked."

Actually, I wouldn't say I liked Lester. Too much of a by-the-book guy, but now wasn't the time to speak ill of the dead. They had a habit of reappearing to call you out.

I pulled out my phone and showed pictures of the two I killed. "Do you recognize either of them?"

"I recognize the demon. Pretty low-level. He was here earlier in the week, spending like he was loaded. He and his buddy hired two of my girls for the night. Figured he scored big," Fre-Fre replied.

"These two," I said, tapping the screen, "not only carried some major hardware but were blazingly fast. One was able to cut me. I have to believe they were juiced."

Fre-Fre let out a long whistle, then whispered to one of his minions, who walked off toward several dancers. Fre-Fre was concerned, and rightfully so.

Jean frowned. "What does it mean to be juiced?"

"Basically, a very powerful angel can temporarily give someone some of their power in exchange for a favor. Usually, that favor is assassinating a rival," Fre-Fre replied.

"To recap, a powerful celestial being wanted Kye dead. So, they paid a couple of angels, gave them some weapons, and then juiced them," Jean recounted, trying to piece together the situation.

I finished my drink. "Yes, to make it worse, to be able to juice two angels enough to handle those weapons means it's a top-rung angel."

"And now, the two biggest heavyweights short of God and Satan are on Earth. You have to wonder if there is a connection," Fre-Fre said, shaking his head.

"Don't forget Death," I added, hoping Carl was listening.

The club owner smirked, then looked around. "Getting better at brown-nosing, are we?"

Fre-Fre's runner returned with two of his dancers and interrupted the conversation. One was young, still sporting most of her feathers. She must have just Fallen. She thought I was her next customer and gave me an angelic smile.

The other dancer's name is Cara, and she's a veteran I have had a few unfortunate run-ins with. The feathers on her wings were fake, but her clientele didn't care. She gave me an intense look of hate. "He ain't a customer, sugar. He's one of Death's guys, and I'm tellin' ya, this is going to go badly."

The first dancer broke into tears. "I ain't done nothing wrong. You gonna kill me?"

I glanced at Fre-Fre. "Is my reputation that bad?"

He shrugged. "You aren't exactly on everyone's Christmas card list."

"I guess not," I said and turned my attention back to the Fallen. "Honey, no. I'm not going to kill you. I just have some questions for you two. What's your name?"

"Don't say nothin' to him. It will lead to no good," Cara cautioned.

"If you two want to keep working here, you will answer his questions," Fre-Fre warned. His tone was all business, and there was an implied threat. Being fired from his club included some nasty ramifications.

"Honey, last time, what's your name? I won't ask again."

She was scared but looked me in the eye. "Tania, it's Tania. What do you wanna know?"

"Two nights ago, a demon came in and hired you two for the night," I showed her the picture. "What can you tell me about him?"

Tania's face lit up. "That's Iggie? He's nice. Treated us well. I think he really likes me."

"Why is that?"

"He had a big, important job today. Then he was gonna take me to his palace in Hell." She giggled and stared at the picture like she was in love. When angels and demons fall, it devastates them. Many kill themselves before Fre-Fre can get to them, while others turn to the drugs which Fre-Fre supplies. He does restrict the drug flow. He wants them happy, not hooked. Tania was very happy at the moment.

Cara rolled her eyes. "He had no intention of takin' ya anywhere, other than a romp in the back," she said, then hesitated. "You killed him, didn't ya?"

"Yes, him and an angel but not before they killed another Arbiter, then tried to kill me. They were pretty juiced and would have continued killing if I hadn't stopped them."

Realizing that Death may be looking for recompense for the killing of his employee, Cara's look of hatred turned to fear. "He and his buddy just kept bragging about moving up and how much gold they were gonna make—paid us really well. If I'd known what they were up to, I would've said something. You tell Death I don't know nothin'. I'll give the gold back if it helps."

Tania was pretty clueless, but she knew that something was going on if Cara was spilling her guts. "You can have all mine, I spent some, but I'll work it off."

"I don't want your gold. However, can I see it for a moment?"

They both had their gold strategically hidden. Don't ask me where. You don't want to know. Both girls poured their coins on the table. Several of Fre-Fre's guards now eyed the glittering pile intently.

"Anyone who tries to take their gold will face Kitten," I warned, and the guards found new places to look.

I picked up a couple of coins. Gold has an incredible ability to pick up energy from its holder. I felt for the hidden energy, and what I got didn't make sense. I put the two coins in my pocket. Both girls started to protest but caught themselves. I pulled out two different coins and added them to the piles. The coins I added were worth ten times what I took.

33

"Take your gold and hide it," I said, and they both hastily put their fortunes away. "Also, both of you are now under Arbiter protection. Here, take this." I handed them each a poker chip that I have modified for these situations. "If anyone comes after you, squeeze the chip, and an arbiter will be there in a moment's notice."

As the two dancers turned to leave, I grabbed Cara's arm. "Take this card and call the number." I forced my card into her hand. "This guy owes me a favor. It will cost you what I just gave you, but he'll see to it you two spend a few weeks in Heaven. It will be much safer there. Think what you like, but I don't want you slaughtered simply for talking to me."

Cara's hard stare softened. "Thanks, I'll call now." Both walked off toward their dressing room. Full Fallen angel power turned on. It took everything I had not to call them back for a bit of fun.

"Back to Earth's visitors, why are two superpowers here for one prize?" I asked.

"Their prize is someone that I know little about, which is worrisome," Fre-Fre sighed, losing his smile. "He's way too powerful to be anything other than the product of some upper echelon angels. Someone broke the rules. Those that can get near enough to him can't tell if his power comes from Heaven or Hell."

"Really? That's all that the great Fre-Fre knows about this guy?" I knew the jibe would get under his skin. Especially since he knew that to keep his club open, he needed to provide answers.

"This guy is powerful. I have two agents recovering after they tried to get near him. To be honest, he worries me. Whichever side gets him will gain a heckuva soldier." Fre-Fre slugged down the rest of his wine. Usually, he loves to savor good vintage and must be worried.

"I visited him today, and he tried to take my head off."

"People trying to kill you is pretty standard fare, I would say," the club owner joked.

I chuckled. "Yeah, but not mortals. The weird thing is that he said he didn't want anything to do with Heaven or Hell. This guy's already acting like an angel. Not sure where he came from, but I agree, at least one of his parents is an angel."

The Fallen male dancer that caught Jean's eye came by with more drinks. He stared at Jean like she was the featured cut at a steak house. She was looking him over like he's her main course. That she still had her clothes on showed she had some self-control.

Jean put her drink down and flashed me a smile. "Meet you at your house at eight a.m."

"Make it nine," I called, but I don't think she heard me as she followed the server.

I turned my attention back to my host. "I need information and will pay well for it."

"Come back tomorrow night, and I should know more," Fre-Fre said, sipping a fresh glass of wine.

I headed to the private room I pay dearly for to keep my activities confidential. Cassi had made herself comfortable on a sofa with a drink. I keep a selection of clothes here in case of a wardrobe malfunction. She was now wearing my favorite—a red dress that accents every delicious feature of her heavenly body. An added bonus was that it came off with the pull of one string. The dress covered just enough so we can walk out the door and not get ambushed by a horde of horny angels.

I offered her my arm, and we walked out via my private exit. I enjoyed having her with me, even under these circumstances. I had a thing for her before things fell apart and still do.

"Where's your car?" she asked as we enter the parking lot.

"Honey, tonight we fly first-class," and with a snap, we stood outside my LA home. I have enough wards set up around the place that it's best to enter the old fashion way, through the door.

I owned the house along with a few dozen other properties held under various shell corporations. I bought the land and built this place when I sold Death the land to build his Earthly headquarters. I made a fortune on that sale. Death finds it amusing that I live on Earth as most Arbiters refuse to. They can get whatever mansion they want in Death's realm. I tried living there, but it was not for me. It never felt real. So, I bought as much land in the early 1900s as I could afford, then slowly sold it off over the next hundred years. Most of what I purchased was in the Los Angeles area, but I also own property in almost every state and most foreign countries.

This place is my dream home. The view of Los Angeles is breathtaking, and the scythe-shaped pool is always the perfect temperature. My pipedream is to retire here someday. I very much doubt I will live long enough to see that happen.

Cassi made herself at home and poured me a drink. She sauntered toward me, giving me a full Fallen blast. "Do you have my stuff?" she asked as she handed me a glass and snuggled up against me.

I downed my drink. "Yes, but that comes later." I'm tired and have had a few—time to enjoy myself.

I knew better than to start this in my living room. I usually have to replace broken furniture, but I don't care. I pulled the string on her dress, and it dropped to the floor. Cassi has a body that just won't quit, and she knows it. Her wings appeared, adding to the moment.

I threw my coat aside and ripped off my shirt. While celestial beings don't possess magic, we do have incredible physical strength. My wings emerged, and Cassi jumped in surprise.

"Mmm, those are new. I do like the addition," Cassi cooed. With a flap of her wings, she launched herself into me. I grabbed her as we crashed into the sofa, taking out a lamp and several vases. Two of the sofa's legs snapped, sending us to the floor. We tumbled to a stop with me on my back and Cassi on top.

She grabbed my belt, and with a snap, she ripped it off. She sat back on her knees, belt in hand. "Now, this could be fun."

Not to be outdone, I sat up, grabbed her by the waist, and lifted us into the air. I'm still getting the hang of flying and crashed Cassi into the ceiling. Great, my ceiling has my girlfriend's butt print on it.

Actually, not a bad conversation starter, and I decided to keep it.

We hang, suspended above the room until I did a mid-air roll, and then tried to land us on my piano—her favorite place to have sex. I'm not sure why, but I'm happy to oblige. Unfortunately, our landing was harder than expected, no pun intended. The piano's cover cracked and caved in, causing the piano to let out a mournful chord.

We're both pretty sturdy, and Cassi was more turned on than injured. "I see you finally bought a bigger piano," Cassi whispered into my ear.

I smirked. "Nothing but the biggest for you, my dear."

****

Several hours later, she's lying in my bed, and I grabbed my kit. She let out a gasp and grabbed my arm as I injected my 'Heaven' concoction into her thigh. Her body shuddered, then relaxed. A moment later, she drifted off to a deep sleep. I could set off fireworks and not wake her.

For angels, living in Heaven or Hell was like a constant IV feed of heroin. On Earth, they only get a small dose of that feed, and withdrawal symptoms show within a few days. It's one of the reasons angels spend little time on Earth without special precautions. Since the Fallen can't return home without help, they eventually waste away like a junkie going cold turkey. Some, like Cara, adapt and will live another century or two. It's why the Fallen will do just about anything to return home, even for a few days. For some, it's the only way they can survive.

My Heaven concoction mimicked the energy of Heaven. By tomorrow, her mind will be fully restored, and her feathers will regrow. It will only last a week or two, but I can't give it to her again for a few weeks. I'm still trying to figure out how to get her back into Heaven permanently. At least, without her becoming some angel's plaything.

I laid next to her and brushed a few strands of hair from her face. I put my head on her chest and fell asleep in seconds.

# Chapter Eight

At eight, banging at the door reminded me that Jean didn't hear my message about meeting at nine. I stumbled to the door, every muscle in my body reminding me of its painful existence. After battling two angels, Death's punishment, and an hours-long romp with a Fallen, I wasn't moving quickly.

"Hold your damn wings!" I yelled as the doorbell rang for the umpteenth time. After dying and becoming an Arbiter, I had to relearn how to cuss. On one of my first assignments, the soul was this loud-mouth lady who wouldn't shut up and constantly complained about me. I lost it when she said something nasty about my parents. Out of reflex, I told her to "Go to Hell." It turned out she was supposed to go to Heaven, and it took me two weeks to retrieve her from Hell.

I paid dearly for that one.

I opened the door to find Jean. She seemed refreshed and glowing, a sign of a successful night with her waiter friend. She gave me a surprised look and then suddenly concentrated on a piece of art behind me.

"Could you at least put some underwear on before you answer the door? What if I was a Girl Scout selling cookies?" she asked, still focused on the not-so-fake Van Gogh behind me.

"Why, what's the problem?" I grinned. To make her even more nervous, I began to bounce up and down, but stopped when my head began to throb.

"Christ, you're going to hurt yourself," she said, then pushed past me.

I laughed. "If you want me fully clothed, then next time, listen when I say nine am."

Jean viewed the wreckage of my living room. "And what the heck happened here? Were you attacked in your own home?"

On cue, Cassi emerged wearing one of my shirts. It's about an inch too short, perfect in my opinion, and Jean picked up on the message.

"Ah, Ms. Kilford, nice to see you again," Cassi said with a bit of a smile. "If I had known you would be here so early, I would have dressed appropriately.

"Excuse me while I take a quick shower and get dressed," I said and left to avoid the awkward conversation about to happen.

Twenty minutes later, I returned, dressed and smelling much better. Cassi and Jean were chatting in the kitchen.

Cassi kissed me and handed me a cup. "Coffee?"

"Oh, yes. So, what are you two girls talking about?"

"Just getting to know each other," Jean said with a knowing smile. I got the hint I had been the main topic of conversation, probably not in a good way.

Before I could reply, red lights flashed, a disco ball dropped from the ceiling, and 'Stayin' Alive' blasted from the speakers.

"Sorry," I yelled as I typed a code into a panel on the wall. The lights turn off, and the music stopped. "That's my home alarm." I glanced at the disco ball still suspended in the air. "I guess I need to get that fixed. Now to find out why my alarm went off."

Cassi shook her head. "Stayin' Alive? Really? You couldn't have a normal alarm?"

"I like my alarm, and I happen to like that song if you don't mind." Believe it or not, I liked 70s music.

A quick check revealed two of Heaven's angels lurking just outside my property line. "Looks like I picked up a tail. It probably won't be too long before Hell sends some as well."

"Which means I'm not going anywhere," Cassi said with a sigh. "The second I walk out that door, one of them will be on me in a flash."

"As opposed to..." Jean began.

I cut her off. "You can finish that thought later. With this case, they wouldn't hesitate to kidnap Cassi and use her against me as leverage. Is that okay with you, Ms. Kilford?"

She blushed and bowed her head. "Of course."

"Cassi, they don't know about you yet, and we need to keep it that way. They also don't know I can travel, so I'll take you to my other home. I paid cash to keep it hidden from prying angel eyes." I wasn't thrilled that I was letting someone who worked for Death know about it. You never know when you might need a hiding place. Luckily, I had more than one backup home.

"Get dressed and pack your stuff. When you're ready, I can take you there." I ran my hands through my hair. This day hadn't started off the way I had hoped.

Jean watched Cassi walk out of the room. "She has stuff here?" Jean asked, trying to be nonchalant and failing.

"Yes, she does. Do you have a problem with that?" My head hurt, and she wasn't making it any better.

"You know, she doesn't blame you for what happened to her," Jean said, changing the subject.

"She told you?" I asked, incredulous. Memories I had suppressed now bubbled to the surface.

"Just the highlights. She was overly ambitious, and another Arbiter tricked her into giving him some valuable information about an important soul. He used that against her and awarded the soul to Hell. In retaliation, her superiors kicked her out of Heaven."

"There's way more to the story than she let on. I wasn't thinking, and by the time I realized what was going on, it was too late. I made that Arbiter pay dearly enough that Death wasn't happy with me. He couldn't argue my logic, but he still had to punish me." I have several scars on my back, and they ache every time I see a whip.

"What I'm really interested in is what you did to her. Last night she acted like a strung-out whore. Today, she's a smart, intelligent woman. Also, she feels different today, like an angel. How'd you do it?"

"If I had something that could do that, and Jeremiah found out about it, he would kill me in an instant. If not him, then definitely someone from Heaven would," I said, staring intently at her.

"Okay, forget that I asked."

"Good, because if they come after me, and I find out you told anyone, my last act will be to run Kitten through you."

With eyes wide in shock, she simply nodded. Cassi returned dressed like a runway model in a short skirt, high-heels, and perfectly applied make-up.

"Wow, the tension's pretty thick. Were you two talking about me?" she asked.

"Just getting to know each other," I said and grabbed my phone. "Time to go. After I text Renaldo, that is."

"And he is?" Cassi asked.

"A guy that owes me a favor. You won't be able to go out until things blow over. He'll make sure you have everything you need and will provide you with some company when I'm not there. He's a Fallen also, but also gay, so don't waste any time trying to sleep with him," I joked and gave her a wink. He's bisexual, but If he even thinks of touching her, I would cut off his dick, and he knew it.

"I do like a challenge," Cassi quipped with a smile.

I texted Renaldo and gave him the basics. I took Cassi's hand, and with a snap of my fingers, we were in my place in London. I got Cassi settled, then headed back to Jean so we can get to work.

"Time to go visit our new guests."

"You mean Lyzark and Eizan?"

"Yes, I sent messages to both that I would be visiting."

Jean cocked an eyebrow. "And what makes you think they won't try to kill both of us when we get there?"

"I might have mentioned that Jeremiah would be monitoring and may join the party if it got interesting."

"Then let's go!"

# Chapter Nine

I grabbed a brown paper bag from my desk and handed it to Jean. "Whatever you do, don't open this, and don't drop it." Before she can reply, I snapped my fingers, and we're back in LA, on a street corner a few blocks from Lyzark's camp.

As we made our way toward Lyzark's headquarters, it's easy to feel his power and see its effect. The street had been blocked off from vehicle travel, and there was quite a bit of foot traffic. Prostitutes that generally don't even open their eyes until 3 pm were already selling their wares. We passed by a fleabag hotel that advertised rooms for twenty-five dollars for fifteen minutes. From the anxious looks of their customers, they wouldn't need the full fifteen minutes. On either side of the street, makeshift booths where drug dealers peddled their wares alongside various black-market vendors with stolen merchandise. It felt like this part of LA had become one huge illegal flea market.

As we neared Lyzark's location, the booths get fewer, and security increased. Several of Lyzark's low-level demons eyed us, but a couple decided to be brave and moved to the center of the street. I pulled Kitten and let her demonstrate her strength. A wave of power burst from her, and the festivities came to a grinding halt, and the thugs hesitated.

"We're on arbiter business, and Lyzark expects us. Get in my way, and I will turn you into hamburger." My threat worked as we passed groups of demons lining either side of the street. Every one of them gave menacing looks but maintained a respectful distance. I suppressed a laugh. Compared to what we were about to face, these demons were pups. Jean received a few catcalls but ignored them. She pulled her sword and gave it a few practice swings. She was incredibly fast and graceful.

The catcalls stopped.

We approached Lyzark's stronghold, and I took a deep breath. If this went bad, Jeremiah had better show up. If he didn't, it would be a blood bath, mostly mine.

Lyzark had commandeered a local hotel for his stay. The outside looked like it hadn't been painted since it was built a century ago. We entered and found the inside to be a different story. The place was spacious and decadently decorated with golden statues, large paintings of nudes, and more chandeliers than I ever thought possible. Everything looked very expensive, but none of the décor matched—as if someone just randomly bought stuff off the internet and hoped it matched. I looked for the Amazon boxes but saw none.

In a way, it reminded me of my LA home until I hired an interior decorator. The first time she saw the inside, she just about fainted. Her initial thought was to burn the house down and restart. I nixed that idea. It cost me a fair penny, but she did a great job. I still don't have the heart to tell her that I kept the velvet painting of dogs playing poker. It was still hung in my bedroom.

Stepping inside, a couple of female demons wearing dresses that barely covered anything greeted us. I moved closer to one to get a better view.

"Hey, big-boy. Ready for the best time of your life," the demon whispered into my ear.

I shook my head. "Sorry, she'd get jealous and end up killing both of you, but I would love to know where you got your dresses." I glanced at Jean. "I think I know someone who would love to see this on you."

When Jean pulled a pair of throwing knives, the two demon sirens ran off, and I held up my hands. "Just kidding!"

Jean frowned as she stowed her knives. "You know, I think you were right. Damnit, they didn't tell us where they bought those dresses."

I held up a price tag. "Got that covered."

Jean grabbed the price tag. "Thanks, but I didn't see this hanging on their dresses. Where did you find this?"

"I don't think you want to know," I replied, and Jean laughed.

Feeling quite smug, I scanned the area finding an assortment of fine foods sitting on a large round table in the center of the room. Everything from chicken fingers to caviar awaited the lucky visitor. A quick arbiter check confirmed there was nothing wrong with any of it, except the cheap champagne, which was laced with enough cyanide to kill an elephant. I can honestly say it would. I had a case where a soul killed an elephant with cyanide. He's in Hell being trampled by elephants hourly. Do this job long enough, and you'll see just about everything.

I grabbed a stuffed mushroom and warned Jean to avoid the drink.

She wistfully stared at the rows of glasses. "Damn, I love a good champagne."

"Don't worry. The good stuff is coming," I said as we walked toward a set of massive double doors.

Two large gargoyle-like creatures each grabbed a rung and grunted as they struggled to open the heavy doors. I waited until they were completely open before entering. Making Lyzark wait, even for a few seconds, was a power play. I'm sure he'd do the same to me, but I was first. Petty, maybe. Important, yes.

Lyzark sat on a throne in the middle of a large open room. Four Large gargoyles sit in each corner. As we walked in, Lyzark threw scraps of meat to them. Hell's lord leaned back in his throne made of gold, gems, and skulls. It's so ostentatious that I was at a loss as to why anyone would have built it in the first place.

Lyzark ignored me and turned his attention to a barely dressed demon who was doing her best to seduce him. She arched her back, doing her best to pull his face to her. Her hips do a slow grind on the demon lord, and she had his full attention.

I watched, mesmerized until my attention was diverted to a Fallen Heaven's angel. She was in chains lying on the floor in front of him. It took me a second, but I recognized her as one of Fre-Fre's girls. She was a little bruised and bloodied, but otherwise, she looked okay. When Fre-Fre heard about this, he'll kick every demon out of his club for a month. That's assuming he hadn't sold the girl to the demon in the first place.

Jean moved toward the Fallen, and I grabbed her arm. When she looked at me, I shook my head, and she stepped back. It was obvious the Fallen was an attempt to piss me off and throw me off my game. He should know better, so I decided to return the favor. I marched over to a table full of demons and grabbed their bottle of champagne. I took a swig from the bottle, then put on a nasty face as I spat the champagne out over the demons.

I hurled the bottle at the back wall, sending shattered glass and champagne everywhere. "It's like I told you, Ms. Kilford. If you want good champagne, you have to go to Heaven."

The room went quiet, and all conversation stopped along with the halt of the demon lord's lap dance. Lyzark was particular about his champagne, and my comment got under his skin, which was a good thing unless he kills us. Lyzark pushed the siren off his lap and grabbed his sword. To be square, it was delicious champagne, and I resisted the urge to go lick up what was left off the ground.

Lyzark stood six-foot-nine, muscular with perfectly groomed long brown hair. What's unusual was he's in his demon form, which technically is against the rules. Heaven and Hell have quite a few rules about being on Earth. Chief among them was that they must take human form when visiting. To see him in his demon form was unusual. Despite the rumors, demons don't have pointy tails or horns. Lyzark's skin is dark red, but demons, like humans, come in many colors. He does have a pronounced forehead with a ridgeline at the top. His eyes are a crimson red with light red sclera.

Lyzark smiled when he spotted Jean and blasted her with his demonic energy. Demons usually only did this for their own kind as part of their mating ritual, but clearly Lyzark was taken by Jean. I have to say the guy had power. Even I was thinking of hitting on him after that blast, but Jean didn't flinch. She completely ignored Lyzark, which could have been construed as an insult to him. If anything, she was flirting with the captive Fallen angel. I'm impressed. She played this game well.

Lyzark leered at Jean then glared at me. "And why shouldn't I kill you, Mr. Dodson, for your insult?" He put his sword down and picked up a battle axe that's almost as tall as he was. He gave it a slow twirl.

"Because I'm not sure that Kitten would allow it." Kitten flashed Death's gift of her newfound power to help make my point. "Plus, I bring something much better than what I just threw away."

I motioned for Jean to hand me the bag she carried, and I pulled out a bottle of bourbon. The bottle glowed in a rainbow of colors that reflected the light. There was an intoxicating feeling just staring at the colors, and Lyzark eyed it hungrily.

"If you're willing to answer some of my questions, I will share a glass or two with you and then leave the bottle."

"A lot of good that will do me," Lyzark growled.

Normally, he would be right. This particular brand of bourbon is both magical and enchanted. The enchantment prevented demons and angels from enjoying its content.

"That's where you are wrong. I have full ownership of the bottle. I can give it to anyone I want, no enchantments. But, in exchange, I also get the Fallen angel."

I had Lyzark's full attention. This wasn't just any other bourbon, and for him to own a bottle would give him bragging rights throughout Hell. Even Satan would barter to get a shot.

"Why would you want the Fallen ba...?" The demon gave me a confused look then waved his hand. "Never mind, crazy arbiters. Done." The chains dropped off the Fallen angel. She's crying and tried to crawl to me. I walked to her and knelt.

"Did Fre-Fre sell you to him?" I asked. She shook her head between sobs. I handed her a coin that should cover her costs for a few days. "I'm sending you to Fre-Fre. Give him this coin and tell him I will come for you later."

I snapped my fingers and sent her back to the club. Long term, she was going to be a problem. Fre-Fre was protective of his Fallen. If she were taken without his permission, he would ban all demons from his clubs, and I know Satan loved her weekly steak.

"Thank you, Kye, for taking care of that problem for me," Lyzark said.

It was my turn to be confused. "Um, you're welcome? Except, why was she a problem?"

Lyzark looked around the room. "If you don't know, then we should leave that for a future conversation."

I was baffled by his comment but decided to let it go. "Then, let's drink." I opened the bottle and poured Lyzark a double shot, and let him take the first drink.

It was a small sign of respect, and he drank it slowly. About halfway through, he looked at me nervously. Realizing he thinks I might have poisoned the bourbon. I poured a shot and tossed it back to prove it was safe.

The liquor burned going down, but what comes next was its specialty. The bourbon was distilled by a small group of warlocks who found a way to infuse magic into it. Magic that can heal both physically and mentally. I feel the aches in my bones disappear. My worries, fears, and anxieties all went away. Right now, all was good with the world. The best part, my senses were heightened. Without even looking, I knew the position of each one of Lyzark's goons, the weapons they possessed, and if they were getting ready to attack.

I poured a glass for Jean. She took a sip, then another, then downed it. She smiled then dropped into a nearby chair.

We enjoyed another round and then handed Lyzark the bottle. He happily poured his lieutenants drinks. I felt a decent buzz coming on and settled into a chair. The bottle will refill itself in a minute, another plus. It will do that for a year after it's opened.

"Now for my questions," I blurted, my buzz intensifying. I paused to make sure I have my thoughts straight.

Lyzark's had enough of the magical liquor to be friendly but not drunk enough to want to fight. He fell into his throne and nodded. "Pleasure first, then business. Ask your questions, Arbiter Kye," he roared with a slight slur. Demons and angels can't hold their liquor no matter what they say.

"The prize. He's obviously the spawn of someone not from Earth. Is he from Hell?"

Lyzark flinched. He didn't want to let that type of information out. But to lie to me now would be a severe infraction. I knew I would get truthful, albeit incomplete, answers.

Lyzark frowned as he concentrated on what he would say. "No. As far as I know, his power is not from Hell. His sire is not one of Satan's angels. His power is impressive, and he is very dangerous," Lyzark paused. "I don't like any of this."

"Do you think his sire could be one of Heaven's angels?"

"I don't think so. But if he is, it would have to be Eizans. Very few from Heaven would be able to sire a mortal. Even fewer could give their offspring that much power," Lyzark said. "This prize could be the start of the war we all know is coming."

With Lyzark's statement, the room went quiet. To see someone as powerful as Lyzark concerned had everyone worried.

I waited a minute to see if he would add anything more, but nothing more came. "Has anyone gotten close to him?"

"No, not without starting a fight. He's powerful and very knowledgeable. Do you know when Death plans on taking him? I will need to prepare," Lyzark said, standing.

It looked as though my question and answer time was up. "No, he hasn't notified me on when which isn't unusual. I don't usually push for information unless it's critical. Death is not a very patient person."

Lyzark nodded. "I could say the same for my boss." He put out his hand, and I shook it. He kissed Kilford's hand, and we left. Jean did a slow catwalk out the door, knowing full well Lyzark was watching.

After leaving Lyzark's place, we walked a couple of blocks. After making sure there were no prying eyes, I snapped my fingers and returned us to a couple of blocks from my L.A. home. I slipped up when I sent the Fallen to Fre-Fre. Lyzark will now know that I can travel. I'm counting on him working his way through the bottle I just gave him. Which meant his people wouldn't know until he sobered up. I figured those watching my house would assume we snuck out without them seeing.

Next up on the itinerary was a visit to God's right-hand man. But I needed my head clear before dealing with the celestial lord, which meant heading back home.

# Chapter Ten

**W**e walked back into my house, and Jean looked around with a look of surprise. The place was spotless, and Cassi's ceiling butt print was gone. Damn, I should have told my maid not to fix that. Oh well, there's always next time.

"That's amazing. How did you get your place repaired so quickly?"

"Planning and a fantastic maid."

Jean gave me a questioning look, and I tried to hide my smile. "This has happened before."

Jean stared at the missing ceiling print then cocked an eyebrow.

"Okay, maybe not that. I keep multiple sets of furniture in a nearby storage facility. As for my maid, she's one of Death's former aides. He's had several since I started working for him, and he usually ends up killing them when they fail to anticipate his needs. When he lost his temper with his last aide, I called in a favor he owed me. In reward for some 'special services' rendered, he reassigned her to me. Now, she cleans my house, runs errands, and generally makes sure that my household is cared for. In exchange, I helped her become the CIO of some social media company where she makes great money. Through a few shell corporations, I now own forty-five percent of her company. It wasn't hard to arrange."

"You just can't be normal, can you." Jean quipped and plopped into a chair. "Back to Lyzark. That was pretty good bourbon, but why was he willing to talk for a bottle of whiskey?"

"Because it's great bourbon, and no one from Heaven or Hell can buy or even steal a bottle. That means owning one put him one step ahead of anyone else in Hell, including Satan," I responded, without really thinking about it. Instead, I pondered Lyzark's words about the Fallen in chains.

Why couldn't he talk about her there?

"Why can't they get any?" Jean asked as she closed her eyes and eased further into her chair.

"The bourbon is made by a small group of secretive warlocks. Not so long ago, they got into a tiff with an angel and a demon. The whole thing blew up, leaving a warlock, an angel, and two demons dead. The remaining warlocks barred angels and demons from ever drinking their bourbon. God intervened and negotiated the sentence down to five hundred years. Every bottle produced since then has an enchantment that prevents angels from drinking it. I just happened to have a few bottles that don't have that enchantment."

"So, warlocks know about God and Satan?"

"No. Only the head warlock, Mistress something or another, who led the negotiations. I think she knows. In this case, the warlocks thought they were dealing with another magical group," I said. Time to find out what my partner really knew. "What do you know about warlocks?"

"Very little. They're difficult to kill but, I'm trained to deal with one if necessary," Jean replied. I laughed, but she doesn't.

"My training was entirely centered on how to kill all sorts of entities. Other than eliminating a mark, I learned just enough so I can track them down if necessary. I just don't know who they truly are other than a target," she said, stone cold.

The trained killer emerged, and I felt her essence. It wasn't pleasant, but compared to a reaper, it was perfume. Her reply did confirm what I pretty much already knew. Jeremiah insists his employees learn everything about who they deal with. Which is usually the last thing taught. If she doesn't know who her targets are, then her training must have been cut short.

"Jeremiah only taught us about the most common forms, wizards, warlocks, dragons, and a dozen others. But he said there were many more. Is it true? How many different life forms are on Earth? Are there aliens?" In seconds, the hardened assassin had turned into a curious researcher awed by the world.

I sighed. "God created more than just Earth and man. He created Satan, Death, angels, and an entire universe, then let them do whatever it desired. In return, the universe has created things that I don't think even God expected." I truly meant every word. I have seen so many strange things walk by me that nothing surprised me anymore.

Jean sat upright, wide-eyed. "You mean there *are* aliens?"

"You died thirty years ago, became an employee of Death, have met angels and demons, and you're surprised that there may be life on other planets?"

"Well, um, yeah," she replied.

I had to give her credit. At least she was honest. "Yes, there are all sorts on Earth. You already mentioned wizards, witches, and even warlocks. I do suspect that warlocks and others may have found a way to travel to other planets. I don't have definitive proof, but I've encountered some beings that could not have originated on Earth. Their souls were completely wrong compared to a human. I have been around for about a hundred years and have met many. You will, too, if this case doesn't kill us."

"Can we travel to other planets?"

I suppressed a laugh. I asked the same question almost a hundred years ago. "Death is quite clear on the matter. Our domain is Earth, and Earth is where we must stay."

I recognized Jean's crestfallen look. It's the same one I wore when I was told I couldn't leave the planet. To be honest, I haven't been bored since becoming an arbiter, so I really can't complain about not being able to explore the universe.

I moved to the window to check on those sent to tail me. There were two demon angels and the two from Heaven watching me. What's different was two new Heaven's angels walking past my house. It's clear they're casing the place, looking for a way in. The four original observers closely watched the newcomers.

"Things are getting interesting outside," I said, and Jean joined me in time to watch as the two Heaven's angels sent to tail me confront the newcomers. There was a little pushing until the weapons broke out, then no one moved.

"Should we do something?" Jean asked, reaching for her sword.

"No. Best not to get involved with Heaven's business. I've been on the job for over a hundred years and have never seen anything like this. The two on the left are Eizan's men. Challenging their authority could almost be considered treason by some."

The group broke up, and it looked like the show was over. The two newcomers wandered off, trying to play it cool. Something told me I'd see them again.

"Curious. I wonder who sent the new arrivals."

Jean didn't respond. She just stared out the window.

"Okay, time to go visit Eizan." I handed Jean another bottle in a paper bag. "We'll take a walk, lose anyone who may be following us, and then pop over to Eizan's place."

"We can't drive? I kinda like the idea of a drive."

"Normally, I would, but an automobile is too easily manipulated by a celestial. I prefer not to be ambushed by our angel friends outside."

She nodded, and we headed out the door. Both sets of angels started to follow us, but they're clueless about tailing people. We hopped through a few hedges, and we lost them.

We traveled another block to a vacant lot with trees. The trees blocked the view of anyone that might be watching, making this an excellent spot to leave from. I was about to pop us over to Eizans when I spotted a pair of Heaven's angels pointing guns at us.

"Look out!" I yelled and tackled Jean. A series of shots peppered the tree where we stood. To Jean's credit, she rolled away from me, stopped with her back to a tree, and assessed our situation. The bag I gave her firmly in her hand and its contents thankfully unbroken.

Another round of bullets hit the trees around us. It's small arms fire, which is weird. With all of the weapons available to celestials, why would they use mortal weapons?

"Why aren't you shooting back?" Jean asked.

"With what? I don't carry that kind of weapon," I responded. What did they teach her in training?

"Why the hell not? You never bring a sword to a gunfight. Everyone knows that!"

"The reason I don't is because it's stupid. Those guys are about to die. This is an amateur move unless...," I searched for another presence and found it rapidly coming our way.

"I'll take out the two shooters. You need to delay the huge thing that is about to attack. Just keep it busy long enough until I can help," I ordered.

She began to argue, but I didn't wait. Pulling Kitten, I brought up a shield and stepped into the line of fire. The first couple of blasts hit my shield with only minor damage. The average mortal bullet won't kill me, but they do hurt.

Using Kitten's energy, I grabbed the next volley of bullets, and I redirected them back to the shooters. One of the attackers took a round to the head and dropped to the ground. The other angel took one in the shoulder then disappeared. The fact that the one sported a new hole in his head was dead tells me those weren't average bullets. I will have to worry about that later. One problem down. Hopefully, Jean was okay.

A loud crash diverted my attention to where Jean was battling a giant demon. He's easily six-foot-eight and three hundred pounds of pure muscle. Impressively, he was on the defensive as Jean was a whirling blur with her sword. Her speed was incredible. The demon was backing up, but I began to suspect it had more to do with tactics than him losing the battle.

Kitten's blades grew to full length, and I leaped into the battle thinking I had the element of surprise. Somehow, the demon knew I was coming and countered my swing with incredible ease. We were going at the demon at full speed, and he was holding up amazingly well. We were at a stalemate. Unless one of us makes a colossal blunder, we'll be at this all night.

In situations like this, I like to do one thing. Cheat. I maneuvered around to where Jean left the bottle of bourbon. With a quick flip of a wrist, I tossed the bottle directly at the demon. A demon's greed will always get the better of them. At least that's what I was counting on.

The demon spotted the bottle and swung to break it, then realized what it was and stopped to catch it. That gave Jean just enough time to take the demon's head off, sending it bouncing to my feet. The body flopped to the ground, but I caught the bottle before it smashed on a rock.

Jean picked up the head. "He still has a look of greed. I can't believe he fell for that."

I jogged to where the dead angel should be, but the body was gone. There was enough angel blood on the ground for me to assume the angel is probably dead, and someone retrieved the body.

I kicked a rock in frustration. None of this made any sense. I jogged back to inspect the dead demon and checked his neck for an ownership tat. He had the markings of a direct report to Lyzark. At this point, I'm tired of being lied to by just about everyone, including Jean. There was something she wasn't telling me. She was too well trained to be fresh out of training. I've seen several of Jeremiah's assassins, and none could wield a sword as well as her.

I grabbed the bottle and the head. "First, we're going back to talk to Lyzark and find out why we were attacked. Then, we're going back to my house, and you are going to tell me everything you left out!"

She and I were going to have words. But first, I needed to deal with this decapitated head and the demon that caused this mess.

# Chapter Eleven

I snapped my fingers, and we landed as near Lyzark's digs as I could get. He'll have plenty of demonic protection, and I didn't want to set off any of his wards. We headed toward his location, and, at first, the demon guards ignored us. But when they noticed the decapitated head, we got their undivided attention.

As we neared his location, it was time to start the fun. "Lyzark! Come out here. I want to know why you sent one of your killers after me. Death will hear about this."

An ugly group of demons with weapons approached but backpedaled at the mention of my boss's name. Few low-level demons want anything to do with Death.

Lyzark stomped out of his hotel. "Kye," he bellowed. "This better be good. I was in the middle of..." he began but stopped when he saw the head. The two demons that had followed us now flanked him. I can't say I have ever seen two demons more scared in my time as an arbiter.

"I brought you an offering. We had a civil conversation, but you try to have me killed afterward. Why?" I yelled but got my answer almost immediately when Lyzark's expression turned to one of confusion.

He scanned the crowd gathering. "Inside. I guarantee your safe return," he offered and stormed back inside, taking both doors off their hinges.

Against my better judgment, I followed. A demon's guarantee of safety ranks right up there with 'No new taxes.' We followed Lyzark as he entered his throne room. He cursed and lashed out at anything or anyone near him. He wanted everyone gone, and there was a stampede to get out of his way.

He planted himself on his throne and took a long swig of the bourbon I gave him. "I will answer your questions, but I need to hear what happened first."

"We left my house, and your two demons followed us. Suddenly, we have two Heaven's angels shooting at us using modified mortal weapons. I killed one, and then we got jumped by this guy." I held up the head, and Lyzark winced. A small pool of black, demon blood formed on the floor under the dripping head. "Now, tell me why he was trying to kill us?"

"I don't know why he attacked you," Lyzark replied as he stared at the head.

"I know he works directly for you. You're honestly trying to tell me he did this on his own?" I asked, incredulous.

"Yes. His name was Rusk, he worked for me, and he was also my friend," Lyzark paused and stared at the bottle in his hand. For him to show any emotion was telling. "He said he had a plan that would generate a lot of gold for us, not to mention quite a few Fallen. He was always working on schemes, and I didn't question him. Rusk fought hard to be at my side, and he deserved my trust. I last saw him two days ago."

Lyzark focused on me, his eyes blazing red in anger. "My demons lost you, then found the dead angel, and you two fighting Rusk. How do I know you didn't attack him?"

"You have my word that he attacked us. I can have Death verify that," I said and hoped he didn't call my bluff. It's not a pleasant experience. Similar to a colonoscopy without sedation.

The blazing red in Lyzark's eyes dimmed when he concluded I hadn't initiated the attack on Rusk. "This has to be related to the new prize. But how, I know not. Someone must have paid him a lot to attack you. Especially with a bodyguard as well trained as Ms. Kilford."

Kilford smiled and blushed, and I gave her a hard stare. She quickly looked the other way.

"Do you want the head? I am assuming those two can tell you where the body is." I tried not to show any sympathy. Lyzark looked upset, but this could be an act.

"Leave the head. We'll retrieve his body and arrange for an appropriate send-off for Rusk."

I dropped the head and marched out. Back on the street, the host of demons eyed us, careful not to get too close. Killing Rusk was a feat worth respect, and I slowed my walk. Most of the demons were merely watching us go by. A few make a fist and bumped their chest. It was a sign of respect that I have never received from a demon. In fact, it's rare for them to show that type of respect to anyone outside of Satan's domain. It felt amazing, and I enjoyed it until a thought came rushing from the back of my mind. The respect was genuine, which meant any demon that killed Kilford or me would be highly honored.

I snapped my fingers, and we returned to the front door of my home. At this point, it was clear I could travel at will, and I didn't need to hide the fact anymore. Plus, I didn't want to give any demon a chance to win some honor.

I turned off my home security, let us into the house, and headed straight to the bar. Any buzz I might have had from our meeting with Lyzark was gone, burned away during the attack. I poured myself a tall shot and tossed it back. I poured two more, handed one to Jean, and dropped into a chair, my throat burning.

I took a minute just to clear my head. There was a war going on in my mind between the different thoughts that raced through it. I closed my eyes and tossed back another shot, and let the burn clear my head of everything except Jean. The one thing that was clear, Jean had been lying to me about her role. Since I met her, all sorts of warnings had gone off in my head about her. She was assigned to me for a reason, and I needed to know why.

I turned my head toward Jean. "Now, I want the truth. Who the heck are you? And why were you assigned to me?"

I didn't even try to hide my anger. She's lied, or at least hiding the truth, and I needed answers.

"My name is Jean Kilford, and I have been training under Jeremiah," she said and moved toward the window. Her usual cat-like walk gone, replaced with a nervous pace.

"That would be a great start if we were at an AA meeting. Don't try to lie to me and tell me you were randomly chosen for this assignment. Anyone trained under Jeremiah would know everything there was about an arbiter, the war, and a host of other stuff you have no clue about. Your ability to use a sword tells me you aren't just another of Jeremiah's minions. Tell me what is going on and why *you* were assigned to me, or we will continue this conversation with Death himself."

I hate being lied to, especially someone who is supposed to have my back.

"Okay," she said as she brushed her hair back. "About thirty-five years ago, I died and was recruited by Jeremiah. I was in a group of six that trained under Jeremiah. Somewhere along the line, I ended up having an affair with him," she paused.

I was as puckered up as you could get. Death had partnered me with Jeremiah's love interest. If anything happened to her, Jeremiah would make me his play toy.

"It lasted about a year. He told the rest of the team I was training elsewhere, which we were, but every night, after training, I joined him in his bed," she blushed again, and I let it go. "Jeremiah personally trained me, but it ended when I was hit by a trainer and almost died. I was out for several months. Eventually, I rejoined the rest of the team for about twenty years. I was two years away from finishing when I was pulled into this mess."

"Did he say why he assigned you to this case?"

"No, he just said that I was the best fit for this assignment."

Could this get any worse? Jeremiah pulled a personally trained pupil, not to mention his lover, out of training early and assigned her to me. I needed to figure out his end game. Had he hoped she'd get killed in the mix to eliminate an affair gone wrong? Was she a key to solving this case?

The war in my brain fired back up. I believed she was telling the truth, but her story didn't add up.

Jeremiah can take an almost dead arbiter and restore them in minutes. Why was she out for months? I needed to talk directly with Jeremiah and possibly Carl. That part was obvious. How to do it without getting myself killed was the tricky part. Celestials like Jeremiah and Carl typically deal with messy affairs by killing everyone involved.

"Let me make myself clear. Lie or omit the truth to me again, and you will get to see the sword of retribution in action. Am I clear?" I said, and Kitten added a growl.

She looked at me then to where Kitten was stashed in my jacket. "Deal."

"We'll continue this conversation later. For now, we need to go visit Eizan."

"I agree, but I think you have something to take care of first," she said and pointed out the window.

I looked to where she's pointed and spied a teenage demon hiding in the bushes across the street. Can this day get any better? The kid pointed at us and then back to himself.

"He wants to talk to us. Shall I let him in?" Jean asked.

"Absolutely not. You think the average teenager on Earth is a monster? They don't hold a candle to a teenage celestial. They have absolutely no impulse control." I took a deep breath. "Plus, his parents or handler have to be nearby for him to be here."

"Why do you say that?"

"Remember what I said about the Fallen and losing their connection to Heaven or Hell?" Jean nodded. "It's even worse for children of angels. Most can only be on Earth a couple of days before they starve to death. The energy coming from Heaven or Hell is like mothers' milk to them. Without it, they die, usually going insane in the process." I had a bad feeling about this. "Who would have brought a youth with them?"

Jean remained silent and stared at the kid. She slightly lifted her hand as if she wanted to reach out to the kid. I've seen that look before, and I call it the 'Mom' look. It's relatively common among arbiters who had kids when they were mortal and now must deal with a child's soul. I usually see it on women but have seen it on a few of my male colleagues. "You had kids before you, uh, became an employee of Death?"

She shook her head. "No. I never had kids."

Her response caught me off guard, and I wondered if she was lying again. I would have bet anything she's had kids, but for whatever reason, I believed her. I'm missing something here. I was just not sure what.

"They can't be all that bad, can they?" Jean asked, breaking my train of thought.

"They are worse than you can know and will cause all kinds of trouble. A loose teenage angel once caused a war just to see what it was like. We need to get rid of him quickly," I said and almost laughed at the absurdity of my statement. One does not just simply return a demon child to Hell.

"I am assuming when you say, 'get rid of him' you mean return him to Hell." Jean gave me a look telling me she is now on the demon child's side.

"You don't understand. He shouldn't be here. Whoever brought him here needs to take him back." The bad feeling from earlier rushed to the front of my mind, with a picture of a demon head. "Ahh, Hell! Rusk better not have brought him here."

This couldn't get any worse, and Jean just stared at me, confused.

"If Rusk brought him here, then he has no one. If we just send him back to Hell, he would be slain immediately or sold into slavery. What they do to their slaves is beyond barbaric."

Without waiting, I snapped my fingers and appeared a few feet behind the kid. I pulled Kitten just in case he was looking for some glory. He whirled, and the terror on his face was genuine. He stood about five-foot-five and looked to be in his early teens. Impressively, he held himself proud, not cowering, not reaching for a weapon. He's afraid but handled himself like a veteran warrior. I had to give him some credit.

Demon and angel children mentally mature at a much faster rate than mortal children. A demon child will often score their first murder by the time they are thirteen or fourteen. Demon youth were expected to start learning how to kill, using sex to lead mortals astray, and an assortment of other morally corrupt tricks when they become teenagers.

"Are you going to kill me?" he asked and tried to put on a brave face.

"No, I typically don't kill people without a good reason. Do I have a reason to kill you?" Kitten let out a quiet growl, and I was impressed that the kid didn't pee his pants.

"I was helping Rusk when he attacked you," he replied. I expected him to lie but believed him. This kid doesn't act like a demon child.

"Hmm, I guess I do have a reason," I mused and let him squirm. "Tell me everything you know about the attack, and I will consider letting you live." I had no intention of killing an unarmed kid, even if he was a demon. The effect on this kid was immediate, and he spilled his guts.

"Rusk came and got me earlier. He told me to wait in the bushes. When he gave me the signal, I was supposed to stab you with this," he said and whipped out a demon blade. "But he never gave me the signal."

Kitten heated up, ready for a fight, but the kid dropped the blade and backed away. His eyes desperately searched for an escape route. I could almost see his mind whirling, working to find a way out of this.

"Don't move," I ordered as I picked up the weapon.

Demon blades are made from an ore only found in Hell, which makes spotting their weapons easy. Typical demon blades are entirely black and can vary in length from four to forty-eight inches. Most are drab affairs with little or no decoration. That's not the case here. The handle was gold with lines of encrusted gems swirling around it and matched with an eight-inch long blade with a curved point. The length indicated it's meant for a demon child. It's beautiful and worth a lot.

I stowed the knife in my belt. The kid stared at it; he wanted it back but said nothing.

"I'll give the blade back to you when it is safe." Now, I asked the question that I didn't want to ask, "Are you Rusk's son?"

The demon shook his head. "No, I am, uh, was his ward."

His response didn't make sense. Why would Rusk entrust a weapon this expensive to a lowly ward? It was the type of blade a demon father would bestow upon his demon son when he became a man. A ward is just a hair better than being a slave in the demon world. I've never heard of a demon saying a nice word to their ward, let alone handing them an expensive blade—Another strange piece to this puzzle.

I checked the kid out. He looked in good shape. He probably hadn't been away from Hell for that long, at least one good thing.

"How long have you been his ward?"

"As long as I can remember. I liked Rusk. He treated me well and only beat me when I really deserved it." Tears formed in the kid's eyes, and he tried not to cry. The kid was losing it and probably would give anything to be anywhere else. "What am I going to do without him?"

I should have told the kid to run, headed back into my house, and forget about the whole thing. What am I going to do with a demon child?

My frustration boiled over. "Christmas almighty. Can I not get a break today?" I yelled to no one. I lowered Kitten and paced. The kid took a step back and expected the worst.

"Do you have anyone else in Hell to go back to?"

He shook his head, and the tears flowed faster. Oh, dear Death, what did you get me involved in? As much as I want to, I couldn't leave the kid. As an arbiter, I should send him back to Hell. Let them deal with it. Most arbiters would, and that's why I don't get along with most. Sending that kid back to Hell would mean either death or a life that I wouldn't wish on my enemies.

"Just wait for my signal, then come to my door. We'll figure out how to get you home." The kid looked up expectantly, and I needed to set the ground rules. "But I'm warning you."

I extended Kitten to her full form and pointed her at the kid. Her blade mere inches from his head. I gave him a dose of my arbiter power to impress upon him the seriousness of the situation.

"Destroy anything in my house, lie, betray me, or do anything at all to get in my way, and I will cut your head off," I said. I tried to get Kitten to growl, but she knew I was lying and gave a half-hearted meow. It didn't matter. The kid was fixated on Kitten's blade.

"I'm going back to my house and will signal you in a few minutes," I said. The kid nodded and stared at Kitten.

I snapped my fingers and expected to return to my house. Instead, I was in Death's office.

Why me?

# Chapter Twelve

C arl sat at his desk and studied a document. I waited patiently until he looked up. I was in no hurry to interrupt someone who could wipe out your very existence out with just a mere thought.

"Kye! Glad you could come. I understand you have some questions for me."

I wanted to point out I hadn't told him I had questions, and I didn't have a choice about coming to his office. But I preferred to live and stowed my comments. He motioned to a chair, and I sat.

"How much do you know about Jeremiah and Jean?" I asked. Carl doesn't appreciate beating around the bush, and I won't waste his time. A slight smile showed surprise at my direct approach, hopefully in a good way.

"As you probably expect, I know everything. I was delighted to see Jeremiah find someone to love. He has spent many millennia perfecting his craft. He needed some joy in his life."

"How did it end? I asked Jean, but her answer just doesn't jive with the facts."

"I am not sure it is over." Carl stroked his beard as if looking for the right words. "Maybe just on hold. As for what happened between them, you will have to ask Jeremiah. I don't think it's my place to share that information," Carl said and returned his gaze to his papers.

I suspected my meeting had come to an end, but he surprised me again when he looked up with a cocked eyebrow. "What are your plans for the kid?"

"I'm not sure. He hasn't given me a reason to kill him. But if I don't do something, he'll starve to death. Hell, killing him may save him from some nasty suffering," I said, hoping that would suffice.

Death leaned back in his chair, a quizzical look on his face. "Do you plan on killing him?"

This was the part where I'm supposed to be a stone-cold killer and say yes. My mind said yes; however, my heart said no.

"Probably not. If I can, I'll figure out a way to get him back into Hell with someone who won't sodomize him for their own pleasure."

Carl smiled. "Good. I'm glad my faith in you is well placed. Put some trust in the kid. It will pay off in the long run," he said, with a don't-be-an-idiot-and-ignore-my-advice look. "To help you, I have a little present for you. There is someone I want you to talk to, a Mr. Bush."

"Another prize?"

"Not exactly. Just someone that I think you need to meet with. He has some insight into your current problem."

Before I could reply, I appeared back in my living room. I really hate being bounced around like a toy.

"Where the heck have you been?" Jean asked.

"Death wanted a quick conversation."

Jean frowned. "That can't be good. What did he want?"

"To get an update and to tell me that we have someone we need to talk with," I said and unlocked my front door. I opened it and waved to the kid.

He looked up and down the road to make sure the coast was clear, pulled his hood over his head, and hightailed it to my house. Once he crossed the threshold, he stepped to the side and put his back to a wall.

Jean glanced at me. "Kye, introduce me to your new friend."

"Kid, this is Ms. Kilford. Jean, this is ah, the kid," I said, realizing I didn't even know his name.

Jean gave me an evil eye. "Pardon Kye's lack of manners, Jean Kilford. And you are?" she said and extended her hand.

I rolled my eyes. The kid won't have an idea what a handshake is. Demon wards are more likely to be beaten or raped than taught this type of etiquette.

"Rusk called me Tassis," he replied. He shook her hand, which I hadn't expected. There may be more to this kid than I thought.

"How long have you been away from Hell?"

"A couple of hours. Rusk came and got me right before he attacked you."

I grabbed his collar and pulled his face close to mine. "Did he tell you anything about the attack? Did he mention if anyone else was involved? Anyone at all?" I was desperate for information.

"No, he just came and got me. Gave me the knife, told me where to hide, and said I wasn't supposed to move until I got the signal," Tassis replied. The eagerness in his voice to prove he was trustworthy made me believe him. He was in a bad situation and knew it.

"What I don't get is how he knew where we were going to be? We weren't followed, but he knew." I let him go and ignored the evil stare from Jean. Something didn't jive, and too many thoughts bounced around in my head. I needed to concentrate on one and let the rest stew for a while. Hopefully, my subconscious would figure out this mess.

"Are you hungry?" Jean asked Tassis.

The kid's eyes lit up, and he nodded. His natural red eye color is slightly faded, and his hunger was a sign that the adverse effects of being away from Hell had begun. I hoped I was wrong, but I've dealt with enough situations like this to know the progression. Luckily, eating would slow it.

I pointed to a doorway. "There's brisket in the fridge. Save some for me."

Jean led Tassis into the kitchen, and I followed. As she took the brisket out of the fridge, he tried to push past her and grab it.

Jean pushed him back. "We will warm this and eat together."

The demon blushed and apologized, confused by his actions. To me, there was no confusion. Tassis had a day, maybe two, before he starved to death. He will become violent, and his anger will consume him. When that happened, I'll have to kill him.

We ate, well actually, the kid devoured most of the food while Jean and I snacked. Tassis seemed better with a full stomach. He excused himself to use the restroom, and I waited until he left before speaking.

"We need to go see the person Death wants us to talk to," I stated as I wiped up the gravy on my plate with the last biscuit.

"Well, then let's go. Is there an issue?"

"Yes, what the heck are we going to do with him?"

"He comes with us," Jean said flatly. She crossed her arms and gave me a look that said she had made up her mind. She's supposed to be one of Death's assassins yet didn't act the part.

"Are you nuts? We don't know what we are getting into. This kid could end up getting himself, or worse, us killed," I argued. I hoped she would see reason. I knew she wouldn't, but I had to try.

"Then he can just stay in your house until we come back," Jean replied and grinned. I'm boxed in, and she knew it.

"That ain't happening. I guess he comes with us. But I'm warning you. I'm not sticking my neck out to save this kid."

Jean ignored me.

Tassis returned and scanned the room for something. "Do you have anything for dessert? Rusk always had dessert. He said it was the best part of any meal," his voice trailed off as he realized Rusk was not coming back.

Jean put an arm around him. "Of course, there is! Rusk was right. Just give me a minute to find where Kye has hidden his sweets."

She rummaged through the fridge but will come up empty. Cassi would have polished off any kind of sweet.

I excused myself and headed out of the room. With a snap, I was at my favorite bakery. Why? I had no idea, except that I hoped that a sugar high would keep Tassis alive a little longer. I bought a triple-chocolate-something cake and headed back.

Tassis' eyes grew wide as I placed it in front of him. "Yes, you have to share."

"I will. Rusk always said that sharing shows strength," Tassis replied, not taking his eyes off the cake.

There was much more to Rusk than I thought. Since when does a demon lord teach a ward morals? I'm beginning to believe I would have liked Rusk.

Jean smiled at me. "You will have to tell me where you kept that hidden."

She winked, and I ignored her. If she thought I was getting soft on the kid, she's wrong. At least, I kept telling myself that.

Jean cut the cake and gave us each a slice. I expected the kid to demolish his piece in seconds, but instead, he took his time. I have spent a fair amount of time with demons and their offspring. Yet, I have never seen a powerful demon treat their ward, as well as this kid has been treated. Tassis identified himself as Rusk's ward, but Rusk treated him like his own son. In the demon world, a ward is only slightly better than a slave. They cook, clean, and generally are grunts expected to stay out of sight. Either Rusk was a major softie, or there was more to this story.

Kilford stared at Tassis. I can't tell if she struggled to understand the kid like I am, or her motherly instincts to protect their young were kicking in.

"Okay, tomorrow we need to make a trip to visit a client. Tassis, if you can keep your promise about behaving, you can come."

Tassis smiled and nodded. "That's awesome. Thank you."

This was a bad idea that would most likely end up with me getting hurt or killed. I just couldn't come up with a better idea.

"Now it's time to get some sleep." Tassis began to argue, but I cut that off quickly. "Look, Jean and I have had a long day, and if you want to come along tomorrow, you won't argue."

He went quiet and nodded his acceptance.

"You can take the last room on the right. Jean, can you spend the night here? I want to check up on Cassi, make sure she isn't doing anything stupid."

She gave me a knowing smile. "Something stupid in another one of your shirts?" she quipped, and I just glared in return. "Sure, but I want a bed, not a sofa, to sleep on."

"The first bedroom on the left has a very comfy bed. Good night all!" With a snap, I landed in my London home.

Cassi was thrilled to see me, and after a couple of drinks, we're in my bedroom ripping each other's clothes off.

Afterward, we snuggled in bed, and I enjoyed the feeling of her body against mine. I've had many lovers over the last century, but Cassi was the first person I wanted to spend time with. Arbiters aren't supposed to have love interests—too easy for someone to use them as leverage. There's also the problem that she has to return to Heaven to survive. My angel cocktail will only last for so long, and its effectiveness on her was waning.

I could ask Death if I could retire in Heaven. He would probably grant my wish. There were at least a dozen of Heaven's angels who owed me favors. That might be enough to get Cassi back in.

"What are you thinking about so hard? I can feel your mind buzzing," she said as she stroked my chest.

"This case," I lied. "It has me worried. I have a bad feeling it could blow up big time. To make things worse, I now have this demon kid staying at my home with Kilford. I have to figure out what role they play in all of this."

"I didn't know she was staying at your house. She's very pretty. Do you like her?" Cassi asked, and I felt her body tense. Was she jealous?

"She seems to be a good person and is a pretty good partner," I said. Her body did not relax. If anything, it grew more tense. "But that's it. She has a love interest, and I'm keeping my distance."

Cassi smiled and swung her leg over, straddling me. She stretched her arms and arched her back, knowing full well where my eyes were laser-focused. She leaned forward and put her hands on my shoulders. "I'm glad to see you haven't lost your interest in me."

I wanted to tell her that I would never lose interest in her, but she stretched farther forward and pulled my head to her.

The last thing I heard before my libido took over was Cassi whispering. "I hope you never do."

If she only knew the truth about my feelings, she would never have to worry. I just need to man-up enough to tell her.

# Chapter Thirteen

The next morning, I returned home for a quick clean-up and fresh clothes. Kilford's made breakfast, and the kid ate anything he could get his hands on. Out of self-preservation, I grabbed some bacon and a cup of coffee before they disappeared.

"I didn't realize cooking and cleaning were part of Jeremiah's training," I quipped.

I ducked as a throwing knife, courtesy of Jean, zipped by my head and embedded itself in the wall behind me. Tassis gave Jean an appreciative look then returned to his food.

Jean turned to put a dish away. "Any other questions?"

I chuckled. "Nope. I'm just glad to see he taught you something useful."

Another blade flew by my head, and I decided I needed to change the subject. I grabbed my phone and checked my arbiter app. To my surprise, our meeting was in New Orleans, or NOLA, as the locals refer to it.

I have a love-hate relationship with New Orleans. It's a great city to visit and have fun. But, every time I've gone, I ended up dealing with things I've never seen before. Most of my arbiter brethren hate being assigned there. For better or worse, there was never a dull moment when you visited the Big Easy.

With a snap, we landed in the financial district. I let out a breath, happy we didn't end up on Bourbon Street. Nothing too strange happens there, at least from a celestial perspective. I just hate the party crowd.

After a short walk, we approached a small group of bodyguards positioned around the front of a four-story building. The guards were decked out in matching black suits. The bulges under their jackets indicated they were heavily armed. A black Maserati screeched to a stop, and the group moved into position to welcome the driver. He climbed out wearing the type of suit that tried to look like it's casual wear—even though it costs more than your yearly salary. I know; I own a couple.

I approached the new arrival with Jean and Tassis in tow, and two guards moved in to intercept me. A quick blast of my arbiter power, and they wandered off confused. The others reached for their weapons.

"I wouldn't do that if I were you," I said and shook my finger at them. "Mr. Bush, we just want to talk. No harm, no foul." I needed this to go peacefully.

The driver stared at me, then Jean. My eyes flashed gray, a warning that he needed to take me seriously, and his expression changed. "Neat trick. However, you'll need an appointment to see me."

"Mr. Bush, Death sent me. Should I tell him you didn't want to talk with his emissary?" My eyes glowed gray, and his guards backed up.

Bush smiled then took off his sunglasses. It only took a second for me to realize why Death sent us here. He's the mirror image of Joshua. Jean took a quick breath as she came to the same conclusion.

Joshua and Bush were identical twins.

"Are you a reaper?"

I'm glad he asked. It gave me a clue of how much he knew about celestial beings.

"No, believe me, if I were a reaper, you wouldn't have to ask."

Reapers have an aura unlike anything else I have ever experienced. Their mere presence can make the average mortal assume a fetal position. Being an employee of Death, I'm immune to it. The only non-celestial being not affected by a reaper's aura are cats.

I once watched a cat stroll up to a reaper, vomit a massive hairball on its foot, then walked off to take a nap. The funny thing was the reaper was too afraid of the cat to do anything. Death loves cats, and his employees pay a heavy toll if they harm a cat unnecessarily. Consequently, reapers give cats a lot of respect and avoid them if at all possible.

I'm not a cat fan, but I put out bowls of food for the local strays to discourage reapers from making unannounced visits.

"In that case, why don't we head up to my office?" he offered, with a slight bow. Scowls from his bodyguards told me they weren't happy, but they parted as we walked to the elevator. Bush pushed four, and we were on the fourth floor in no time.

We emerged into an open area, and his 'office' was the entire floor. There were multiple desks, sofas, and workstations scattered around the room.

We're greeted by a tall receptionist in a pin-striped suit and an unusual lapel pin. I knew the symbol from somewhere but couldn't place it. As she walked toward us, her cat-like stroll could rival Jean's. The two size each other up, and it was clear they have taken an instant dislike to each other.

"Mr. Bush, you have unscheduled guests," the receptionist greeted with a well-practiced smile.

"Yes, we are meeting for just a few minutes. Everyone, this is my personal assistant, Darlene." She gave a crisp and very mechanical nod to the group, and Bush continued. "Can you please clear my calendar and bring us coffee and some of those sandwiches?"

Darlene nodded and looked at Tassis. "And what would you like, young man?"

I cringed at her question. Demons are taught to fight for the respect they are due. Tassis's upbringing would make him believe he was equal to Bush and me. By singling him out, Darlene had inferred he was somehow inferior to the other males in the room. The receptionist will pay for her comment. I just wasn't sure how.

"Coffee, black with three sugars. A dash of rum would be good also," he answered, then stepped toward her. He was only inches from her and stared into her eyes.

Her perfect smile wavered.

"I think we can skip the rum, for now, just the coffee for him. Thank you," I said and pulled the demon back. I hoped he'd settled his score, but I suspected he hadn't.

The receptionist nodded and hurried off. Bush chuckled, and I joined him until an annoyed look from Jean shut us down.

"Not sure I have ever seen her rattled before. That alone was worth meeting with you," he said and motioned for us to sit. The chairs were very comfortable, and I settled in.

Darlene returned with coffee and sandwiches. Tassis' eyes followed her everywhere, and the effect on her was apparent when I'm forced to catch the food tray before she dumped it in my lap.

"Mr. Bush," Tassis said, and I almost stopped him. But if I interfered with him establishing his position in the group, I would be his next target, and I didn't want to have to kill him. "I would like to trade for her. I have a lot of gold and other items that may interest you."

70

I just about spit out my coffee at the expression on the receptionist's face. Bush's coffee had stopped midway to his mouth. He had no idea how to respond.

"I am not a thing to be bargained with! Who do you think you are?" the receptionist shouted after she regained her senses.

"I apologize. I thought Mr. Bush owned you," Tassis offered, and I watched as the receptionist relaxed, which was a mistake. "Then I will deal directly with you. How much for you to serve me? I have considerable resources and have been told I am good at pleasuring a woman."

Tassis' expression was perfect. There was no sense that this was a joke. He could very well have asked to buy her car. My entire body shook, and I tried not to burst out in laughter. But I had to shut this down before it got out of hand. "Tassis, we came here to discuss my business, not yours. Continue your negotiations at another time." His nod signaled his honor had been satisfied.

The receptionist turned and fled to the other side of the room. I put my fist in my mouth and tried not to laugh out loud. Bush was also trying to control himself, and we both failed. The disapproving look from the assassin quieted us. She didn't enjoy the banter, and I guessed it was time to get back to what we came here for.

Bush stifled a last laugh. "So, what can I do for you?"

"Well, Mr. Bush, we're here about your brother."

"Please, call me Ken. Tell me, what has my brother done now? Cured cancer, eliminated homelessness, or saved kittens from trees?"

"Not to my knowledge," I replied, trying to keep us on track. "Can you tell me about your parents?"

Ken shifted in his chair and turned to one of his guards. "I need some privacy. Please clear the room, including you, Darlene."

He sighed. "This may take a while."

# Chapter Fourteen

The room emptied in record time. Darlene wasn't thrilled and made it a point to be the last out the door with a "You know how to reach me if you need me."

Once we were alone, I continued. "You were saying?"

"We don't know who our birth parents are," he began. "There was little documentation to be found. Somehow, we were surrendered for adoption one day and adopted the next. No one can explain how it happened, and they don't seem to care."

I sighed. What happened had all the earmarks of celestial interference. There have been a few cases where children have been returned to the mortal world. For reasons unknown to me, Death is in charge of this, and I've been involved only once. Standard operating procedure in these cases—minimal documentation and as much celestial magic as needed.

I nodded and urged him to continue. "From the few official records available, we were adopted when we were three months old. Our adopted *parents*," he said, "raised us until they both died when we were sixteen."

The tone in his voice made me wonder. "How did they die?"

Bush looked down, silent for a moment. "We were just getting full control of our powers. At the time, my brother was the rebel, always looking for a fight. We ran into some creatures we knew were not from Earth. Joshua picked a fight, and a couple of them died. I tried to negotiate peace with them and failed. Later, they found out where we lived. One day, when we were at school, they killed our parents." A tear glittered in Bush's eye, and his face flushed. He took a couple of ragged breaths.

"When we came home and found them, we went ballistic. We knew who did it and tracked them to an underground complex. We were in such a rage our powers took control of us. By the time we came to our senses, we had wiped out every single one of them." Bush stood and walked to a window.

Jean sat stone-faced. I'm a bit of a sucker for sad stories and struggled to keep it together. Tassis walked to Bush and put his hand on his arm.

"I just lost the person I wanted to call my father. He told me of the curse that we, who have power, must endure. It is called the Blood Lust, and it will take over when horrible events occur. Do not blame yourself for those deaths. The only thing you can be held accountable for is what you did afterward," Tassis said and stared Bush in the eyes.

Bush looked back at Tassis, seemingly unable to say anything. So far, this kid had been a source of entertainment and knowledge. Hopefully, I can keep him alive long enough to get him back into Hell.

When Bush remained quiet, I prompted him to continue. "What did you do next?"

Bush wiped a tear from his face with the back of his hand. "My brother and I took different paths. I decided never to rely on anyone ever again and used my powers to become a very wealthy businessman. My brother decided to atone for his sins and used his powers to help those that couldn't help themselves. After a couple of run-ins when our new lives crossed paths, I moved to New Orleans to give us some space."

"Successful with eight bodyguards waiting for you when you arrive at work?" I noted.

He laughed. "At first, I didn't have any. I don't really need them. With my powers, I can take care of myself. But I found that many of those I wanted to work with wouldn't give me the time of day without them. Evidently, if no one wants to kill you, then you're not a player in my field." He took a breath and paused. "So, I hired a few bodyguards, staged a couple of attempted assassinations, and suddenly everyone wanted to work with me. Craziest thing I've ever seen."

"About your powers, do you know where they came from?" Jean asked.

"No, although I suspect Heaven."

I leaned forward, intrigued that he would know the difference. "And why is that?"

"Well, I've dealt with a few demons. Even visited a place they said was Hell. Looked a lot like Vegas if you asked me. I've picked up a few items during my visit, and the energy in them is not like mine."

Ken walked over to a six-foot-tall round cylinder sitting in a corner and put his hand on it. I felt him send energy into it, and the energy is unusual. It was a combination of powers from Heaven, Hell, and Earth. How he pulled it off, I had no clue. The cylinder split into two parts revealing a whole selection of goodies. Most were expensive looking— watches, gold-plated gun, etc. There were several items I recognized that were from Hell. One was something that could be very helpful if I could get it to work.

Ken waved his arm toward the large cylinder. "Feel free to check out my toys."

I walked over and pulled out the gun. It's beautiful, lightweight, and the bullets contained demon magic. Meaning they could kill another celestial. I left it in my left hand as I pulled out what looked like a short tree branch, careful to block the energy that emanated from it. "Do you mind if the kid holds the stick?"

"Be my guest. I was never sure why they gave me that. They just said to keep it in case of emergency," Bush replied.

"Tassis, please take this. I'm not sure this will work, but just in case, do not let it touch anyone else. Do you understand?" I asked while I put the gun back. Tassis hesitantly walked over. The look in his eyes told me he was scared but didn't want to show it to the others. The energy in it won't harm him, even if he couldn't use it. But it could harm Bush.

He reached out and gently took it from my hand. His eyes went wide, and he let out a satisfied sigh. After thirty seconds, he handed it back to me. I did a quick check on the amount of residual energy when I noticed something strange. It was a hidden tracking chip stored in the base of the stick. I've used that trick before, and it's easy to detect if you know what you are looking for.

"Thank you. I feel much better. I couldn't use all of it," Tassis said, looking quite content. The bags that had formed under his eyes were gone. His overall skin color was now a little darker.

Jean knelt next to Tassis, appraising him. "Do you mind letting the rest of us in on what just happened?"

"Demons call it a Feast Stick. Whoever left it was making sure they had a lifeline in case something went wrong."

The looks from Jean and Bush told me they still didn't understand.

"Being away from Heaven or Hell for any length of time is hard on an angel or demon. To make remaining on earth easier, each side has developed a way to store energy in an object and retrieve it later. Typically, it only works for the creator and their immediate family," I said.

Tassis frowned. "So why did it work for me?"

"Ken, was the demon you were working with named Rusk?" I was pretty sure of the answer, but his nod confirmed my guess. This helped, but still didn't explain why Tassis, a mere ward of Rusk's, could use it. Only Rusk's family should be able to use the stick.

"That's why I could use it. It was Rusk's," Tassis said excitedly, then his face fell as he remembered his mentor was not coming back.

Bush eyed Tassis, and I was sure he was about to ask a question that the kid would prefer not to answer. I took him by the arm and escorted him out of earshot of Tassis. "Rusk was like a father to him, and he's dead."

Bush had been staring at Tassis, but his head snapped back to me at the news. He tried to feign a frown, but my news was important to him. He didn't know the demon was dead, and I guessed that Rusk's death was bad news for him. If Bush knew Rusk, did he know about the attack that killed Rusk?

"Poor kid, that's got to hurt. What are you going to do with him? I didn't think angel or demon kids could survive on Earth," Bush said. "He can keep the stick. It's of no use to me."

His look of concern wasn't related to Tassis, of that, I'm sure. Plus, his gift to Tassis was suspicious. With his car, bodyguards, and office, he is successful and probably ruthless. Where his smarts couldn't get him, I'm sure his powers did. Having a heart on top of all that would be a rare combination, and I would have to watch him closely. Giving something like the Feast stick away so easily had a meaning. What it was, I'm wasn't sure until I remembered the tracking chip. Pieces of the puzzle began to fall into place.

"Thanks, he will need to use it again tonight, when we are at home," I lied and set my trap. "Can you hold on for a second?"

When he nodded, I turned away and woke Kitten.

*What is it now? Do you want me to kill him?* Kitten asked.

*No, just tell me how powerful he is?*

*Hmm, he's powerful. Almost as powerful as you, which makes him dangerous. He can travel, and I can tell he has recently. Be careful. He seems very cunning.*

*Thanks, Kitten.*

*You owe me!*

*You got to kill three angels. I would say I'm still on the plus side,* I said. Kitten liked to keep a running tab, and I have learned to be very thorough on my credits and debits with her.

*True, but I have some additional information...*

"Is everything okay?" Bush asked.

I pulled myself from my thoughts and what Kitten told me. I'll have to let her kill something soon. One key tidbit she revealed—Darlene was a demon. I'm impressed. To be able to hide her true nature from an arbiter meant she had some real power.

I returned my attention to the current situation. "Yeah, just checking on something. Tell me, why didn't you mention you just visited your brother?"

"Hmm, very good. How did you figure that out?"

"The big clue was the shield around your brother. It didn't move when he did, which meant that someone else was controlling it." I tried hard not to act smug.

"My brother called me when the angels and demons began to show up. He put up a shield, but I am much better at that sort of thing. I popped over there with an item I picked up from Rusk. It worked well at powering shields. I was getting it set up when you two arrived."

"It was you that I saw when he disappeared."

"Yes, I was surprised that you spotted me so easily."

"Lots of practice," I said and checked the time on my phone. "We have to go, but I may return if I have more questions. You need to be careful. It won't be long before Heaven and Hell make the connection between you and your brother. They are very interested in your brother and wouldn't think twice about using you to get to him. Considering the situation, you may be in more danger than your brother."

"I already came to the same conclusion. I'm very good at hiding, and I think it's time I disappear for a while."

"Are you two ready to go?" I asked Tassis and Jean.

Tassis looked hungrily at the stick, then nodded. Jean glared at Bush until he realized he missed his cue.

"Tassis, you can keep the stick if you'd like. Consider it a gift from me to you," he said, with a smile that if I didn't know better, I would think was genuine.

Tassis smiled, then before Bush could react, he hugged him. "Thank you. Someday I would like to talk to you about Rusk. I want to learn as much as I can about him."

We walked outside, and I felt like it was time for a little distraction. I needed time for the ideas flying around in my head to come together. We're in New Orleans, and what better way to have a little fun than to take a tour of this great city.

Death's Arbiter

Which meant it's time to visit Uncle Bud.

# Chapter Fifteen

ncle Bud is the 'unofficial' caretaker of many of the NOLA cemeteries. When weird things happened in a cemetery, he's the guy that gets the call to take care of it. Bud's mortal but can see celestials and other magical entities. Over the years, I've encountered around a dozen or so like Bud—mortals that can see magical entities. Why they can and others can't, I have no idea. I took the liberty to give him enough information about Heaven and Hell to know how to deal with their representatives. All he knows about me is I make sure souls get to their correct destination.

The less he knew about Death, the better.

Over the years, he's dealt with a whole lot of supernatural stuff along with the homeless, gangs, drug dealers, and others. He always has money for anyone needing a handout and is a regular at the local homeless centers, dropping off food and other supplies. Bud's a good man with a good soul, and I've already made arrangements for him to spend eternity in Heaven.

Today, I tracked him to one of his favorite haunts, Saint John Cemetery-Mausoleum. He's good friends with several resident spirits, and he liked the vibe of the place.

"Kye! Great to see you," he shook my hand then gave me a bear hug. "Would it hurt you to age a little? Makes me look bad."

He looked past me and spotted Jean. "Well, this is a pleasant surprise. Did you finally get yourself another girlfriend? You can call me Uncle Bud."

"Jean Kilford, nice to meet you. I'm Kye's partner, not his girlfriend. This is our friend, Tassis."

Uncle Bud smiled at Tassis, then extended his hand. "I haven't seen a demon youth around here in a long time. Welcome to New Orleans." Bud pronounced New Orleans like the locals, with two-syllables. Some can do it with one, was the running joke.

Tassis shook his hand. "I would like to hear about this previous girlfriend of his."

"That was a very long time ago, and I'm not sure what happened to her."

My happy mood soured at the thought. "Tracey was killed by an angel. He was upset that she had just sent a soul to Hell that he wanted."

"So, you killed him in revenge?" Tassis asked, a little too eagerly.

"Nope," I growled and scanned the cemetery. "I wanted to, but Death warned me not to kill him. So, I cut off his wings, along with a couple of other things, and handed him over to Satan. He eventually was returned to Heaven, and I got into a lot of trouble. Later, he tried to exact his revenge." I smiled. "He's currently listed as missing."

These were hard memories for me. I had cared for Tracey and ended up going down a dark hole for a couple of years. I channeled my anger over her death into my work. Anyone that got in my way those years paid dearly. It was the very reason that Kitten selected me to wield her. My ability to hold anger, use it, and channel it, was perfect for her.

A polite cough pulled me from my thoughts. Bud and Jean have backed away and nervously stared at me. I'm not sure why until I realized I'm holding Kitten in my hand, and her blades were out. How long had I been just standing there?

I stowed Kitten. "Sorry."

Uncle Bud put a hand on me. "Kye, is there something you need from me?"

"Yes, actually there is. I'm hoping you could give us a tour of the local cemeteries and point out some of the highlights." I tried to plaster a smile on my face.

"Excellent idea. I would love to. Especially if you could help me with an issue," he said, clasping his hands and looking down at his feet. He's spooked about something. Considering that Bud has seen a lot for a mortal, it must mean something bad must be going on.

"Sure, I will do whatever I can. What's the issue?"

"There's something very evil in the area. I think it has killed at least two people, and several of my resident ghosts are missing. It's gotten to the point that I avoid the cemeteries at night."

"Any information on it?" I asked and hoped this would be a quick and easy fix.

"I've only seen it from a distance. Not even sure if I really know what I saw." Bud took a breath and rubbed his hands together. "Out of the corner of my eye, I see this moving black fog. I turned to look at the fog, and it formed into a person. The next day that person was found dead. It's even got my resident demon worried."

Jean gave me a questioning look.

"The demon's name is Trey and hides in local cemeteries," I explained. "Lyzark wants him dead, so he spends as much time as he can away from Hell. Pretty anti-social and prefers to be left alone. Avoids trouble as best he can."

"You have what's called a 'Vapuer,' which means vapor in French. It's a type of wraith," Jean offered, surprising me.

She shrugged when I cocked my head. "What? These are the types of things I have been trained to deal with."

I shrugged my shoulders. "Okay."

Jean continued. "They are tough to kill until they take form. They will find a spot to hide and watch for days, or even weeks, for their next victim. After they pick a target, they come alive at night and form into a pretty good likeness of them. They're excellent trackers and never fail to find their prey. They feed off the victim's fears as they are tortured."

While Jeremiah's group usually dealt with issues like this, I have killed a couple of vapuers over the years. Death isn't a big fan of non-mortals killing mortals. Consequently, when something like this is reported, one of Jeremiah's hit squad is sent to eliminate the non-mortal. With Jean being my partner, it will be up to her to report it.

"How do they pick their targets?" Uncle Bud asked.

"First, the victim as to touch the spot where they are hiding. They like to hide on large black surfaces and can mimic the look and feel of the object they are hiding on. Second, they pick someone they know will be frightened the most; they can sense it when touched. People like military special forces, firefighters, and cops aren't good targets for them."

"Yeah, so far, a teenage girl and an elderly man were killed. Very brutally. My cop friends won't even talk about it," Uncle Bud said. "So, how do you get rid of one?"

Jean jumped with a ready answer. "Not easy. They can spot a non-mortal from a distance, which makes killing them hard. When it's hiding, Kye couldn't get within fifty feet of the vapuer without it spotting him. But once it forms, our weapons can eliminate the wraith."

She left out that usually, there was only a short window from when a vapuer formed and when it killed.

"Then we have to find out where it's hiding and wait for it to transform," Tassis added.

"Any hints on how to track a vapuer down?" Uncle Bud asked.

"They like spots out in the open. They also like lots of foot traffic nearby. Parks and malls are their favorites along with tourist spots such as monuments," I replied. "The key is that someone has to touch the object they are hiding on for the vapuer to select its prey."

"Well, my guess would be City Park, but it's huge. I could spend days looking and not find it," Uncle Bud said, clearly worried.

"We'll start where you spotted it the first time. We might pick up a scent. The issue is it can travel for miles in its vapor form. Most humans can't see it, but those who have seen a lot of supernatural events can. Also, if your cop friends can tell us where the victims visited, we can narrow down the spot," Jean said, then paused. "One thing going for us is that once a vapuer picks a spot with a successful kill, it won't abandon it unless forced to leave."

"Okay. My cop friends will help me. They're spooked and will take help in any form, even from an old man like me. But it'll take a couple of days." Uncle Bud took a deep breath then his famous smile appeared. "Now, let's take that tour!"

We spent the day visiting many of NOLA's famous cemeteries. Uncle Bud knows his stuff, and even I learned a lot.

We visited famous graves, took a trolley ride, and spent a lot of time in City Park. We spotted a vendor selling ice cream, and I gave Tassis money to buy some. Even though he's a demon, he was still a kid. The look of pure joy on his face made my day. He grabbed Jean's hand, and they made a run to the stand. I hadn't felt this alive in a very long time. I caught Uncle Bud staring at me.

"Now tell me. Why'd you stop coming around?"

I knew the question was coming, and he was due an answer.

"I was going to lead with the whole busy arbiter thing. But I owe you the truth." I took a breath and pulled my thoughts together. "Uncle Bud, you're a wonderful person, and you bring out the best in everyone around you."

"Thanks for the compliment. I suspect a 'but' coming."

"You are a reminder of the humanity that I have lost. That I was once a person, just like you, alive. I had hopes, dreams, my faith, and when I died and became an arbiter, those things changed."

I watched Tassis take his first lick of an ice cream cone and some dribbled down his face. Jean laughed then wiped his face with a napkin.

"When I last saw you, the reminder was too much, and I had to leave." I turned toward him. "What I failed to realize is that I needed you to help me keep what humanity I had left. To prevent me from becoming another celestial automaton. To remind me that the souls I'm working with are as precious as just about anything in this world."

I looked back to Tassis and Jean and enjoyed their smiles. Uncle Bud's hand rested on my shoulder, and I just listened to the world.

"Thank you for helping me remember what it was like to be mortal. I promise I will visit more often," I said and vowed to keep that promise.

"Kye, deep down, you're a good man. Remember that. Also, remember, when you visit, bring your bourbon!" He laughed, and I quickly joined. The man doesn't realize how much bourbon he is going to receive.

I gave him a bear hug. For the first time in years, I felt like a person—not just an arbiter. I am Kye, and I am more than my work.

Tassis and Jean returned, and I released Uncle Bud. Jean eyed me but said nothing. Tassis handed me an ice cream cone, and it's the best thing I have had in a long time.

"There are a few spirits I would like you to meet," Uncle Bud said.

We headed off to another cemetery, and I strolled along, just enjoying the view. It's a beautiful day, and for just a little while, I could forget what I do and what I was.

"That's the first genuine smile I've seen on your face. You should share it with Cassi," Jean remarked.

"I hope too, Jean. I hope too."

Jean gave my shoulder a playful, albeit painful, punch. "You'd better."

We saw quite a few spirits, but all from a distance. Most knew we worked for Death and did their best to avoid us, fearing we may try to take them back to Heaven or Hell. A few waved to us, and two flipped me off.

"Friends of yours, Kye?" Uncle Bud asked.

"'Friends' may be the wrong term," I replied and received a round of laughter from the group. "Most spirits on Earth are here because they don't like the outcome an arbiter recommends. Those two died in a car crash running from the cops. It was a minor crime, and the cops weren't interested in chasing them until they side-swiped a school bus. They died five minutes later. For whatever reason, Heaven didn't want them, so it was off to Hell for them. That meant a pretty bleak existence, so they made their escape and returned to Earth. They were lucky. Most don't make it back. I guess they blamed me for not letting them go to Heaven.

Heaven was dead-set against taking them, but they'll never accept the decision."

"What will happen to them?" Tassis asked.

"Assuming they don't pick a fight with someone, or something, much stronger than them. They'll probably fade away in another year."

"Ahh, here she is. Elena, please come over here," Uncle Bud yelled. Several people walked by and glanced around. They can't see the approaching spirit and looked at Uncle Bud like he's crazy.

"Bud, who are your delicious guests?" she asked, then spied me. Her smile faltered, but she quickly composed herself. "Bud, I didn't know you were friends with an arbiter. Should I be worried?"

"Elena, this is Kye. He's a good friend. You have nothing to fear from him. Isn't that right, Kye," Bud stated, eyeing me.

"Quite right, we're enjoying the day, and I'm off duty. It's nice to meet you, Elena." I gave a slight bow.

She smiled and looked to the others. Bud introduces Jean and Tassis, and they exchanged pleasantries. I was about to find out more about Elena when I spotted a fierce spirit storming our way.

And it's heading straight for Kilford.

"Jean, behind you!"

# Chapter Sixteen

J ean turned, spotted the spirit, and pulled her sword, ready for battle. Most celestial entities have a way of identifying themselves: God's angels have their white light of Heaven, Satan's demons have the black light of Hell, arbiters have a gray light of Death. Reapers don't have their own light like other celestial beings. Their aura of death is more than enough to identify them.

While arbiters and Jeremiah's assassins share a similar gray aura, each is distinct. Jean flashed her aura, and it's a warning the spirit needed to heed. The tip of Jean's sword hovered inches from the spirit. The wayward soul eyed Jean's sword, smiled, then began to hurl all sorts of not-safe-for-work abuse at us.

Tassis' eyebrows raised, impressed with her vocabulary. Since demons revel in such trash talk, it's high praise.

"Tina! That's enough. You're going to hurt yourself!" Elena screamed, and Tina stopped.

While both Elena and Tina are spirits, Tina's aura is visibly darker, almost black. Which could only mean one thing, and it wasn't good.

"You don't get to talk to me like that," Tina replied.

"I didn't know he was yours! I'm sorry. Forgive me," Elena pleaded.

Jean glanced at me and took a couple of warning swings. "Can someone tell me what's going on?"

"Yeah, I think I can," I answered. "These two are spirits who feed off human sexual emotions."

Yeah, they exist. If you ever feel like someone is watching you have sex, there probably is, and they're enjoying it as much as you are.

"Elena must have come across a guy Tina had laid claim to. No pun intended." When it's obvious no one got my joke, I added. "I thought it was a pretty good one!"

The glare I received from the group told me my joke was not in good taste. While I love humor, the dark spirit before me is a problem that I needed to address. "Tina, you look rather dark. Why is that?"

Tina began to scream, and I gave her a full arbiter blast. My power can scare an angel, but it had little effect on the dark spirit. The darkness I saw in her had all but consumed her. It's obvious now that sex is not the only thing she draws energy from now. I pulled Kitten and am surprised when she was already awake and ready. Usually, killing the average spirit doesn't even rate on her scale.

"Tina, what have you done?" I asked. A couple walking by stopped and gave me a scared look. A quick blast of arbiter energy, and they rushed off.

"Those that cross me pay the price. He should not have done that with her!" she growled as she moved a little closer toward Jean.

Jean was ready and gave the spirit a warning swing, her blade barely missing Tina. The spirit watched the blade fly by then rushed toward Jean. Tina thought she could get to the assassin before Jean could bring her sword back across. Jean was too well trained to be fooled that easily. She performed an impressive spin, and her sword sliced through Tina.

Tina stopped and laughed, thinking she was safe, then her smile faltered. The weapons we carry work just as well on spirits. Her smile disappeared, then so did Tina.

"Why? Why did you do that to her? You monster!" Elena screamed and stepped toward Jean. In a blur, Jean whirled, her sword stopping a mere inch from the spirit's face. She raised her hands and backed away from the assassin's sword.

"Elena. Tina killed the man you shared. Something snapped in her, and she's been drawing energy off killing people," I said.

I tried to signal Jean to stand down, but she was in complete assassin mode. Her eyes flicked to me, then back to Elena. The look I received in that instant could send a chill down the back of a reaper.

Elena frowned. "No, she would never do that," she replied, trying to sound confident. In the background, police sirens blared. I suspected someone just found a dead body.

"Yes, she did, and I'm guessing it wasn't the first time. She learned that she could feed off the emotions of those being killed. But killing mortals will corrupt you. It will turn you into a monster and drive you crazy. The Tina you knew was already gone." I hoped she picked up on my warning.

Elena turned away and disappeared.

I glanced at Uncle Bud. "Let me guess. Tina was the one you wanted us to meet?"

Bud looked down and nodded. "Yeah. She was a kind spirit until she got tangled up with a witch. The witch put some sort of spell on her so she couldn't feed. She only meant for the spell to last a day, but it lasted a week. After that, Tina was never the same. I was hoping you could help her."

"I'll need the name of that witch. What she did gave Tina a taste for killing."

"Now, don't go starting no trouble. She made a mistake and tried to fix it. I don't need you killin' some witch over this," Uncle Bud argued.

"I have no intention of killing her. But at least one person is dead because of her mistake, and she needs to know what she did," I replied.

I returned my gaze to Jean as she lowered her sword and her eyes focused on the ground. I know what she's going through. Even though Tina was a spirit, she was still a mortal soul. When a non-mortal kills a human, we feel what the victim feels as they die. It's a rule that the big three (God, Satan, and Death) insist on. The hope is that it will keep celestials from going on a mortal killing spree. Believe me, it's heart-wrenching and hit me hard the first time it happened to me. Jean's a much tougher cookie than I am. She's probably more confused by her emotions than upset.

Reapers do feel the pain from their victim's death, but it's meaningless to them. To be a reaper means you feel almost nothing. It takes a lot to make a reaper feel fear or happiness. Not how I would prefer to live. Carl created them and can make a reaper feel whatever he wants. But he created them, and it's his prerogative.

Jean let out a breath and looked up. She had already shaken off whatever was bothering her. Like I said, she's a tough cookie.

We strolled for a while, trying to enjoy the day. Jean was in a good mood. Assassins are always in a good mood after killing something. I'm not sure why. We spent the day visiting shops and meeting various spirits. It took some persuasion, but many of the local spirits opened up to us.

I'll have to return at some point. I could tell several were ready to leave their ghostly lives. I can't have Bud involved in the process, and I need to do it without letting the reapers know. To be on Earth means these souls escaped from a reaper. One of the few things that upset reapers, and when they find a wayward soul, they kill it.

I think it's about time to head home, when I got a whiff of decaying flesh. Sure enough, I spotted a reaper watching us from across the street, and I nodded to it.

There's nothing pleasing about reapers. To arbiters, they have a slight scent of rotten flesh. To those they are ferrying to Hell, it's an overwhelming stench. For souls whose destination is Heaven, I've heard it described as a sweet scent of decaying fish. I knew this reaper, and she owed me a few favors. Reapers hate owing anyone, but I provide them with certain services they craved. She gave me a nod, and I excused myself to find out what she wanted. Jean eyed us closely but said nothing.

She wore the typical reaper uniform of an immaculate black robe. Reapers keep their robes amazingly clean at all times and leave only their face and hands exposed. That's all I have ever seen or wanted to see of a reaper. From under her hood, I could see her face, which is a skull with a semi-transparent gray skin cover. With wisps of hair sticking out the top, she looked like a rotting corpse.

The worst part? Reapers don't have eyes. Jeremiah says it's because not even a reaper wants to see what they do to their victims. Instead, black skin covers their eye sockets, leaving only small slits. There are black orbs behind the slits. I looked into one once, and I didn't sleep for a week.

Their hands are skeletal, with a small amount of grayish skin and muscles covering them. An unusual feature is their finger bones stick through the tips of their fingers. Some reapers file the tips to a razor-sharp point. I asked one once why they did it, and he responded with, "it looks good."

Those passing by couldn't see the reaper but unconsciously adjusted their course to go around it. Still, most felt a chill and looked around in fear. Despite the warm weather, many shivered and zipped their jackets as they walked by.

"Latvius, what do I owe the honor of your visit?" I asked, but I knew why she was here.

"The old man, he is a friend of yours," she stated, rather than asked.

"Yes, he's one of the best men I have ever met. Are you here for him?"

"Yes. I know you have made deals to make his afterlife a good one. I would like to settle my debts with you by delaying his death." Reapers are not known for their conversation skills and tended to be to the point.

"We have done a lot of business together. This would settle some of our debt." I'm about to begin negotiations when an idea hits me. "But I have a deal for you and a few of your friends who owe me. They could settle some of their debt also."

Latvius smiled, revealing rows of pointed teeth, and the hair on the back of my neck stood. I prefer it when reapers don't smile. "Please continue. I am listening," Latvius replied.

I wrapped up my deal with the reaper, feeling quite good about myself, and returned to the group and motioned to Uncle Bud. We moved off to a safe distance.

"Was that a reaper?" he asked, and I nodded. The fact he saw the reaper spoke volumes. "Was it here for me?"

"Not entirely. Some of the other reapers owe me, and she was here to make a deal," I said, trying to be casual about talking with a reaper.

"Do I even want to know what ungodly things you've done that reapers owe you favors?" I detected a slight hint of disapproval in his voice.

"It's not like that," I replied. Bud's scowl told me he didn't believe me, so I tried to explain. "Reapers are kept on strict leashes. If they go off on their own, they can cause quite a bit of trouble. Which means when they aren't guiding or hunting a soul, they're locked up." I took a breath and looked around to make sure no one was listening. "I provide them with a place to go and enjoy themselves. Well, as much as a reaper can enjoy themselves, I guess."

Bud's confused look told me he's not understanding, "Movies, specifically anything gory, they love. The more death, mutilation, or horror the better. I can't tell if it is comedy or porn to them, but they love the stuff."

Bud laughed. "My life's been so boring without you, but tell me." He rubbed his chin, then asked the question I hoped he wouldn't ask.

"What part of your conversation was about me?" He raised an eyebrow and gave me that fatherly don't-lie-to-me-son look. "I want the truth."

"I'm sorry, but you're on the reapers list to die soon. The favor I just called in will give you a few more years."

"Well, if it's my time, then why shouldn't I go now?" he asked, surprising me.

"It's not like that. Your death is not part of some grand plan. If you do or don't die, it will not affect God's or anyone else's plans."

I hoped I was helping him but evidently not.

"So, my life has no meaning?" Uncle Bud said. His smile told me he was playing with me.

"Your life has meaning, but man's 'Free-will' has so buggered up this planet there's simply no plan left that anyone knows of."

I'm not convinced that's true. But I've been at this for over a hundred years, and if there's a plan, I don't see it.

"One last thing, I need the name of the witch that cast the spell on Tina," I asked to change the subject. "Someone will find out what happened. If I go, she gets a warning. If anyone else goes, she may die."

Uncle Bud sighed, then gave me the information. With our discussion over, we went in search of Tassis and Jean. We found them exiting a beef jerky shop, each loaded down with bags of treats.

"Do I want to know where you came up with the money to pay for this?" I asked.

Jean flashed one of my credit cards then put it in her pocket. "You forgot to ask for this back."

"I don't remember giving it to you, but since we work for the same company, I'm not going to complain."

Finally, it was time to head home, and after some tearful hugs, we were ready to leave.

"Kye, you promised me you would visit again soon. I'll hold you to it," Bud said.

"We have to come back for the vapuer, but after that, I will be back before you know it."

I snapped my fingers, and we traveled to a new safe house I own in Colorado. Tonight, some bad stuff would happen, and I wanted to make sure we were someplace no one could find us.

# Chapter Seventeen

W e landed in the office of my Colorado home, and I'm not happy about it. While I don't hide my house in LA, I have spent a century quietly purchasing additional homes. I secured each from attack or detection and made sure no celestial being knew about them—especially those who work for Death.

In the last few days, I've revealed my London and Colorado homes. Each house took years to prep and a heckuva lot of work. Some of the wards needed to help hide each house take months to create. I'll have to sell them after this mission. If Jean knows, then I'm willing to bet Jeremiah will know. Nothing to be done for it now.

"Make yourself at home. My maid keeps the house ready and the kitchen fully stocked. There are several bedrooms down the hallway. The room at the end is mine, and I would stay out. There are enough wards and safeguards to kill just about anyone who tries to break in."

Jean smirked. "I do love a challenge."

"Well, be careful. One of the traps wipes out this entire house and will kill angels, demons, or any of Death's employees.

"Okay, I think I'll avoid your room."

"Good idea. On a different subject, I have to make a couple of visits and will be back soon."

Jean frowned. "Don't kill the witch. You'll only stir up a hornet's nest."

"Why does everyone think I'm a murderous psychopath?"

Jean winked. "Oh, I don't know. From what I hear, you tend to kill a lot of things and carry a weapon called the Sword of Retribution. Which does tend to make one think you're a deranged killer. Personally, I find murderous psychopaths' kind of sexy if it makes you feel better."

"Actually, I find that weird," I said as I cocked my head.

With a snap of my fingers, I was in a suburb of NOLA, in front of a small home in the middle of a residential neighborhood. It's a track home with a small lawn, a two-car garage, and a flower garden by the only window.

I shook my head. This is what the modern magical world has come to. Instead of a dark forest and boiling cauldron, it's cable tv, homeowners associations, and a hybrid car in the driveway. As I approached the door, I heard laughter coming from the house. I peered through the glass in the door and spotted a group of women sitting around a table drinking wine.

I rang the doorbell.

A woman in her early thirties opened the door. She's attractive with a nice figure, and her auburn hair accented her green eyes. I also detected magic emanating from her.

She smiled. "Well, hello! I'm Jenna. They told me Aubrey's dad was coming to the meeting, but they didn't tell me he was hot." She switched her glass of wine to her left hand and held out her right.

Well, why not. I gave it a brief kiss. "I do love your shirt." It said, 'I may be a devil in disguise' with a buxom she-devil smiling. Jenna can definitely give the she-devil a run for her money. If the clasp on her overburdened bra broke, someone could get killed. I'd give the clasp a nudge, if I thought she wouldn't detect me doing it.

She giggled and brushed the hair from her face.

I gazed at her for a minute before I remember what I'm here for. "Sorry, but I'm not Aubrey's dad."

"So, you're not here for the scout meeting? Even better." She winked.

"Nope, I'm here to talk about Tina and the spell you put on her," I replied.

Her reaction was dramatic. Jenna's smile disappeared, and her welcoming look turned to a frown. "Uncle Bud sent you, didn't he? I told him I would fix her."

"Bud asked me not to come, but I didn't have a choice. Tell me what happened."

Jenna sighed. "Well, my boyfriend and I were at his place, having a little adult fun, if you know what I mean."

"Yes, please continue."

She grinned. "We were enjoying ourselves when I spotted Tina watching and enjoying herself."

"Interesting. Please continue," I urged. At least I confirmed what kind of spirit Tina was.

"I was fine with it. Ken, my boyfriend, didn't notice her, and it added a little kink to the setting. The next time I visit him, she decided to join in just as we are finishing. Ken isn't magical and had no clue why he felt something he couldn't see groping him. It completely threw him off his game, but the spirit loved it. Later, I told her if she did it again, she would pay. A week later, she tried again, and I threw a simple spell to scare her. She disappeared, and I thought it was over."

"But it wasn't."

"Unfortunately, no. She just couldn't stay away. By then, Ken started getting paranoid, and our sex life is falling apart. So, we come back to my place to do the deed. But a few nights later, we're back at his place, and she showed up. I'm ready and cast a spell so she can't feed off our energy, and she disappeared. I thought it would last only a day, at most."

"Instead, it went on for several days," I interjected.

Jenna nodded. "Uncle Bud called and told me about what was going on. I tracked her down and removed the spell. By then, Tina was pretty desperate. She couldn't feed and was starving and acting erratically. Just as I cast the spell I thought would fix her, she disappeared again. I've been trying to track her down to help her. If you know where she is, I think I know how to make this right."

Jenna's eyes are watery, and I expected tears any second. Especially with the news I have for her.

"It's too late. She's dead."

"Well, no duh, Captain Obvious. She's a ghost," she said and dabbed at her eyes with her sleeve.

"No, I mean. She's permanently gone. There's nothing to save."

"Oh, God, no. What happened?" Her eyes filled with tears, and remorse was written all over her face.

One of her friends wandered by, saw Jenna crying, put her arm around her, and gave me a nasty look. "Jenna! What's wrong?"

I flashed a police badge I carry just for these situations. "A friend of hers was killed, and I have just a few more questions."

"I don't think..." her friend never finished as Jenna cast a spell over her. The woman looked dazed and wandered off.

Jenna watched her friend walk away, then turned back to me. "Sorry. Tell me what happened."

I checked to make sure no one else is listening. "When Tina couldn't feed off sexual emotions, she went with something strong enough to get through your spell."

"And what was that?"

"She killed someone and fed off them as they died."

Jenna froze, and I wasn't sure she was breathing. I waited a moment and continued. "Eventually, Tina attacked the wrong person and was killed."

Jenna's a blubbering mess. I wanted to console her, but she indirectly caused two deaths.

I handed Jenna a tissue from a box on a nearby table, and she wiped her tears.

She took a deep breath and straightened her shoulders. "So, what happens next?"

"Nothing. Except you will be more careful with your spells. If you run into any more wayward spirits, contact Uncle Bud. He knows how to find me."

Her smile returned, along with her seductive look. She arched her back while stretching her arms, and I waited for the bra to explode, but it didn't. "And if I need you for something else?"

In my eyes, Jenna went from a seductive siren to a repulsive being. She just found out she caused two deaths, and now that she knew she wasn't in trouble, she hit on me. The witch is a much better actor than I gave her credit for.

"Call me for anything other than a problem spirit, and I will let my sword do the talking," I warned as I pulled Kitten partway from her sheathe.

Jenna backed away with her hands up. Satisfied she received the message, I stowed Kitten.

With a snap of my fingers, I returned to my Colorado home. I needed to leave before I decided to let Kitten teach Jenna the lesson she deserved.

# Chapter Eighteen

I ain't sure why Lyzark wanted a down-and-out demon like myself to lead this mission, but I'm not going to let him down. The crazy bitch that offered me the chance didn't actually say that Lyzark had given the orders, but she wore his crest. I've been looking for my break to move up for a long time, and I ain't going to miss my chance.

Being a bottom-of-the-barrel demon means I've been stuck in the shithole pits of Hell, cleaning some of the most disgusting stuff you can think of. Imagine the worst of Hell's demons, then imagine what their shit looks like. Yep, I clean that up. But not anymore. Lyzark's aide made it clear—kill the targets, and I'm sittin' pretty as a rich and powerful player. Screw it up, and I'm roasting over someone's firepit.

"Listen up, you bottom-dwelling vermin—we gotta job to do!" I said, with as much authority as I could muster.

"Anything you say, *Slay*," a short, fat demon name Olis shouted, and the group laughed. Olis has been calling me Slay since he'd gotten here, knowing it pissed the heaven out of me. I ordered him to call me Slayer, but the ass ain't listening.

I brought along a couple of extra soldiers for just this very reason. I pointed the sword the bitch gave me and pushed a button. Flames roared out and devoured the mouthy little demon. His dying screams echoed, then all went silent. I now got everyone's attention, and their fear felt good. This don't happen often, and I soaked in the moment.

"My name's Slayer. Anyone else gotta beef with me?" I asked, and a few 'No problems, Slayer' later, "Good. I'm the boss. Mess with me, and you die."

After everyone nodded, I let them in on the plan. "Our job's simple. We follow this thing," I held up the small box the bitch gave me, "to where our targets are hiding. There will be three of them, a couple of

Death's people and one demon kid. We kill 'em and then return very rich demons." The group roared their approval, then went quiet.

"Um, uh, Slayer, sir?" the biggest of the group asked. The brute's name is Chog, and he's enormous. His fists are half my body size, and he could kill any one of us by just sitting on us. Lucky for me, he's as dumb as a rock. Even for me, outsmarting 'im is a cakewalk.

"Yeah?" I'm interested in what he's gonna say. It was the most I have heard from the oaf, ever.

"You know Satan wants us to use the term angels. She said calling us demons is an insult," he said, looking proud of himself. The others nodded as if he has just said something profound. I can't believe I chose these idiots.

"Do this task, and I'll call you dumb asses anything you want. Until then, you're demons," I said.

I raised the sword, and everyone ducked. I can't afford to lose the big guy, but it don't hurt to instill a little more fear. I cringed as he was right, and I hoped Satan hadn't been listening.

I opened the thing mortals call a cell phone. After five minutes, everyone is anxious, and I was nowhere near getting the cursed thing to work. I lifted the sword to my mouth and whispered. "I can't get the phone thing to work."

A few seconds later, I jumped as the aide appeared. The bitch is a tall blond in a neat pin-stripe suit. Lyzark's seal is on a pin fastened to her jacket lapel.

Denz, a demon almost as dumb as Chog, let out a, "Hey, baby. Wanna party?"

Before he can react, she punched the mouthy demon. He bounced off a wall, and then she grabbed him, flipped him onto his back, and buried a knife in his chest. Crap, I'm outta spare demons for the raid. With Denz dead, I only had six demons left.

"Anyone else?" she asked, and the place went quiet.

The aide scanned the room and spotted me. With a groan, she walked over and grabbed the phone out of my hand. "Between you and Bush, I've just about had it." She pushed a couple of buttons and shoved the phone back in my hand. "Just follow the dot, you idiot. Call me again before it's done, and I'll cut your dick off with a rusty axe."

She left in a flash of light, leaving everyone looking at me like I was an idiot. "If we fail, I'll kill each of you before she can get to me. Is that understood?" I received a nod from each.

I studied the blue dot on the phone. It told me our targets are located in a desert region mortals call Afghanistan. I know little of mortals, or earth, and I ain't got a clue as to what a desert is. I pushed the *Travel* button, and we landed outside a cave in a mountainous area. The heat felt wonderful, and I let my crew catch their breath. I looked around the area and turned up nothing. Literally nothing. No people or animals, and the vegetation, what little there is, looked like it was dying.

I preferred Hell to this place. Yeah, this place was hot, but where were all the souls to torture, creatures to hunt and kill, and where the heck were the females? Even where I live in Hell, there's enough females for everyone. They ain't much to look at, but better than nothin'.

There's nothin' to be done about, and I took a moment to enjoy the heat. At least I did until a sense of dread crept over me. Somethin's really wrong, and I just wanted to get my ass out of there and return to Hell. The looks on my crew's faces told me no one else felt it, which didn't make me feel any better. This lot was about as stupid as they come. Whatever coin they earn will be gone in a week—wasted on booze and renting Fallen angels. I might spend a little on a Fallen, but my goal is to buy me a better job. Nothin' fancy, just something that don't involve picking up shit.

I wasn't sure where the sense of dread was coming from. But earning coin was useless if you're dead. Maybe cleaning up shit isn't so bad after all. At least I'd be alive. But that ain't an option. If I bailed on this assignment, we'd be hunted down and tortured for disobeying orders. I decided to take a different approach that might keep me alive. Demons are greedy creatures by nature, and that might be my ticket to staying alive.

"We need to get this done. An extra bag of gold to whoever gets the most kills," I said, and there was a rush to get in the cave. I ducked as Chog tossed a demon who tried to get in front of him. He landed hard on a pile of rocks but managed to drag himself back into the fight.

I waited until the team was in, and I followed, making sure I had a clear path to the exit. About ten feet from the mouth of the cave, we broke out our light sticks and continued on. It was getting colder the farther in we went. Made sense, I guessed. My sense of dread had gone nuts in my mind, and I let the crew get farther ahead of me. We continued forward, and the phone thing said we were almost there.

I heard voices in the distance. It must be our three targets, and I signaled the team to be quiet, and we crept forward as silently as possible. We rounded a bend, and the feeling of dread had me by the balls. The nervous looks from my team told me it was affecting everyone except Chog. I don't think he has enough brain cells to register anything other than hunger or lust.

We approached a large opening, and I put my fist up. The group stopped and looked at me expectantly. I quietly counted, "One, two, three, Go!!!" and the team rushed in. I got to the opening and peered around the corner. I'm surprised to see my crew in the middle of a large clearing, surrounded by ten cloaked figures. This ain't right. There were only supposed to be three. But they ain't carrying weapons, nothing to protect themselves. Maybe we caught a break.

I breathed a sigh of relief. Then, a sudden revelation crashed over me as to why they don't have weapons—they're freakin' reapers!

I jackrabbited out of there and hoped my idiot crew would buy me enough time to escape. Seconds later, I heard the screams of my crew as the reapers wiped them out. I tried desperately to stab at the Travel button on the phone, but I kept pushing the wrong button. I hoped the reapers hadn't detected me and needed to keep things that way. So, I whispered into the sword. "We need help!"

The annoyed voice of the aide replied. "What did you do now, moron?"

"You led us to a whole den of reapers, you bitch. Get me out of here!" I said as quietly as I could.

I hoped she would get me out of there. Instead, the phone exploded, taking part of my hand with it. The pain was excruciating, but I was more worried about the noise it just made.

I'm almost out of the cave when a reaper appeared. I pointed the sword at the reaper, and flames engulfed it. The sword began to heat and burned my hand. I surprised the next reaper as I tossed it to him. The reaper caught it just in time for the sword to explode and blow him into pieces. It's clear that the bitch wanted to clean up any loose ends. I don't blame her, except it meant I was a loose end, and she wanted me dead.

I made it out of the cave and ran down the hill. What's left of my hand is bleeding, and I had no clue where I'm headed, but I'm alive.

I kept running until something grabbed me by the neck and slammed me to the ground. It's the reaper I just fried. Smoke billowed off the reaper's robes, and I felt pure hatred coming from it.

"Stop! Don't kill me! I have information to trade!" I desperately babbled.

The reaper pulled a sword from its sheath and held a device in its other hand. A voice from the device screamed not to kill me. I might make it if the reaper just obeyed the voice.

The blade coming toward me told me it didn't.

# Chapter Nineteen

"For Death's sake! I told you not to kill him!" I screamed into the phone. The video feed showed the demon leader of the assault team on the ground with his head a couple of feet from his body.

"He killed another reaper and burned me," Latvius responded calmly. "I will remind you that I do not report to you."

Usually, I wouldn't bother to argue with a reaper, but this one owed me a big favor and failed. One thing that was going in my favor; reapers are a logical lot. They don't understand anger, let alone emotions, and respond poorly to anything other than logic. I just needed to reign my emotions in.

I took a deep breath and slowly released it. "If the tables were turned, how would you react?" I asked as coldly as possible. The silence on the other end of the line meant I hit pay dirt. Latvius realized she made a mistake killing the demon.

"I am sorry for the mistake. To make it up to you, we believe we know where the sword came from and will track it to its source."

"No, don't do anything. I know where the sword came from, and I don't need you causing any more problems. I will let you figure out how much of your debt to me has been paid," I said and hung up.

I tossed the phone onto the desk and returned to the kitchen to find Jean and Tassis cooking up a huge meal. I don't have to eat often. Death has seen to it that his arbiters can go weeks, even months, without having to feed. I still preferred to eat regular meals; it's a simple pleasure that keeps me connected to my mortal life.

"Did the trap work? Did they come?" Jean asked, then flipped several steaks and threw seasoning on them. Her technique was perfect, and the meat looked fantastic.

Jean eyed me as I drooled after the steaks. "For the record, I studied to be a chef before I died. But as it turned out, I was much better at handling knives than I was as at being a chef."

"Well, it looks like you know what you're doing." I shrugged and sat.

Tassis stood next to me and mashed the potatoes. He kept sneaking peeks at Jean. I couldn't tell if he saw her as the mother figure he never had, or he was trying to figure out how to ask her out. With this kid, you never knew.

"Yes, they did. A team of demons showed up tracking the stick and thought they were getting the jump on us. Instead, they found a room full of ticked-off reapers who didn't appreciate being pulled into this mess."

I swiped a quick spoonful of Tassis's mashed potatoes, then gave Tassis a nod. "They're quite good."

Tassis beamed, and I continued. "Unfortunately, the reapers ignored my orders and killed them all."

"How did you know that Ken's admin was a demon?" Tassis asked. "I'm impressed she could hide the fact from me."

"At first, I didn't know. I recognized the lapel pin she wore but couldn't place where I had seen it before. It was Kitten who told me she was a demon, along with several of Ken's bodyguards."

I tried to snag another spoonful of mashed potatoes, only to have Tassis whack my hand with a wooden spoon.

I snatched my hand back in surprise. When Tassis realized what he had done, fear filled his eyes. "I'm sorry I hit you," he shouted. He dropped the spoon and backed away.

"Tassis, it's okay," I offered and tried to get the kid to relax. "The potatoes are wonderful. I couldn't help myself," I added to defuse the situation.

I picked up the offending weapon and handed it back to him. "It's fine, really."

Tassis let out a breath as he relaxed. "Thank you. Jean is teaching me how to cook." He gave her a big smile and continued to mash the potatoes.

So, now I have a demon who likes to cook living with me. I'm not sure this case can get any crazier.

Jean's skills as a chef were exceptional, and the dinner was excellent. I ate as slow as I could. Left to my own devices, I would have inhaled it. But I wanted to take my time and enjoy the meal. I haven't felt this mortal in so long. My laughter was real, my happiness was real, and I never wanted it to end.

After dinner, I grabbed the dishes and a sponge and started to wash. Jean gently took the sponge from my hand. "Why don't you go show Cassi that great smile of yours."

"Thanks." I gave her a peck on the cheek and snapped my fingers. I landed in the living room of my London home to find Cassi and Renaldo each enjoying a book. Cassi put her book down and slinked toward me. Pieces of clothes dropped to the floor with each step.

Renaldo closed his book and set it on the table next to him. "I guess that's my cue to leave."

Cassi put her arms around me. "I'm not sure what happened, but the smile on your face is the first real one I've seen in a long time."

I caressed her face. "It's been an interesting day, and I've been thinking about you."

"You have?" She smiled, and my heart melted.

I put my hands under her arms and lifted her. She instinctively wrapped her legs around me. With a thought, my gray and black wings unfurled and folded around her. We're in our own little world for a moment, and I kissed her.

Cassi pulled back and raised an eyebrow. "And just what do you think you are doing?"

I looked up to the ceiling then back to her. Cassi shook her head. "If you're thinking what I think you are thinking..." She didn't get to finish as I launched us toward the ceiling.

This time, I made sure to leave a note to the maid not to fix the butt print.

# Chapter Twenty

I woke in the embrace of Cassi's white wings. The feeling was unlike anything I have ever experienced. I would have loved nothing better than to remain nestled with her. Unfortunately, that wasn't an option. I needed to see Eizan. With only mild complaints from my lover, I extricated myself and took a quick shower. Today felt like it would be a good day. I just hoped I could make it out the door before Cassi started the argument I knew was coming.

I dressed quietly and headed to the kitchen for coffee, and a peanut butter sandwich, my daily go-to breakfast. I hoped I could sneak out before Cassi woke, but then she entered the kitchen. She wore one of my dress shirts, and that always boiled my blood. Cassi once asked me what she could get me for my birthday. I requested a dozen dress shirts. When she gave them to me, I surprised her when I hung them in her closet. She didn't understand why, until the first time she decided to wear one. We didn't get out of bed for the entire day.

With the look of concern on Cassi's face, I knew what was coming. Worse, there was nothing I could do to prevent it. After a few of these encounters, I have learned to wait for her to make the first move. She poured herself a cup of coffee and sat next to me while I waited for the inevitable.

"You're going to see Eizan today, aren't you?"

"Yes, and I can only hope it will go better than Lyzark's meeting. Going a day without killing a celestial would be nice."

"I know what you're going to say, but I think I should go with you. I can provide backup in case something goes wrong."

I wanted to scream. Without Cassi's heavenly powers, she wouldn't last a second against what I would be facing. I'd probably end up dead just trying to protect her.

"I'll have Kitten ready, and Jean is my backup. Anything more than that will be seen as hostile. Plus, I suspect Jeremiah will keep an eye on things. The less fuss, the better," I said and hoped this ended it.

She toyed with her coffee. "It just might be a great opportunity for me to get back into Heaven."

"I told you I would take you to one of Mikael's parties soon. Much less chance of someone trying to kill you, and a bigger chance of someone helping you to return."

I knew she was desperate, but getting an angel reinstated into heaven doesn't happen often.

I kissed her. "Just give me a little more time. I think I might have an idea on how to get you back to Heaven, but I have to work out a few details." What I said was true. I did see a possible chance for her. It was a long shot, but at this point, we're running out of options.

She stared at me until she was sure I was telling the truth. "Okay, I'll trust you on this one," she kissed me, then pulled back. "For now. My time is running out, and I will not end up shriveling up and dying on this forsaken planet, full of self-absorbed idiots."

I winced. Cassi knew I prefer living on Earth, and she isn't a fan. Her comment wasn't aimed at me, but it still hurt. I was born on this planet and planned to live out my existence here. I tried to let her comment go instead of starting a fight. If my concoction was wearing off, then she must be feeling the withdrawal effects.

I got up and brushed her hand off my arm. "I've got to go."

The realization of her mistake was reflected in her eyes. Before she could apologize, I snapped my fingers and returned to my Colorado home.

# Chapter Twenty-One

I returned to my Colorado home, arriving in my kitchen, then searched for Jean. I found her in the living room with Tassis. I had expected a battle about Tassis wanting to see Eizan but found him happily propped in front of a TV. With a tray loaded with snacks and the cartoon network in full play, he was content to stay.

"Ready to see Eizan?"

Jean smiled. "Follow me." She snapped her fingers and disappeared.

I followed her to a spot in Los Angeles, only a few blocks from where we visited Lyzark. I recognized the area. I once owned the land here and sold it in the 60s for a considerable amount of money and interest in a mall they were building. I later sold my interest in the 80s for another fortune. Several years later, it fell into decline, mainly due to the mall's accountant, who embezzled a large portion of the income. The last of the tenants moved out in the late 90s.

The last time I saw the place, it was a wreck. But not anymore, it now looked like a Beverly Hills shopping center, and I made a snap decision to invest in the place. It will be a short-term investment. A year from now, the next angelic 'in place to shop' will pop up, and this place will be abandoned by the angels, replaced by super-rich mortals. A few years after that, the mall will be abandoned. It's the circle of life for places like this, but for now, it was a moneymaker. I sent a text to one of my business managers to buy as much of this place as he can.

I was surprised to find that Jean had changed on the way. She was now dressed in a red top with a plunging neckline, leather miniskirt, and six-inch high heels. With diamond earrings, a small black purse, and a single gold Choker necklace, she looked like she just stepped out of an issue of Vogue.

We stood near a line of stores that offered all sorts of expensive merchandise. Several of the storefronts featured scantily clad models, who posed wearing the latest fashions. The store nearest us had a male model wearing see-through underwear. Jean eyed the model but blushed when the model winked and turned toward her to flash his wares.

"I wonder if they have my size," I quipped.

"I doubt they come in extra-small. Now, let's go." Jean winked and walked off.

I snorted. "Ouch!"

We headed down the street, taking in the sights, and passed a store that sold perfume. A saleswoman stood outside with a small bottle offering samples. "Miss, would you like a sample?"

Jean smiled. "Why, yes, I would."

The woman sprayed a mist into the air, and Jean walked through it. "I'm sure the gentleman will love it."

Jean walked over to me, leaned in, and whispered in my ear. "And how do I smell?"

I took a whiff and my libido fired up. With great effort, I resisted ripping Jean's clothes off and pushing her into the back seat of a nearby Mercedes. "You, uh, smell wonderful." I backed away from Jean, who now ogled me like a prized stallion.

I realized what was going on. "How much?" I asked.

The saleswoman smiled and pressed a business card in my hand. "Ten thousand dollars."

"For that bottle?"

"It's ten thousand per spray."

My cheap side showed as the price tag put my libido into cold storage. "Sorry, no thank you. A little on the cheap side for me."

I grabbed Jean's hand and pulled her along. She held a funny look, then put her arm around the small of my back. I was a bit confused on what she was doing until she pinched my butt.

I stopped, and she turned to me. Her lips close to mine. "Jean, are you hitting on me?"

Jean gazed at me and smiled. "Maybe," she drawled and nibbled my ear.

I leaned back then cocked an eyebrow. She frowned, slapped me, then pulled away.

"You hit on me, then slap me? What the hell for?"

"Sorry, it must have been that perfume. On the way back, we need to avoid that shop."

I nodded but checked the business card I received. Lucky for me, it had a website where I could order a spray or two for Cassi.

We continued on and admired the sights. If you had a taste for something and the money to back it up, you could find it here. The road was crammed with million-dollar-plus cars, and the average outfit looked like it cost more than most folks make in a year. While I was dressed nicely, I was out of my league. Jean, on the other hand, was dressed to perfection. She even received a few envious glances from those that passed by.

Jean halted in front of a men's clothing store and told me to wait. Five minutes later, she walked out with a black suit jacket and matching shoes.

"Here, put this on," she said and handed me the jacket. It was a perfect fit, and I admired myself in the store's window reflection. I had to admit, it looked great on me. She handed me the pair of shoes that I'm pretty sure cost more than my first car.

"How did you afford…" I began then realized she still had my business credit card. "I'm going to need that card back before you cause it to melt."

Jean pulled the card from her purse and tossed it to me. She pulled out another one. "I got my own now. Yours is maxed out. A dozen matching suits will be delivered to your house."

I stowed the card, a bit worried. That card had a high credit limit.

We walked to where I knew Eizan resided and received a few nervous glances along the way. With our gray, Death's aura, we stuck out among the dozens of Heaven's angels we encountered. Kitten purred in delight. She expected, or maybe hoped for, some sort of action. Angels that passed by felt her desire and gave us a wide berth.

"This is just so wrong. I expected Satan's minions to act the way they did, but I would have thought God's angels wouldn't be so…" Jean stared at two overly dressed angels, complete with fur coats pass by, "so material."

"Don't be too disappointed, even angels need a vacation."

"What do you mean?" Jean asked. It was evident by the way she looked at me, she hoped I could rescue her faith. I've seen this in newly minted Death's employees when their religious upbringing meets reality. Most grew up religious, read the bible, and attended church. They believed that angels were the cloud-hopping, hallelujah-singing warriors of God's truth. When faced with the fact that what was written in the bible doesn't always match reality, they sometimes have a crisis. Despite having died and working for Death, they can't let go of what their parents and preachers taught them growing up.

"Angels love what they do. They work among humans and try to guide them, help them to be good souls. When we were in New Orleans, we passed many, but they kept themselves hidden from other non-mortals, especially demons."

"Then what is all of this?" she asked and waved toward a store displaying gaudy handbags made of gold and covered in gems.

"Can you imagine spending eternity doing one thing? Taking care of others, no time off, no vacations, just the same thing every day? I can't. Eventually, every angel needs a break from taking care of mortals. So, God grants them time away to rejuvenate every century or so. I don't know all of the details, but they're allowed to do pretty much what they want. What you see here is one way they step away from their work. Most take a few months off, relax, enjoy themselves, then return to work."

"Most? And God doesn't mind that some never return to their duties?"

"I think He does, but I don't know for sure. There have been rumors that God deals very harshly with those angels. Angels and demons are pretty tight-lipped about what happens to wayward celestials."

We continued on and approached an old four-story hotel. It was built in the 50s and was *the* place for Hollywood's A-listers to hang out for many years. When the mall was built, it was also restored. But when the mall failed, the hotel was abandoned. The place had been refurbished and looked exactly as it did the day it opened. I should know. I was there when it opened.

Guarding the entrance were two giant angels. I gave them a flash of my arbiter power, but they ignored it.

"Eizan is not here. You will have to come back tomorrow," the first brute said with a grin. The guy looked like a giant mass of muscles with a head. His hands were the size of my head.

I turned to Jean. "Then I guess Lyzark will get this very nice bottle." I pulled out the special bottle of bourbon just enough to show the top of the label.

Doubt flashed across the faces of the two angels when they realized their mistake. I took Jean's arm and attempted to walk away.

The second brute moved toward us. "Wait, is that what I think it is?"

"This?" I held up the bag. "Maybe. But I'm not taking it out of the bag again."

Kitten purred louder. *Please, oh, please let him try something. Anything.*

The first put out his hand. "Give it to me, and I will make sure Eizan gets it."

"Like Hell I am," I quipped. I felt pretty smug about my pun.

From behind, I heard a chorus of moans from those who didn't enjoy it. I turned to find a crowd of angels had formed to watch the antics. A short, heavy-set angel stood in the back collecting money. When he called out "5-1 odds on Death's guy getting' killed," I'd had enough.

"The bottle is for Eizan, and I'm not letting you two swipe it." I pulled Kitten and at the same time went into full arbiter mode. My newfound wings sprouted, smacking two angels in the face. Jean pulled her sword and faced the crowd. All decorum lost, the crowd beat a hasty retreat out of the combat zone.

"There are only two ways this ends. You face down on the ground in your own blood or us walking through with no more games." I hoped for a fight. I wanted to see how Jean would do against these goons.

A voice boomed, ending my fun. "Let them in, and no one touches the bottle. We will speak about this later." It was Eizan, and he sounded irritated. The two goons looked at each other, worried. Their attempt to steal the bottle had landed them in disfavor with their boss. They opened the doors, avoiding eye contact. I wondered if they would live long enough for me to see them again.

We walked down a hallway so over-decorated I wanted to stop to appreciate it. Art and jewelry from around the world lined the walls. Some were priceless works of art, vases, and just about anything a collector of antiquities would desire. The main goal of the hallway seemed to be to demonstrate to the visitor the abundant wealth of the owner.

I was sure Eizan knew about my run-in with Lyzark and Rusk and had expected a visit from me. So, I waited for the thing he thought would put me off my game. Eizan's an expert at getting under his opponent's skin, irritating them to the point of causing them to make a mistake. I'm pretty thick-skinned, so I assumed Eizan would up his game for me.

About ten feet from the doors to his chamber, we found it, actually them. In gold cages, two Fallen angels. They struggled to stay on their feet under a heavy load of gold chains and jewelry. Their wings had been painted gold and clipped. Music played in the background, and the two tried to dance to the rhythm. Each attempted to give seductive smiles but were in such agony, they failed. The two quietly begged for release.

This would be Cassi's fate if I couldn't figure out a way to return her to Heaven. Eizan knew that and would try to use the knowledge against me. Eizan guessed, accurately, I wouldn't be able to stand to see the Fallen suffer.

I popped open the cage doors. "Out."

I pulled Kitten. She purred loudly—something she usually does just prior to a killing spree.

"Are you letting us go?" one asked.

"Nope, I'm taking you to Eizan, then he will let you go."

The two Fallen cowered in the back of their cages. "Eizan will kill us if we do," they pleaded.

I pointed Kitten at one. "You can either die by my sword now or follow me and maybe live longer. You have five seconds to decide." It was a bluff. There was no way I could kill them. Fortunately, my bluff worked, and they climbed out.

Jean jumped when I swung Kitten, leaving the gold chains they wore in pieces on the floor. Eizan's bobbles meant nothing to me. He wanted to get me riled up, and I decided to play along.

"Next time, give me some warning," Jean warned. The tip of her sword pointed at me.

I put Kitten away. "Better stow that. We don't want to give him a valid reason to kill us."

"You don't think he'll be pissed already? You just released his playthings and cut up their chains."

"Nope. They're pawns to be discarded as needed."

We passed through a golden archway and entered into a vast circular room. In the center sat Eizan; his seat could give Lyzark's a run for the gaudiest throne. He's nonchalantly perched upon it with a male and female angel nestled in his lap. Both are naked and did their best to seduce him. The rest of the room was filled with well-dressed angels with their playthings. The amount of debauchery between Heaven and Hell is about the same. Heaven's angels just do it with style.

The two dancers behind me dropped to their knees and started to plead Eizan for their lives. "We were doing as you commanded. He threatened to kill us and cut the chains."

The huge angel waved his hand dismissively at the two and grinned at me. "Kye! My friend, I am so glad to see you again. It has been ages." Eizan turned his attention to Jean. "I see one of Jeremiah's toy soldiers has come along. I have to say your taste in bed partners has improved."

Jean's hands were clenched, and the death stare she gave Eizan was impressive. I waited for her to respond, but she remained quiet. I tilted my head and smiled at the naked, busty female angel sitting in Eizan's lap. She smiled back but averted her eyes before Eizan noticed.

"Speaking of bed partners, how is Cassi?" Eizan continued.

I ignored him and stared at the siren angel. I had to admit, she was every celestial's dream. I paused for another moment to make Eizan wait just a little longer. "Sorry, did you say something? Oh, yeah. Cassi. She's doing fine. Thanks for asking." Eizan sneered, and I pressed my attack. "How's God's lapdog doing? From the look of the place, he isn't happy with you. Does he still tell you when you can crap?"

I'm not sure that angels do crap, but from the sour look I received, I hit home. The two angels in his lap eased their way from him. My eyes lingered on the female angel as she sauntered toward an exit. Eizan's face now held a red tinge, and had moved his hand to his sword.

"Now that you boys have had your little pissing contest, can we get on with business?" Kilford interjected.

Worried that I may have overstepped, I continued. "Yes. Maybe it's best we do."

Eizan nodded, removing his hand from his sword, and I continued. "I'm willing to gift this bottle to you for some information and job reassignments for these two. Something that doesn't involve being sodomized or used as a slave."

Eizan gave me a confused look. "Why would you trade for something you already own?"

"What do you mean?" I turned to Jean. Her look of confusion matched Eizan's.

"I was told the Fallen were yours. That you wanted to have something to play with when you arrived. I must admit, I was surprised when they were delivered. I didn't think that was your style."

I looked at the two Fallen warily, wondering what kind of trap they represented. "I know nothing about them."

Eizan must have had the same thought. He pointed toward two of his aides. "Get Gantor in here."

The aides looked at each other, not sure which one Eizan had pointed to. When the head angel ordered, "Now!" Both ran out of the room.

Eizan paced around the room, and the tension in the room rose. The angry angel stood about six-foot-six, with blond hair and heavily muscled. His skin was a pure, light white. No freckles or scars, not a single imperfection. He wore a see-through silken white robe that flowed to the floor. Underneath, he only wore what I assumed was a tiny white bikini bottom. When he turned away from me, I realized he was wearing a G-string. I averted my eyes and blinked to burn the image from my mind. Jean stared intently at the ceiling.

A few tense minutes later, an aide returned. "We found him in his room. When asked about the Fallen, he disappeared. We have not been able to find him, your eminence."

"Release the wolves. Track him down," Eizan bellowed, and everyone in the room cringed.

"We did, sir, so far without luck, your eminence," the aide replied and ducked his head in fear when Eizan roared, grabbed his throne, and hefted it over his head.

I readied myself for Eizan to throw the huge chair at me. But jumped in surprise when my phone chimed.

I held up my hand to Eizan. "Hold that thought." Eizan frowned as I checked my phone. It was a text from Uncle Bud.

*Someone is following me, and I found where the vapor thing is hiding. Meet me at the old ice cream shop.*

I showed the text to Jean. "Go get Tassis. I will signal my location when I'm there."

Jean nodded and disappeared. Eizan lowered his throne and picked up his sword.

"I have to go take care of another emergency. Let me know what you find. Send the two Fallen to Fre-Fre's place, and I will hand over the bottle later."

Leaving Eizan to his temper tantrum, I snapped my fingers and disappeared.

# Chapter Twenty-Two

That evening, Jean and I stood on a street corner in an older part of NOLA, waiting on Uncle Bud. I had expected to meet him this morning, but he sent a cryptic message several hours later saying he lost whoever was tailing him. I thought he was safe until he messaged me that he saw the vapuer following him. For a vapuer to start tracking during the day was unusual but not unheard of. His last message was that he was heading our way.

I had avoided returning to this place for many years. The area was a mixture of empty lots and abandoned and decaying buildings filled with the remnants of mom-and-pop shops. Many of the stores have been abandoned, including a dry cleaner that I used to frequent. The store's sign hung by one corner and swayed with the breeze. Next to it, an ice cream store I visited with Tracey before her death. The place was somehow still in business, and Tassis was inside getting an ice cream cone. The kid is crazy about ice cream and can't get enough.

In my mind, I envisioned the place as it was in its heyday. I watched my first post-death girlfriend Tracey walk out of that very shop, ice cream cone in hand. She held a smile that always brightened my day. The vision shifted to that of Tracey's broken body lying lifeless in front of the shop.

I shook my head to pull myself from those dark memories. Bud wasn't here, and that worried me. I needed my mind on the problem at hand.

Jean's hands were clenched, and she stood still, almost rigid.

"Shall we make a bet? The kid comes out with at least four scoops," I said, mainly to distract myself.

Jean scanned the area, her eyes darted to each person on the street. Her hand slowly moved to her sword. I waited for her response. When she didn't, I reached over and touched her shoulder.

"What the…." she yelled as she batted my hand away and pulled her sword.

I jumped back and put my hand on Kitten. "I think you need to relax."

"Don't do that to me," Jean hissed, then stowed her weapon.

"I asked you a question, and you didn't respond, so I touched your shoulder." I paused and hoped she would relax.

"Sorry, but something's wrong. My instincts tell me we are being watched. But my senses aren't picking up anyone." Her eyes twitched in every direction.

*She's right. We're being watched,* Kitten warned.

*Yeah, I feel it too. But from where? I have tried to scan for others, and I'm getting nothing. Something is blocking me.* Being an arbiter, I can identify any other celestial being in my area. But I couldn't sense anyone, not even Jean.

*A reaper across the way. Two angels down the block disguised as drunks. The woman pushing the broom in front of that store is a demon. The clerk in the ice cream store is also a demon. There are a few others,* Kitten offered.

*Wow, quite a few celestial beings for one spot, and I can't sense any of them. What gives?*

*Someone who works for Death is using their power to block you two. Unlucky for them, their power won't work on me.*

I leaned closer to Jean in case someone tried to listen in. "There are angels, demons, and even a reaper in the area, but for some reason, my senses are blocked. Kitten can sense them."

When she didn't respond, I contemplated the risk of another tap on her shoulder. Finally, she responded. "Something is trying to block my senses also, but I have spotted them all."

The opening to 'The Second Line', a Mardi Gras favorite, played on my cell. That meant Uncle Bud was calling, and I quickly picked up. "Bud, where are you?"

"That things' after me," he wheezed. His breath puffed into the phone, and the chain of his old bicycle rattled in the background. "I'll be there in a second."

Out of the corner of my eye, I spotted the headlight of Uncle Bud's bike coming toward us in the distance. He passed under a streetlight, and I see Bud pumping his legs as hard as he could. For an old man, he was moving fast. I sprinted toward him. Down the street, the fog of the vapuer slinked along the ground as it chased after Bud.

I was twenty feet from Uncle Bud when a reaper and a demon materialized on either side of him, grabbed him off his bike, and then the three disappeared. His bike rolled on before it crashed into the curb.

I stopped to catch my breath. The vapuer had halted and moved into the shadows. I stood in the middle of the road and scanned the area. Whatever was blocking me seemed less powerful here. I could now sense Jean's approach but found no one else. The drunks were nowhere to be seen, and a broom lay on the ground where the demon had been cleaning up.

Jean skidded to a stop next to me. "What just happened?"

"Someone just kidnapped Uncle Bud. I think I know who's behind it. But we need to find Bud fast," I huffed. "I just need to figure out how."

Someone had targeted Uncle Bud as someone I cared about. That meant they would try to use him as leverage against me. If that failed, they would kill him.

"I think I know how to find him." Jean nodded toward the vapuer. "It's searching for him."

I beamed as the vapuer became a spinning mass. "Whoever took Bud may be able to hide him from us but not from that vapuer."

Vapuers are amazing trackers. I don't know how they do it, but once they pick a victim, they can track them anywhere. Fifty years ago, a vapuer picked a wizard as its target. To avoid dealing with it, the wizard used his magic to return to his home in Germany. Two weeks later, the vapuer arrived at his home. Unfortunately for the vapuer, a reaper arrived at the same time to claim the wizard's soul. The reaper dispatched the fog and took the soul.

Bud's vapuer spun for another minute, then sped away. "We need to follow that thing," I ordered and sprinted after it, but when Jean didn't move, I stopped and ran back. I grabbed her arm to pull her along, but she dug in her heels, leaving two skid marks on the asphalt.

"Come on. We're losing it," I urged.

Jean said nothing, and she ran back to the ice cream store.

Just as she got to the shop, two bodies erupted through the store's front window and crashed to the ground. Tassis landed on top of a demon while he flailed away at her with a black demon knife. While the demon was at least three times Tassis's size, she was fighting for her life. She cocked her legs and launched Tassis off her. Tassis sailed backward before he slammed into the asphalt and dropped his knife. He rolled and stood, then let out a horrific howl. The she-demon howled in response.

Tassis tilted his head, first left then right, to stretch out his neck. He then knelt and picked up his knife, and faced the demon. He tossed the knife back and forth between his hands as he moved toward the female demon but stopped when Jean yelled to him. "Tassis, we need to save Uncle Bud."

Tassis's expression changed from anger to one of calm. "Okay," he replied. He stowed his knife and walked to the demon. "I'll call you later."

The she-demon smiled, kissed his cheek, pushed something into his hand, then walked back toward the store. Tassis watched the demon slink back into the store then jogged to Jean. My eyes followed the woman as she strutted away. I had to admit, Tassis had great taste in women.

Jean eyed Tassis. "She seems nice."

Tassis nodded his head vigorously. "Yeah, I think I like her."

While I was glad that Tassis had met someone, it wasn't the time for young love. "Can we concentrate here? Uncle Bud's in trouble, and we've lost the vapuer."

"Relax. I have its scent," Jean replied and headed off.

I put my hand on Tassis's shoulder. "She's cute. Did you get her number?"

Tassis held up a piece of paper with a phone number on it.

"Good, now let's go."

We ran for a mile before we turned down a long alley. Now that we were a distance from the stores, I found my ability to sense celestials had fully returned. At least one thing had started going our way.

Jean continued to follow its trail for a distance until we approached an old warehouse district. Most of the buildings were covered in graffiti, and weeds grew through the cement driveways. These hadn't been used in years.

I had just about given up hope of finding the vapuer, when Jean spotted it down the road passing under one of the few working street lights. She moved into the shadows of the warehouses and crouched. Tassis and I followed. I pulled Kitten and scanned the area. We were in the perfect spot to be ambushed if we weren't careful.

Up ahead, the vapuer spun in confusion.

Jean glanced back at me. "Something made it lose Bud's trail."

I began to worry that it wouldn't pick the trail back up when it came to a stop and headed down a dark street.

We followed, but it stopped again. Jean put up her hand to warn us not to move. The vapuer continued on, but Jean waited.

Jean looked to Tassis. "Tassis, you need to leave. The vapuer can smell Hell's scent on you, and it's interfering with its link to Uncle Bud."

"How do you know?" I asked. Arbiters have extremely powerful senses, and I caught only a whiff of Hell on Tassis.

"It's what I am trained for. I can smell scents even bloodhounds can't pick up. Vapuers can also. Trust me on this."

"I believe you," I said to Jean. "I may have a solution, but we don't have time for explanations."

I pulled Kitten and used my arbiter power to mute Hell's scent on Tassis.

"Just stay a little behind us, so the vapuer doesn't detect you," I warned Tassis.

Jean turned and followed after the vapuer. We tried to stay in the shadows of the buildings we passed. Lucky for us, most of the streetlights were burned out, which helped shroud our movements. We slowed when we got about a hundred feet from it. The fog now moved at a snail's pace. We followed until Jean stopped.

Jean pointed across the road. "What are those two doing?"

I spotted two individuals sneaking along on the other side of the road. They stopped when they saw us. From their energy signatures, they were warlocks. While the two caught my eye, I found the warehouse they stood next to much more interesting. It looked old with the windows boarded over. Two giant sliding doors on the front had come off their railing and leaned against the building. Debris and garbage littered the front. Remnants of an old metal fence stood surrounding the place. A "Keep Out" sign hung by one bolt.

I was fixated by the place and unsure why until I detected the slight aura of magic around the building. I used my arbiter power to look past the magic. The disguise of an old and dilapidated building disappeared, replaced with a view of a brand-new warehouse. The place was spotless. The windows still had their manufacturer's stickers.

*That warehouse is well hidden. It would take someone very powerful to perform that magic,* Kitten said, which confirmed my thoughts.

The warlocks continued on and entered into an alley next to the building, and I motioned Jean to continue. As much as I would have liked to know what the warlocks were up to, I had bigger issues to deal with.

We caught up to the vapuer and followed at a safe distance.

Eventually, it came to the corner of a building and edged around it, then backed up. The fog stretched itself out into a long thin smoke stream and snaked around the corner.

Once it was out of sight, Jean ran to the corner, and we followed. I peered around and watched as the vapuer moved along the base of the building, staying in the shadows. A half-block down, a tall demon in a leather jacket guarded a door, unaware of the attacker that approached. The vapuer must have known it needed to get through that door, and the only way was through the guard.

"This should be interesting," Tassis whispered.

Jean nodded and smiled. She was enjoying the hunt.

I was also interested, but for a different reason. Tassis and Jean wanted to see a good fight. To me, a magical creature created by the evils of Earth was about to go up against an evil created by Satan. The average mortal weapon can't kill demons, angels, or even arbiters. So the question was: with the vapuer being magical, could it kill the demon?

The vapuer snuck along until it was just behind its target, when the demon turned and looked down. He spotted the vapuer and tried to pull his knife. The vapuer sprang and wrapped itself around the demon. The guard struggled, with one hand up to stop his attacker from locking itself around his neck. When the demon dropped to his knees, it looked like the vapuer had won. But the demon slipped his hand free, pulled a knife from his pocket, and stabbed the vapuer. The vapuer screamed and fell away. It reformed into the shape of a human with long claws and launched itself at its target. The vapuer scored a hit when its claws slashed the face of the demon. In a last-ditch attempt, the demon swung with his knife, and the fog dodged just in time. When another swing barely missed the fog, it backed away.

"We need that vapuer to win," I warned Jean.

Jean nodded and pulled a throwing knife from her belt. She stepped around the corner, and with no hesitation, launched it. The knife sailed down the street and embedded itself in the neck of the demon. I'm impressed. That was a long throw, and she nailed it.

The demon clutched his throat as blood poured from his body. He then passed out and would be dead in a minute. The vapuer approached the body of the demon, still in its human-like form. Its head turned toward us, seemingly evaluating us. It returned to its sphere form and launched itself into the door the demon had been guarding. The fog bounced off with no effect. It tried several times more, but the demonic seal around the door meant it wasn't going to get through it without some help.

"Here goes nothing," I said and walked around the corner. I pulled Kitten, and she grew to full size.

As I approached, the vapuer continued to slam itself into the portal but stopped when I approached.

"Back up," I ordered and pointed to the street with Kitten. When it didn't move, I pointed Kitten at it.

The vapuer hesitated then backed away.

As I examined the portal, Tassis approached and stared, his mouth open. "This should not be here. If Satan or Lyzark finds out about this, demons will die."

"Agreed," I replied.

"What's so special about it?" Jean asked from behind. I jumped, pointing Kitten at her.

Jean smiled, and I so wanted to wipe that smile off her face. "Would it hurt to make just a little noise? I almost killed you."

She giggled. "I was in no danger. Now, what's up with the door?"

Tassis placed his hand on the portal, but nothing happened. "It's broken."

"Here, let me." Jean approached and threw a vicious kick at it. Any other door would have crumbled, but it didn't budge. She danced around swearing while massaging her now injured foot. "Okay, what's up with this damn thing?"

I suppressed a grin at Jean's antics. I pointed Kitten at the vapuer that had begun to creep toward me. "It's an entrance to Hell and shouldn't be here. There are only a few doors to Hell, and they typically are well guarded."

Jean raised an eyebrow. "What do you consider well-guarded?"

"Fort Knox, for one," I replied as I grabbed the dead demon's arm and dragged him past a now stunned Jean to the door. I opened the demon's hand and placed his palm against the door. The portal shimmered, then the sound of locks opening let me know my hunch had been correct. I grabbed the handle and pulled it open.

"You're telling me there's an entrance to Hell in Fort Knox?"

I nodded. "And a door to Heaven. There are others, but we can discuss them later. Next time you see Rodin's 'Gates of Hell' look a little closer."

I walked past a stunned Jean and poked my head inside. I was met with the typical eyeful one thinks of Hell. Rivers of lava, flames, explosions, and the mournful wailing of thousands of souls.

I stood back and bowed to the vapuer. "After you."

It didn't hesitate and hurried through the doorway. I'm impressed. With the door open, waves of Hell's energy lapped over me. I knew the vapuer had to feel it also, and I didn't think it would go in.

Jean peered in and shook her head. "Yeah, no. I don't think so."

Tassis walked by her and entered. "I really do wish they would update this. It's so old."

Jean gave me a questioning look.

"Step through, and you'll find out. Or is Jeremiah's great assassin too afraid?" I unsuccessfully hid a smug look.

"Asshole," Jean replied as she walked by.

I followed Jean in and am hit by a blast of heat and the smell of sulfur. An overwhelming sense of dread now tried to creep in and cause me to doubt my choice to enter. It's to be expected as it's part of the security features to keep mortals, and others, out. When I have to visit Hell on official business, they turn this feature off.

With a wave of my hand, the dread and the heat were blocked and no longer affected me. Jean stood still, a look of concentration on her face. She was probably fighting an internal battle of wanting to run away.

I grabbed her by the arm and pulled her along. She initially struggled and tried to pull away. After we traveled a distance, the view and the fear disappeared. Jean relaxed, and I released her. We were now in a long hallway; the walls shimmered red to light the way.

Tassis hugged Jean. "You should be nicer to her," he said and frowned at me.

"Would Rusk have been 'nice' to you in that situation, or would he have let you learn a lesson?" I growled back.

Yeah, I was a jerk for letting her experience this, but Jean needed to learn or die.

"What just happened?" Jean asked as she took a few breaths to calm herself.

Tassis took Jean's hand. "There are security measures to keep the unwanted out."

Jean frowned as she realized her mistake. "That was pretty stupid of me."

Anyone that worked for Death should know enough to use their energy to block Hell's energy. She failed to realize what was going on.

I smiled. "Agreed, but you learned a lesson. Something Jeremiah would have taught you."

"Okay, lesson learned. Now what?" She studied the hallway and took a couple of steps before she stopped. She ran her fingers across an etching of an angel, wings spread wide in the wall. Each placed strategically down the hallway. "Traps, I'm assuming."

Tassis touched the nearest angel. "Yes, but poorly done."

His eyes lit, and his skin began to shimmer a matching red. I sensed him using his Hell's energy to reach out to the emblems. The etched angels all began to vibrate, and then their wings wrapped around their bodies. Their faces now looked like demons.

Tassis released his breath, and his eyes and skin returned to normal.

Jean patted the demon's back. "Great job, Tassis."

Disarming the traps helped, but his use of Hell's energy disturbed me. Now that he was back in Hell, and probably fully charged, I wondered if I could still trust him. I knelt in front of him. His smile faltered as he looked at me. Jean held his hand, and I had to remind myself that even though he is a demon, he is still a kid.

I locked eyes with him. "Thanks for doing that. It helps a lot, but now I'm concerned."

"You are worried that now that I'm in Hell and have all my powers, I'll betray you."

I nodded, once again the kid showed smarts.

"You and Jean killed Rusk, but only because you had to. I respect that. But you've taken me in and protected me. Rusk taught me loyalty and friendship mean everything. Which means I won't betray you. But the person that caused this has taken someone I like. I'll do everything in my power to save Uncle Bud and kill those that took him."

Tassis was juiced on Hell's energy, and the hatred that emanated from him was palpable.

I stood, satisfied with his response. "And we got your back, no matter what. Now let's go get Uncle Bud."

# Chapter Twenty-Three

W e jogged down the hallway, hoping to catch up with the fog, and stopped at a junction. I checked left, then right to figure out which way to go. I caught a glimpse of a twitching foot sticking out of an adjoining hallway to the right. I ran to it and found the dying body of a demon with the vapuer wrapped around its neck.

The vapuer unwrapped itself from the demon and curled up a few feet away. When I first saw it, the thing was a dark, dense fog. Now, I could see right through it. The thing pulsed as I studied it.

Kilford came around the corner, sword out. She surveyed the pulsing vapuer then lowered her sword. "It's dying."

"Yeah, and that's a problem." We needed to get to Uncle Bud fast, and the vapuer was our only hope.

"If we can carry it, maybe it can still guide us," Tassis offered.

"We can't. Out of reflex, the vapuer will try to kill anything that it touches," Jean replied. I stared at her in amazement. She was a walking vapuer encyclopedia.

Jean shrugged. "What? I find vapuers interesting, and spent a little extra time researching them. I just don't know of a way to carry one."

"I know how, and after this is over, you need to have Jeremiah teach you."

I sighed. I never thought I would be carrying an evil creature through the bowels of Hell to rescue a friend.

I concentrated on the vapuer and channeled my energy toward it. A disc, made out of a bright gray light, formed underneath it. The vapuer slowly rose and floated in the air.

I moved toward the fog, Kitten in hand. "Which way?"

A wisp of smoke extended and pointed down the hallway. I knew it wouldn't be long before Hell's security systems detected us, and I broke into a run. The vapuer floated ahead of us and was quick to guide us through a maze of hallways.

We halted in front of a massive metal door. The thing was a good twelve feet tall and ten feet wide and looked like a bank vault.

"Nice job..." I began to say to the vapuer but stopped as I watched what was left of it dissipate. "Damn, hopefully, Bud is behind that door."

I put my hand on the hulking door and racked my brain for a way to get past it. I was about to see if Kitten could cut through it when I heard the thundering sound of boots. I turned to find Lyzark and three of his guards have blocked our return path.

"Kye, what in Satan's name are you doing down here," he eyed Tassis. "And what are you doing with Rusk's..." Lyzark caught himself.

I smiled at Lyzark's slip. I now knew why Rusk treated Tassis like his son. That's because he was.

When Lyzark's eyes moved to Jean, Tassis pulled a dagger with a foot-long blade and planted himself between Jean and Lyzark. The kid had guts. I had to give him that.

Lyzark studied Tassis and furrowed his brow. He tried to glare at the kid, but with the corners of his mouth turned up, it was clear Lyzark wasn't mad.

"One of your men kidnapped a friend of ours and brought him down here through an illegal portal. We're here to rescue him."

"An illegal portal? That's not possible," Lyzark replied.

"It's true! And if anyone wants to call me a liar, let them step forward now," Tassis threatened, dagger ready.

If Lyzark's chest expanded any further, his shirt would rip to shreds, and the flying buttons would kill us all. He drew his sword then stared at the kid. "I won't call you a liar because I know you can't tell a lie. Rusk trained you too well. But tell me why someone would do this?"

Tassis gave me a pensive look, and I urged him on. "Go ahead, son. Prove that Rusk's faith in you was justified."

Tassis nodded but remained silent. I began to worry he wouldn't respond when he squared his shoulders. "I believe the ones that created the portal were the same that got Rusk killed. That was a mistake they'll pay dearly for."

Tassis's eyes burned with a glower that sent a shiver down my back.

Lyzark arched an eyebrow. "Do you think you can kill those responsible for Rusk's death?"

"Yes, but I don't plan on letting them off that easy. I want them to look me in the eye as I carve their guts open."

Lyzark's eyes went wide. Even he wasn't ready for the kid's desire for revenge. "Then I will open this door, and we will fight together. But first, give me that." Lyzark put his hand out for Tassis's dagger.

Tassis hesitated then handed the weapon to him. Lyzark snapped his fingers, and one of his guards drew a black shortsword with a golden hilt from a sheath and handed it to the kid. "If we are going to fight together, you need a proper sword. Rusk wanted you to have this."

Tears welled in the kid's eyes as he ran his hands over the inscription in the sword. It's written in Hell's speak and translates to *Bringer of fire and blood.* Tassis took a couple of swings, and the biggest smile I have ever seen on a demon erupted. Jean sniffed, and I turned to find tears running down her face. She looked at me and dabbed at them. "His first sword. I hope he gets to kill something soon."

I was a bit shocked. "Yeah, every parent's dream."

Jean missed my sarcasm. "Yes. Yes, it is."

I decided to let it go; we had more important things to worry about. "Sorry to interrupt, but a good friend is in there, and we've got to get him out. But I'm not sure how to get in there." I was worried that Lyzark would kill me for interrupting his moment with Tassis.

"I'll handle this. Stand back," Lyzark ordered.

We stepped to the side as the demon moved toward the hulking door and placed his hands on it. His eyes became raging balls of flames. He grew in size and now stood over ten feet tall. His body began to glow, and heat radiated off him. Soon his shirt began to smolder, and he ripped it off. Grabbing the door, his red-hot fingers sank into the now melting metal.

He let out a deep howl as he strained against the vault. The sound of metal bending and breaking filled the air before the hunk of metal broke free. He hefted it above his head, and the sound of his roar echoed down the hallway. His guards only had a moment's notice before he launched it in their direction. They flung themselves off to the side of the room to avoid being squashed. A loud *clang* reverberated when the hunk of metal crashed to the ground.

Tassis moved next to Lyzark. "Now we fight! For Rusk!"

Lyzark looked down at the kid and screamed, "For Rusk!" and the two rushed into the room. I tried to enter but jumped back to avoid being run over by his guards, rushing to join the battle.

We entered into a large room filled with at least two dozen demons.

I instantly recognized the room as a demon torture chamber. It's fifty feet deep and twenty-five wide, with dark metal walls. The ceiling is thirty feet up, and all that I could see was a raging fire. If there is actually a ceiling behind the flames, I couldn't tell.

The place was a who's-who of torture devices. Along the walls, iron manacles hung from the wall. A Brazen Bull, where a prisoner was placed inside a bronze replica than roasted alive, sat to one side. A fire was lit underneath, and muffled screams emanated from it. Several tables with victims strapped in, were littered around the room, each surrounded by demons holding whips and other weapons. One demon held an electric saw and was in the process of cutting off a leg when she looked up. A more modern device, an electric chair, sat to the right. Two demons were removing the fried remains of a body but dropped it when they saw us.

In the center of the room, Uncle Bud hung from chains wrapped around his arms. I worried for a moment that we were too late, but he rolled his head and looked at me. A demon with a chain in his hands stood next to him. The chain was covered in blood, and from the looks of Bud's wounds, he had been worked over pretty well. Bud looked barely alive, and my blood ran hot.

Our entrance caught the demon torturers caught off guard, and the ones next to the doorway didn't stand a chance as Lyzark, and Tassis cut them down in seconds. Those further from the door grabbed whatever weapons they could, and the battle ensued.

Kitten roared to be let loose, but this was my kill, not hers. I pulled Kitten and used my magic to launch myself over the battle and landed next to the demon with the chain. Before he had a chance to move, I cut the chain he held then cut off his arm that had been holding it. Without thinking about the consequences, I dropped Kitten and grabbed the chain and wrapped it around his neck, and pulled. Intentionally releasing Kitten meant that while we were still bound to one another, she was free to do as she pleased. That included killing me.

But I didn't have time to worry about that. Around me, chaos ensued. Tassis let out a war cry, and from the corner of my eye, I could see him shredding through the demons. Lyzark ripped apart a demon and used the two halves to pound the others. Blood and gore flew everywhere. Jean had lowered Bud and hacked the chains that had bound him.

My gray arbiter aura surrounded me, and my anger yearned to be released. I lifted the now choking demon, and my desire to kill him nearly overcame me, but I needed him alive, at least for now. I tossed him into the air, like a ball at the end of a chain, and I spun him around. Kitten flew about trying to cut the demon but missed when he swung by. She roared in anger at me for interfering. She wanted the kill, and I wouldn't let her have it.

"This one is mine!" I screamed. "He'll spend eternity wishing I had killed him. Don't get in my way!"

Before I realized what I was doing, I sent several blasts of my arbiter energy at Kitten, each barely missed her. When I stopped, Kitten halted in mid-air and pointed at me. My only concern was making the demon pay, and I ignored Kitten. He flew around the room on the end of the chain, and everyone ducked to avoid being bowled over by the flying demon. With one last swing, I released the chain. Hastily, I opened up a portal and sent him to a holding cell somewhere only Death, and a few of his employees, knew where. I've been there a few times, and it's the scariest place I have ever been. Even reapers were afraid to go there.

With the release of the demon, I dropped to the ground. Between the blasts that I fired at Kitten and the energy I used to open the portal, I had nothing left. Kitten was sure to kill me for my transgressions, but I didn't have the energy to worry about it. I closed my eyes and tried to bring my heaving chest under control.

I felt a presence, then heard Tassis ask, "Are you dead?"

Opening an eye, I found Tassis's face a mere inch from mine, and I jerked in surprise.

"I guess not."

Tassis backed away, and I opened my other eye and spotted Kitten as she floated nearby. My sword approached slowly and retracted her blades. I plucked her out of the air and stuffed her back in my jacket.

*About time you manned up,* she offered.

I chuckled. That's when I saw Uncle Bud lying on the ground. Jean was trying her best to heal him and had propped his head up with her jacket. Bud looked toward me and gave a weak smile. His left eye was swollen shut, and he bled from multiple wounds. Marks from the chain covered his body. I smiled back; he was alive. But then a chill ran down my back when a reaper appeared a few feet from Bud. I scrambled over to my friend and took his hand.

"How are you, old man?" I asked as tears formed in my eyes.

"I've been better, but who you callin' old?"

I laughed. "Sorry."

"I think your friend there is waitin' on me," Bud replied and unsteadily pointed to the reaper.

"He probably just wants another video. Let me go talk to him."

"They do like their porn, don't they?" Bud tried to laugh but broke into a coughing fit and sprayed blood across the floor.

I stood and approached the reaper, Kitten back in my hand. His name is Canten, and I've worked with him a few times. About as straight a shooter as a reaper could be.

"It is his time. I know you want him to live longer, and you can heal his wounds, but you cannot fix the pain his mind is suffering. The only way to wash away the memories of what was done to him is to let him make his journey."

"He's going to Heaven. There's no arguing on this," I growled.

"Then, that is where he shall go. I'm told that for what he has done, he will be among the honored in Heaven. I will check on him regularly to make sure all is well with him."

I didn't want Bud to go but knew it was his time and nodded. "Thank you. I will check on him also."

Canten gave a slight bow and moved past me. He knelt next to Uncle Bud and put his skeleton hand on his chest. "Uncle Bud, it is time for you to take your place in Heaven. That is where you will spend eternity." Canten put his other hand over Bud's eyes, and Bud smiled.

"It's beautiful. Kye, you should see it!" Bud exclaimed. "I'm ready."

The reaper glowed then disappeared. Bud's body relaxed, and he was gone.

Lyzark approached. "I will have his body delivered to you when you are ready.

"Thank you."

I wanted to cry, scream, to do anything to release the anguish I felt. But no tears came.

Revenge was the only thing that would ease my aching heart.

# Chapter Twenty-Four

I should have been exhausted, but the anger of losing Uncle Bud fueled my passion for revenge. Lyzark eyed me but broke eye contact when I glared back. My grip on Kitten was so hard I could feel my bones ready to snap.

Jean approached. Splatters of demon blood cover her clothes, and blood streamed down her cheek from a cut. With a wave of her hand, the cut healed. The assassin was smiling, and I thought all was well until she slapped me. "Kye. Concentrate. We need to stop those that did this."

My head snapped toward her. The sting from her slap felt good, and I was tempted to return the favor. I wanted to rage, destroy everything and everyone in sight. However, her slap was a reminder that there was a better way to get my revenge. A few deep breaths later, and my rage reduced to a simmer.

"You're right," I replied. "But don't ever slap me again."

"Or what?" Jean asked with a twinkle in her eyes.

"Or I will let Kitten kill you," I warned with a smile.

The twinkle in Jean's eyes disappeared, and I waited for a response, but there was none.

In the background, Lyzark and his guards were policing the bodies. When one body spasmed, the demon lord ran his sword through it, and the others joined in until the body was nothing but a bloody pile of bones and gore. Lyzark tilted his head back, spread his arms, and broke into a song. It was a demon ballad about vanquishing your enemy. While extremely graphic, the tune was catchy, and I joined in.

Lyzark trotted over and put his arm around me for the last stanza. In full voice, we finished with:

*And then we kill again!*

We laughed and patted each other's back.

"Thank you, Lyzark, for your offer to take care of Bud's body." I took a breath to control my emotions. "Besides the guy I just sent to lock-up. Did anyone else survive?"

Cursing behind me provided my answer. We turned to see Tassis had a demon strapped to a table. The prisoner's toe rolled away on the ground as blood spurted from his foot. The demon wasn't much taller than Tassis and had orange skin. His size and skin color told me he must work in the tunnels in lower regions of Hell where being shorter is advantageous.

"Listenin' up, you son of an angel. When I get out of here, I'm gonna..." the prisoner didn't get a chance to finish as Tassis stuffed a filthy rag into the demon's mouth.

Tassis smiled as he ran his finger over a tattoo on his prisoner's arm. "I like your tattoo. I think I will take it."

The young demon pulled his dagger and slowly carved the tattoo off his prisoner's arm. The muffled sounds of the prisoner cursing reverberated throughout the room. If it had been a mortal on the table, I would have expected him to pass out. Demon's revel in pain and torture, and this is nothing to them.

Tassis held up his trophy as he removed his captives gag. "Very nice. I think it will look good on my wall. Now, you will tell me everything, or I'll remove the rest of your toes and will keep removing body parts until there's nothing left."

"I can't. They'll kill me," the demon snarled, then spat at Tassis. "Plus, I ain't afraid of no kid."

"We shall see." Tassis raised his sword, paused, then brought it down with force and severed the demon's foot.

The demon shrieked, then gritted his teeth as he sneered at Tassis. "Is that all ya got? I've been tortured by some of the best."

Tassis let out an evil laugh. "I ain't even started."

Tassis concentrated on his hand, and a flame erupted from it. He pointed his now flaming hand toward the bleeding end of the demon's leg. Like a blow torch, the flames shot out and seared the end of the leg, and stopped the blood loss. The overwhelming stench of burning flesh filled the room as the demon howled in pain.

Lyzark beamed proudly at Tassis, then elbowed me. "Rusk taught him that."

"Actually, that's quite impressive. Heal your subject's wound to keep them alive longer," Jean added. "I'll have to talk to Jeremiah about incorporating that in his training."

It took a second for me to pull my jaw off the floor. These two were actually enjoying this. *Heck, I need new friends.*

Tassis placed the end of his sword on the demon's other leg. "I can do this all night, and then I will kill you. What's it going to be? You tell me everything, and I may let you live. Keep silent and die a painful death."

"No more, please. I'll tell you everything!" the demon begged and began to sob.

Tassis's face fell in disappointment. Lyzark and Jean's faces had the same expression. *Yep, I really need new friends.*

No one moved, and I stepped forward, afraid that Tassis would continue torturing the demon. A different approach was needed to make sure I got the information I needed. Tassis did a great impression of the 'Bad Cop' role. Now I'll play the good cop. "What's your name?"

"It's Tharcus."

"Okay, Tharcus. Tell me why you kidnapped that man," I pointed to Uncle Bud's body, "and tortured him."

"Pirq told us it was to get back at you. But I know the real reason. Promise me you won't let him kill me, and I'll tell you," Tharcus sobbed. He bled from the cuts that Tassis had made, and his burnt leg still smoldered. This guy was in so much pain—he couldn't lie if he wanted to.

"You tell me the truth, all of it, and I'll make sure he doesn't kill you."

"Pirq, the guy you threw with the chain, he's been disappearing a lot and wouldn't tell us where he was going. So, I followed him the next time he took off. He met up with an arbiter he called Lester. Never got the dude's last name." Tharcus closed his eyes and took a few deep breaths.

I picked up a club from a nearby table and tapped his footless leg. "I need details."

Tharcus howled as he thrashed against his restraints. "Okay. Okay. I just need a break."

I tapped his leg again, and the demon continued. "Lester wanted Pirq to capture your friend, torture him, then dump his body next to Lyzark's throne."

I raised the club as a warning. "Why next to Lyzark's throne?"

"He, he wanted you to find it."

I whispered into his ear. "Why did he want me to find Bud's body?"

"That arbiter, man, he's nuts. Promised Pirq he would rule Hell if he helped. He's trying to start the war, you know, *the* war between Heaven and Hell. But he wants Death to be part of it. I only heard a little of his plan. Something about givin' some guys special swords, and they'd start the war. That's all I know. I swear."

I looked him over and agreed, he had nothing more to tell. I pulled Kitten, and she extended her blades. My body tingled as my arbiter power energized. It's an amazing feeling, better than any drug high.

"You said you wouldn't kill me! You promised!"

"I promised that I wouldn't let Tassis kill you," I said, and I looked away.

"Whew, for a second I thought you were going to kill me," Tharcus replied.

I looked back at him as I raised Kitten and brought her down with a *thud*. My eyes followed his head as it rolled off the table.

"That was for Uncle Bud."

Lyzark moved next to me and studied the dead demon. "That was nice work—for someone who isn't a demon. If you ever get tired of working for Death, I have a spot for you."

I smiled—that's a big compliment from a demon lord. "Thanks, I'll remember that."

"What happens next?"

I took a breath to clear my head. "I need to talk to Pirq in his holding cell."

"I'll go, too."

"Sorry, you can't. I need him in Death's holding cell, and that's definitely a place you can't go. It's not a place any demon or angel can go without serious consequences."

"I can handle anything..." Lyzark began, but I put up my hand.

"Think about the worst that Satan could do to you. Then double it. Death knows many different ways to destroy a person. But I can let you watch, and afterward, he's yours."

Lyzark sighed. "I can accept that. But if he dies before he's turned over to me, you will pay."

"Understood."

I prepared to visit my prisoner when Jean put her hand on me. "I work for Death, so that means I'm going."

"You can go, but you have to be careful. The things that guard the place are some of the evilest things I have encountered..."

Lyzark clearing his throat interrupted me. I glanced at him, and he raised an eyebrow as he glared at me.

"Present company excluded," I corrected and nodded in deference to the demon lord. "As I was saying, to be in that cell, you would need to use your energy to protect yourself. Since Jeremiah hasn't taught you how to do that, I will need to do it for both of us."

Jean raised an eyebrow. "If you're using your energy, why do I have to be careful?"

"Because I will barely have enough energy to protect you and me, meaning it will be weak. Touching anything will break it. You do not want to be in that cell without protection."

"Fair enough, can we go?"

"Just give me a moment," I said, I walked over to the wall and waved my hand, and a video feed of Pirq displayed. He was in a fetal position, rocking and crying. The bloody stump where his arm once was, was healed courtesy of the entities that protect those cells. Their main job is to make sure no one escapes, even by dying.

"Lyzark, you can watch the party from here."

Lyzark approached the image and admired the scene. Pirq shook violently and begged for death between whimpers. "I don't know what is being done to him, but I would pay to know. Just name your price. Anything."

"Sorry, trade secrets. Now, the fun part," I said and snapped my fingers.

# Chapter Twenty-Five

The holding area Jean and I appeared in was the last place I ever wanted to be. There was a buzz coming from all around. It was irritating like nails on a chalkboard amplified over surround sound. A white spotlight highlighted Pirq, but whatever the source was, I couldn't see it. There were no solid walls or ceiling. Just a fluid blackness that ebbed and flowed all around us. What makes up the walls was why I didn't want to be there. I call them the 'Darkness' and what they are, I have no idea. To be honest, I don't want to know.

To me, the Darkness represents evil incarnate.

I once interrogated a high-ranking angel in an area like this. Instead of answering my questions, he decided to escape by entering the Darkness. Moments later, the things spat him back out, and he crumbled to the floor, shaking and babbling like a baby. It took a full hour of him whimpering before he could form coherent sentences. His fear of returning to the Darkness caused him to answer every one of my questions truthfully. He was eventually returned to Heaven for sentencing. According to Death, despite God wiping the angel's mind of the event, he was never the same.

Even with my magical block, I felt them, and it wasn't pleasant. Not the 'my dad just found out I lied to him' type of unpleasantness. More like 'you're tied up, naked, covered in raw meat, and a thousand starving rats are running toward you.'

Jean stared intently at the barrier. I knew she must have been trying to figure out what the Darkness was made of. Something I tried once but quickly gave up.

"Jean," I said, trying to get her attention. "You don't want to look too closely."

"Why?" She didn't even turn her head when she replied.

"Death warned me to avoid looking at them for too long as his creatures prefer their anonymity."

Jean looked at me as her face went pale. She slowly turned her gaze to Pirq.

Tapping into Kitten's power, I waved my hand, and my protection from the Darkness was extended to Pirq. The Darkness is quite powerful, and while I probably had enough energy by myself to protect all three of us, I didn't want to risk it.

Pirq's body relaxed, but he continued to whimper, and I gave him a moment to pull himself together. I've interrogated enough prisoners here to know that his mind had been overwhelmed by fear, and it would take a minute for him to register that the fear was gone. Soon, he removed his remaining hand from his face and peeked out with one eye. When he saw Jean and me, he opened the other and tried to sit up. His entire body still shook, and he tried to speak, but he only sobbed and stuttered.

Jean kicked him. "Time to get up." She was in full assassin mode, and cold hate rolled off her in thick waves. She turned her gaze to the Darkness, and it backed away from her. I always believed that the Darkness feared no one, but Jean proved me wrong.

Pirq sat up and took a deep breath. "I, uh, am…, uh, trying," he stuttered.

Jean pulled her foot back for another kick. "Try harder!"

Pirq flinched. "Okay! What do you want? I will tell you anything, do anything, just get me the hell out of here."

I was impressed. Kilford knew how to motivate. I stepped closer to Pirq. "For starters, you're going to tell me everything you know about Lester."

"I can't do that! The second I tell you this thing will kill me." He lifted his arm to show his forearm. There was a tattoo of a scythe on the back. I ran my hand over it and recognized the magic in it.

"Son of a bitch, when I get my hands on Lester…" I growled.

Jean frowned. "So, he has a tattoo. What's the issue?"

"Lester, that asshole, stole my invention. That's arbiter energy that looks like a tattoo. I created it to track souls under my protection. It's similar to an electronic ankle bracelet the police use for those under house arrest. The tattoo lets me monitor where a soul goes, what they say, and even terminate them if they break my rules."

Jean eyed the tattoo like it was gourmet chocolate. "Wow, that would be handy. Can you teach me how to do it?"

"If you're good, maybe as a Christmas present."

"Excellent, I would..." Jean trailed off, then cocked her head. "Do we celebrate Christmas?

I sighed and pointed at Pirq. "Can we concentrate on the task at hand?"

"Um, sorry, yeah."

I glared at Jean and then returned my attention to Pirq. "You don't have to worry about the tattoo right now. This room is designed to block any access. Lester doesn't even know you're here."

Lester did a poor job recreating my tattoo invention. It wouldn't have worked while he was in the deeper parts of Hell and definitely wouldn't work here, which was good. That meant Lester didn't know we had his guy.

"Lyzark! Check the bodies of the demons that were with this guy. If any of them have a tattoo of a scythe, don't remove them from the room."

Pirq's head swiveled, trying to find Lyzark, then turned his attention back to me. "What do I have to do to get out of here?"

I laughed. "You think after what you did to Bud, you're getting out of here?"

Pirq whimpered and curled into a ball. "Either kill me or get me out of here."

I grabbed his hair and pulled his head toward me, nose-to-nose. "You will answer all my questions, truthfully, omitting nothing. If you do that, you might have a chance of leaving here. Lie once, and the Darkness will have you for eternity."

Pirq grabbed my arm. "Honest? You'll get me out of here?"

"You have a slight chance if you prove valuable to me."

"Okay, okay, I got something for you."

"Let's start with you telling me everything you know about Lester."

Pirq sat up and wrapped his remaining arm around his legs, and began to rock. "A while ago, Lester was workin' a soul my boss really wanted. My boss don't take losing good. He'd kill his mom if it made him coin. I tried givin' Lester some gold for the soul, but he laughed at me. He was about to send the soul to Heaven when I panicked and told him I knew of a place where he could get any weapon he desired."

Pirq went quiet and started muttering to himself.

I knelt next to him and whispered into his ear. "The Darkness has left you alone because of me. Start talking, or I will give you to them."

I stood, and he grabbed my hand. "No! I'll tell you. Ya gotta promise me that only you hear what I got to say."

He glanced at Jean. "It's safer for everyone." Pirq then mouthed, "the two swords."

I nodded to Jean to leave, and she shook her head. I tilted my head and waited.

"Oh, alright," and she disappeared. I waved my hand, and the feed to Lyzark stopped. I also put up a block to keep anyone else from listening in. The Darkness rippled faster in irritation. Anger radiated from the things, but it couldn't be helped. My gut told me that I needed complete secrecy and that included the Darkness.

"This better be good. I'm pissing off those things, and they will take it out on you."

"Yeah, it is. My papa used to be a big deal in Hell. Had Satan's ear, and if you believed him, her bed. That was until he was caught bangin' a Heaven's angel. Rumor has it that Satan sliced 'em both in half." Pirq went quiet and resumed his rocking.

"Clock's ticking Pirq, another minute and no real info, and you're a plaything for the keepers of this cell."

"I'm gettin to that. Anyhows, my pap's told me Satan selected him to hide away some things that she didn't want anyone else to know about. Dangerous things. I didn't believe him, even made fun of him till he took me to the place once. More shields, locks, and curses than Hell itself. Took 'em a full hour to get us through. There's stuff stored there that shouldn't exist. Papa called the place 'The Eye.'"

*Oh, dear Death. What have you got me into?*

"Do you mean 'The Eye of God'?"

The Eye of God is a place where celestial weapons are stored. Specifically, weapons that could be extremely dangerous if they fell into the wrong hands. Why it's named the Eye of God, I have no clue. God, Satan, and Death each have a private entrance to the Eye. They're allowed to designate their own Keepers to place weapons there and make sure nothing leaves without authorization. Jeremiah was the sole Keeper for Death until I had my run-in with Kitten. Now, I'm a Keeper also.

"Yep, that's it! I can take ya there. When Paps died, Satan had me take his place. Not much to do now. Once a year, I go and count everything. You get me outta here, and I'll take you. I ain't gonna say a thing. Promise."

I shook my head and turned away from the idiot. The big three keep the existence of the Eye under wraps, and Death placed security precautions on his Keepers to kill them if they revealed information about the Eye. I was told that Heaven and Hell had similar precautions. But if that was true, how was Pirq still alive?

Fearing that the Darkness may try to kill Pirq, I extended my energy to push the Darkness farther from him.

*Keep close tabs on the idiot. Someone may try to kill him.*

Kitten growled. *Let me kill him. It will be kinder than letting the Darkness get him.*

*I would, but I need him a little longer.*

*You'd better hurry. I know what the things in the Darkness are. Death created them at the same time he created me. I'm only a little more patient than those things.*

*You know the Darkness?* I asked, stunned.

*Yes, before I met you, I used to come here often. I can't say we are friends, but we do respect each other.*

*Let's talk about this later,* I stated and turned my attention back to Pirq.

"Let me guess. You took Lester to the Eye. What did he take?"

"Only a couple of swords. Made 'em happy. Wanted to take a few other things but couldn't. Rules. Things can only be taken one at a time for cleaning and other stuff. You try'n take out more, and all sorts of alarms go off, and Lester couldn't bypass 'em. The swords are a set, so he could take both."

He was telling the truth. The weapons stored there are dangerous, and one of the many rules about the place was you can take only one item out at a time. Every once in a while, one of the big three runs into a problem where they needed to borrow a weapon. What worried me was that when that happened, I received a notification. Lester removed a pair of swords, and no one was notified.

"Tell me how he took the swords without anyone knowing about it?"

Pirq's head snapped toward me but said nothing.

"Answer, or I will give you to them." I nodded toward the Darkness.

He sighed. "I ain't sure. Lester did something, and he thinks he can do it again. But he can't get in without me."

I reached down, grabbed his arm, and placed my hand on his tattoo. Pirq screamed, and his body spasmed as my energy entered his body. I removed Lester's tattoo and replaced it with one of my own. He slumped to the floor when I released his arm.

136

Pirq's eyes fluttered, and he groaned as he sat up. "Why'd you do that? I didn't do nothing."

"Sorry, I forgot to deaden the nerves."

He glared up at me. "You did that on purpose."

"Yes, and I enjoyed it. You should be happy about it because we're getting out of here. I will warn you that you'd better behave when we leave. I put my version of the tattoo on you. That means if you cross me, I can send you straight back here and give you to those things."

Pirq nodded. "Okay, where we goin'?"

"We're heading back to Hell. You're going to call Lester and tell him you have to go to the Eye to get something for Satan."

# Chapter Twenty-Six

I snapped my fingers, and we were back in Hell with Lyzark, his bodyguards, and Jean. Lyzark sharpened his sword as he ran it back and forth over a stone. He glared at me then returned his attention to his work. Jean stood near a body strung up as a target against a wall. My name had been spray-painted on the corpse, and several of her throwing knives were embedded in its chest. She glanced at me and, without looking at her target, threw another knife. It struck perfectly in the 'K' painted on the body. Lyzark dropped his stone and threw his sword. It landed in the letter 'E'.

I knew the two would be mad at me for blocking them out of my conversation with Pirq. But I hadn't counted on them being this furious.

"Guys...I had to..." My explanation was cut short by Pirq, who, despite missing an arm, took a victory lap to celebrate his release. He stopped, arched his back, and screamed, "Woohoo!"

The assassin and the demon lord's heads both snapped toward Pirq. Jean readied her sword, and Lyzark jerked his from the demon target. The two hunters headed straight for the demon, who danced around, oblivious to the approaching danger.

"Guys, stop! We need him alive!"

Pirq turned and screamed when he spied the two advancing on him. I've never heard a demon scream as much as this one.

Lyzark swung his sword, narrowly missing the one-armed demon. "Creating another portal into Hell has endangered us all. He must die for what he has done."

I ran to place myself between the demon and his would-be killers. "Agreed, but he's the only one that can help us catch Lester. Plus, he knows about the *you-know-what* place."

Lyzark shrugged. "What you-know-what place?"

"You know," I said slowly and pointed to my eye. "The *you-know-what* place."

The demon lord cocked his massive red head then smiled. "He knows about the Eye of..."

My eyes went wide as the demon lord had just let Jean and his remaining guards in on a huge celestial secret.

"Shit, I shouldn't have said that out loud," Lyzark lamented as he glanced at Jean then back to me.

"Nice job. Anyone else you might want to tell?" I mocked. "Try using a megaphone next time."

Lyzark pointed his sword at my neck. "I should cut your head off for talking to me like that."

I readied Kitten and stepped back. Jean responded by turning her sword toward Lyzark. Lyzark's bodyguards were busy trying to figure out who was the bigger threat.

"How do you know about the, uh, place?" Lyzark stole glances at Jean, clearly worried about what the assassin might do.

"Now it's the *place*? You should have thought about that before you blurted it out. As for your question, I was assigned by Death."

Lyzark nodded and lowered his sword but still held it ready. "And how does Pirq know?"

Kitten groaned. *Don't these idiots talk to each other?*

*Evidently not, which is strange. He should know all of Satan's Keepers.*

Something was wrong, but I couldn't figure out what. "You don't know that Pirq is one of Satan's Keepers? Forget I asked that. It's clear you don't. The thing we should be worried about is that Pirq took Lester there, and Lester borrowed a couple of swords."

"Okay, guys. Can you let a girl in on whatever the heck you are talking about?"

Lyzark and I stared at each other and then turned to look at Jean. Telling Jean was a major no-no, but considering the situation, neither one of us had the guts to tell the assassin she couldn't know.

"Kye, she does not know?"

"Thanks to you, she does now," I replied. Desperate, I tried to come up with a solution.

Kitten sighed. *It would help if you used your brain every once in a while—just make her your backup.*

I nodded. *Good idea. I would have thought of that eventually.*

*Sure.*

"Everyone stow your weapons. Kitten has a way out of this mess, but nothing happens until the weapons are put away."

Lyzark sheathed his sword and signaled his guards to do the same. Jean surveyed the room for further threats, then stowed hers.

Technically, I was supposed to get Death's approval first. But there was no moving forward until Jean knew the rest, and I was pretty sure Death would agree. I surprised Jean when I placed my hands on her shoulders and looked her in the eye. "Jean, I designate you as my Eye of God Keeper back up. I'm sorry for what is about to happen."

She gave me a confused look as I stepped away. A white aura enveloped her. "Kye? What did you...?" Her body spasmed then went rigid, cutting off anything else she wanted to say.

I figured Jean would want to kill me after the procedure, but it was required by Death. Despite her clenched mouth, I heard her muted screams, and her body twisted and jerked. I went through the same procedure, and it was painful. As my backup, she had to receive the same safeguards as I had to prevent her from revealing the secret.

The white glow faded, but I knew this wasn't over. I needed to warn her what would happen next. "Heaven's precautions are complete. Hell's, then Death's are next."

"Kye, you son of a..." Jean growled before her body went rigid again.

A black and red haze enveloped her, which was then replaced by a gray one two minutes later. When the haze began to fade, I moved to catch her before she fell.

"Someone get me a chair," I yelled as Jean slumped into my arms.

The scraping of something heavy being dragged across the floor caused me to glance over my shoulder. Lyzark's guards were dragging the electric chair toward us.

I glowered at the demons. "You've got to be kidding me."

The guards looked at each other, grabbed a different chair, and helped me ease Jean into it. Her eyes fluttered, then she looked up at me. She tried to speak, but only gibberish came out. She frowned and slurred the words, "When I'm able, I'm gonna kill you."

I smiled. "You can try, but you're the one that wanted to know, and this was the only way. Otherwise, Death would have been forced to kill you."

"Doesn't matter," Jean said slowly and fumbled for a knife in her pocket.

The buzz of electricity flowing and the lights dimming interrupted our fun conversation and told me someone was using the electric chair.

"Again," the demon lord ordered.

Lyzark had made himself comfortable in the electric chair and had hooked himself up to it. His body twitched as the sound of electricity flowing filled the air. He laughed, seemingly enjoying the shocks.

Watching him, I realized that something was amiss. He had let out the secret, but nothing had happened to him. The protections that I, and now Jean, had placed on us should have kicked in. Looking back at Pirq, I now had to wonder why he hadn't been killed when he let Lester into the Eye.

Walking to the electric chair, I pushed aside one of his guards, turned the power knob to maximum, and hit a big red button. A loud buzz filled the air as Lyzark's body twisted and writhed. I hit the button again, and the power flow stopped. The demon lunged at me, but his convulsing body refused to cooperate. Instead, he fell to the floor in a heap.

"Kye, if she doesn't kill you. I will."

I knelt next to the demon lord. His hands still sizzled from where he had held the electrodes. "You son of a..." I checked myself when I realized that I was about to compliment him. "Sure, while you're trying to kill me, why don't you explain to Death how you let out a big secret and wasn't immediately punished. Or how Pirq was able to take Lester to the Eye and is still alive."

Lyzark made several attempts to stand, and I backed away. Kitten purred, waiting for him to attack. With the help of his guards, Lyzark made it to his feet. Holding on to a chair, he swayed in place but remained upright.

He glared at me for a moment, then suddenly smiled. "Now that I have thought about it. I think we should forget about this whole thing. I have forgiven you for trying to kill me, and I think it's best we just move on," Lyzark said and turned away.

"Nope, not gonna work. I want to know why, or we bring in our bosses."

By now, Jean was back on her feet. She tossed one then another of her dark gray daggers into the air. As each came down, she snatched them from the air and threw them. Lyzark remained still as the daggers flew past him and embedded themselves in the chair on either side of him.

Lyzark surveyed the two daggers quivering in the chair and gave Jean an appreciative look. "If you must know, Satan put me in charge of her Keepers. I can grant access to those I feel worthy and am in charge of keeping the secret safe."

I nodded. "Well, it looks like you failed. You still haven't answered my question on why the required protections failed."

Lyzark waved a dismissive hand at me. "Kye, have you learned nothing about us. Rules mean little to demons. Plus, those that I have told about the Eye, know that if they betray me, they will die. Had I known that Pirq was a Keeper, I would have made sure this would not have happened."

"Wait, you'll what?" I yelled. "You haven't implemented the required protections because no one will betray you? I just put Jean through the wringer, and you think your threats are sufficient. News for you, Mr. Demon Lord, demons are greedy, and for the right incentive, anyone will betray you." I paused and lowered my voice. "I'm sure Death will be interested to hear this."

"Guys. If someone doesn't tell me about this Eye thing and why I just went through hell, people are going to start dying," Jean warned as she tossed another dagger into the air.

Lyzark clenched his lips shut. When he glanced at me, I cocked my eyebrow, waiting for a response. When it was clear he would not answer, I decided to press my case. "I will tell you as soon as Lyzark clears his guards out."

"No need. I think we all know," one of his guards replied.

It took all my willpower not to let Kitten carve this idiot up. I placed my hand on Kitten and walked toward Lyzark, stopping when we were mere inches apart. The demon glared back at me, but his confidence was gone. "When God and Death hear about this, I wouldn't want to be you, Lyzark. That's assuming Satan already knows about your mistake."

Lyzark's now pale-red face told me she didn't know, and Lyzark would have some explaining to do.

I walked over to a chair and took a seat. "As for the Eye. Its real name is 'The Eye of God.' Why? I don't know. My guess is that since God built it, he got to call it whatever he wanted. To understand the place, you need a little background. Satan getting kicked out of Heaven was a lot bigger deal than what the Bible led everyone to believe. There was war, a bunch of super-powerful weapons created, and a lot of celestials died. When peace was declared, everyone was so relieved they just buried their weapons wherever they could find a spot on earth."

"Really? Their best idea was to bury the weapons on earth?" Jean asked.

"Yeah, you would think that someone would have been worried about that much firepower being left wherever anyone could dig them up. As you can probably guess, a mortal found one of the weapons. Quickly there was a race to find more, which ended up with all sorts of bad actors in possession of some powerful weapons. Chaos ensued, and a whole lot of mortals and celestials died."

Noting that Pirq had remained too quiet, I spotted him edging his way toward the exit. I tapped Jean and nodded toward the escaping demon. Seconds later, she sent a throwing knife soaring toward him, and it embedded itself in the wall after taking off the tip of Pirq's nose.

The demon let out a stream of curses but went quiet when Jean pulled another knife. I pointed at a spot next to me. "Stand there and don't move."

Pirq moved to the spot, giving Jean a wide birth. Pirq held his bleeding nose with his remaining hand but remained quiet. Jean sheathed her weapons and sat next to me. I continued. "After cleaning up their mess, the big three decided the weapons needed to be locked up."

"Wow, very smart of them. Only took killing a bunch of people to realize that," Jean snarked.

I nodded in agreement. "So, God created a place where the weapons could be stored and out of the hands of the power-hungry. The weapons can still be accessed if needed, but each deity can only take out one at a time. This was to prevent someone from arming their forces with some super-powered weapons."

Jean frowned. "Why weren't they just destroyed?"

Lyzark cut in. "Satan told me she had put her own power into many of the weapons created. The power in them has long since been corrupted, and she can't pull it back. If she destroyed her weapons, it would be like killing part of herself. God and Death are in the same situation, or at least that's what I was told."

"I heard the same thing. Teams are still searching for any remaining weapons, but most have been found and stored at the Eye," I said.

"Not all," Lyzark interrupted.

Jean frowned. "And what do you mean by that?"

I glared at Lyzark, and he remained silent.

Her eyes went wide. "Kitten was one of the weapons, wasn't she?"

Lyzark decided now was the best time to inspect his sword. I finally nodded.

"Yes, Kitten was created during the holy war."

Kitten growled and shifted.

"Why wasn't she locked up like the rest?"

Kitten escaped from her sheath, and I grabbed her before she could slip away. Her blades grew to full size, and she let loose a stream of curses.

Jean drew her sword. "Kye, are you threatening me?" Her voice was low, and she had positioned herself in a defensive stance.

"I'm not. Kitten is. You need to remember that she is a sentient being. She heard what you said."

Jean studied Kitten, then sighed and relaxed. "Kitten, I'm sorry."

I waited for Kitten to attack. She wasn't the forgiving type. I just about fainted when Kitten retracted her blades and purred.

"But I want to know how you got to keep Kitten while the rest of the weapons went into the Eye."

Lyzark nodded. "I have only heard part of the story. I would like to hear the rest."

The rest of his guards took seats and stared at me expectantly.

"Okay, I guess it's storytime," I said. I took a breath and made myself comfortable. "It was a long time ago. I was in a very dark place after the death of Tracey, an arbiter that I had been dating for over twenty years."

"She was the one that Uncle Bud mentioned?" Jean asked.

"Yes," I said and paused to sort my thoughts. "After her death and my revenge on her killer, I locked myself in my house. Jeremiah tried to coax me out by asking me to help him locate a weapon. He was searching for some relic that assassins used. A bronze jug that would poison the wine being poured, but only for a specified target. It sounded interesting, so I went with him. We found it in a sarcophagus in a middle eastern country. We were preparing to leave when I spotted Kitten and foolishly picked her up. She'd been in a deep sleep, and somehow, my touch woke her. When she saw Jeremiah, she went berserk and tried to kill him. I stopped her, and then she tried to kill me."

I took a deep breath as everything about that time reminded me of Tracey. "I don't remember much of what happened next. According to Jeremiah, I let out some primordial scream and tried to break Kitten on a boulder. Kitten and I then spent the next two days trying to destroy each other. If anyone got too close to us, we tried to kill them. Exhausted, I passed out, and when I woke up, I found Kitten on my chest. Anyone that tried to touch her, including Death, she attacked. I thought Death was going to eliminate both of us, but instead, he worked it out with God and Satan so I could keep her."

Silence set in, and for once, I enjoyed it.

Lyzark interrupted my peace. "Satan and God had no choice but to allow it. Death created the sword and put his own energy into it. To destroy it would be like killing part of himself. Per their rules, God and Satan would have had to destroy one of their own weapons. Neither wanted to do that. As long as Kye uses the sword appropriately, he is allowed to keep it."

"And he has used the sword appropriately," Jeremiah's voice came from behind me.

He stood next to Pirq, hand on his sword. Eizan stood behind the two with his fists balled. Being in Hell couldn't be comfortable for the angel.

Kitten growled—having these three in the same location was a bad sign. If history was any indicator, a lot of people were about to die.

Eizan whipped out his sword, and before I could stop him, he beheaded Pirq. The demon's body dropped to the floor, and his head rolled and stopped at my feet. "But Pirq didn't follow the rules. Lyzark, you should be next for what you did, but we don't have time."

I picked up Pirq's head and did my best to suppress my anger. "Eizan, you moron. Pirq was my best lead in finding Lester. You shouldn't have killed him."

Eizan sheathed his sword. "I know, but there are immutable rules we must follow when it comes to the Eye. Rules that state Lyzark and his guards should be dead for knowing about the Eye without having the proper precautions. But, considering the circumstances, we will address this at a later date." Eizan smiled. "I'm sorry that your lead is now a *dead end*."

The angel gave a triumphant smile, and even Jeremiah smirked at the attempt of a joke.

"Why Eizan, a pun. How absolutely mortal of you," I quipped.

Eizan gave a slight bow. "I learned from the best."

"Thank you, but rules aside, killing him makes finding Lester harder." I tossed Eizan the head. "That means you get to clean up the mess. Afterward, we need to talk about what's going on, but I don't want to discuss it here. We need somewhere private, just immediate family."

"I'm not your family, but I agree we need to discuss the situation," Lyzark replied.

"Kye, I didn't think you had any living family," Eizan chimed in.

I blew out a breath in frustration. They still had a lot to learn about humor.

"He meant just the four of us," Jeremiah said and suppressed a chuckle. "Kye, when will you learn that they are very literal?" He turned to the other two. "The meeting place, now."

Eizan and Lyzark disappeared. When Jeremiah turned back to me, I held up my hand. "This is not going to go well for you. It's time that the truth came out."

Jeremiah sighed. "Yes, I know, but it's time to go." He then tried to put a hand on me, and I stepped back.

"I've got to make a quick stop and will join you afterward."

"Be quick, those two will be drunk in no time."

"I will."

Jeremiah's eyes followed Jean as she walked by pretending not to be interested in our conversation. He turned and followed after her. As much as I would have loved to listen in on the lovebird's conversation, I had to check on something.

It was time to visit the Eye.

# Chapter Twenty-Seven

I appeared in a tunnel in front of a large rock wall covered in gems of various colors. All were brightly lit, which meant that the security precautions from Death, Heaven, and Hell were active and ready to blast me into bits if I failed their authentication procedures. Occasionally, I have found the remains of some poor thief who somehow found this place and tried to break in.

Pirq was right. For most Keepers, it would take an hour to get through the locks and security precautions. But years of practice, and with Kitten's help, I was through in only a couple of minutes. The rock wall disappeared, revealing a short hallway. I walked through and entered the weapons locker. It was a modern, data center looking place with clean, white walls and floor. On the wall to the left was Hell's entrance, and the wall on the right held Heaven's entrance. In the center of the room were eight neatly arranged rows of six-by-six cells separated by sheets of glass. The rows were labeled A through H, with each cell numbered.

Each cell contained a weapon created by one of the big three, and I strolled to the last row, admiring the weapons. Among them was the poisonous pitcher that Jeremiah and I found the day I met Kitten. An empty square sat near the end where she should be residing.

"H8. You sank my battleship," I chuckled.

*I never sank a battleship, but I helped sink a merchant ship once about....*

"Kitten, it was a *joke*. You need to catch up on modern history," I said.

*Sorry.*

There was a new square, H9, which was also empty. From the scratches on the floor, something had been stored there.

"So, you weren't the last weapon to be found. I'm guessing this is where the swords are supposed to be."

*Yes, they were discovered and placed here last year.*

Kitten's response surprised me. "And how do you know that?"

*I like to keep tabs on this place and my deadly associates that live here.*

"What can you tell me about the missing swords?"

*Nothing beyond what I already told you.*

"Well then, let's get a little more information on our newest inhabitants."

Kitten didn't respond as I approached the back wall. I reached out to activate the hidden archival system but paused when I thought I heard a noise. I waited, but all was quiet. I scanned the area, and nothing was out of place, yet something didn't feel right. The security protections in place keep the weapons stored here inactive. In theory, I was safe, but for some reason, I didn't feel safe.

Every time I have visited this place, I felt only the energy from the inactive weapons. The energy I felt now wasn't quite the same. I scanned the place but detected nothing unusual. I walked back to the pitcher and stared at it. Something was different, and I couldn't figure out what until I realized what I was missing.

The dust. Or better stated, the lack of dust.

One of my duties as a Keeper is to come here every twenty-to-thirty years and wipe these things down. I don't mind as it bothers me to see such beauty dusty. I last cleaned over fifteen years ago, and there should be some dust.

Yet the pitcher was clean. So were the rest of the items.

*Do you notice anything different?* I asked Kitten mentally, worried.

*Only that there is a lot of energy in this room. Be careful.*

The hair on the back of my neck stood up, and I drew Kitten. Her blades grew, and I waited for something to happen, but nothing did. I slowly walked to the back wall, ready for an attack. Reaching the wall, I put my hand on it. The white wall dissolved, replaced with a workstation and a large monitor. Situated next to the workstation was a big red button labeled 'Trouble', and I almost pressed it. In theory, all sorts of backup should arrive if I pushed it. Knowing the big three, it was linked to a bomb to wipe the place out.

*Keep watch. Something isn't right,* I said to Kitten and leaned her against the desk.

*I would hurry if I were you. The energy in the room means something is about to happen.*

Ignoring Kitten's warning, I punched up the record on H9. It contained basic information like when the item was discovered and where. There was a link to a video, and I clicked on it. An image of Pirq appeared, and I tapped 'Play'.

*"Yeah, this is Pirq. I was notified that a team found a magical sword, and I retrieved it from them. I put the location where we found it in the thing here. I tested the sword to see how much energy it held but found little. Was wrapping up the report when I got called back. They found a matching sword. Tested it in the field, and it's pretty damn weak also. Brought it back and put the two in H9."*

I shook my head. "Pirq, you idiot. You have to test the two together in…"

*Kye, we have a problem.*

In the monitor's reflection, I watched as several swords rose into the air. This was definitely an 'oh, crap' moment, and I hit the big red panic button. I blew a sigh of relief when the only thing that went off was a siren. Turning to face the onslaught, I grabbed Kitten just as the first sword came at me.

Normally, I enjoy a little swordplay, but this was not fun and games. A quick swing and the attacking sword dropped in two to the ground.

I began to panic when every weapon in the room began to move. *What the Death was going on?*

An arrow flew toward me, and I used Kitten to bat it away. My mind raced, how could these things be activated, and when was my backup coming?

The answer to the second part of my question was answered when Jeremiah and Jean appeared in the doorway I came from. Lucky for me, I had failed to close it behind me. Seconds later, Lyzark and Eizan appeared on opposite sides of the room.

"Kye, what's the emergency," Jeremiah shouted. In response, a spear launched itself toward him. With a quick swing, Jean knocked it down.

"I don't know what started this," I shouted back and watched as the room's inhabitants headed for the new arrivals.

Lyzark drew his sword and swatted away a pair of daggers that flew at him. "That's one! Let the games begin," Lyzark roared as he engaged a cutlass intent on separating the demon lord's head from his body.

From across the room, Eizan yelled. "Two down. Bring me a real challenger." His request was answered when a Gladius, a sword favored by Roman soldiers, nearly sliced him in two.

"I know what's causing this. Look for a black stone about the size of a home wireless router," Jeremiah yelled over the clanging of weapons.

Jean gave him a strange look, and I wanted to ask how he knew about wireless routers, but there was no time.

I swung Kitten as fast as I could to keep a pair of machetes from slicing me in two.

I had just sliced one of the machetes in half when Kitten warned, "Duck!"

I dropped to my knees just in time for a boomerang to fly over my head and embed itself in the wall. It shuddered, trying to free itself until a slice from Kitten ended its life.

The sounds of battle rang out as we were trying to keep from being beheaded. Eizan and Lyzark continued their kill call out, trying to one-up each other.

Eizan yelled out, "Four," as he used his sword to cut a spear in two.

Lyzark held up a broken Sai and countered with "Five!" It proved to be a mistake as he missed a Bollock Dagger flying towards him and it embedded itself in his shoulder.

"Shit, you rotting pile of..." Lyzark screamed as he pulled the weapon from his shoulder. He threw it to the ground and swung his sword to destroy it.

With his concentration on destroying the dagger, he didn't see the spear hurling his way. I was about to warn him when Jean made a flying leap over the sword she was battling. She snatched the spear mid-flight, then hurled it toward a wall next to me.

I glanced at the spear still wobbling in the wall. "Be a little careful there!"

Jean smiled and resumed her battle with the sword.

It was only a matter of time before one of us would be killed, and we needed to find the stone controlling these things. Out of the corner of my eye, I caught a glow coming from a wall near Jeremiah. It was square and about the right size.

"There," I pointed to the wall.

Jeremiah put a hand on Jean, and they disappeared only to reappear in the corner.

Jeremiah yelled, "Cover me," as he tried to get to the stone in the wall. After a minute of pounding on the wall with his sword, he turned back to help Jean fend off an onslaught of arrows.

"I can't get to it," Jeremiah called.

Desperately, I looked around for anything to destroy the stone. My eyes rested on the spear Jean threw, still trying to free itself from the wall behind me.

*I need you to hold these things off so I can destroy that stone.*

*I can give you maybe thirty seconds,* Kitten responded.

I released Kitten, and she continued to spar with a pair of jewel-laden swords. Taking a quick step, I grabbed the spear. It was solidly embedded in the wall, and I struggled to pull it free. It was taking too long, and knew I would have to give up soon.

*Kye, hurry!*

Putting a foot against the wall, I pulled with everything I had. The spear broke loose from the wall, and I caught myself before I tumbled backward. Spotting the glowing spot in the wall, I heaved the weapon as hard as I could and hastily put up a shield for what I knew was coming. But just as I released, Jean stepped into the path of the oncoming projectile.

"Jean!" I yelled, and she jumped out of the way just as the spear passed by where her head had been. The spear slammed into the wall and pierced the stone. The stone exploded, sending nearby Jeremiah to the ground, and shards of the wall bounced off my shield. With the stone gone, the remaining weapons dropped to the floor with a clang.

I grabbed Kitten and staggered backward. Leaning against the wall, I took a few deep breaths. Eizan was bent over with his hands on his knees. Lyzark ran his hand over his shoulder injury, healing it, blood still running down his chest. Jean pushed part of the wall that had come down onto Jeremiah and helped him up. He had multiple cuts, but they were actively healing.

Eizan staggered over to Lyzark and put his hand on Lyzark's shoulder. Their combined energy healed the wound.

"I believe that was eight for me to your six," Eizan gloated.

Lyzark nodded. "I'm a bit tired of beating you, so consider us even."

Surveying the room, a good third of the weapons stored here were now shattered or broken. The head of an axe slithered toward its broken handle. Jeremiah swung his sword and sliced the head in half.

I stared at Jeremiah with a raised eyebrow. "That's a bit cold."

Jeremiah huffed. "That axe and I had history. It tried to kill me a couple of times, and he had it coming."

Lyzark chuckled. "So Kye, what the Satan did you do?"

"I must have set off a trap but not sure how." I glanced at Jeremiah. "What was that thing we destroyed?"

"It's part of Death's security precautions. If someone manages to get in while the alarm systems are still on, that stone could activate the weapons and kill any intruder. You turned off the alarm systems, so this should not have happened."

"I'm guessing it was booby-trapped by Lester."

Jeremiah's head snapped toward me. "It was Lester that Pirq brought to the Eye?"

"Yes. We need to discuss this, but not here. He may have left other surprises."

Jeremiah nodded. "I agree. I will send a team to sweep the area and check for any other traps he may have left. They will remain and protect the Eye until we can reinforce our security measures. Now, follow me to where we will meet."

I was about to argue, but he, along with the other two, disappeared. It didn't surprise me when Jeremiah left Jean.

Jean glared at me. "Where did they go?"

"They said to follow, and I sense their trail. Don't you?" I asked, trying to play innocent. Jean wasn't invited as she was going to be a central part of the conversation.

"Oh, well, I do sense something," Jean said, then disappeared. She'll be really pissed when she finds herself back at my house, alone.

I snapped my fingers to get out of there before Jean figured out she had been duped.

## Chapter Twenty-Eight

I expected to meet Jeremiah and the group but landed near Fre-Fre's club. It took me only a moment to realize that Death must have redirected me again. I should have been pissed about being way-laid, but I sensed something was wrong. The fountains in the area flowed full stream with their special effects, and performers were doing their acts, but there were no customers. Tension hung in the air with at least twenty of Fre-Fre's security goons positioned throughout the area, weapons out. One approached and took off his sunglasses. He had the same speckled eyes as his boss.

"Arbiter Kye?" the man asked with an accent that sounded like a combination of Australian and French.

I nodded as I scanned the man. He carried six weapons, including a full-length sword. It was hidden in a place I didn't think would be comfortable at all.

"Fre-Fre just informed us you were coming. We did not expect your arrival for another thirty minutes. Please follow me."

He turned and walked off, and I reluctantly followed. Three additional guards joined and formed a box around me. Their eyes scanned for potential trouble as we walked. I wondered if they were taking me prisoner, but their eyes never looked to me. They seemed more concerned about external threats. Why Fre-Fre felt that I needed protection was curious and disturbing.

We entered the foyer with its four familiar doors. Interestingly, a sign on the blue door read, "Closed for Renovations." Fre-Fre never closed his business's doors during the day, preferring to close in the early morning hours only when necessary. Even then, he could renovate a room in only an hour. Something was going on.

Fre-Fre stepped through the Blue room door, saw me, and waved for me to enter.

"Let no one in unless I authorize it," he ordered and closed the door behind us.

Inside, the place was a mess. Overturned table, splattered food, and at least six bodies created a tableau of death and destruction—a stark contrast from Fre-Fre's normally pristine standard of operation. I walked over to the first body, and I recognized him as Spike, Fre-Fre's talent manager. It looked like he died mid-transition to, or possibly from, his wereyote form. His neck had been slit, and his body rested in a pool of bright-red blood.

The bodies of several more dead wereyotes littered the area. I then spotted something that is rarely seen. Next to the body of a wereyote was a reaper, her head separated from her body. A black sludge oozed from her neck. It wasn't often that I came across a dead reaper. When a reaper dies, its flock retrieves its body immediately. For one to still be here was unusual to say the least.

I examined her head, looking for her flock's insignia. Reapers love to kill and won't hesitate to kill another if they can get away with it. To protect themselves, reapers will join a flock, a celestial gang so to speak, for protection from other reapers. Their insignia is similar to a gang tattoo and represents the flock they belong to. But the skin where the emblem should be on this reaper had been removed, post-mortem.

"Someone doesn't want us to identify her," I said and pointed to the spot with the missing skin.

Fre-Fre examined the area I had indicted. "No one has touched the body that I know of. I will check my security cameras."

I knew this reaper from someplace but couldn't place her and tapped my chin trying to recall where I knew her from. When nothing came to mind, I waved my hand toward the carnage. "What the heck happened here?"

Fre-Fre sighed, surveying what was left of his club. "When you sent the Fallen given to Lyzark back, I began investigating how this could happen. I haven't authorized selling a Fallen in a long time. I only sell one when the Fallen requests it. Something wasn't right, and I soon found several other Fallen missing. So, I went looking for Spike and found him sitting at that table over there with several of his pack members."

Fre-Fre pointed to a large corner table. The table was on its side, the contents of the meal spread across the floor. It looked like the main course was various cuts of raw meat.

"As soon as I called him over, he knew he was in trouble and tried to run, but my guards blocked him. He went full wereyote, along with his tablemates, and it was a free-for-all. I yelled for my guards to take him alive. That's when this reaper started killing anything in its path."

Just when I thought I had seen everything. "What was a reaper doing in a restaurant?"

"I suspect she was watching Spike and his group. The reaper ordered food, and it had just arrived when things went south. When Spike tried to escape, she eliminated anyone that got between her and Spike. Her mistake was to try to kill me."

I nodded, and my respect level for Fre-Fre increased ten-fold. I've never heard of a non-celestial that could kill a reaper. "A reaper ordered food? How many reapers do you serve?"

Reapers don't eat, ever.

"She was the first."

I spotted a woman wearing one of Fre-Fre's uniforms lying on the floor. Her uniform was covered in, what I assumed was, her own blood. "Who's this?"

Fre-Fre sighed. "Such a waste. When Kassandra fell, I recruited her to dance in my other club, but her angel girlfriend disapproved and wanted her to do something else. Today was her first shift as a waitress."

"What happened to her?"

Fre-Fre knelt next to the woman. "When Spike morphed, she was right next to him, and she was holding a tray of meat. Spike killed her simply for being in his way." Fre-Fre shook his head. "She was so excited about her new job."

I sighed and stared at the dead Fallen. Despite having her neck ripped out, she still looked beautiful. As a Fallen, her soul had no place to go. She was gone, and this was Lester's fault somehow. I knelt next to her and covered her body with a tablecloth.

"Did any of Spike's group survive?"

"Yes. Spike. As soon as he saw his friends getting slaughtered, he tried to make a run for it. We have him tied up in the back."

I looked back at Fre-Fre in confusion. "Wait. I just saw Spike's body over there."

"That was his twin brother. When the reaper came for Spike, he hid behind him." Fre-Fre shook his head. "Spike sold out his own brother."

I wasn't surprised. Wereyotes are pack animals and typically fight together. But, an Alpha like Spike won't hesitate to sacrifice a pack member or two to survive. I followed the club owner to a back room where Spike was bound to a table. He was bloodied and bruised and raged against his restraints. His bonds were tight, and the four guards stationed near him kept a close eye on him. He tried to morph to his wereyote form, and one of the guards slammed a short baton into his stomach.

His transformation stopped.

He turned his head toward us, and his eyes widened to saucers when he saw me.

I took Kitten out and let her blades grow to full size. She let out a purr, expecting to kill something soon. As I approached Spike, the four guards backed away. Spike scrambled harder, his nails dug into the table, and his feet pounded as he tried to break loose. I lowered Kitten's blade until it barely kissed his neck. In my mind, all I saw was the vision of the dead waitress—gone forever.

"Start from the beginning and omit no detail," I threatened. It took every bit of my willpower not to carve the wereyote alive.

"Will you, uh, let me live if I do?" Spike stuttered, and a stain spread across his pants. He gulped when the blade touched his neck.

"If you tell me everything, I will let a Fre-Fre decide if you live or die."

"That's fair, I guess. I, uh, started renting some of the Fallen out to those with enough coin for just a few hours at a time. It was good money, and no one got hurt," Spike blurted out.

Fre-Fre slammed a fist into Spike's groin. "Except the Fallen weren't paid, and they were forced to work. You threatened to kill them if they didn't."

Spike screamed like a soprano on speed and writhed in pain. "I wouldn't have killed them. It was just a threat."

He clearly was less than brilliant if he thought that answer would help him. Fre-Fre delivered a second punch. At that point, I was pretty sure what was left of his balls were now located somewhere near his armpits, and I gave him a minute to recover.

"But you did something worse. Didn't you?" I pressed Kitten's blade against his skin. A small shimmer of blood began to flow.

"Yes! Yes, I did. An arbiter came to see me. Wanted me to deliver a few Fallen to Lyzark and Eizan as playthings. Paid me a lot, and I figured out how to hide the missing girls."

I eased up on the blade. "Did this arbiter have a name?"

Spike cautiously lifted his head. "He didn't give me a name, just handed me a lot of coin, then gave me the addresses where I should deliver them to. I got the first off to Eizan easy enough. The Fallen that went to Lyzark put up a pretty good fight."

I pressed the blade harder against his neck, another trickle of blood began to flow. "Yeah, I saw the results. Tell me, is this the guy?"

I held up my phone to show him a picture of Lester.

"Yeah, that's the guy."

"His name is Lester, and I want him dead. Anything else you can tell me before he decides your fate?"

Spike licked his lips and started his transformation but stopped before he was punched again. "Yes, I do. Something I think's really valuable, but I gotta have your word that you'll release me. Alive and with all my limbs."

The club owner grabbed Spike's head. "There ain't no info you got that's worth saving your miserable life. Not after what you did."

"I do. I do. I think I know how you can find where the guy and his buddy are hiding."

This had my attention. "Buddy, what buddy? You didn't mention anyone else."

"I hadn't got to that part yet. Hard to talk with a blade cuttin' my throat. But I'll tell you how you might be able to find them, but I gotta live, and you need to protect me." Despite a blade to his throat, he thrashed around, looking for someone. "If he finds out I told, I don't want to think what he will do to me."

The club owner frowned and looked at me, questioning. We were both thinking the same thing. Who could he be more afraid of than us?

Fre-Fre shrugged. "I want this piece of shit dead. But I have to admit, I really want to know who he's afraid of. Make the deal."

"You tell me everything, and if I find it helpful, we will let you live. As for protection from this guy, you're on your own. But if I get to him first, you won't ever have to worry about him again."

The wereyote nodded a little too violently then screamed when it caused Kitten's blade to dig deeper. I pulled her back. "Good. Good, so your man, Lester. I met him by the old car dealership down the way. He's supposed to pay me the rest of the coin for delivering the Fallen. Said he had more work for me. But he showed up with this other guy. Crazy-ass-looking dude. Blood all over his shirt and a weird sword. Swore it hummed. Lester hands me the bag of coins, but the other guy starts getting all worked up. Lester was yelling at 'im, but he ain't listening. The guy scared the hell out of me. I ain't never seen anyone with eyes like his. He was possessed."

Spike licked his lips and looked around. I wasn't sure if he was trying to figure out an escape path or he was looking for the guy.

"The guy starts screaming that he has to kill me. Well, I ain't no fool. I go full coyote, grabbed the bag of gold in my mouth, and take off. He chased me, and he's fast. He almost got me. But I had a couple of guys as backup—both huge as mountains. One carried a special gun—dude said it would kill anything, including angels. Well, he got off a couple of rounds before the dude chasing me splits him down the middle. My other guy pulled his sword, and they went at it. I didn't stay to find out who won."

It was my turn to frown. A wereyote can run at incredible speeds. Not too many can catch one. But what worried me was the gun he mentioned. The gun itself wasn't special, but the bullets were. They were created by a powerful demon eons ago. The things could kill just about anything, including angels and demons. When Satan found out about what the demon had done, she went ballistic. Anyone caught with them was executed on the spot, and Satan sent out a hit squad looking for the remaining rounds. The running rumor was that the demon that created them was still alive, and Satan tortures him to this day.

While the bullets were a concern, the fact that the guy chasing Spike got hit twice and survived meant he must have had a celestial object that kept him alive. I know of only a few items that could do that. Kitten is one of them, which gave me an idea.

"Did you say the sword hummed?"

The wereyote nodded. "Yeah, it was a faint hum, but I'm sure it was coming from the sword."

I nodded as it made sense. It was the sword that somehow kept him alive.

"You said you know how to find where Lester's hiding. What you told me isn't enough to save your hide."

"Yeah, Yeah, I got more. I think I know how you can find your guy, Lester."

"You think? You think? I am predicting a very short lifespan for you," I growled. This guy was playing games, and it was time to end this. I raised Kitten and prepared to cut this piece of junk's head off.

"Wait! Let me explain. You know I can smell really good cause, you know..."

"Yeah, we know, a wereyote. Move it along."

Spike held still, but his eyes continued to search for an escape route. "I prefer coyote. Anyhow, Lester, you know, is always spot clean, but the scary guy, he ain't. I smelled salt on him. Not just any ole' table salt. It's got a real sweet scent, like roses. I ain't never smelled anything like it before. Can't be too many places that smell like that."

"Hmmm." I mulled over Spike's clue.

Spike's right. It was a solid lead. He had held up his part of the bargain, but I didn't want to let him go, especially after what he had done. But I had given him my word and I couldn't renege. I walked out of earshot of the guards, and their boss followed. Spike could still hear us with his coyote hearing, and I used my energy to block him from listening.

Fre-Fre eyed me closely. "Kye, does this help you find where Lester is hiding?"

I paused, trying to give me time to figure out a way out of letting the wereyote loose. "Yeah, it does. Only a few places exist that match what he's talking about."

"And this other guy? He's the soul Lyzark and Eizan were on tracking on earth?"

I nodded. "Yes. The one you were going to get me more information on."

Fre-Fre cleared his throat. "Uh, yeah, sorry about that. Been a bit busy." The club owner waved his hand toward Spike. "So, you think this prized soul got his hands on a special sword? Maybe one of a set?"

I had been staring at my shoes, but my head snapped toward the club owner.

He smiled. "Don't be too surprised. I've been around long enough to have heard about them. A guy carrying a sword takes two magical rounds and survives? Only a few things can explain that."

"One of these days, we're going to have an honest conversation about who and what you are?"

Fre-Fre chuckled. "Sure, but in the meantime. Do we let Spike go? He held up his end of the bargain."

I groaned. I didn't want to let him go. The face of the dead Fallen burned into my memory. "I don't see any way around it. But he needs to pay for what he did."

"You gave your word. Now let him go."

The owner was too calm, which worried me. I headed back to the prisoner and swung Kitten, cutting a rope binding his arm. The wereyote yelped, then realized he still had his hand. I cut the other three bindings, and he sat up.

I pointed Kitten at the wereyote. Her tip a mere inch from his nose. "We're letting you go, but I never want to see you again. If we meet again, I will not hesitate to kill you."

Spike scrambled off the table. He backed away but stopped and looked down. "Can I have my other shoe back?"

Fre-Fre launched himself over the table. "You'd better run!"

The wereyote dashed through the door. I doubted I would see him again.

I stowed Kitten then slammed my fist into the table. Letting Spike go was the last thing I wanted to do. From the white-knuckled fists of the nearby guards, they were pissed also. The only one who didn't look angry was Fre-Fre. The club owner wore a smile that hinted at a plan.

"What aren't you telling me?" I asked.

"Well, the Fallen that he killed, her name was Kassandra. Her girlfriend is an angel named Nakita. Nakita didn't appreciate others enjoying one of her girlfriends, so she asked me to reassign her to be a waitress as a favor. She's not going to be happy that Kassandra is dead."

I laughed and felt much better. Nakita was a tracker and hunter. If a non-human does something it shouldn't and runs, Nakita was sent to find it. Nine out of ten times, she ended up killing what she hunted.

Fre-Fre grinned and held up a shoe.

"And you kept Spike's shoe so she can hunt him."

## Chapter Twenty-Nine

**T**en minutes later, I joined Jeremiah and the others in a hunting lodge created for meetings between the celestial superpowers. I was usually invited as most times it was something I did that necessitated a meeting.

The walls and cathedral-style ceiling were made of large, bare-timber logs. There were no doors, and only a few opaque windows mounted high on the walls to light the place. Large, wrought-iron chandeliers, each with dozens of lit candles, hung overhead. The heads of dozens of different creatures, including a few humans, were mounted on the walls. A full-sized, stuffed Wooly Mammoth stood in one corner. Excalibur, embedded in a large stone, sat nearby.

In a corner near the fireplace, a Hell Hound curled up into a ball. He never lifted his head, but his bright red eyes followed my every move. Next to it sat a white Angel Wolf. Its piercing white eyes tracked me also. The wolf raised its head and bared its teeth. Kitten returned the growl, and the cowered animal lowered its head with a whimper.

I had tried to convince Jeremiah we needed our own pet to bring to these gatherings. After a fair amount of nagging by me, he announced he had found the perfect pet, which immediately made me suspicious. At the next meeting, he brought a rat the size of a greyhound. Jeremiah called it his 'Reaper Rat, ' and Lyzark had snickered at the name.

Unfortunately, the overly sensitive rodent attacked Lyzark, and the Hell Hound jumped into the fray. Five minutes later, the rat lay dead in the middle of the floor with Eizan's sword protruding out of its back and the place in shambles. The Hell Hound took two full days to recover, and Jeremiah was barred from bringing any more pets. The monster rat's head was subsequently mounted on the wall.

A large fireplace sat to one side. It was lit, and Hell's Fire happily danced among the logs. A Hell-flame spotted me staring at it, smiled, and exploded. Embers flew across the room and landed on a rug. Moments later, the Hell-flame erupted from the smoldering rug, and it continued its dance.

The demon lord looked to the Hell Flame burning the rug, and said, "That's enough of that." The flame leaped back to the fireplace. With a wave of his hand, Lyzark repaired the rug. I once asked why we didn't decorate with fire-retardant materials. Lyzark responded with, "Hell's Fire would consider this a challenge. Best not to tempt fate."

Near the fireplace, Eizan and Lyzark lounged in huge, high-back leather chairs, each nursing a drink. Jeremiah stood by the bar, a worried look on his face.

I walked to the bar and poured two bourbons. I handed one to Jeremiah, grabbed his arm, and steered him toward two empty chairs facing the celestial lords. We sat, and I surveyed my audience. Lyzark and Eizan were relaxed, nothing seemed to be worrying them. Jeremiah tried to play it cool, but he was on edge. I have known him for almost a century, and he has tells just like everyone else.

Lyzark set his drink on the table next to him. "Are you going to tell us why we are here?"

"I am, and you definitely want to hear what I have to say, but I have a little business to transact first," I said, then looked to Heaven's number one angel. "We started a transaction before things went a little off course."

I stood and handed Eizan the bag with the bottle of bourbon I had promised him. He pulled the bottle out and admired the sparkling colors.

"I'm holding you to your word on this one," I warned, mainly to emphasize he was not to try to figure out how to weasel his way around our deal.

Eizan looked up and smiled. "The two Fallen that were left for you will be returned to you unharmed."

His response caught me off-guard. I had completely forgotten about them. "I don't want them. They were left as some sort of trap by Lester."

Eizan smirked. "Well, if you don't want them, I can always use a couple of playthings to keep me entertained."

"Yeah, I don't think so. Send them to Fre-Fre. Now back to my questions."

"As for the information you require, please ask."

"The prize, Joshua, what do you know about him?" I sat and waited.

"You mean the prize and his brother?" Eizan asked, waiting to see if I reacted.

"Yes, both." I wasn't surprised he knew about the twins—Ken and Joshua. But I would have loved to know how he found out about Ken.

"Unfortunately, I'm not going to tell you anything about them you don't already know. Neither is of Heaven, but both are quite powerful." Eizan paused and glanced at Lyzark. "What I can tell you is someone from Hell has been trying to recruit both to Hell's cause."

"It is not I," Lyzark growled. "It must have been Pirq."

"I know Pirq wasn't working with you. But there is someone in Hell that Pirq was working for and aided Lester. Maybe you know?" I asked Eizan.

Eizan frowned. "That, I don't know." He paused. "Tell me about this Lester character. He seems to be the instigator of this whole mess."

"Lester was a by-the-book-arbiter who wasn't happy that I was promoted above him. The man absolutely loathes me. He faked his death, trying to kill me in the process. According to Pirq, he wants to start the war between Heaven and Hell."

Jeremiah broke in. "How do the brothers play into his plans?"

I wasn't ready to release that information yet. I needed my boss to tell his secret first.

"All in due time," I replied, and I smiled at Jeremiah as he glared back at me. "Before I release my secret, I think it's time you told yours."

"I'm not sure what you mean," Jeremiah quipped, but from his nervous look and shaking hand, I knew he was lying.

"Should I invite Jean to this gathering?" I asked and hit pay dirt when Jeremiah looked away. Up until that moment, what I had was conjecture at best. Now I knew the truth.

Jeremiah got up to pour himself another shot. "No, please don't. She doesn't even know."

I had been taking a sip and spewed it out. "How could she not know?"

The two other celestials leaned forward in their chairs, eager to hear more.

"Okay. I think it's time I tell everyone," Jeremiah took a deep breath. "The two prizes, Ken and Joshua, are my sons, and Jean is their mother."

Eizan and Lyzark looked at each other, their jaws nearly reaching the floor. Lyzark snapped his fingers, and two bags of popcorn appeared. Each grabbed a bag, sat back in their seats, and looked to Jeremiah expectantly.

Jeremiah continued. "We were in love, and to be honest, I didn't think she could become pregnant. I've been with Death for a very long time and have never heard of something like this happening."

Jeremiah then went quiet.

Lyzark let out a laugh. "You were banging someone that reports to you, and you're surprised you knocked her up?"

Jeremiah jumped to his feet, hand on his sword. I launched from my chair and positioned myself between Death's right-hand man and the demon lord. "He's crude. But he's right. You were a bit naïve on this one."

"But that isn't how it works for us. You know that, Kye," Jeremiah pleaded.

"I do." I turned and glared at the other two. "And *so* do they. They're just jealous."

Lyzark and Eizan looked down at their drinks. I wanted to rub it in, but the dejected look on both told me I had already made my point. God's angels and Satan's demons can, with permission, procreate. Satan and God dole those permissions out sparingly to the count of maybe once every decade. Tassis was the first demon child I had encountered in twenty years. The two celestial lords were centuries old and had probably seen the birth of Jesus but had only been given permission to be a father once. It was clear they both longed for that chance again.

When Eizan made eye contact, I could see the hurt in his eyes.

"Congratulations on being a father," Eizan said, then looked back at his drink.

"Yes, congratulations," Lyzark added. "But how did that happen? I thought Death forbade his people from having children."

Jeremiah nodded. "He has. So when it happened, I decided I needed to hide the boys. I wasn't sure what Death would do to them or Jean."

"If Death were to create his people instead of recruiting souls, this would not have happened," Eizan said.

I nodded as he was right. A majority of God's and Satan's angels were originally created by the big two. Procreation by those angels created most of the rest. Death took a different route. His people, except reapers and maybe Jeremiah, were born on earth, and when we die, all that remained was our soul. The Big D then recruited us into service. We are pure energy that manifests itself how we want. Death somehow has blocked our ability to procreate, but there have been rumors of a few pregnancies over the centuries. How they happened, I had no idea.

Eizan smiled and stretched his legs. "I'm impressed that it took this long for us to find out. But please, go on, tell us what happened."

Jeremiah stared at Eizan, and I worried he was about to attack the angel. Instead, he took another drink and continued. "The birth of the twins was nothing like what happens for humans or even angels. Instead of giving birth, her body returned to its celestial form. She glimmered, and I lost my breath at her beauty. That's when there was an explosion that sent me flying. I watched as the twins were literally ripped from her. Power flowed over me like I had never encountered. Worse than a star exploding. When it was over, I had burns from head to toe. Jean collapsed to the floor, and the boys floated, landing next to her. It took everything I had to save her, and it took two full months for her to regain consciousness."

Jeremiah paused and took a breath. "When she woke, she barely remembered who I was or even who she was. She had no recollection of giving birth. Death had been adamant about not allowing his people to procreate, and I was afraid of what would happen if Ken and Joshua were found out. I couldn't detect any power from them, so I hid them on Earth. I assumed they would be safe. But I was wrong."

"You hid your sons on Earth and thought they would be safe? Maybe you should have been more worried about the welfare of those on the planet and what your sons could do to them," Eizan warned.

"They were fine until Lester found out about them and pushed them into using their powers," I said, trying to divert some blame from Jeremiah. "Also, it didn't help that agents from your two sides started recruiting them," I said to throw a little shade back at them. I liked Jeremiah. He made a mistake but so had everyone in the room.

"So, we know about Jeremiah's indiscretion. Gabriel's trumpet, we even know about *your* indiscretion, Kye. Speaking of that, you can't hide Cassi forever," Eizan said, not even trying to hide his threat.

He expected to get a rise out of me, but, in this case, I was way ahead of him. "I won't need to as you're going to restore her to her previous position. I might even demand a promotion for her."

Eizan stood and drew his sword. Even Jeremiah gave me an appreciative look.

After a few tense moments, Eizan sat and placed his weapon across his lap. "And how do you plan on making me do that?"

The room went quiet, and I paused, letting the tension build. It was my turn to release a secret, and I enjoyed the moment. If I could have played background music to match the tension in the air, it would have made the scene.

I laughed and took a sip of my drink. "Did you really think I was going to attack you? You might want to hold off on any more of that bourbon for a while."

Eizan ran his hand along his blade. "Then, for the sake of clarity—and your life. What do you propose?"

"What if I tell you about the existence of a Berserker sword? Technically two."

# Chapter Thirty

L yzark bolted upright, sending his chair flying. His sword now pointed at me. Kitten purred, enjoying the show and possibly some angel killing. I sat and watched the spectacle. Jeremiah smiled, leaned back in his chair, and took a sip of his drink. Eizan stood, sword drawn, but his confused look told me he didn't know what a Berserker sword was.

"You had better be joking, Kye," Lyzark said as his chair slid back into place, and the two celestial heavyweights eased back into them.

Eizan watched Lyzark down his drink then turned his attention to me. "What is a Berserker sword?"

"They're weapons that Satan should never have created!" Lyzark roared and threw his glass into the fireplace, sending his Hell Fire scrambling. "Had I known they had been recovered, I would have destroyed them myself."

Lyzark hopped up, grabbed a bottle of rum, and took a long drink, and I decided to fill Eizan in. "During the great war, Satan created a pair of sentient swords. Effectively sibling swords. Each sword by itself imbues its owner with strength, stamina, and excellent healing powers. When given to a pair of biological siblings, they become a literal holy terror. Two siblings that wield Berserker swords would be almost invincible. They can fight for days with no break, wounds heal in an instant, and they have incredible strength and speed."

Eizan's eyes went wide as he realized the danger the swords created.

Lyzark belched and glared at Eizan. "Satan created the swords and gave them to two demon brothers. They had killed over a hundred Heaven's angels when the war ended. Satan wasn't able to persuade the brothers to release the swords. It took her three days of battle to kill them."

Eizan looked first to Lyzark, then me. "And how does this relate to Lester and Jeremiah's sons?"

"Recently, I was attacked by two angels, one from each side." Eizan gave me a look as he hated calling demons *angels*.

I continued. "At first, I thought they had been juiced and given some pretty powerful swords. But I now know that they were both carrying berserker swords."

"And how do you know that?" Jeremiah asked.

I frowned at him then tilted my head toward the other two. This was a dramatic moment, and I wanted one of the other two to ask that. It was a bit childish, but I enjoy melodrama as much as the next arbiter.

Lyzark rolled his eyes. "Yes, please tell us how you know this." He then frowned. "Your accusation, if true, could be a breaking point and the start of a deadly war."

"You're aware of my sword?"

It was Eizan's turn to roll his eyes. "Yes, we are all aware of the sword you call Kitten."

"She recognized the two swords when we battled them. They are equivalent to her cousins. Death created her in response to Satan creating the Berserkers. During battle, Kitten will cut through all but the most powerful swords, but she barely dented these."

There was a pause as everyone thought about the implications.

Eizan massaged his temples. "Their very existence is disturbing, and if Jeremiah's sons have the swords, it could be the start of a war that would destroy everything. If you help us find and destroy the swords, I will consider restoring Cassi to her previous position. You will also earn favor in my court."

"And you will earn favor in my court as well," Lyzark said. He shakily sat back in his chair.

The revelation had spooked the entire group. Jeremiah used both hands to take another drink.

"Thank you both for your offers. It will take all of us to track down and destroy them."

Lyzark let out a belch. "And where did Lester get two Berserker swords?"

"They were found by the teams searching for weapons from the great war. Unfortunately, they found one, tested it, realized it was from the war, and sent it in. They found the second and did the same, not realizing their true nature. Had they tested them together, they would have found out what the swords truly were," I said, then I let them stew.

"I don't understand. Why was it important to test the two at the same time?" Eizan asked. He's more of a 'give me something to kill with' type and had not studied weapons and their history.

"That's because Berserker swords are sentient beings, somewhat like Kitten. When the team tested the first sword, it hid its true nature. Same with the second. Had they tested the two at the same time, the swords would not have been able to disguise their true identity."

"So, if Lester's end game was to arm the brothers with the swords, why did he give two of his minions the swords to kill you?" Jeremiah asked.

"I believe he was searching for the brothers, but his work as an arbiter was getting in the way and needed to fake his death. So, he gave the swords to a couple of low-level angels and paid them a lot of coin to kill me. I think he gambled on the fact that they would fail. He just needed to establish his death, and I was his patsy."

I stared at Hell's Flames, trying to work out my thoughts. "I'm guessing that he plans to make sure that one brother ends up in Heaven and the other in Hell. Then give each a sword and wait for the war between Heaven and Hell to start. Those boys are very powerful, and you throw in Berserker swords and..."

"You have Armageddon," Jeremiah said, finishing my sentence.

"Correct. I'd bet my last coin that Pirq was also working with someone other than Lester, and that effort interfered with Lester's plans. Whoever it is, maybe trying to recruit both brothers to Hell's cause."

Eizan frowned. "That means we need to get to those brothers before either plan is enacted."

"And how do you propose we find them? They've both disappeared, and we've had no luck finding them," Lyzark said.

"I have a lead on where Lester's hiding, but we won't have luck with finding the brothers without their mother's help." I grinned.

"It's time their mother found out about her sons."

# Chapter Thirty-One

I tossed two gold coins into a plate then handed it to Lyzark. "My bet is that she tosses him around, even sucker punches him, but he lives."

Lyzark laughed. "She's going to try to kill him, but Death prevents it." He added his coins to the ante.

Eizan rubbed his chin and threw his coins in. "I don't know. Hmm, yes, she kills him."

We stood at the end of a large room, easily fifty feet by fifty feet. The walls were smooth rock, and the only features were a door to an observation room on one side and another door on the other end. Where the second door led to, I had no idea. Jean and Jeremiah were at the opposite end of the room from us. We chose this place because it could survive a nuclear blast. But knowing Jean, the three of us weren't convinced it was enough.

Jeremiah had the unfortunate task of telling his girlfriend that she was the mother of two grown sons. The fact that he hid it from her until now was not going to help. Jeremiah had begged us to let him keep his weapons, but we felt it best that both parties were unarmed.

Eizan smiled. "It's beginning."

Jeremiah rubbed his hands together, then reached over and put them on Jean's shoulders. All was quiet, and I could almost hear Death's lieutenant telling her the news.

"You did what?" Jean screamed and slugged Jeremiah in the gut. He doubled over, but she pushed him upright and punched him in the face. He stumbled backward and slammed into the wall.

"I called it. The sucker punch," I boasted.

Lyzark growled. "It ain't over."

"Wait! I did it to save you!" the panicked man said, righting himself. He pushed himself away from the wall and backpedaled as his apprentice menaced toward him.

"Save me? Save me! How could not telling me about getting me knocked up and giving birth save me!"

Jean turned toward us with a snarl and pointed at me. "Why didn't you tell me about this, Kye? You're going to pay. You are all going to pay!"

"Ah, shit," I said. The three of us retreated to the room on the other side of the window. It wouldn't stop Kilford from killing us, but it would give us more time to escape. I made sure I was a half-foot behind the other two to give me a head start.

I hit a button on the wall, and a microphone turned on. "Jean, I just found out, and that's why he's telling you."

I just lied and threw Jeremiah under the bus, but between the two, I liked my chances of facing him. He gave me a dirty look, and I'd better do something, or I'd be a target for both of them.

"Jean. He had to, or you'd be dead, along with your sons."

Jean's chest heaved, and she looked confused. She frantically scanned the area as if trying to find something to destroy.

Jeremiah approached slowly, arms wide, gray blood dripping from his broken nose. "If you would let me explain, I think you would understand."

He had almost reached her, and I knew what was coming. I tried to hit the microphone button to warn Jeremiah when she stepped toward her lover and turned. Grabbing his arm, she threw him over her shoulder. He landed with a grunt and rolled to his hands and knees.

The assassin glowered over him. "Okay, now I'm listening."

"Death has one unbreakable rule—*Do not procreate*. It's the one rule he has always told me that he would enforce. If Death found out about the boys' birth, I was afraid he would kill them and you. I couldn't let that happen."

He leaned back and sat on the ground. "Kill me if you want. But I did it because I love you." He pulled out a hunting knife and slid it to Kilford.

"How did he get a weapon?" I demanded. "Both of you were supposed to search him."

Lyzark laughed. "Did you really think I would body search him?"

I glared at the two celestial lords. "Cowards."

Jean picked up the dagger, strolled to Jeremiah, and put it to his throat. A tear rolled down her face while Jeremiah gazed back at her.

She pulled the dagger back, and I was sure she was about to strike.

Jeremiah arched his head back, exposing his neck. "I have always loved you."

I expected her to kill him when she turned and threw the weapon. It sailed across the room, shattered the window, and impaled itself in the wall behind us. I gauged the distance between Jean and me. That was an impressive throw.

I looked around to plan my escape when everything went dark. A beam of light from an unseen source lit the not-so-loving couple. A separate spotlight shone on me. I then found myself lifted into the air and floated toward the two. Jeremiah looked into the darkness as I glided to a stop about ten feet from them.

I turned to see what Jeremiah was staring at, and a man emerged from the shadows. I could tell by his aura it was Death. But he looked like George Washington. Military suit and all.

"Hey George? Where's your boat?" I joked before my brain could tell me to keep quiet.

My head turned to noise from above, and I watched in horror as a wooden boat headed straight toward me. I dove out of the way just as the boat crashed onto the ground where I stood.

"Happy now, or should I find a cherry tree?"

I waved my hands when an ax appeared in Death's hand. "No thanks. I'm good." I needed to learn to shut my mouth around Death.

Jeremiah pushed Jean behind him and took a defensive stand.

Death raised a hand. "Relax, you two are safe, and so are your sons. Assuming we can find them before they do something so stupid that even I can't save them."

Jeremiah remained frozen. "But your rule..."

Death smiled. "Jeremiah, you saw what happened when your boys were born. If you weren't there, they would have all died. That's the reason I have banned my people from reproducing. I was tired of watching mothers and children perish in childbirth. God created humankind and their souls and set the rules on how they exist. It was either ban procreation or watch more innocents die. I think you can understand that."

Jeremiah nodded, then frowned. "I do. But how were Jean and I able to have the boys?"

"First, because I trust you, and my mandates have never been binding to you. Also, because you deeply love Jean, and she loves you." Death cocked an eyebrow at Jean. "I suspect God added a backdoor mechanism that gives the power of love the ability to overcome my block. It's rare, but it has happened before." Death took a deep breath. "When I found out about the twins, I realized that by not telling you the whole truth, I put you in an impossible position." Death extended his hand. "If you will forgive me, the boys will be welcomed home if we can stop them in time."

The two shook hands. Death considered Jean as she glared at the two. "Don't think just because you two made up, I'm okay with what happened. Until my sons are safe and sound, there will be no peace."

Jeremiah's head bowed, and he turned away.

Death stared at her, tapping his chin. "Fair enough. Then let's find those boys. Kye?"

Every eye turned toward me, and I got off the ground only to start gliding toward Death. I was done with being pulled where Death wanted me to be and snapped my fingers and appeared next to Jean.

"Yes, George?"

Death laughed. "Very good. Now, as for your idea to have Jeremiah admit his mistake." He paused, and the room is quiet except for the echo of Death's voice. "It was a very good one, I must say. Which means you get the honor to lead the search to find the missing boys. Whatever resources you need are yours for the asking. God and Satan have given you access to their resources also. I have taken the liberty of bringing those that I think can help."

Death disappeared, and the lights came back on. Around us were dozens of arbiters, reapers, angels, demons, and a few I have no clue what they were.

# Chapter Thirty-Two

F re-Fre stood in the back, a confused look on his face. My body tingled like I just drank a hundred cups of coffee. It only took me a moment to realize that Death effectively 'juiced' me.

Cassi now stood to my left. She was dressed in white combat fatigues, and her wings were out. Every third feather was missing or falling out, and her wings had taken a brown tinge. Bags were under her eyes, and she looked tired.

The Heaven formula I gave her was waning, and I needed to do something. My body still tingled, and an idea formed. If God and Satan gave me everything I needed, then maybe I could help her. I took Cassi's hand and sent a charge through her. She blazed white, and I caught her as she dropped. Her eyes fluttered, and she took a deep breath.

Her wings were now white, and the missing feathers regrew. The bags under her eyes were gone. She smiled and kissed me.

I enjoyed the moment until a voice seared through my happiness. "Cassi, so good to *see* you again. How are the hummingbirds doing?"

I recognized the voice of Keitz. A fellow arbiter and the moral opposite of me. Where I take the occasional bribe but make sure justice is done, Keitz would send his mother to Hell if there was coin in it. His reference to the hummingbirds must be to the tattoos that Cassi had inked under her breasts. If he referenced a fox, I would run Kitten through him.

I glared at the arrogant arbiter and then eyed Cassi. She turned red-faced and won't meet my gaze. "Kye, I just danced. That's it. Nothing else. I was desperate."

She began to cry, and Keitz smirked. Wrong thing to do to the man now in charge of you.

"Glad you're here, Keitz. I have an assignment for you."

The arbiter grinned. His team had a reputation for being relentless trackers, but their leader had pissed me off—time for a little revenge.

"I need you to go over every detail from the attack where Lester faked his death. I need to know who was killed and if there were any clues."

The man's grin faltered. "Sorry, everything was taken to Death's dumping ground. Probably burned by now."

I felt like the cat that was about to eat the canary. "Nope, not burned yet. I just checked. Don't get too dirty. I need that information ASAP."

I snapped my fingers, and Keitz and his team were now knee-deep in a field of celestial waste. I should've told them they were about a mile from where they should be searching but didn't. After all, they were good at tracking.

I collected myself to make sure I didn't say anything that might destroy my relationship with Cassi. Long-term.

"The next time you're desperate, you see me. If you had followed my plan, you wouldn't have had to dance, or other things, for Keitz."

Cassi sobbed. "Kye, it was a while ago, and I only..." I interrupted her pleading by sending her back to Renaldo. I believed her, but I don't know how many dances and not-quite going all the way favors she had done. We would have our reckoning later when there wasn't a crowd.

My anger flared, and I felt the darkness that I lived with after Tracey's death, nipping at the edge of my consciousness.

*Kye, now's not the time. You need to focus. Going there won't help,* Kitten said.

If I didn't know better, I would say I heard sympathy in her voice.

I looked around, and everyone had backed away. Kitten pulsed in my hands, fully extended. Fear showed in the eyes around me. This wasn't the way I wanted to introduce myself to the team.

I breathed deeply to control my anger. Kitten retracted, and I stowed her. The tension in the room dropped, but every eye tracked me. They were waiting for my plan. Which would be great, except I didn't have one other than showing up where I thought Lester was hiding and hope he was there. I needed Lester to go back to his hiding spot, at least for a little while, to corner him.

It would help if I knew who was working for him. Finally, the first part of a plan began to form. It was a long shot, but it was all I had.

"Okay, everyone, listen up! There are several things we need to do. First, we need to know who the enemy is."

"And how do we do that?" Lyzark asked.

"Easy, I need you and Eizan to pull all of your people from Earth. Anyone that doesn't return home consider a traitor. Anyone who tries to return to Earth without permission consider them a traitor. Don't kill anyone too quickly. We need information. Also, take as many Fallen home with you as you can. When you have everything under control, track me down."

Eizan chuckled. "No angels or demons on Earth. This should be interesting." He disappeared along with every angel in the room.

Lyzark roared with laughter and vanished, followed a second later by his demons.

Jean looked unnerved. "What's so damn funny about no angels or demons on Earth?"

Jeremiah cut in. "Having Earth abandoned by Heaven and Hell has only occurred twice before. Each time, Earth plunged into chaos shortly after. It usually only takes a few months. I think the last time they called it World War II."

"Let's hope this ends quickly," I replied. "Everyone else, you have the same orders. No celestial entity should be on Earth except Jean, Tassis, and me. At least until we have everything under control."

Jeremiah gently placed his hand on Jean's shoulder. "Jean, I made a mistake. I really thought he would kill you and the boys. I couldn't bear the thought of losing you."

Jean stared at his hand then stepped away. "I know you did what you thought was best to protect me...but it doesn't mean you shouldn't have told me earlier."

Jeremiah nodded. "I see that now. Can you forgive me?"

Kilford sighed. "I, uh, don't know."

Jeremiah was teary-eyed as he walked away then disappeared, along with the reapers and the other arbiters. Jean gazed at where he disappeared, and tears flowed down her face.

Those left began to disappear, except Fre-Fre. "Sorry, I ain't leaving Earth. Too much going on."

"Considering most of your clients won't be coming for a few days, I'm not sure what you'll be doing."

Fre-Fre grinned. "I have plenty of non-celestial staff and customers to stay open. That said, I have to believe I'm here for a reason."

"Yep, you nailed it. I need you to keep as many of the Fallen that decide to stay. Also, any angel that does not return home I need to know about. Lastly, I need you to be ready."

Fre-Fre's grinned disappeared. "Ready for what? Not sure I can do much if Armageddon happens."

"Lester is going to cause as much chaos as possible. That could include sending his troops to attack your clubs."

"I ain't letting no one screw with my clubs," Fre-Fre growled. His body pulsed, growing and shrinking. He took a deep breath, and the pulses stopped. "I will prepare."

The club owner disappeared. I wasn't aware he could travel. Another clue to help figure out what he was.

Tassis nudged me. "Well, fearless leader, what's our next move?"

"We're going hunting for Joshua and Ken."

# Chapter Thirty-Three

e returned to my Colorado home to give me a few minutes to think. I had an idea on how to find one of the brothers, but fear of a falling cherry tree drove me from the bunker. Feeling a little hungry, I decided to whip up something to eat. I'm not great at cooking, but I needed the distraction.

I picked up a frying pan. "How about some omelets?" I asked and received two confused looks.

"You can cook?" Jean asked.

I arched an eyebrow. "Of course, I can cook."

Jean looked up at the fire detector on the ceiling. "Does that thing have fresh batteries?"

"Very funny, and the answer to your question is, yes, it has fresh batteries."

I didn't want to tell her the last time I pan-fried some fish, the alarm went off, and it took me twenty minutes to clear the smoke. By then, the batteries wore down, and I had to replace them.

Jean walked over and took the pan out of my hand. "Here, let an expert do it."

I walked away a little dejected. "I can cook...but I guess you are a chef."

"Now, back to our problem." Tassis frowned. "How do we find Lester or the twins? We have nothing on where they may be."

"We do have a clue. Spike told me about a sweet salt on Joshua. There are several undiscovered underground salt mines with a sweet scent."

"Chop these, please. Without cutting yourself." Jean placed a cutting board, a knife, and a couple of tomatoes in front of me. "So, we check those places out and hope we find them?"

"Actually, I have a better idea. I think we may be able to track Ken and hope he leads us to the others." I smiled and waited for my moment to show them how clever I was. "We will use the Arbiter app on my phone."

Jean looked up from cracking eggs. "Let me guess, you slipped a tracking device on Bush?"

"Yes. I'm betting that when you picked up the gun from the container in Ken's office, you put a tracker on it, hoping he would take the weapon wherever he went," Tassis added.

Well, crappy diem. "Really? You couldn't let me have just one moment to shine?"

Tassis patted my arm. "It was an excellent idea. Assuming he took the gun, and he hasn't discovered the tracking device."

I scowled at the two. "If you have a better idea, hit me with it."

Jean shrugged and tossed a pat of butter into the pan, and it began to sizzle. "I do think it was a great idea. Is that enough adoration, or does your ego need more stroking?"

I was half-tempted to send her to help Keitz in the waste field. No doubt she would kill the sexist ass within the first ten minutes of her arrival. But I needed her if we did find the twins.

I grinned. "I think Jeremiah would prefer that you leave the stroking..."

Jean blushed. "Kye, don't even start."

I chuckled, then handed Jean the cutting board full of chopped tomatoes. Pulling my phone out, I opened the arbiter app. While I liked the app, it wasn't the easiest thing to work with. I couldn't figure out how to connect it to my tracking device.

Jean poured eggs into a pan then topped it with seasonings and chopped veggies. The smell wafted toward me, and it was wonderful.

My hunger didn't help my frustration at not being able to get the app to connect to my tracking tag. Fearing I would smash the thing into pieces, I gave up and tossed the phone onto the table. "It looks like you can't connect the two."

Tassis grabbed the phone. "Please let me do it. I'm very good with these things."

"I'm telling you they won't..."

"Done!" Tassis exclaimed and handed the phone back to me.

Jean looked at me, and I knew a snarky remark was on its way, and I cut her off. "Not one word or you're with Keitz."

"Wouldn't dream of saying anything. Now, can you find Ken?" Jean asked as she slid an omelet onto a plate.

"Yes, it has tracked Ken's gun to..." I did a double-take on his position then looked back to Jean. "He's in one of Death's holding cells. Either this is some sort of trap or a very brilliant place to hide."

Jean frowned. "Why wouldn't Death know about it if he was there?"

"His holding cells are jam-packed. There are probably hundreds, if not thousands, of prisoners coming and going. Plus, technically, Bush is an employee of Death via his family. The Darkness that guards the prison won't know one employee from another."

"Or it's a trap," Tassis warned.

"Good point. I'll alert Death and Jeremiah just in case. But, with my new powers, we should be okay. This does mean that you can't go, Tassis. You can go hang out with Lyzark for a while."

Tassis's eyes lit up. "I would like that."

With a quick thought, I sent Tassis to Lyzark. Jean stared where the demon had been, a wistful look on her face. She liked the kid, and she was afraid of losing him.

"Tassis is a good kid and looking for a father figure to replace Rusk. But he won't forget about you. You're probably the first real mother figure in his life."

"Better not," Jean grumbled, tossing the omelet into the trash bin. "Can we get moving?"

I stared at the lost omelet in the bin. "I thought we were going to eat first."

Jean placed her hands on her hips. "You can take us to a nice restaurant after this is over."

I sighed, grabbed a candy bar strategically hidden behind a bread box, then held it up. "In that case, I'm not sharing."

I blinked, and we appeared in the middle of a stately room. It wasn't exactly what someone would expect when describing a holding cell in Death's prison, but I recognized the place. Expensive furniture, pieces of art, and thick, luxurious rugs littered the room. Nearby a water fountain flowed, the water a sparkling gray. A well-stocked bar stood in the corner, and that was where we found Ken, holding the top of a running blender. Two margarita glasses lined the counter, already salted, and readied for the pour.

He waved when he spotted us, grabbed another glass, and salted it. "Not the company I was expecting, but I'm happy to see you. Hell, or should I say Death? I'm happy to see anyone."

Jean's eyes were glued on her newfound son. She was probably trying to figure out how to tell him that she was his mother.

Ken handed us both a drink, and I took a sip. "Very nicely done."

"Thanks. This place looks great, but with no one to talk to, it's a bit boring." Ken looked around. "I'm not even sure where this place is."

His eyes flicked to Jean and then back to me. Her eyes still bored into Ken.

I took another sip. "It's one of Carl's VIP holding cells. Meant to protect high-profile souls while we process them. Sometimes, if one side gets wind that a soul isn't going their way, they will try to kill them so the other side doesn't get them."

I walked to a blank wall and waved my hand. A monitor and workstation appeared.

"Don't bother. The Reaper on the other end is useless. Won't tell me a thing," Bush lamented.

I grinned. A reaper's day was about to go very badly. "Hmm, please try again. I'm very interested in seeing who you are talking to."

"Sure, but all reapers look the same to me." Bush walked over and tapped the monitor.

I moved to the side, out of the view of the camera.

A few seconds later, the image of a reaper appeared. "I told you, Mr. Bush, Mr. Lester has not told me when he is returning."

Ken looked at me, and I signaled for him to cut the line, and the screen went blank.

"I recognized the reaper, and I'm going to have a conversation with him. Why don't you two get to know each other," I said.

Jean nodded. "Ken, we need to talk. Maybe we should sit down. Also, we might want to refill the blender."

Jean led Ken to a pair of chairs, and I turned my attention back to the reaper Ken talked to. He worked for Latvius, and since she kept pretty close tabs on her flock, she must know about Bush. Time to use some of those super-powers that Death gave me.

I closed my eyes and concentrated on what I wanted. When I opened my eyes, I was in another prison cell—not the good type. The reaper monitoring Bush stared at me in disbelief. Before I could mouth a word, it charged me. With a flick of my hand, Death's creation was blasted backward into the black wall. The Darkness grabbed onto the reaper, and it let out a howl that sent chills down my back. I gave the wayward employee a moment to learn his lesson and then ordered the Darkness to release its captive.

The reaper dropped to the floor. "What am I doing here? I'm supposed to be monitoring Mr. Bush. Latvius will hear of this."

I knelt next to him. When he tried to reach toward me, I waggled my finger.

"Touching is a no-no. Failure to comply will result in me giving you to those things." I motioned toward the wall.

The reaper bowed his head. "I will serve."

"Good, now tell me your name."

"Gus."

I bit my lip from laughing too hard. "If you're messing with me, the consequences will be quite severe."

Gus raised his hand. "My real name is Metaro, but I made a few mistakes, and Latvius has ordered my name to be Gus until she decides otherwise."

This time I didn't try to hide my amusement and laughed out loud. "Okay, Gus, why are you guarding Mr. Bush for Lester."

"You don't know? He's a high-profile guest. Orders came from Death himself."

I shook my head. "Death didn't order this. Who assigned you to do this?"

"Latvius. She said that Death wanted him to stay here. Why I do not know."

"Are you aware that Lester hired a couple of angels to kill me, then faked his own death?"

The reaper paused for a moment. "I was sent to collect the swords that were used during the attack. But I was told an attack was staged to make everyone think Lester was dead and to capture the swords. I did not know they attacked you."

"And you swapped the weapons with replicas?"

Gus nodded. "Yes. Lester said they were powerful swords that Death wanted locked away."

"Hmm. Why would Lester have a reaper collect them?"

Gus looked up at me. "Because the swords won't work for us. When I picked them up, I could feel them trying to connect to my soul. Reapers do not have souls. So there was nothing for the weapons to connect to. To us, they're like any other sword."

I hadn't realized that, but it made sense. "Thank you for the information. If you keep cooperating, you may survive this. Anyone else that you know of that is also working with Lester and Latvius?"

Metaro shook his head. "No, I only met with the two."

I pointed at my captive, and he floated toward the wall. The Darkness in the wall shivered in anticipation. "Last question, any idea where Lester and Latvius are now?"

Metaro's arms flailed as he tried to steady himself. "I don't know where they are, but I overheard Lester tell Ken that he should head to the salt mine if he changed his mind. That's all I know, by Death's name!"

I should have killed him. There are protocols about high-profile cases, and he bypassed all of them. Someone, most likely Jeremiah, will cut him up as an example of what happened to those who don't follow protocol. But that's Jeremiah's call, not mine.

I released the reaper, and he fell to the floor. "You'll stay here and cool your jets while I find Joshua."

Gus stood. "You're giving me jets to cool?"

I sighed. When will I learn? "No, it's an expression meaning you're going to stay here until someone either releases you."

I paused for the effect, although I know it's lost on a reaper. "Or kills you."

# Chapter Thirty-Four

en looked up when I reappeared in his holding cell. He held Jean's hand, and both were in tears. I had to assume that Ken now knew about his parents.

"Everyone okay?" I asked.

Ken dabbed at his teary eyes with a handkerchief. "Considering I just found out that my parents are alive and work for Death, I guess I'm doing okay. But I don't think I'm ready for any more surprises for a while."

Jean just nodded and placed her hand on Ken's back.

"I hate to interrupt the family reunion, but Gus the reaper," I bit back a snicker, "mentioned he overheard Lester instructing you to go to a salt mine if you changed your mind about something. What does he want from you, and where is the salt mine?"

Ken put down his handkerchief. "Lester has a grand plan for his rise to power. For it to work, he wants Joshua aligned with Hell and me with Heaven. Why? I don't know. I don't trust him and told him I wasn't going along with his plan. I tried to convince my brother not to get involved, but ever since he got a hold of that sword, he doesn't listen."

"And the salt mine?"

"He told me if I changed my mind, to let Gus know, then head to an underground mine he uses. I'm supposed to wait for him there. I've only been there once, and the place is hard to describe. It's beautiful, but it felt..." Ken's voice trailed off as he stared at Jean.

"Let me guess. It feels like home," I added.

Ken's head snapped toward me. "Yes. How did you know?"

"I think I know the place and should have guessed Lester would use it as a hiding place. I can explain later, but we need to head there now and end this."

Ken shook his head. "He told me he hated the place and only went there when he has to. If I go, he'll probably make me wait a couple of days before he arrives. If you want to catch him, you need to force him to go there."

I was about to reply when Kitten interrupted me.

*Kye, I pick up a distress call from Lyzark. He's calling for backup.*

"We'll have to worry about that later. Lyzark's needs our help."

Jean looked up. "Lyzark needs *our* help? That can't be good."

I nodded as I pulled Kitten, and she heated up, extending her blades. Jean drew her sword, and a gray aura surrounded her. A calm hostility emanated from her. Not to be outdone, I flowed into my Arbiter mode.

I snapped my fingers, and we landed in the corner of a large one-room cabin. Dead demons, angels, reapers, and at least one arbiter lay scattered across the floor. Sunshine poured through an open door.

"What in Death's..." I didn't get to finish as the sounds of battle thundered from outside.

Jean ran out the door first with me right behind her. Outside, the chaos of war raged with at least a hundred battling it out. To my right, Jeremiah warred with three demons and two angels. His sword blurred as he struck down his opponents, and the five stood no chance against Death's head of security.

Jeremiah glanced over at me. "Glad you could join. I marked the bad guys in black."

His words confused me until a reaper with a large, black dot on his chest attacked me with a hatchet. I swung, and Kitten cut the hatchet, and then the reaper, in half, and it was on. Kitten roared, she had tasted blood and wanted more. My body tingled, and an overwhelming desire to kill overtook me.

One of the reasons Kitten selected me to wield her was that I could match her desire for blood and rage. Most would be overwhelmed by her. For me, she fueled my rage, and I hers.

I stepped toward my first target, and before I could cut the angel's head off, Jean ran her sword through the angel. She moved on to her next kill, leaving a trail of dead bodies wherever she went.

"Not fair! Save some for me!" I yelled and sprinted toward a group of ten. A demon stepped into my path and tried to take my head off. He attacked from his right-to-left, and I swung Kitten to match his swing. He expected our swords to collide and stop. Instead, his reward was half of his weapon now on the ground. As he registered what just happened, I removed his head. Three dead demons later, and others turned and ran.

Jeremiah ran his sword through a female angel then, with her still impaled on the sword, he dueled a reaper. The reaper not only had to contend with Jeremiah's lightning-quick sword but also the angel flopping about, stuck on his sword. Jeremiah pulled his sword back and took a huge swing at the reaper. The reaper raised his sword to block the downward swing. What he failed to realize was Jeremiah wasn't swinging at the reaper, he was tossing the flailing angel off his blade. The body slammed into the reaper and knocked him to the ground. With a thud, Jeremiah ended the reaper.

The enemy realized it was a losing cause, and more disappeared. But fighting behind me told me things were not done. I turned to find Jean sparring with a man whose gray aura told me he also worked for Death. The two were a blur as they went at each other.

Jeremiah stepped forward. "Go find Lyzark. I'll back up Jean."

"Who's the guy?"

"A classmate of hers and someone she really hates. Now go!"

I would have loved to stay and watch two top-notch assassins duel to the death, but I ran to find Lyzark. Cresting a hill, I found him sword-to-sword with my prize, Joshua Arbol. Their blades blurred as the two battled. Both bled from various wounds, but Joshua looked excited, energized. Lyzark sweated, but a hint of a smile on his face told me he too enjoyed the battle. I'd join the fracas, but superpowers like Lyzark don't like to share. He'd as soon kill me for interfering.

*Joshua's sword is one of the Berserker swords,* Kitten warned.

Lyzark fell back onto one knee with the tip of his sword on the ground. It looked like he was in trouble, but I recognized the move. When Joshua tried to do an overhead swing to slice the demon in half, Lyzark pivoted out of the way on his knee. With no sword to collide with, Joshua's momentum sent his sword plowing into the ground. Lyzark continued his pivot, stood, and tried to cleave Joshua in half with a downward swing.

I thought it was over, certain that Lyzark's sword would slice Joshua in two. Instead, Joshua leapt to the side, narrowly missing Lyzark's falling blade. He rolled then stood unsteadily. Before Lyzark could react, the twin threw a dagger at the demon, and it glanced off the demon's shoulder.

My hopes that Joshua had survived the attack unscathed were dashed when he staggered backward, holding his side. While he managed to avoid a fatal strike from Lyzark, he still received a deep slice across his side, and blood gushed from the wound.

I realized I had to step in and ran toward the two, putting on extra speed to get to him and wrestle the sword from Joshua. But just as I got to him, Lester appeared, wrapped an arm around my prize, and disappeared.

# Chapter Thirty-Five

y frustration boiled over as I stomped around looking for anything to kill, but any remaining enemy either lay dead or dying.

"Shit!" I screamed to no one in particular.

Lyzark sat on a log as he tried to heal his injuries. For a celestial, a cut from any other sword would heal in a second. But as I discovered, Joshua's sword was different, and Lyzark's wounds healed slowly. Jeremiah approached, put his hand on Lyzark's shoulder, and added his power to the demons, and the wounds disappeared.

Lyzark looked up. "Thanks."

I looked for Jean and found her limping up the hill toward us. In her hand, the decapitated head of her classmate. Gray blood oozed from a dozen cuts. As she approached, I noted that while the injuries were healing, it was at a slow pace. A clear sign Jean was exhausted. Jeremiah hurried to her and reached out to help, but she held up her hand. "No. Kye will help me."

She approached me, and I'm expecting her to attack. Her chest heaved, and sweat dripped off her face. The blazing gray light in her eyes told me she was still in battle mode. Worried she would kill me without even thinking about it, I crept forward, keeping Kitten in one hand. I used my other to help heal her wounds. One was on her left butt cheek, and I briefly placed my hand on it to close the wound. I snatched my hand back before she could try to cut it off.

"Did you enjoy that?" she growled and threw the dripping head at me.

"Really? All this death and destruction, and I'm enjoying myself closing up your butt cut?" I turned and walked away from her, trying to put as much distance between me and the enraged assassin. To be fair, yes, I'm a teenage boy at heart and enjoyed it a little, but no sense in letting her know.

"Kye," Jean called after me. "I'm sorry. Thanks for helping me."

I halted, turned back, but said nothing in fear she would figure out my ploy.

I surveyed the carnage. Besides the four of us, there were twenty-to-thirty arbiters, and a couple-dozen angels and demons left standing from our side. The bodies of those lost in the battle lay all around. "Jeremiah, what in Death's name happened here?"

Jeremiah wiped the blood from his weapon. "After everyone was supposed to leave earth, we detected this camp. We thought there was only five-to-ten of Lester's soldiers. But when Lyzark and I arrived with thirty of our warriors, we found over fifty. We called for backup, but a sentry spotted us, and we attacked before they had a chance to get organized. We killed a good many of them before they were able to regroup. By then, reinforcements had arrived."

Lyzark continued. "Things were going well until Joshua showed up with an arbiter and two swords. He drew one and howled as the sword energized him. He then tossed the other sword to Lester. Lester joined the fight but ran like a coward when he saw you."

"My guess is Lester wore gloves?" I asked.

Jeremiah nodded. "He was. Probably to keep from feeling the effects of the sword."

"About the swords, I was surprised that they were not more powerful. My opponent was excellent, but nothing I haven't dealt with before. I'm not sure why we are that worried about them," Lyzark remarked.

"That's because the berserkers' full potential is realized when both are in use by siblings. Only one was activated, and even that kept you busy. When they're both in use, they are much stronger."

Lyzark frowned. "Then why didn't the arbiter fight?"

"Because Kitten was here," I said, and Kitten purred her approval. "She's the only weapon that can beat a Berserker sword one-on-one. You two could have kept Joshua busy, meaning Lester would have had to take me on by himself. He's too much of a coward to start a fight he isn't sure he can win."

Jean used a rag to clean her blade then stowed her weapon. "What do we do next? Lester, Joshua, and the swords are gone, and we don't have many leads."

I nodded and tried to look like I had wisdom that everyone thought I had. Looking around the camp, I wondered how this many of Lester's army were able to hide from us. I was about to impart my newfound wisdom when Jeremiah cut me off.

"I think we should search the camp. We need to figure out how they hid from us," Jeremiah offered. The others nodded their heads as I glared at him.

"Nice job, Jeremiah," Jean commented. "Why didn't you think of it, Kye?"

She walked off before I could respond. I gave Jeremiah one last scowl and walked in the opposite direction.

"What did I do now?" Death's right-hand man called after me.

*Okay, help me find something,* I asked Kitten.

Kitten purred. *And why should I do that?*

*Because the sooner I find something, the sooner you get your revenge on those swords.*

*Do not call them swords! They are abominations and should not exist. I will help you only because I want this planet clear of those swine. Now go to the center of the camp. The device hiding the camp is there.*

I scanned the area to get my bearing. The closer I looked, the more this camp was a perfect circle. A dozen or so tents lined the outskirt of the area, forming a circular arc. I walked toward the fire pit and extended my senses.

*That's it. I think you might actually have a brain,* Kitten purred.

I chuckled. *That coming from a sword.*

I stopped at the edge of the firepit. A few embers still smoldered, and I picked up a nearby bucket of water and dosed the remains. A shovel leaned against a tree, and I grabbed it and began to dig. With the second strike of the shovel, I was reworded with the sound of the shovel hitting metal. With a little more digging, and I uncovered a three-foot by three-foot metal box. I dug around it until it was clear, then picked up the box and placed it next to the pit. It was surprisingly light and cool to the touch. Considering it had been in a lit firepit, something was off.

*I would not open it if I were you. That is if you want to continue living.*

I heeded Kitten's advice and let out a loud whistle. "Found it!"

Lyzark arrived first, followed by Jean and Jeremiah.

"What is it? Lyzark asked.

"According to Kitten, it's what's hiding this camp. She told me not to open it if I wanted to live."

"Ah, yes. Better to leave this to your superiors." Lyzark grinned at Jeremiah. "I think Jeremiah should open it."

"And why me? Why can't you do it?" Jeremiah fumed. His gaze darted from me to Lyzark. He was uncharacteristically nervous.

"Because I'm still recovering from wounds from *your* son," Lyzark grumbled.

Jean lunged at Lyzark, her blade at his throat. "He's my son also, and you almost killed him."

Lyzark didn't move as he stared back at Jean. He then raised an eyebrow. "I never said he wasn't your son. It is also the reason he's still alive."

A look of doubt came over Jean's face, and she lowered her sword. "Um, uh, sorry. I guess I owe you an apology."

I stared at the assassin, her response was completely out of character.

Lyzark shook his head. "No, apologizing is a sign of weakness." He then took a deep breath. "Now that I have Tassis to look after, I am realizing that being a parent is much harder than I thought."

I was utterly dumbfounded. Lyzark was a cruel and deadly demon. He murdered his way to his position and has held power due to his ruthless nature. Some of the things he has done would turn the stomach of a serial killer.

"Okay, I'll open it," Jeremiah let out his breath then raised his hand toward the box.

"I wouldn't do that if I were you," Eizan interrupted as he approached the group.

Jeremiah lowered his hand. "Do you always show up late to the party?"

"Well, we had our own party with similar results." Eizan looked around and surveyed the carnage. "We followed Kye's advice, tracking down any missing angel who did not return home as ordered. We found one and tracked him to another camp. It took a little while to eliminate the treasonous angels."

"Great news, but how does that relate to opening the box?" Jeremiah asked.

Jeremiah was usually a calm and patient person, but he was tense, and I was pretty sure Eizan would play this out as long as possible to provoke him.

I grinned. Time to sound wise and all-knowing. Okay, maybe just smart. "You found a similar box. Probably used it to find us."

Eizan's Cheshire cat grin disappeared. "Mr. Dodson, you take the fun out of everything."

I bowed. "I learned from the best. Let me guess. If Jeremiah opened the box, he would have been blasted by a powerful energy force. Not enough to kill him but enough to take him out of the game for a while."

Jeremiah whirled on Lyzark, sword drawn. "You tried to set me up, you son of a whore!"

"I merely went along with what Kye was saying. By the way, how did you know about my mother was a whore?" Lyzark asked. From the look on his face, he was completely serious.

Jeremiah cocked an eyebrow, and I waited for his next attempt at an insult. "Pretty obvious."

Lyzark chuckled. "Really? Thank you. My mother was a powerful and resourceful woman, and I loved her, even though she wouldn't tell me who my father was."

Jeremiah's face changed to one of complete confusion. "I'm, uh, sorry for your loss."

"No, don't be. She was a great mother, and she was very proud of me," Lyzark sighed. "Actually, her last words were 'I'm proud of the demon you have become'. She said it right after I ran my sword through her."

Lyzark dabbed a tear from his eye. Eizan tried not to laugh and turned away, his shoulders shaking.

Jeremiah ran his hands through his hair. He was too prim and proper to truly insult Lyzark.

Jean interrupted our fun. "Can we get back to the matter at hand? If we can track the other boxes, maybe we can catch Lester and wipe out his army."

I shook my head. "Too obvious. Lester probably knows we can track the other boxes and either has moved his soldiers or using them as expendable bait. Knowing Lester, he's going to concentrate on the swords and the brothers. My guess is that he has explosives at the other two camps. We show up, and he wipes out his troops and us."

Jeremiah placed the box on a tree stump and ran his hands over it. I could feel his power from ten feet away. He straightened then turned to us. "While I agree Lester has most likely laid a trap, but we need to find those other camps. I believe I know how to do that."

I was about to reply when I received a message via Kitten from Renaldo. Someone had broken into my London home. I frowned at the message. The magical alerts I had put on the place were quiet, if there was a break-in, they should have gone off. I was considering what that meant when Kitten interrupted my thoughts.

Death's Arbiter

*We need to go, now*, Kitten ordered.

# Chapter Thirty-Six

"Something's going down. We've gotta go," I said to Eizan. I grabbed Jean by the hand and returned us to my London home. We landed in the living room, weapons out, to find three demons with their backs to us. Behind them were three angels dueling Renaldo.

The three demons turned toward me—weapons ready. Without hesitating, I roared and lunged toward them. The first moved to engage and swung a hatchet at my head. I ducked and, with a swift thrust, ran Kitten through his neck. I pulled Kitten back and swung, slicing off the gagging demon's head. The second watched his comrade's head roll to his feet. Before he could react, his head then rolled next to it.

The third took a step back into a defensive stance, the tip of his weapon pointed at me. When I didn't move, he raised his sword to attack but stopped when two throwing knives, courtesy of Jean, embedded in his chest.

The demon laughed, patting the knives. "These are supposed to hurt me? I've had worse cuts..."

Jean cut the demon's sentence short when she hurled her sword, and it implanted in the chest of the laughing celestial. He looked down at the hilt of Jean's weapon protruding from his chest. The celestial dropped his sword and fell to his knees. He began to topple forward, but Jean grabbed the dead warrior's head to steady him and pulled her knives, then her sword from the demon. She released the body, and the demon toppled to the floor.

"To answer your question, no. The knives were a distraction," Jean replied to the dead demon.

With the three down, that left three hulking angels that had Renaldo cornered. The Fallen was covered in blood, and his right arm dangled at his side. But with his left, he swung his cutlass with efficiency and kept the three intruders at bay. Confident that their demon brethren would hold us off, they hadn't even turned around.

A fatal mistake on their part.

Crossing the room quickly, I sliced the wing off the first angel, and as she screamed, I swung again and beheaded the second. The third and largest of the angels confronted me, an ax in one hand and a machete in the other.

The angel sneered. "I am going to have fun cutting you into pieces and listening to your..." What he was going to listen to, I will never know as Renaldo's cutlass erupted from his chest. The angel's face registered surprise before falling forward and smashing my coffee table. I never did like that table, but he didn't have to destroy it.

Whimpering behind me caused me to turn to find the angel who lost a wing, now throat-to-sword with Jean's blade.

I tossed my canister of healing cream to Renaldo. "Where's Cassi?" I asked, afraid I arrived too late.

"Fre-Fre's," he gasped as he applied the cream.

I growled as I turned my attention back to the remaining angel. "Tell me who sent you, or I will see that Death uses you as a plaything."

"All I got is a first name. An arbiter named Lester," the angel cried.

I nodded to Jean, and she swung, taking the angel's head off.

"I meant for you to knock her out, not kill her. I might've needed her again."

She shrugged. "Then be more clear next time."

"Never mind, we need to get to Fre-Fre's," I ordered.

We arrived at Fre-Fre's and found him defending the entrance to his club. The owner was barely recognizable. He stood twelve feet tall and looked like a series of boulders cobbled together. The only thing recognizable was his head and shoulders atop the boulders. He led a ragtag group of angels, demons, and a few that resembled Fre-Fre. A demon came at him, and the owner ripped him apart before he could land a blow.

The square in front of the club, normally filled with performers and those out for a stroll, had been transformed. The once beautiful fountains that Jean and I had enjoyed were now quiet, and their water turned black and red from the bodies that floated in them. More bodies lay strewn about the square. An enemy force of demons, angels, and reapers now occupied the square and faced Fre-Fre's group.

I spotted Cassi being carried into the club by an angel and a werewolf. At the sight of blood covering her wings, my anger boiled, and Kitten purred. The enemy hadn't seen me yet, but they would.

My anger took over as my vision dimmed. I heard nothing other than my heart pounding, demanding revenge. My wings sprouted and spread, and I combined my power with Kitten's. My mind and hers were now intertwined. This was a suicide mission, but I didn't care. Those who had hurt my lover were about to find out the true meaning of 'a fate worse than death'.

I shouted and released my arbiter power. The resulting shockwave caused the enemy forces to cry out and face me.

"You only have one choice. Put down your weapons, and I may let some of you live." My arbiter-powered voice echoed off the walls. The enemy soldiers looked at each other questioning, but none lowered their weapons.

"Death it is!" I sprinted toward the group swinging Kitten faster than I have ever done before. My tunnel vision only showed me those that were falling to my blade. I heard Jean raging behind me, and her battle cry was pure joy.

Fre-Fre's group attacked, and it was a back-and-forth battle. But soon, I found myself back-to-back to Jean, surrounded by the enemy. Fre-Fre's group remained in front of his club, but at least half their numbers lay dead on the ground. The enemy retreated just outside Kitten's reach. I'm not sure what they were waiting for, but I was glad for the break.

Jean nudged me. "Ten coins say I kill more than you do."

I chuckled, admiring the blood dripping from my sword. I snatched a glance at Jean, and we're both covered in cuts and wounds. Nothing fatal, but we both needed the time to heal.

A three-foot-tall wall of bodies surrounded us, making it harder for our attackers to get to us. Still, they had the numbers in their favor.

A demon stepped toward us, evidently the leader of the enemy force. He glared at us until his eyes turned a fire-red. Holding out his hand, an arc of energy erupted, splashing over his army, and their eyes now matched their leader's.

"What the heck just happened?" Jean asked.

I shook my head. This was not a good situation. "Somehow, he just juiced every single one of them," I said. My voice was hoarse from screaming.

"That doesn't sound good. Can Kitten help?"

*No. I'm not much help here. I have to say this isn't looking good for you two,* Kitten warned.

*Don't you mean the three of us,* I replied.

*No. I'm in no danger from them. They are not strong enough to hurt me. But you are in trouble. Together, we can kick the ass of any one of them. But with enemy charged up. They will overrun you and Jean. Unless someone comes to your rescue, this could be the end of our relationship.*

I sighed. *Aren't you Lil Miss Sunshine?*

*Sorry. I will say we've had a good run.*

"Kitten says we're in trouble without backup," I replied to Jean.

The group's lead pointed his spear at me. "This ends now, no prisoners." His warriors roared in response. His voice now sounded strange, like three people speaking at the same time.

"Well, I thought this was a suicide mission. Time to see if I was right."

I was about to go on the attack when an energy surge washed over me. Jeremiah, Lyzark, and Eizan then appeared in a circle around me.

I glanced at Jeremiah. "Thanks for coming, but I think you picked a bad time to join the battle. It's a bit lopsided."

Jeremiah surveyed the group. "I agree, but maybe they'll find a few more to even the odds."

I eyed Jeremiah. "Am I missing something? You guys are good, but not this good."

"Kye! Go slow. I wagered you would kill about fifty," Lyzark cut in.

I lowered my sword and frowned at Death's lieutenant. "What is he talking about?"

Before Jeremiah could reply, the enemy leader broke in. "Are you finished whining? It's time for you to die."

I growled at him. "You'll get your shot, but for now, just shut the hell up."

"Hell has nothing to do with this Kye," Lyzark retorted.

I blew out a breath. I really needed to watch what I say. "Sorry! Now, back to my question. All I see is a huge group of super-charged celestials all around us. And the five of us in the middle. So, I ask again, what am I missing?

"Don't you remember?" Jeremiah asked and pointed at me. "The big three super-charged you, and it's time for you to really use that power."

"What the..." I began but stopped when Eizan and Lyzark also pointed at me. "This can't end well."

Beams of gray, white, and black flowed from the three celestials and slammed into me. I screamed in pain as the beams bored into my chest then slowly engulfed my body. My only sight was of the bright lights surrounding me. I helplessly fought against the energy as it streamed into my body. While the pain was beyond anything Death had ever dealt me, it also felt wonderful. It felt like I simultaneously had my balls in a vice while I had the longest orgasm a man could ever have. I couldn't decide if I would need counseling afterward, or a cigarette.

As fast as the power hit me, it stopped, and I dropped to my knees. My body buzzed from the residual energy, and I waited for it to stop. After everything that had happened, I should have been exhausted. But instead, I felt energized, more alive than I had ever felt. I stood and took stock of my situation. Arcs of electricity raged over my body. Flames of gray, white, and red dripped off Kitten. My muscles rippled, and I felt like I could rip a car apart with my bare hands.

*This is f'ing amazing. Time to kill everyone,* Kitten exclaimed gleefully.

*Not quite yet,* I replied.

Jean stared at me in awe. "Are you alright?"

"He's alright. Just super-juiced," Lyzark replied.

"Then let me return the favor," I said.

I pointed toward the three celestial lords. A burst of energy flew from my hand and enveloped the three. Lyzark grew in size, now almost ten feet tall. When he glanced toward me, his eyes blazed red like the fires of hell, and his sword glowed a matching red. Eizan now matched Lyzark's size. Blue and white flames drip from his sword, and his eyes were a blinding white.

But the most frightening of the three was Jeremiah.

He towered over the other two, engulfed in Death's gray color. His pure black eyes were frightening. To look into them was to look at death itself.

As I stood, a lightning bolt struck me. I expected to be reduced to a pile of ash, but instead, the power passed through me, and I howled in delight.

I held up Kitten, and another lightning bolt struck us. Kitten now sizzled with electricity. I pointed her at the enemy leader, and a bolt flew from my blade and vaporized the demon.

"Kill them!" I raged. "Kill them all!"

# Chapter Thirty-Seven

T he enemy turned and ran for their lives. When one stumbled, those behind him climbed over him. Anyone too slow was either trampled or ran over. They only got a little way before they found their path blocked by an invisible shield. I smiled as they frantically clawed at the shield to try and get past it. But there was no escape for them today.

The demon leader was right. It ended today. Just not the way he expected.

I spotted a line of reapers toward the rear of the group and dove into the mix after them. "That's ten dead, and the reapers are mine!" I yelled.

"Not if I get to them first. My count's twelve," Jean screamed back and swung her sword at an errant angel. "Make that thirteen."

I stole a look at the assassin, and I'd never seen her happier. A huge smile was plastered on her face. She was killing anything and everything that got near her. The assassin was in her element, and I veered left to avoid getting too close to her. I wasn't sure she could discern friend from foe at this point.

I reached the line of reapers, and they just stood and stared at me. Their calm demeanor a stark contrast to the chaos all around. When a retreating demon attempted to push past a reaper, he was cut in half by the reaper's scythe. Death had made reapers hard to kill, and few in the retreating army worried them. But with my newfound powers, I killed two before the others realized I was a threat.

I knew I needed a couple of them for information. "Jean, get that one and keep him alive." I hoped she heard me as I went after a different reaper I knew all too well.

Leaping over several bodies, I brought Kitten's edge to the neck of a reaper. "Nice to see you, Latvius."

Latvius dropped her scythe and raised her hands. "It is good to see you again, Arbiter Kye."

"After I'm done with you, I'm not sure you'll be happy to see me."

The reaper tilted her head. "I don't think you will kill me. I have information you need, plus I have been a loyal reaper to Death for a long time. He would be upset if you killed me."

"I don't want to kill you. I do think a few others will when they find out you're trying to start the war between Heaven and Hell." I waited for the proverbial "How did you know?", which never came.

Latvius shook her head. "What are you talking about? Lester told us he just wanted to pay you back for everything you did to him. He said if we helped him, Death would let us start killing humans again. We just want to go back to the old ways when reapers took lives."

Her gazed turned toward something behind me, and I realized everything had gone quiet. I glanced back, and found Jeremiah, Eizan, and Lyzark staring at me expectantly.

"We need to send Latvius someplace to make her pay for her crimes," I said, and Latvius didn't flinch. Pain meant little to reapers, and even Jeremiah's power was not enough to scare her.

"I have that covered. Death wants to have a conversation with her and her traitor friends," Jeremiah said, wiping the smug look off Latvius' face.

"No, wait," she screamed and vanished.

One-by-one, the rest of the attackers began to disappear. "God and Satan made similar requests of their people," Jeremiah added.

"That's good news, but I need to know that Cassi is okay. Everything else can wait." I stepped forward, but the world began to spin, and I felt my face hit the ground. I groaned and rolled onto my back, trying to figure out which bus just ran over me.

The spinning world slowed, and the image of Jeremiah peering down at me came into focus. Well, all three of him, that is.

Jeremiah, or should I say one Jeremiah', smiled down at me. "You used up all of the juice the big three gave you."

My body ached, and I haven't felt this hung over since the 60s. It turns out, LSD and I don't mix well.

When there was only one Jeremiah, I sat up. After a minute, I put my hand out. The Death's Lord grabbed it and hauled me to my feet.

I took a breath to clear my head. Once I was sure I could walk, I staggered into the club to find Fre-Fre in his human form. He was naked short of a red-and-white checkered tablecloth around his waist. The club owner looked pretty banged up with cuts and bruises on his chest and arms. He took a quick slug from a bottle and handed it to me.

Fre-Fre grinned. "I assume you're going to pay for the damages to my club? Not to mention the loss of business."

I handed him my company card. "Seems only fair, but Death will need to approve those charges." I took a swig from his bottle then spit it out. It was horrible whiskey, and I wasn't a fan. "Since when do you drink the cheap stuff?"

"You just don't know your Scotches, son." Fre-Fre jerked a thumb toward a back door. "Cassi's in the back getting patched up. I have to give her credit, Kye. She swings a mean blade."

I made my way to the back, and my anger cleared my hung-over mind. When I got my hands-on Lester, what I would do to him would make Death blush.

I found her with her shoulder bandaged up and blood splattered over her wings. An angel bandaged a cut on her hand and looked up as I approached. "You must be Kye. I'm Samantha."

I nodded and stared at Cassi.

Samantha put a piece of tape to hold a bandage in place. "She should be as good as new in a little while. Whatever weapons they used has made the healing process slow. Give her a little time, and she'll be fine."

"Thank you," I replied.

Relief flowed over me, and I almost knocked Cassi over when I threw my arms around her. I held her for a moment, just grateful she was alive. I shouldn't be this attached to anyone, but I didn't care. I released her to check her wounds.

"How are you?" I asked.

Cassi gave a weak smile. "I'm fine, just tired."

The angel aiding her froze and frowned. "You're feeling tired?"

Her wounds didn't look too bad. But the exhausted look on her face told me something was wrong.

Cassi closed her eyes and leaned back. "I think I just need a nap."

Samantha put her hand on Cassi's forehead. "We're losing her. I don't understand what's happening."

Alarm bells went off in my head. I mustered every bit of my arbiter power and scanned her. I cringed when I identified the poison in her system. It's a poison made from a plant called Eden's Weed. It was planted by Satan in the original Garden of Eden. Garden is a complete misnomer as it's much more like a jungle.

The weed is a particularly potent poison for celestials and has since been banned by God and Death. After it was used to kill some of her own personal guards, Satan also banned it. God cleared Eden of it, but like most weeds, he was never able to completely eradicate it.

I realized her attackers must have coated their swords with the poison. I used my power to remove the poison, but she didn't respond. There's a cure for it, but it takes days to brew, and Cassi didn't have that much time.

I slammed my fist into the table. My lover was fading, and there was nothing I could do about it. Short of intervention by someone powerful, she wouldn't live long.

"Sorry, I hurt you," Cassi whispered. "Kye, I never betrayed you. I just danced."

"I know, I know," I said as tears rolled down my face and I could barely breathe. My heart ached, and I should be mad at her, but the thought that I was losing my love burned everything else away.

"Cassi! Cassi! Stay with me," I shouted. I tried shaking her, but she didn't respond.

I turned at the sound of someone running toward me. "Kye, I think I have what you need," Jeremiah shouted.

Jeremiah stood with the possible solution to our problem in his hand.

"Death said you would need this," he said and handed me Heaven's version of a Feast stick. The thing glowed with Heaven's power, and I pressed it into Cassi's palm.

For a moment, Cassi remained still, and I feared it was too late. Her body began to glow, and waves of energy emanated from her. I waited for her to move, fearful that even the power of Heaven could not save her.

Jean burst into the room, "What's going—oh, Kye."

I held my breath, and Jean put her arm around me. Together, we waited for any sign that Cassi would live. But the waves of energy coming from her ceased, and as time wore on, I began to shake. I took a ragged breath, and my pounding heart felt like it was being ripped from my body.

But when I put my hand on Cassi. All went quiet.

My true love was gone.

# Chapter Thirty-Eight

My world began to crumble, and I slumped into Jean's arms. Pain like nothing Death could dish out raged through me. Jean held me as I sobbed in her arms.

"This isn't how it was supposed to go," Jeremiah bellowed, pushing Jean and me aside. "I have one last trick to try."

Climbing onto the table, he positioned himself over her like he was going to do CPR. Overlapping his hands, he placed his hands on her chest. With a deep breath, his body began to glow Death's gray. With the first compression, the gray light flowed through his arms into Cassi. Her body convulsed like a defibrillator had hit her. Samantha screamed and backed away.

Jeremiah paused, and I looked on hopeful. But when Cassi didn't move, he shocked her again.

The sound of my beating heart went quiet. Without Cassi, I was done. There was nothing left for me, and I was ready for Death to take me for the last time.

Jeremiah tried again and again. But after the fourth time, I had given up hope. "Jeremiah, thank you, but she's..."

I couldn't bring myself to say the words.

"No, she's not!" Jeremiah raged. He sat up, took a huge breath, and his eyes lit with a bright, gray light. The sound of electrical arcing over his body filled the room. He glared with a snarled face, and Jean and I took a step back in fear.

Overlapping his hands again, he placed them on Cassi's chest. With a jerk, he did one more compression and yelled, "Live!"

The energy racing over his body struck her, and her body convulsed so hard it threw Jeremiah from the table. Cassi's back arched as she took a deep breath.

"Kye, she's alive!" Jean screamed when Cassi took another breath.

I grabbed Death's Lord by his hand, hauled him to his feet, and wrapped my arms around him. "Thank you for saving her," I cried.

Jeremiah stood stock still, his body tense. He gently patted my back like I was a rabid badger about to strike. To say my boss wasn't used to emotional displays from his employees was an understatement.

"It's the least I could do," Jeremiah replied. "Can you let me go?"

I laughed and released Jeremiah from his awkward situation.

Cassi's eyes opened, and she looked at me. "Kye. Wha, what happened?"

I pulled my love into my arms and held her. The sound of my heart beating again reassured me we would both survive.

"You were poisoned. Jeremiah saved you. The swords of the angels that you and Renaldo fought…" I began but realized the swords that had poisoned Cassi may have cut Renaldo.

We needed to get to him before it was too late.

I grabbed Heaven's stick, found it still held energy, and tossed it to Jean. "Get this to Renaldo. I need to stay with Cassi."

Jean nodded and disappeared.

I returned my attention to Cassi as she tried to sit up.

I put my arm behind her back and helped her up. She laid her head on my shoulder, and I fought back my tears.

"Thank you," she whispered. "I'm feeling much better, but I do tingle a bit."

I let out a laugh through my tears. "Considering how much energy Jeremiah pumped through you, I'm not surprised."

I clung to her, happier than I had ever been. She wrapped her wings around me, and I enjoyed the moment. I could have held her all day, but she eased back. Using the tip of her wing, she wiped a tear from my face.

I laughed. "Thank you." As she pulled her wings back, I noticed they now held a gray tinge. I wondered if that was an after-effect from Jeremiah's rescue and how long it would last.

Five minutes later, Jean reappeared, and I hoped the smile on her face meant he was still alive.

"Renaldo's fine. It turns out, only one of the angel's swords had the Eden's Weed on it," Jean reported.

"That makes sense," Cassi replied. "When they attacked, Renaldo engaged the demons, and I took on the angels."

Jean frowned. "He also wanted me to pass along that he says he's sorry."

"Why is he sorry?" I asked. "He just risked his life protecting Cassi and has nothing to be sorry for."

Suspicious, I looked to Cassi.

She turned her focus to the ground and pulled away. "I know why, and I owe him, and you, an apology."

"Cassi? What did you do?" I asked, my happiness slipping away.

My lover looked up at me. "I was going stir crazy in that place. I just needed to get out for a few minutes. I convinced Renaldo that if we disguised ourselves, we could go out, and no one would know. Obviously, someone did."

I wanted to be angry with her, but after almost losing her, I couldn't. "You almost got yourself and Renaldo killed." I took a deep breath and wrapped my arms around her as she began to sob.

I pulled back and kissed the top of her head. "Do something like that again, and I'll kill you myself."

Cassi grinned and nodded. "Promise?"

I laughed. "I promise." I checked Jean and Jeremiah. "What about you two?"

"What about us? You plan on killing us too if she breaks her promise?" Jean teased.

"No, but don't tempt me," I quipped. "I meant, are you okay?"

Jean looked herself over. "Only scratches. Jeremiah? Are you..." She glanced at Jeremiah, and the look on her face softened. "You're hurt."

She reached over to Jeremiah and touched a cut that spanned his chest. Gray blood oozed from the wound. To him, it was a scratch that would heal soon. But judging by the look of concern on Jean, she was sure it was much more serious.

"Does it hurt?" Jean sidled closer and, with a flash, healed his wound.

Jeremiah lovingly gazed down at her. "Just a little."

I knew he lied but couldn't blame him for playing it up. His wound had healed, but she kept her hand on his chest. He gazed down at her with a goofy smile, and she smiled back.

Jean began to caress his chest. "Oh, sorry," Jean said and tried to pull her hand away.

Jeremiah caught her hand and placed it back on his chest.

"Thank you for healing me," Jeremiah replied.

They stared into each other's eyes until a crash from another room broke their concentration, and they pulled away from each other but continued to gaze into each other's eyes. Jean smiled and brushed a few strands of hair away from her face. Her eyes flicked to Jeremiah's, then to his chest.

A general awkwardness filled the room, and Cassi shook her head. "Really?" she mouthed. "You brought me back for this?"

Jean stepped forward and ran her finger along Jeremiah's chest where the injury had been. He stared back, his eyes locked on her.

Cassi whispered in my ear. "Do something? I may die again from the awkwardness!"

I waved to Jeremiah. He turned his head toward me, and I mouthed, "Talk to her."

"About what?" he mouthed back, and I shook my head. How can one of the most powerful beings in the universe not know how to talk to a woman?

"Anything," I mouthed back.

"So, Jean," Jeremiah began, then hesitated. She gave him a dreamy look that he returned. "Still cleaning your sword like I showed you?"

Cassi slapped her forehead, and I looked for any type of weapon that could take me out of the misery of watching these two lovebirds.

Jean nearly swooned at the ridiculous question. "Oh yes, every day. Just like you said. That oil you recommended works perfectly."

"Fantastic," Jeremiah replied, then went quiet.

"Are all of Death's people this clueless?" Samantha whispered.

Cassi glared at the angel, then turned to me and whispered, "Help him!"

"How?"

"I don't know, but help him before we all die of awkwardness," she whispered.

I caught Jeremiah's eye and mouthed, "Date." He nodded and turned to Jean.

"What's today's date?" he asked, then gave me a quizzical look.

*Please just let me kill them,* Kitten pleaded. *Torture would be less painful than this.*

I held Cassi back as she pulled a knife and glared at Death's Lord.

"Really? Ask her out on a date." I mouthed, then rubbed my temples. I could only hope that more reapers would attack and save us from this agony.

"I'm not sure. I can check..." Jean replied, looking bewildered.

"No, I mean. Sorry, I found this great restaurant in Italy. Would you like, you know, to go get some food there...with me?" Jeremiah asked.

"You mean like a date?"

Jeremiah gazed at his love. The silence became unbearable, and I stepped forward and slapped the back of his head.

He glowered at me then returned his gaze to Jean. "Yes, a date."

"I would love to," Jean replied. I half-expected Cassi and me to be pushed out of the room as Jeremiah's chest swelled.

They gazed at each other, and I waited to see if they would jump each other and rip their remaining clothes off. I needed to end this madness. "Okay, Cassi needs to go rest up. Jean needs to talk with her son, and we need to go meet Eizan and Lyzark to figure out our next move."

Jeremiah eased toward Jean, and she didn't back away. Her hand had now slid to his belt buckle.

"Jeremiah," I yelled. When his eyes flicked to me. "Eizan and Lyzark. Bad guys still loose. World ending. Remember?"

"Yes, agreed," Jeremiah nodded, clearly not having heard what I said.

He pulled Jean close, and she had a hungry look in her eyes. I was sure she would throw him to the ground and have her way with him. I pulled my cellphone. It took great videos but decided against using it.

I needed to break them up. "Okay, guys. I'm going to strip, and we can make it a threesome. Maybe Cassi can join when she's up to it. Samantha, are you up for some fun?"

Jeremiah didn't even flinch. "That sounds great, Kye…Wait, what did you say?"

He looked at me, and I cocked an eyebrow.

Jeremiah sighed, then returned his attention to Jean. "I have to go, but maybe we can catch up when I get back."

"That would be great," Jean cooed.

"Then it's agreed. Samantha, can you take Cassi back to my London apartment? I will send my maid to clean the place up and some arbiters for security." When she nodded, I grabbed Jeremiah's arm. "It's time to go."

He nodded, and we're about to disappear when Jean cocked her head. "And why is it I can't go with you?"

I turned toward the assassin. "Because I need you to go interrogate Bush and learn everything you can about him and his brother."

"Why me? Why not Jeremiah?" she put her hands on her hips and glared at me.

I tried to muster my best 'this is serious' look. "Because you're their mother, and Joshua has already tasted the energy of a berserker sword. By now, he's hooked. His only chance to survive this is for his mother to connect with him." I stepped toward her. "And that's you. Or do you want to leave their fate to Mr. Personality here?"

"Wait," Jeremiah protested. "I'm full of personality. Remember that joke I told last year?"

We both glared at the superpower until he threw up his hands and looked away.

Jean tried to continue her death glare, but her conviction was gone. She broke eye contact as uncertainty set in. "I don't know how to be a mother. How can *I* help my sons?"

"No one is born knowing how to be a mother or a father, and no one's perfect at it. It's just on-the-job training. You're their only hope, and you have to try. You were great with Tassis, and I have faith you will save your sons."

Jean looked down as she bit her lower lip. When she looked back, I could see her conviction had returned. "I will go talk to him, but if I find out this was simply your way of getting rid of the only woman in the group, I will cut off your balls." She turned her head to Jeremiah. "Both of yours."

When she glared back at me, I could see in her eyes that she meant every word. At this point, my balls hid somewhere around my heart. I nodded, and she disappeared.

Jeremiah chuckled nervously. "We'd better go."

I covered my groin. "Agreed."

## Chapter Thirty-Nine

 e returned Cassi to my London apartment to rest up. Jeremiah sent a squad of his assassins to back up the arbiters I had sent to protect the place. Samantha would stay and monitor Cassi and Renaldo.

After getting Cassi settled, we headed back to the hunting lodge, and Jeremiah wasted no time pouring himself a stiff drink.

A drink sounded like a good idea, but then I spotted a buffet on the other side of the room. I struggled with the thought that Death's Lord and the other two superpowers would eat buffet food. That was until I opened one of the containers, and it was stacked full of steaks. Not the destroy your teeth with gristle type but *eat this and then argue with yourself about which is better, sex or the steak.*

I put a huge piece of meat on my plate and moved on. I added a few more items and headed to the bar. I passed the three super-celestials with drinks in hand and hunger in their eyes.

As they placed their plates on a table, I stumbled and propped myself against the bar. On the table, the image of Cassi lying dead appeared. My heart pounded in my chest as I dropped my plate on the bar and grabbed a stool to prop myself up. When no one else reacted, I had to believe I was hallucinating.

*She's alive, Kye, remember that,* I said to myself.

*Only because Jeremiah saved her, she almost died because of you.* A voice responded.

I wasn't sure where the voice came from, but it was right. As long as Cassi was a Fallen, she would be a target for those trying to get to me. I looked at the others, and they acted as if nothing was wrong.

I grabbed a whiskey bottle, and I tried to pour myself a drink, but my hands shook too hard. Using both hands, I took a long drink from the bottle then slammed it down on the bar. The brown liquor burned its way down my throat, and I took a few breaths to regain my composure. I dared a look at the table, but this time it was just a table, no Cassi. I managed to pour myself a drink and waited. When I was sure the image was not coming back, I eased my way to a chair near the others.

My fellow diners were already elbow-deep into their food, and I guessed there would be no pre-dinner conversation. With my hand still shaking, this was fine with me. My hunger roared its desire, and I grabbed my plate and dug into the feast. Eager to forget all about the image.

Ten minutes later, I tossed my plate onto a table and waited. Lyzark gnawed on a turkey bone like it was the last piece of food in the world. He grunted and tossed it into a corner, adding to a pile he'd deposited there.

I sank into my chair, my belt strained from my full tummy and took a sip of my drink.

Jeremiah frowned. "Are you alright? You look a little pale."

"Yeah, I'm fine, just ate too fast," I lied. Not wanting to discuss my hallucination, I tried to change the subject. "What gives with the buffet?"

Jeremiah gave a Cheshire Cat grin but said nothing. Eizan and Lyzark avoided my stare.

Lyzark waved his hand. "We are the leaders of legions. We need no reason to eat well." He gave a forced laugh, but Jeremiah laughed heartily, and Eizan glared at him.

Jeremiah's laugh turned to a snort at Eizan's glare. "Don't look at me like that. Tell him, or I will."

Eizan looked away, so Jeremiah continued. "It's their wives. They decided their husband's diets were too meat-rich and are forcing them to eat vegetables at home."

I was confused. "Why would immortals need to worry about their diets?"

Eizan and Lyzark avoided my gaze, and Jeremiah cackled. He leaned over and slapped Eizan's arm. "Come on, tell him. You had your fun when I was forced to admit my affair with Jean. You can do the same."

Eizan's eyes flicked to Jeremiah, then back to me. "If you must know. Lately, Lyzark and I have been exchanging, uh, personnel, and well. It's, uh, left us a little drained, and our wives have noticed."

I knew I would enjoy this and let out a chuckle as the two glared at me. "You mean, you two have been exchanging lovers and then didn't have enough juice to do the deed with your wives?"

Lyzark leaned forward and tried to stare me down. I shook my head. "After the shit that just went down, that ain't gonna work on me."

Lyzark's glare disappeared. "You would make a great demon. But, yes, you have captured the situation correctly. Tell anyone, and I will gut you. No matter the consequence."

I had met Eizan's wife, and she was a freight train, and a nuclear bomb wrapped together. Lyzark's wife was equally dangerous. If I tell anyone, one of those two will kill me for embarrassing their family. "Don't worry, your secret's safe with me. But I would recommend the oysters next time. They're supposed to increase your stamina."

Eizan growled. "I will not stand for your jokes."

"Actually, I'm not joking. It works for mortals."

Eizan's eyebrows went so far up his head, I wasn't sure where they ended, and his hairline began. He stood and made a beeline to the buffet table, followed by Lyzark.

"Oysters!" Lyzark ordered. "We need oysters."

A demon appeared with two large plates of oysters. He shook as the two lords descended upon him and ripped the plates from his hand. He was replaced by an angel with two more plates. This went on for several minutes until both collapsed into their chairs.

Both moaned from their gluttony, but Lyzark leaned forward and looked between his legs. "I think it's working."

Eizan checked out Lyzark's groin, then his own. "You're right! It is!

Jeremiah put his head in his hands. "Oh, dear Death. Can we get on with the meeting?"

"Yes, please," I pleaded. We needed to steer the conversation away from Lyzark's raging boner. "I think we have a lead on where Lester and Joshua are hiding."

Eizan looked up from his study of his groin. "We do too. His army is consolidating in an area in northern California. Lester was spied there, but he was seen alone. We are amassing our forces to wipe out the traitors."

"How many in his army?" Jeremiah asked.

"About a hundred, but more are streaming in," Eizan responded.

Jeremiah frowned. "How did he amass such an army? How could so many abandon their mission."

Eizan and Lyzark shook their heads.

"It's the berserker swords. They have the ability to enslave those around the sword owner. Watch." I pulled Kitten and tapped into her power. I then took that power and spread it across the room.

Eizan looked up in surprise. "That's amazing. I feel the attraction to your sword."

I nodded. "This is one of the abilities the swords were given when they were created. After seeing the potential for abuse, Kitten was given only a small amount of that power when she was created."

I released Kitten's power and stowed her. "You three felt it, but it barely affected you. With the stronger pull from the berserker swords, your foot soldiers would be hard-pressed to resist. I would not be in a hurry to wipe out his army. Once the swords are gone, the attraction will vanish."

"I'm in no hurry to slaughter those under the sword's control, but they are preparing for battle. What would you have us do?" Lyzark asked.

"Position your army near theirs, then wait. We want his troops to feel the hopelessness of a battle. It will reduce the pull of the berserker sword." I wasn't confident about my last statement. Kitten and I tried to work this out, but she only knew the basics about the other sword's power.

Jeremiah interrupted my train of thought. "Kye. What's the rest of the plan?"

"I'm hoping that our troops will scare Lester and Joshua and force them to return to their hiding spot. We'll need to take Jean and Ken and hope we can convince Joshua to give up his sword. I can guarantee you that it won't be easy. He may be too far gone and may want to fight to the death."

Jeremiah took a slow breath, nodded, but said nothing.

I shook my head as the next part of the plan wasn't any easier. "While you're saving Joshua, I'm going to kill Lester."

# Chapter Forty

I walked around a colossal redwood and admired the beautiful forest. We were about ten miles from the Pacific Ocean in northern California. This area is part of what is known as the Emerald Triangle. It's where hippies came to "drop out" and live in harmony with nature. Which, of course, meant growing weed. Their offspring embraced the economic benefits of commercializing pot and prospered. The legalization of marijuana hasn't hurt their income.

One of the downsides of working for Death means pot barely affected me. But it's always fun to smoke with mortals, then mess with them when they're high. I would let my eyes flash gray or disappear to Death's domain and back, resulting in some freaked-out mortals. Pizza and cookies always managed to calm them down.

I chuckled then realized that any mortals growing pot here would have been killed when Lester's soldiers arrived. Nothing I could do about that now, but if everything went well, Lester's army would surrender, and this wonderful place would remain intact.

Lyzark and Eizan stood near a map floating in the air, while Jeremiah stood on a nearby ridge. The plan was simple: act like this was a staging area for our army and prepare for a battle we all hoped would never come. Troops would arrive throughout the day, and Lester would think the battle was tomorrow. Hopefully, it would force Lester back to his hiding spot and give us the perfect chance to rescue Joshua and kill the wayward arbiter.

The two leaders were positive that Lester's spies had infiltrated their armies and were watching them. They had scripted out their next moves to convince Lester's spies we would attack tomorrow. Lyzark and Eizan were thrilled to prove their acting skills, sure an Oscar was in the bag. It turns out the two watched a fair amount of television. I knew that Lyzark owned an interest in several porn studios but never thought he would watch anything else.

The issue was—neither of them could act.

From twenty feet away, Lyzark announced, "Eizan, my dear friend, how are our plans going?"

Lyzark majestically swept his arm toward the map. Eizan looked around, stuck out his chest, and then marched the whole two feet to the map and responded. "Well, Lyzark, my old friend..."

I jogged over and interrupted the two would-be thespians. "Excuse me."

Both looked confused since it was clear I was not in their script. "Yes?"

I was about to school them on acting when I noticed a smorgasbord of food and drink nearby. I turned an appreciative eye to a few bottles of wine sitting on a table. Someone had good taste. Eizan followed my gaze. "God provided the food, and Death provided the wine."

"And what did Satan ante up?" I hoped for some of her tequila. Her collection was unmatched. But I noticed Eizan tried his best not to meet my gaze. Lyzark suppressed a laugh and stared at a nearby box.

I looked to where Lyzark stared and spotted a pallet loaded with boxes. I read the label on a box and almost squealed. "You've got to be kidding me. Are those X-1's? I didn't even know they were out yet!"

I ignored the look of confusion on the two celestials and rushed over to a box marked 'Large'. Ripping it open, I pulled out two dildos. The company that made these was rolling in cash, and I was sure Satan owned it. There were rumors that she personally designed all products sold.

I held up the sex toys to the two leaders. "These are amazing. They are made of a..."

"Are you sure you're not a demon?" Lyzark cut me off then grinned. "But you're right. These are the best. Check out the contour of the..."

Eizan interrupted. "And just what are your plans for those?"

I blushed as I stowed them in my jacket pocket. "They're for, uh, Fre-Fre's girls." Well, it was partially true. I noticed a couple of backpacks with suspicious bulges. "And I'm assuming that you two are stocking up in case the oysters fail to raise the dead for your wives?"

Both studied the ground like they'd lost a contact lens.

Eizan changed the subject. "Can we get back to why you interrupted us?"

I motioned for them to move closer. "Guys, you're staging for a battle. Not reenacting Macbeth."

The woeful looks I received surprised me. These two were not known for being sensitive.

"I thought we were doing quite well. Don't you think, Eizan?"

"Yes, of course. I performed my role for Shakespeare, and he applauded."

I suppressed a laugh. "You didn't happen to have a sword in your hand when you performed?"

Eizan puffed his already expanded chest. "Of course, I was using it as a prop."

"Uh-ha." I could see I wasn't getting through their massive egos. "I didn't say you weren't doing great. But every great play has a director guiding their stars. I'm just trying to help."

Their slow nods meant that I might have pierced their thick ego shields. "This scene calls for more intrigue. Play it quieter, deadlier. If you do, you will nail it."

Both eagerly nodded. Our little consult broke up, and Eizan walked to the map and took a deep breath. He hunched his shoulders and began to tap his fingertips together, then spoke in a deep, raspy voice. "Our troops are here and here. By tomorrow we will be ready."

He sounded more like a talking frog than a general leading his troops. I suppressed a burst of laughter when Lyzark put his hand over his mouth and furrowed his brow in an attempt to look contemplative. The result made him look like he was severely constipated.

As I walked away, Lyzark tried what I thought was a Yul Brynner imitation, but he wasn't even close. The 'King and I' will be forever ruined for me.

I approached Jeremiah. "Ready?"

He nodded. "Yes. Jean and Ken are in position. I guess they had a long conversation and have gotten to know each other."

Death's right-hand man didn't move. I wasn't sure what he stared at, but I could almost feel his mind racing.

"What's the matter?" I asked when the silence grew awkward.

Jeremiah gave me a look of despair. Whatever internal argument that raged in his mind was clearly still in progress. "I have two sons, and I don't even know how to address them. Do I say, 'Hi, son!' or call them by their names? Do you think they will call me Dad?"

Jeremiah's a good guy and has always treated me with respect. I wanted to help him, but never having had kids myself, I wasn't sure how. "All I can say is go slow. Use their given names and hold off using the term

215

*son* until they signal it's okay. Be prepared for some yelling and resentment. Forgiveness is hard. Remember that."

"Why would they be upset? I didn't..." Jeremiah paused and frowned. "I suppose abandoning them on Earth would not promote familial affection. How can I overcome that?"

"I don't know. You were trying to do the right thing but messed up. Go with that and show them that you're a good guy and will be there for them."

"You think I'm a good guy?"

"If you ignore all of your stupid rules and your lack of humor, then yes."

Jeremiah laughed. "Well, you do ignore my rules. That must mean you like me."

"And there's that lack of humor again."

We both laughed. I did like the guy, but he was my boss with a dark side and had eliminated employees that crossed the line. Even ones that considered him a friend. "Ready?"

Jeremiah nodded, and I signaled Jean.

This should be simple. Rescue Jeremiah's son, kill Lester, and destroy two berserker swords.

What could go wrong?

# Chapter Forty-One

e appeared in a cavern with Jeremiah right behind me. Jean and Jeremiah's son, Ken, stood ten feet to our right. The place was a hundred feet deep and three hundred feet wide. Toward the back, a large pool of crystal-clear water. A grayish light emanated from it. The walls were covered in a hodge-podge of red and pink salt clusters that glowed, lighting the area. Tunnels sat on either side of the cavern that I knew, from experience, were both blocked several hundred feet down.

Stalagmites and stalactites adorned the cave. I could never remember which one hung from the ceiling and the one that rose from the floor. I pulled out my phone to look it up, but there was no cell coverage. Putting the phone away, I realized I was a bit apprehensive about facing Lester. There were few weapons that could hold their own against Kitten. The berserker swords definitely could.

I've been to this cavern many times. The pond's a great place to take a dip, and the power from the walls invigorated me. This underground sanctuary was thousands of years old. It had been used by thieves, runaway slaves, and those trying to escape arrest or hide from pursuers. Early in my career, I was tracking down a wayward soul and discovered the cavern. I loved it so much I ran the few inhabitants out, collapsed the entrance to the tunnels leading in, and cleaned the area up. A few other arbiters had found the place over the years, but we have tried to keep it a secret.

I think I know who told Lester about our secret, and he will pay.

Jean's eyes grew wide as she took the place in. "What is this place? It feels almost like—home."

I grinned. I knew the feeling. "Only someone who works for Death would enjoy the ambiance here."

"Why? This place is wonderful."

"Because of its horrific creation. But I have to say, Lester made a great decision to hide here. I really should have guessed it." I breathed in the air and let the energy make me feel whole again..

Jean punched me in the arm. "Are you going to tell me, or do I have to beat it out of you?"

"Ouch! Okay, okay. You know you have a lot of pent-up anger. Maybe if you and Jeremiah got a little..." I received another punch in the arm and stepped away from the assassin. "Easy on the arm, slugger."

Jean gave me an evil look, and I continued. "Many thousands of years ago, this area was above ground—a peaceful meadow if the reports are true. What I learned is one of the celestials, or one of their minions, ditched the berserker swords in that pond. It was deep at the time, and they thought no one would find them. Obviously, they didn't put a lot of thought into it, or they would have thrown them into the ocean. Eventually, a drought dried the pond, and two brothers found the swords, each taking one back to their respective homes. The power of the swords corrupted their minds, and they soon suspected the other of trying to kill them. The brothers, with the help of their sword, each raised a small army, and a war was waged here. The power of the swords corrupted everyone nearby, and hundreds fought to the death. By the time Death could send anyone to check out the situation, everyone was dead, and the swords were gone."

I paused for dramatic emphasis. "Death visited this place, found men, women, and children all brutally killed. One of the arbiters reported finding a small boy still holding the knife he plunged into his mother's chest, her sword still lodged in his stomach. From the firsthand reports, it was a horrific scene, and even the arbiters that accompanied Death were disturbed by it. Death buried this place inside a mountain and created this cavern. All reports written up about the incident were sent to a special archive that took me forever to break into."

I turned and looked into Jean's eyes. "As to why it feels like home to you. We are children of Death, and death is our nature. Places that have seen massive killings entices us, feeds us. Morbid, but true."

Jean shivered at my statement. "You mean like cemeteries?"

"No, people rarely die at cemeteries. More like battlefields, hospitals, retirement homes, and comedy clubs."

Jean frowned. "Comedy clubs?"

"Yeah, a lot of acts die there." I tried to say with a straight face but failed, and she slugged me in the gut.

Jeremiah and Ken talking distracted Jean while I recovered.

"At least they are communicating," she whispered as she glanced back at the two men.

For his part, Jeremiah was scanning the cavern, but his eyes kept flicking to his son. Ken was doing the same. "Should I try to help?" I grunted as I turned toward them, still hunched over in pain.

Jean put her hand on my arm, and I stopped. "Let them be. They will figure it out."

I nodded and raised my voice. "You two go that way. Jean and I will go this way."

Ken and Jeremiah warily looked at each other, then nodded. They walked toward the opposite tunnel, keeping a distance from each other.

Jean and I headed in the opposite direction to the other tunnel. But as we approached the tunnel, a man stepped out of the shadows.

It was Joshua, at least what's left of him. His matted hair and the huge bags under his eyes told me he was under the control of the berserker sword. His face was pale, and he was skin and bones. His clothes hung off him, and his face was emaciated. He held a sword with a gloved hand and pointed it at us. The glove looked like those used by powerline workers, very thick, and it covered most of his forearm. Kitten heated up and warned me that it was one of the berserker swords, and I resisted taking her out. The fact that he wore a glove meant he was not completely consumed by the sword's power.

"Hey Joshua. My name's Kye, and this is Jean," I said as loud as I could and hoped Jeremiah and Ken heard. The sound of two sets of feet running told me I was successful.

Joshua glanced at me, then stared at Jean. "How do I know you? How?"

Ken approached and stopped next to Jean. "Brother, they are...Joshua, what happened to you?"

"I'm fine," Joshua screamed. "Tell me who she is?"

Jeremiah approached, and Joshua's eyes locked onto him, and he pointed his blade at Death's lord. "And him? Why do I know him?" Tears began to stream down his face. "Help me, brother. I don't know what's happening."

Ken took an easy step toward his sibling. "You know them because they're our parents. They've come to help."

"Our...our parents?" Joshua stuttered. He stared at Jean, then Jeremiah, then back to Jean. The look in his eyes told me we might have a chance. "How did you find them?"

"Just put down the sword, son, and we can talk," Jean pleaded.

His sword began to tremble, and then the blade drooped toward the ground. Joshua gave his brother another pleading look, and tears rolled down his face. I thought we had convinced him when a sinister voice from the tunnel broke the moment.

"Don't do it. It's a trap. They're not your parents."

# Chapter Forty-Two

Lester emerged from the tunnel carrying the other berserker sword. He wore the same thick glove as Joshua, but I could see the top of another black glove underneath the first. He was taking no chances with the sword's power. But his bloodshot eyes and pale complexion told me he had already used it. For as long as I knew Lester, he had been portly. Now, with a gaunt face and his perfect, by-the-book suit hanging off him, it was clear he had used the sword.

"Brother, he's lying. All of our lives, we've made each other the same promise. What was it?" Ken shouted to get Joshua's attention away from Lester.

"No, uh, no lies between brothers," Joshua replied.

"That's right. I've never lied to you. I'm telling the truth about our parents."

"He's lying to you now. What is the sword saying to you? Listen to the sword," Lester urged.

"Don't listen to him, Joshua. You're wearing gloves for a reason. The only person you should be listening to is Ken," I said softly. "Listen to the only person you know that has never led you astray."

Joshua's eyes darted back and forth and eventually locked onto Ken. "You're right, brother. You've never lied to me."

Joshua switched his sword to his left hand, pulled off his glove, then switched the sword back. He rounded on Lester, pointing the blade at the now terrified man. "It's you that has lied to me," he hissed. "Every step of the way. The things I have done because of you. You must die!"

Lester smiled at Joshua then blinked. His smile faltered as he looked around in surprise.

"If you were trying to use the power of the sword to transport yourself, don't bother. Death sealed this cavern after we arrived," I said and enjoyed as Lester squirmed.

"Joshua, I, I never lied to you...Look out!" Lester jerked and pointed his sword toward a wall. Out of reflex, Joshua spun toward the unseen intruder, and Lester used the opening to run away.

I plowed into Joshua, pushed him into the wall, knocked the sword from his hand, and ran after Lester.

Just before entering the tunnel, I yelled back. "Take care of Joshua. Lester's mine."

I stopped just inside and placed my hand on the wall. Behind me, the passageway sealed shut. The other end of this tunnel was blocked by Death's shield. No one was getting out of here without my permission.

With a thought, the light coming from the walls ceased and plunged us into darkness. Arbiters can see in the dark quite well, but like any creature, it takes time for our eyes to adjust. From further down, there was a clang, then a thud, followed by Lester swearing in pain. Lester must have found Death's shield.

He was trapped in this tunnel and had to know that he would not leave alive. Any of the big three celestials could snatch him, but he was mine as a gift for tracking him down.

With a thought, the walls glowed again, lighting the passageway. In the distance, Lester picked himself up off the ground. He turned and glared at me.

"It's over, Lester. Drop the sword and come quietly."

Lester's laugh echoed through the tunnel. It was the first time I had ever heard him laugh, and he sounded a little maniacal. The fugitive stalked toward me, removed his gloves, and swung his sword. He stopped about ten feet from me, his pupils fully dilated.

He took another swing and advanced toward me. "I should have killed you myself instead of sending those two idiots."

I pulled Kitten. Her blades heated and expanded to full size. She growled, ready to take over and destroy the berserker sword along with killing Lester.

I growled back and let my pent-up anger fuel my hatred. My energy flooded over Kitten. *He's mine!*

*Someone's in a mood,* Kitten replied. *I'll make you a deal. You get to kill Lester, but I get to destroy the swords?*

*Agreed.* I replied, surprised by how well the negotiations went so easily.

Lester eyed me with a look of uncertainty. "Are you ready to end this, Kye?"

"Sorry, yes. Kitten and I were arguing over who gets to kill you. I won. But first, tell me, how'd you do it?"

Lester cocked his head. "Do what?"

"Fake your death and convince the reapers they had the right weapons."

Lester laughed. "It was amazingly simple. Once I had the swords, it was easy to convince others, including reapers, to help me. I found a relative of mine, a great grandson, who looked amazingly similar to me. He could have been my doppelganger. I ordered a recruit to seduce him and convince him to get the same tattoo as mine. She lured him to the building, and I killed both. I put a little of my energy into him and made sure a reaper that worked for me found him first. He swapped the real swords with imitations. Everyone bought it hook, line, and sinker."

I gave him a nod. "Very impressive. But tell me, how did you convince Rusk to try and kill me?"

"I've been collecting Fallen and hiding them away. That Talent manager Fre-Fre hired would line several up, and I would get every third one. When I showed Rusk my collection of, uh, *talent* and a large mound of coin, it wasn't hard to convince him."

I thought for a moment. "One last question. Rusk knew exactly where to ambush me. How did you track me?"

Lester roared in laughter. "Your cellphone, you idiot. Easy enough to track."

*Ah, crap. That was a stupid move on my part.*

"Good point. I have to say, you seemed to have planned everything. But why do all this?"

Lester's eyes went wide, and his face flushed. His knuckles were white from the tight grip he held on the sword. He took another step and pointed his blade at me. "Because of you!" he said, jabbing the blade toward me. "The swords revealed everything you did to destroy me. I should have been the leader of the arbiters, but because of you, I was relegated to a piss-ant position."

The wild eye look he gave me told me he was strung out on the power of the swords. Probably too far gone to reason with, but I had to try.

"Per the rules, I have to offer you a chance to surrender before I kill you."

"I think, in the end, you will find that it is you that will die," Lester said, then lunged toward me, lifting his sword for an overhead swing.

I deflected it downward, and his blade plowed into the ground. Countering with a backhand swing, I hoped to decapitate my opponent, but he pulled back just in time. I nicked his cheek, and drops of blood rolled down his face.

He wiped them off with the back of his hand and smirked. "You've been practicing."

Two more drops rolled down his face, and he wiped again, his smirk gone. He had expected his body to heal his wounds, but it didn't.

My turn to smirk. "Not healing like you thought?"

"Doesn't matter. Once you're dead, I will have plenty of time to heal." Lester lunged and swung his blade with incredible speed. I barely had time to deflect his swing and counter. He was a little more cautious, and he blocked my counter-attack.

"Time to die, Lester." I swung Kitten as fast as I could. We were a blur of swords and movement. Neither scored any hits, and after a flurry of attacks and counterattacks, we paused, each taking a few steps back.

My chest heaved, and my arms ached. Lester leaned against the wall, panting like a dog.

"You could just give up. It would be easier," I spat between breaths.

"You could just let me go. *That* would be easier," Lester retorted.

I took a deep breath and straightened. "After what you've done, you're going nowhere."

I stepped forward, and Lester swung. This time, I took things slower, watching for opportunities. Several times an opening appeared, but I feared that Lester was trying to lure me in.

Finally, I spotted an opportunity I liked and took it. Lester had swung a little too far to his right, and I drove my sword into his left shoulder. I kept pushing and slammed Lester into the wall. I grinned and readied my celebration, but my thrill of certain victory was short-lived. I had left myself open and now had Lester's sword in my left shoulder as a reward.

Well, shit. That wasn't supposed to happen.

# Chapter Forty-Three

Lester and I stared at our perforated shoulders, then back to the other. His look of confusion matched mine.

"On the count of three. One, two, three..." I pulled back and stifled a scream as his sword was jerked out of my shoulder. Something fell from my jacket pocket, but I ignored it as the pain soared through me. "Son of a bitch," I muttered.

Lester remained quiet as he leaned against the wall and tried to staunch the flow of blood. I did the same, but when I moved my hand, to my amazement, I watched as my wound began to stitch itself back together. After my last encounter with the sword, it took the power of Jeremiah to finally close my wound. Seeing it heal itself was not what I had expected.

*I figured out a few things after our last encounter,* Kitten purred. *It will still take time for your wound to be fully healed, and you need to be careful.*

Lester studied his bleeding shoulder, saw it wasn't healing, and glared at me. "How?"

"I guess I have better friends than you," I joked.

Lester pushed himself away from the wall then glared at an object on the floor. It was the head of my X-1. I pulled the other half from my pocket. "Now, look at what you did."

"You brought a dildo to fight me?" Lester shouted.

I reluctantly nodded. "Uh, yeah."

Lester screamed in rage. "Can't. You. Take. Anything. Seriously?"

I shrugged. "It's not like I had planned on using it on you. You're not my type."

I thought my joke was funny, but Lester let out another scream.

*You may not be as funny as you think you are,* Kitten offered.

I laughed at the ridiculous notion. *Of course, I am. He's just upset.*

"And you wonder why I want you dead?" Lester pointed his sword at me. "Time to end this."

He took a deep breath. His sword glowed a bright blue then began to dim as Lester began to glow. Lester convulsed as his wound closed.

*What did he just do?* I asked Kitten, shocked by his sudden change.

*He just drew a tremendous amount of energy from the sword to heal himself. He is feeling better, but his sword is weak—attack now!*

I didn't hesitate and swung Kitten, but Lester blocked my swing with ease. Lester smiled, but he missed the part where Kitten just put a large nick in his blade.

He rained blows onto Kitten faster and harder than we have ever encountered. It took everything Kitten and I had to block his onslaught. My shoulder sent electric jolts of pain every time our swords collided. My wound was healing, but I continued to lose blood, and my legs began to feel rubbery, and my vision blurred. The only good news was the number of nicks in the berserker kept climbing, and they were much deeper.

*Almost there,* Kitten reassured me.

I wasn't sure where *there* was, but I hoped we reached it soon, or he was going to take my head off. My strength was dwindling, and I could only defend against the onslaught. Kitten fed me energy, but I was fading. If I couldn't rest soon, it would be over.

Lester's attack slowed as his breaths became shallow, but he continued to rain blows. I had been forced to retreat, and we had made our way just short of the sealed end of the tunnel.

Just as my back touched the wall, Kitten yelled, *Now!*

Not knowing what I was supposed to do, I swung Kitten down onto Lester as hard as I could. As expected, he brought up his blade in defense. Our swords clashed, and Kitten split the berserker sword into two. Kitten continued, cleaving off my opponent's left arm before plowing into the ground.

Lester dropped to the ground, grabbing his severed stump, and tried to staunch the flow of blood.

"Lester, it's over," I rasped.

He gazed at his shoulder, gushing blood, then back at me. With a huff, he stood but swayed in place. He must have known he didn't have long. "I know what Death will do to me, and I won't give him the satisfaction."

He turned what was left of his blade and pointed it at his chest. He grunted as he tried to push the sword into his chest, but between the blunt edge of the sword and the loss of blood, he couldn't. Screaming, he turned and ran toward the tunnel wall, trying to ram the broken weapon into his heart. But just as he was to slam into the wall, he disappeared. The sword remained and clanged to the ground.

*I'm guessing Death wanted a few words with Lester,* Kitten offered.

I thought we were done when Kitten continued. *Swing me again. We need to destroy that sword.*

*Not sure I can, but I'll try,* I responded and lifted Kitten above my head. With the last of my energy, I brought her down as hard as I could onto what was left of Lester's sword. The berserker sword shattered. I felt, more than heard, a scream coming from the cavern.

"What was that?" I asked, collapsing to the ground. I waved my hand, and the entrance opened.

*That was the other berserker sword dying. They were a matched set and powered each other. When one dies, so does the other.*

I retracted Kitten's blades and stowed her in my jacket pocket. I stood and staggered back into the cavern. Joshua lay on the ground with Jeremiah kneeling next to him, his arm on the man's chest. I could only guess that the loss of the berserker sword was more than Joshua's weakened body could handle.

I wanted to help but wasn't sure how long I had left. Desperate, I searched for a solution when my eyes locked on the pond. Every time I swam in it, I came out refreshed. I wasn't sure if it would help, but I couldn't find any other solution.

"Get him into the water," I ordered.

Not sure they heard me, I staggered toward the pond but collapsed after a couple of steps. Jeremiah rushed by carrying Joshua. Powerful arms lifted me and carried me to the pond.

"Why do I always feel like I do all the work in this relationship," Jean quipped.

I smiled at my rescuer. "Put me in the water."

Jean nodded and lowered me into the pond. From the corner of my eye, I saw Joshua floating near me.

"Tell Jeremiah to jolt Joshua like he did Cassi," I whispered to Jean as she held my head above the water.

She nodded but continued to hold up my head. I put my hand on hers. "Let me go."

"Kye. No, I can't let you drown."

"It's my only chance to survive. Let me go."

Jean complied and released me. My body sank into the water, and my pain and weakness began to diminish. I just relaxed, letting the energy from the water lull me to sleep. I could feel my shoulder wound heal, and my aches and pains vanished. My body was now healed, but all I wanted to do was sleep and forget everything that had happened.

I settled to the bottom of the pond and felt something I hadn't in a long time.

Peace.

## Chapter Forty-Four

itten's voice woke me from my peace. *Kye, you're not going to do something stupid like die, are you?*

*I just need to sleep. Is that a crime?*

*And what about Cassi? What will she do without you?* Kitten demanded.

An image of Cassi smiling filled my mind but quickly morphed into the image of her lying dead on a broken table. I opened my mouth to scream, only to take in a mouth full of water. I thrashed around then sat up, sputtering. Wiping the water from my eyes, I found myself sitting in a couple of feet of water.

Glad the image was gone, I tried to stand. But as I did, the scene around me changed from the cavern and its pond to an ostentatiously decorated room. A seven-foot-tall sculpture of an angel sat in the corner, and on a wall was a massive painting of an overweight angel. The muted, white glow coming from the windows told me I was in heaven. Scattered around me were shards of clear and white-colored broken glass on a bearskin rug. Looking closer at the shards, I realized the white hue was, in reality, angel blood.

A knot formed in my stomach as I looked behind me.

*Ah, shit!* I said to Kitten but realized she wasn't there.

On the floor next to me lay the body of an angel. Blood covered his robes, and stab wounds riddled his body. He lay on the remnants of a glass table. Glancing back at the portrait, it was the same person.

His gray-tipped feathers told me he must have been one of God's original angels. They were a select group of sacred angels, and killing one could be the catalyst of a celestial war. I couldn't be in a worse situation, and panic set in.

Someone had killed an original Heaven's angel. With me sitting in his blood, I would be suspect number one. If Eizan's security goons found me now, especially without Kitten, they would kill me first and ask questions later.

I shook my head to figure out what I should do, but as I did, the image disappeared, and I was back in the cavern.

I racked my brain on who the angel was. His face was familiar, but I couldn't recall his name. I could remember the face of every single angel or demon I had killed, but his was not one of them. So how did I know him?

*Kye, that last image was a premonition,* Kitten began. *I'm not sure where it came from, but...*

Jeremiah's screams interrupted Kitten and pulled me from my thoughts.

"Breathe! Damn it. Don't you die on me son!" A few feet from me, Jeremiah crouched over Joshua doing CPR.

With each compression, Joshua's body convulsed. Waves of power emanated from Jeremiah, washing over me and causing ripples in the water.

Ken sobbed nearby, his arm around his crying mother.

Two things became clear. First, Jeremiah was doing everything he could to save Joshua. Second, he was losing the battle.

Jean tried to hold it together, but when she glanced at me, her flowing tears and look of agony told me she knew this wasn't going well.

"About damn time you got up off your ass," Jean demanded. "Do something to save my son!"

"I just had a near-death experience. Give me a friggin' break," I retorted.

From experience, I knew the only one who could save Joshua was Death. But he notoriously hated being asked to save someone's life. I guess I couldn't blame him, considering Death was his name. For Death to intervene, it was usually a life-for-a-life. I wasn't ready to deal with deciding who should die in Joshua's stead.

I took a deep breath, crawled out of the pond, and contemplated the question that now bounced around in my mind. *Could I live with myself standing by and watching Jean's son die?*

In a way, it was my fault he was about to die. Lester's hatred of me caused all of this. I had no clue what I could have done to change the outcome. But indirectly, it was my fault.

At this point, somebody may have thought that I was about to sacrifice myself to save Joshua. My only reaction would be, 'Aren't you cute'.

No, Death owed me a few favors. Maybe one of them would be enough to convince him to help Joshua.

I staggered to my feet. With the rejuvenating power of the pond, I felt better, but the effects of my near-death experience lingered, and I fought to remain upright. I pulled out my phone to call Death when a man appeared near the edge of the water. His aura instantly told me it was Death, but I couldn't recognize who he was supposed to be.

Finally, after a moment, it dawned on me. "Oh, you're supposed to be Sir..." A cascade of apples rained down on me and cut my question short.

Death gave me a stern look. "Next time, less internal drama and more action, Kye. And yes, Sir Isaac Newton."

I freed myself from the apple pile and managed to stand. I took a bite of an apple as I tried to figure out how Death knew what I had been thinking. Could he read my mind? Better question, did I just use one of the favors he owed?

Carl winked at me, walked into the pond, and approached Jeremiah. "Jeremiah, let me."

Jeremiah looked at him as tears rolled down his face. "Please. Help him."

Carl smiled. "I will, my old friend, but we must hurry."

Jeremiah backed away as Death knelt next to the dying man. He scowled and furrowed his eyebrows as he placed his hands on Joshua. Then, all was quiet as a massive whirlwind of gray and white energy swirled around the celestial. The energy pulsed, slow at first but steadily increased. With a crack, the energy struck Joshua like a lightning bolt. His body went rigid, then relaxed.

The silence grew as we waited. Water dripped in the distance, and its echoes filled the cavern. When Joshua didn't move, I was astonished. How could Death not be able to save him?

Jean screamed, and I jumped when Joshua inhaled a huge breath and then opened his eyes. Jean rushed forward and took the revived man's hand.

Death rose and wiped his brow. "He will live but will require a little more healing when he is ready." Death smiled at his employee. "Jeremiah, I'm sure you can handle that."

Without warning, Jeremiah hugged Carl. The look of surprise on Death was real, and I averted my eyes to the apple I now vigorously chewed. I knew Death's eyes were on me, and I refused to make eye contact. When

I dared look Death's way, it was just in time to see Jeremiah release Death, only for Jean to take his place.

Carl's eyes bulged, and with Death's aversion to being touched, I waited for him to explode. Instead, Jean released him and kissed his cheek. "Thank you for saving my son. I will never forget this."

I almost fainted when a tear rolled down Carl's face. When he saw me gawking, I fully expected to be blasted into another wall, but instead, he smiled. "Don't thank me. Kye called in all the favors I owed him. Isn't that right, Kye?"

For a split second, an internal battle raged in my mind about if I should argue that I hadn't agreed to *all* favors. Luckily, my sense of self-preservation won out, and my head mechanically nodded. "Yes, that's correct."

Jeremiah and Jean hurried over to thank me. Jean hugged me and gave me a peck on the cheek. My boss vigorously shook my hand. Of course, I responded with the obligatory, "It was no big deal."

But it was.

I had held onto those favors in hopes that Death could help Cassi return to Heaven. Eizan had promised to reinstate Cassi, but I knew he would renege on his promise. Cassi was alive, for now, but my best hope of saving her and returning her to Heaven was gone.

Death interrupted the party. "I think the new family needs to head home and have some alone time to heal and get to know each other."

Jeremiah nodded, and the four disappeared. As soon as they were gone, my fake smile slid off my face, and I turned away from Death. Not because I was scared, but because I was disappointed. Somehow, I had just thrown away Cassi's best hope to return to heaven.

"Kye, it's not over. You have a few things to close out," Death said softly.

I nodded but didn't move. Between Lester's sword ripping through my shoulder and losing my best chance to save Cassi, I was too exhausted to clean up the rest of this mess.

"Here, let me give you a little pick-me-up," Carl said as he placed his hand on my shoulder and gave me a jolt of energy. It was like I had just drunk a hundred cups of coffee. I was wide awake and ready to go, but it did nothing for the ache in my heart.

"Kye, I promise you. Everything will work out in the end. Now go check on Lyzark and Eizan."

I looked back to Carl. He smiled, patted my shoulder, and disappeared.

I took one last look at the cavern and snapped my fingers.

## Chapter Forty-Five

I returned to the battle site to find Lyzark and Eizan leaning against a couple of trees, sharing a bottle of rum. Surveying the area, I found hundreds of demons, angels, reapers, and an assortment of others all milling around.

A small orgy was in full force off to one side. Various contests raged on, including a dubious game of knife throwing where the contestant threw a knife at his opponent who tried to catch it. A make-shift hospital was staged not too far off, treating a few knife wounds. An exciting game of tug-of-war where the participants used wing strength instead of arm strength, took place above. In the short time I stood there, more angels and demons arrived to join the celebration.

"What are you two doing, and what happened here?" I asked, gesturing toward the party.

Eizan took a swig of the rum and tossed the bottle back to Lyzark. "We prepped for war when suddenly the enemy gave up. Many weren't even sure what was going on. We figured that you had destroyed the berserker swords that had enslaved them and killed Lester. Afterward, we decided a celebration was in order before we went back to killing each other. Death and God replenished our supplies of wine and rum."

"Did Satan send anything? Tequila maybe?" I asked anxiously, scanning the area.

Eizan looked down and mumbled.

I surveyed the area with the hope of spotting a box or two of Satan's tequila. "Sorry, I didn't get that. What did she send?"

Eizan mumbled again and wouldn't make eye contact. Lyzark spoke up. "She refilled our supply of X-1's and left a note saying, 'Enjoy'. I'll have to thank her later. She is quite generous."

I chuckled as I noted that the pallet had been raided again with a fair amount missing. I tossed the severed X-1 and replaced it with a multi-colored version.

Eizan stood, and Lyzark handed me the bottle of rum. "So, it's true. The arbiter Lester is dead along with the berserker swords?"

I took a healthy swig. "Yes, which means, per our agreement, you're going to return Cassi to Heaven and restore her to her previous position. In fact, I think a promotion is in order."

Eizan took a deep breath, and as expected, he tried to renege on his promise. "I didn't actually agree to return Cassi to Heaven. I just agreed to…" he began, then his eyes glazed over, and his body stiffened. He took a deep breath, and he looked scared. "I meant to say that you are correct. I made the offer and will honor my obligation. I will even grant the promotion. But you must produce her now, and she will leave for Heaven immediately."

I stammered for a response. The only being that could have intervened and changed Eizan's mind was God. While Eizan still held a look of concern, I pressed my advantage. I stepped close to him—our noses almost touching. "I will retrieve her and say my goodbyes. Then you can do what you need to do. Anything other than that, you are in breach of our agreement."

Eizan smirked. "Do you think your sword intimidates me?"

I chuckled and cocked my head. "I think we both know you are going to do as I wish, or your boss will intervene. Again."

Eizan's eyes flicked away then back. We were at a standoff, but Lyzark offered a way out. "You know, Eizan, the way you act like a royal ass, you should have been a demon." Lyzark laughed, and the corners of Eizan's lips went up. "Let Kye say his goodbyes. In the meantime, I'll open some champagne and we can celebrate."

Eizan stepped back. "I guess for some good champagne, I can wait." He broke eye contact and joined Lyzark.

My urge to kill him was at an all-time high, but if I did, Cassi would never be able to return. Watching her wither away was not something I could do.

"You'd better break out a few bottles. Cassi and I have some serious catching up to do," I said and winked at the demon lord.

Just before I disappeared, Lyzark retorted. "When you come back, I want details."

Lyzark then smirked. "After all, the Devil's in the details."

## Chapter Forty-Six

I returned to my London home to find Cassi and Renaldo watching a movie.

Cassi greeted me with a kiss. "I wasn't expecting you back so soon. Just can't keep away, can you?" She stepped back and frowned. "Kye, what happened to you? Are you hurt?"

I whistled when I saw a reflection of myself in a mirror. It wasn't a pretty sight. My hair stood on end mixed with dirt and blood. More dirt covered my clothes which hung in shreds, covered in gray blood.

Cassi frowned then gasped when she ripped open what was left of my shirt. A huge scar graced my shoulder where Lester had stabbed me. Dried blood coated my chest.

"Kye, what happened? You look..."

I pulled her to me as I kissed her. Holding her in my arms made me feel whole again. I never wanted to let her go.

Renaldo stood and headed toward the kitchen. "I'll let you two catch up while I make some popcorn."

I didn't bother to point out there were already two full bowls sitting on the table.

Cassi put her hand on my face. "Please, tell me what happened."

I nodded. "Death has Lester. Lester's forces are disbanded, and the berserker swords have been destroyed."

"Why do I feel a *but* coming?"

She always could read me like a book. "There is, *but* it's a good thing. In return for my services, Eizan has reinstated you into Heaven and your position. He's even given you a promotion."

Cassi bounced up and down, celebrating. I smiled, trying to pretend I was happy.

My love stepped away from me. "This is wonderful. I can return home. No more dancing, no more hiding, or relying on you to support me."

"I didn't mind the last part," I murmured.

She gave me a confused look. "What's wrong with that? I don't understand..." Her smile dimmed as she realized the implications. While we could have the occasional sex session, long-term relations between the different celestial camps were a no-no. It was a quick way to get yourself beheaded.

She looked down at my chest, smile gone. She wanted, no, needed to return home, but now it would be at the price of our relationship. "Kye, I don't know what to say."

"Just tell me that you love me. That's all I need," I lied, turning away from my lover. "We need to leave soon. If we have to go back to my L.A. house to get your stuff, we should do that now."

Placing her hand softly on my shoulder, she turned me back to her. "Yes, I love you. Do you love me?"

My feelings were destroying me, and I wasn't sure how much longer I could hold it together. After all, I have a reputation to uphold. Crying would ruin it. "Yes, I have always loved you."

Cassi smiled. "Then it's settled. We'll leave my stuff at your house until we can figure out how to be together."

*Screw my reputation,* I thought as tears streamed down my face. I had serious doubts about how we could make it happen, but I didn't care. We would be together. I kissed her, then stepped back.

"What?" Cassi asked.

I checked my watch. "I hope Lyzark brought more than two bottles of champagne."

Cassi looked at me quizzically until I began to take off the remnants of my jacket.

I was ripping my shirt off when she picked up my jacket. "What's this?" she asked as she pulled an object from my jacket pocket. "Is that the new X-1?" she asked excitedly. "I didn't even know they were out."

"I didn't know either." I smiled. "And I got two," I said and pulled the multi-colored version out.

Before I could stop her, she swapped X-1's with me. "This one's mine. I will put this one away for later," she said as she put the toy on a table.

"I agree." I ripped what's left of my shirt off then did the same for Cassi's dress.

She pushed me back, surveying me. "You're bloody, stinky, and really need a shower." A grin appeared. "I can help with that."

I grabbed her hand as we headed toward my private bathroom. When she tried to unclip her bra, I placed my hand on hers.

"Let me," I offered.

I pulled her to me. The feeling of her body next to mine drove me nuts. I stared into her eyes as I reached behind her and unclipped her bra.

Cassi cocked an eyebrow. "You're pretty good at that. A lady might suspect you've done that before."

"I'm even better with panties," I replied.

"What do you mean?" She looked to the floor to find her panties several feet away.

"How did you...?

"Shh," I whispered, then kissed her. "Trade secret."

"You're going to have to show me that secret someday," she whispered in my ear.

I guided her to the shower, grabbing a bottle of my special body wash on the way. It's only made in Heaven, and there's a very limited supply. I took my time pouring Heaven's lotion on her body, rubbing it in, then rinsing it off. I wanted to enjoy her wonderful body, and with the lotion, her skin was amazing to touch.

I made sure to go slow, this was not a time to be in a hurry. When I thought I was done, Cassi grinned and unfurled her wings. "Did you forget these?"

I let out an appreciative whistle. "How could I?" I turned her around, poured lotion on my hands, and began to caress her wings.

Her feathers were softer than anything I had ever felt. God created very few perfect things in this world, Cassi was one of them.

When I was done, I reached to open the shower door, but she put her hand on mine. "Not yet." She grabbed the body wash from my hand. "My turn."

She took her time washing my body—not to mention driving me crazy. When she was finished, she ran her finger across my chest. "I think I like this new Kye. What gives?"

"I, uh, finally realized what you mean to me. I don't want to waste a single, precious moment."

She leaned forward, and our lips met. I fought the urge to take her when she placed her hands on my ass.

Leaning back. "Not so fast, miss. You're going to have to work for it."

"If I were you, I wouldn't keep me waiting long," she whispered into my ear .

I opened the shower door. "After you, my impatient nymph."

As she stepped out of the shower, I wrapped a towel around her, then swept her into my arms and carried my love to my bed. "It may be a while before we can be together again. I want to make sure you remember me."

She looked into my eyes, and I was awestricken. How could such a beautiful woman want to be with me? Cassie reached up and caressed my face. "Kye, I won't forget you. We were meant to be together."

I wanted to believe her so much it hurt. But angels are some of the most competitive beings that I know of, and many will forsake anything, including loved ones, to get ahead. It's an obsession with them, and Cassi's not immune to this. I wasn't sure our relationship could withstand that.

I lowered her to my bed and grabbed a bottle off the bed stand.

"What are you doing?" she asked as she removed her towel.

I gave her a quick kiss. "Patience. All in due time."

I used the towel to dry her off gently, then opened the bottle. Warmed from the heater, the smell of lavender filled the room. It was Cassi's favorite.

"Hmm, I love that smell," she moaned.

Starting with her feet, I slowly rubbed the oil onto her skin, pausing only to kiss her where I was about to apply oil. As I worked my way up her legs, she moaned affirmations that I was doing just fine. The farther up her legs I went, the more her affirmations turned to moans of pure ecstasy. Over the years, Fre-Fre's Fallen had taught me many things when it came to pleasuring a woman, and I used everything I had learned.

When I reached her thighs, her body tensed as she let out a scream then arched her back. Time slowed, and every sound of joy coming from her drove me further. I had lost all track of time when her hands grabbed my shoulders, drawing me to her chest. I wasted no time returning to my duty as she guided my head to her and arched her back. When she wrapped her legs around me, it took everything I had not to start the main course.

Finally, I couldn't take any more. The carnal yearning that had been growing in me demanded action. I hauled myself up as my love grabbed my ass and pulled me to her. I couldn't wait, and we began a rhythm that started slow, then built speed. Our sounds of desire filled the room, and I was sure everyone in a mile radius could hear us, but I didn't care. I had never encountered a feeling like this, and I wasn't going to ruin it.

She grabbed the back of my head. "Now!" she shrieked so loud I thought I heard glass shatter.

A bolt of pleasure burned through me. It rolled through me, into Cassi, and back. I think I screamed, but my mind had shut down, forgoing all thought, letting the feeling of the moment overwhelm me.

With one final wave, the feeling passed, leaving us sweaty and clinging to each other. My chest heaved, as did Cassi's. Yet, I kept still, trying not to break the moment.

I enjoyed the feeling of our bodies together and waited for my breathing to slow. Cassi ran her fingers through my hair then kissed me. It was the deepest, most sensual kiss I had ever felt.

She released me then pushed me onto my back. Positioning herself over me, she now cradled me with her legs and scanned the room, looking for something.

"What?" I managed to huff out between breaths.

"Where's that bottle you were using?"

I looked to find it on the floor, shattered from Cassi's sounds of ecstasy.

"Hmm, impressive," I laughed, but Cassi frowned at the fragments.

I grinned. "No worries. There's another bottle on the heater. If you didn't shatter that one also."

Cassi giggled, grabbed the second bottle, then positioned herself by my feet. Opening the bottle, she poured oil on her hands. Then, just as she was about to begin, she looked up.

"Brace yourself. It's my turn."

## Chapter Forty-Seven

C assi and I spent several hours cuddling in bed, cherishing our last time together. After a couple of showers, where we ended up back in bed and disturbing the neighbors, we returned to meet up with Eizan and Lyzark. We found them sitting on the ground, drunk off their asses, and singing. They each had a bottle in one hand and their arm around the other. The song they sang centered around killing and sex at the same time. I had to admit. I was tempted. But when I eyed Cassi, she returned my amorous look with an evil glare, and I decided not to pursue the thought.

After the third chorus, I interrupted the merriment. "Guys. Do we need to come back later?"

"Nope, just good booze and good friends," Eizan slurred, then stood. He swayed in place, trying to steady himself.

"Good to hear. But Cassi is ready to return to Heaven," I said, sure the celestial was about to fall on his face.

Eizan stared, barely remaining upright.

"How many fingers do you see?" I asked, holding up three.

Heaven's lord gazed at my hand. After a minute, he pointed his finger at my hand and jabbed at each of my fingers, trying to count them.

"Three," he replied, triumphant.

"Lucky guess," I retorted.

"Are you ready to return now?" Eizan asked, trying to focus his eyes on me.

"Ah, no. But Cassi is."

Eizan's head slowly turned and stopped when he spotted Cassi. "Of course. That's what I meant."

Cassi stepped toward the Heaven's lord. "Are you okay to do this now?"

He waved her question off. "Of course. Let's begin."

He put his hand out, palm toward Cassi. His eyes turned a brilliant white, and a matching white cloud formed around Cassi. It spun slowly, gathering speed. I smiled; my love was finally returning to where she belonged.

Then her clothes began to dissolve. I realized Eizan was taking one last dig at me by flashing Cassi to the entire camp. It would have worked if he hadn't been so drunkenly slow about it. With a wave of my hand, I put up a gray mist around Cassi, leaving just her feet and head visible. Then, with a flash of light, her wings appeared above the wall. They were restored to their original pearly white.

"Kye, you can drop the wall," Cassi said.

The mist dissipated when I waved my hand, revealing Cassi wearing black leather pants with matching boots. She now sported a black leather jacket with a shirt that showed enough cleavage for several women. I've never seen her wear anything so salacious. Well, as an angel.

Cassi approached, grabbed me by the back of my head, and gave me a kiss I was sure everyone in the camp felt.

When she released me, I staggered for a moment, and she grinned. "That wasn't a goodbye kiss. It was an 'until we can be together again' kiss."

Cassi strutted toward Eizan, and the man's tongue hung out like a horny dog. As she sidled up to him, he went to put his arm around her waist, thinking he was in for a kiss also. Instead, she grabbed him by the back of his head then slugged him in the stomach. The Heaven's lord doubled over then puked.

"That's for being a pervert." She turned toward Lyzark and waggled her finger.

Lyzark grinned but otherwise remained motionless.

She sauntered toward me, angel power blasting. "Until I see you again, Kye."

She disappeared, and I had to pull my chin off the ground. Once I collected myself, I turned my attention to Lyzark. "Your turn."

Lyzark stood then pointed a finger toward me. "I've never kissed an arbiter, but I guess I could give it a go."

He stepped toward me, lips puckered, and I backpedaled away from the overly amorous demon. "I don't mean me. I meant Tassis."

Lyzark halted and shook his head. "I'm not kissing Tassis."

I sighed. "How much did you two meatheads drink?" They both turned and tried to count the bottles lying on the ground. When neither could get past three, I wanted to scream. *Maybe this was what Lester meant about taking things seriously?*

"No. I meant you're taking Tassis back to Hell and not as a slave or a ward."

"Are you calling in a favor owed?" Lyzark slurred.

I laughed. I would if I needed to, but he was too drunk to barter. "What would Rusk say if he saw you bartering Tassis as if he was a thing of little value?"

Lyzark looked to the ground. When he looked back at me, tears rolled down his face. "He would kill me on the spot for treating his son that way," he roared, drawing attention from the entire camp. "And it would be his right. I am ashamed of my actions, and in Rusk's memory, I will raise Tassis as my son!"

With Lyzark's confirmation that Tassis was Rusk's son, it was one more piece of the puzzle. I still didn't know who the demon child's mother was but was determined to figure that out. "Good. When you're sober, I will return him, but let me warn you." I pulled Kitten, and she hungrily stretched to her full form. I then put her blade to the demon's neck. "Mistreat him, and you will have to deal with me."

Lyzark didn't move. He smiled, and I was tempted to take the man's head off. "That may not worry you, but this will. Jean sees herself as Tassis's adopted mother. Mistreat the boy, and you will have an angry mother, who happens to be an assassin, tracking you."

Lyzark's smile disappeared, and his eyes went wide. "Kye, you know I will treat him like a son. I already love him as one."

I relented. "I know you will. He's smart and talented. Give him a chance, and he'll prove himself."

Lyzark cocked an eyebrow. "If I didn't know better, I would say Tassis already has an adopted father."

"I don't know what you're talking about," I tried, but when Lyzark raised the other eyebrow, I sighed. "Yeah, okay. I kinda like the kid. He grows on you."

"Then it's settled. You're officially his Champion." He waved his hand, and energy flowed over me.

"No, wait. I can't…" I began, but Eizan slapped me on the back.

"Too late, Kye. You've been selected, and there's no taking it back."

The two lords staggered away, leaving me muttering to myself. How the heck did that happen? Being a Champion of a demon child was a little like being a godfather, only much more dangerous. I was now responsible for making sure he became the demon he was meant to be. It also meant, if anyone challenged him to a battle, I had to back him up. On the plus side, I now had a free pass into Hell. Being an arbiter, I can get into Hell but only in certain areas. Now, I can go anywhere in Hell Tassis went. When Lyzark sobered up and figured out what he did, he'll be pissed. Worse, Satan will be furious with both of us. Lyzark will want to kill me to make amends with Satan, and I will have to lay low for a while.

Now it was time to unveil the true mastermind behind this whole mess and ask them a few questions. Then, I'm going to kill them.

But first, time to try out my wings and take my maiden flight.

# Chapter Forty-Eight

t felt good to spread my wings and stretch them. My plan was for a short flight to try them out. I would have to be careful and make sure no mortal could spot me. Heaven and Death have teams that wipe the memory of mortals that see a celestial fly. Hell doesn't care. Death gets irritated when he has to send his team out—something I want to avoid.

I ran my hands over my wings for one last check but noticed a change. They were still dark gray with black tips, but now there was a strip of red between the black and gray. I wondered if this was related to my status as Tassis's Champion and admired the bright addition.

I gave my wings a test flap, and my desire to begin my maiden flight overwhelmed me. I extended my wings and enjoyed the feeling of the breeze flowing over them. With several powerful flaps, I launched myself into the air. With the wind on my face and an aerial view of the forest unfolding, it just felt so right.

A screech to my right startled me. Now pacing me was a red-tailed hawk. He screeched again, and I swore he winked.

*A perfect wingman*, I thought as we soared over the forest.

The hawk screeched again, pulled ahead of me, then began to climb. I followed as we flew higher and higher. Adjusting his wings, he slowed, then hovered in mid-air. I almost slammed into him as I flapped frantically to stop. It took me a minute to find the right tempo to keep afloat. But when I did, I took in the view. From this height, the forest extended for miles, and the sight was breathtaking. I never wanted to leave.

With the sound of an impatient screech, I turned back to my flight guide. Shocked, as I was sure it was smiling at me.

"Death?" I asked.

The hawk hovered, then folded its wing and dove.

Following suit, I furled my wings and followed. We picked up speed as we plummeted toward the ground. The hawk disappeared, but I didn't care. The wind rushing over me was exhilarating. I waited until the last seconds to spread my wings. My feet skimmed the ground before I swooped back toward the sky.

Heading toward a mountain, I stayed just above the tree line but was high enough to take in the view of the entire forest. Smoke from a distant campfire let me know it was time to end my flight.

I loved the rush of flight and planned on doing it again soon.

I snapped my fingers and appeared in Ken's office. I gave myself a few moments to let the euphoria of my flight wear off. The room was dark, but after a moment, my arbiter eyes could see just fine.

I found the bottle of bourbon I spotted when we first met Ken. I grabbed it, along with a glass, and headed to a chair in the corner. Along the way, I stopped by the tall cylinder Ken had shown us and opened it to make sure no one had raided it. It was stock full of Hell's treasures, which meant someone was coming for its content soon. I closed it, put a ward on it to prevent anyone else from opening it, and settled into a chair. It might be a long wait before my suspect arrived.

An hour later, a demon woman, wearing a tight-fitting red dress, appeared and headed straight for the cylinder. For a demon to be on earth in their true form meant she was not expecting to encounter anyone else. I wasn't sure who she was, but she seemed familiar. Placing her hand on the cylinder, she attempted to open it but failed. Finally, after a couple of tries, she pounded on it.

"It won't open for you," I whispered.

The demon let out a scream as she whirled toward me, a demon throwing knife ready to launch. I quickly recognized her as Darlene, Ken's personal assistant.

I waved Ken's gun at her. "I'd drop the knife. We both know the bullets in this gun will kill you."

Darlene relaxed and sat the knife on a nearby table. "Mr. Dodson, you scared me. What are you doing here? I don't think Mr. Bush will appreciate you breaking into his office."

I laughed. "Ken's with his family, and Lester is with Death. Both of which you already know." I waved the barrel of the gun toward a chair. "Take a seat. Let's chat about what you've done."

The demon smiled and slinked seductively to a chair. The slit on the side of her skirt opened to her hip, revealing tone, red legs. She unbuttoned her blouse down to her waist, revealing toned abs. Interesting note, demons don't have belly buttons. She made a show of bending over when she sat down to flash her wares. She was beautiful, and a romp with her would be fun, but I had no interest.

"So, what do you want to talk about, Mr. Dodson?"

"Let's begin with your role in all of this."

Darlene smiled and crossed her left leg over her right, giving me a preview of what I could have if I just took her offer. She tried to throw me off my game, but I wasn't buying it, and my eyes were glued to hers.

She uncrossed her legs and sat up straight. Clearly, she recognized she was not going to seduce me. "My only role is as Mr. Bush's personal assistant."

I pulled the trigger and the side of the chair nearest Darlene's head exploded. She jumped to her feet and screamed. "Are you crazy?"

I let the echo in the room die down. Despite what you see on TV, guns are amazingly loud.

"I'll take that as a rhetorical question. Next bullet will leave a mark."

The demon returned to her seat and smiled. "You won't kill me. But before I go, I would be interested in what you know."

This caught me off-guard. Darlene had a proverbial ace up her sleeve, but I had no clue what it was. So, I decided to play along and see what happened. "Okay. Let me see. First, I'm assuming you seduced Lester and convinced him to steal the swords. He was too much of a by-the-book guy to do this on his own. He would have needed someone to give him a push."

She nodded, and I continued. "You were also sleeping with Rusk and convinced him to be a part of a plot to make some gold and land some Fallen."

"Very good, Mr. Dodson. But tell me, how does Tassis play into this?"

I frowned. "I haven't figured that out. I suspect that his mother was more than just a concubine. She must be..." my voice trailed off.

"Ah, I see you finally got there."

I grimaced as I realized what her secret was. "You're Tassis's mother."

"Congratulations, Mr. Dodson, you guessed it," she took a moment to adjust her dress. "Since you've already killed his father, I don't think you will kill me. I saw how you looked at him, and he won't take it lightly if he found out you killed his mother also. Plus, I've made, ahh, contact with Lyzark."

She turned her head to show Lyzark's mark on her neck. "Killing those that belong to him could cause you a lot of grief."

"I have to admit, you're good." I picked up my glass and took an appreciative sip. Ken knew his bourbons. "But I do believe that if I don't stop you, you will spend your life making Tassis miserable. He would probably be better off sold into slavery."

Darlene opened her purse and took out lipstick and a mirror. "Maybe, but you can't be sure." She opened her mirror and checked her make-up. "Unless there's something I am missing?"

I let out a long laugh causing her to drop her mirror. "You missed one important point. Lyzark has adopted him and will love him as a son. If his real mother were never to be found, Tassis will grow up learning to be a demon from Lyzark."

The demon laughed. "I know all about Lyzark and Tassis. He told me everything. He also told me that while you have killed many angels and demons, you only do so out of self-defense. You're not the type to kill someone in cold blood."

Darlene stood and put her hands out in front of her, wrists together. "Here. Put the cuffs on and take me in. It will be your word against mine, and once I get Lyzark in bed, you'll lose."

"I would, but you were right earlier. You did miss something," I said as I cocked the gun. "I will kill to protect others."

"No. Wait!" she pleaded.

"Sorry, I'm Tassis's Champion, and I won't let you destroy him."

Before Darlene could respond, I fired twice. Her body jerked as the shots pierced her chest, and she slumped into the chair. The demon's plans permanently ended.

I downed my drink and walked over to her. Putting my hand on her neck, I checked to make sure she was dead. Demons don't have a pulse. So, I had to use my arbiter powers which told me she was gone.

"Such a shame," I said to no one. She was intelligent, ambitious, ruthless, and beautiful—almost the perfect demon.

I pulled out my phone and dialed a local ghoul named Jake. He's on my speed dial for just such occasions. As I said before, a lot of weird stuff happens in NOLA, and it's always best to be prepared. He will clean up the place, making sure there were no clues that Darlene died here. In exchange, he and his buddies get her body. Ghouls love demon blood and meat but have no desire to anger Satan. They will only take dead demons. A ghoul once attacked a demon, and Satan sent a squad of guards to make an example out of him. They killed twenty-some ghouls before they finished.

I looked over Ken's gun in my hand. I guessed it was circa 1940s and decided to keep it as a souvenir. Once Jake and his crew were done, I would head home.

After solving big cases, I usually host a celebratory bash with at least a couple of orgies. But not this time. Without Cassi to greet me, returning home held no lure.

I now understood the difference between a house and a home.

# Chapter Forty-Nine

T he next few days, I sulked at home, hoping to hear from Cassi. I sent her a few messages, but she never responded. With her reinstated as an angel again, Heaven's rules stated we couldn't fraternize more than the occasional covert quickie. Cassi was home and would survive. That would have to suffice for now.

When my phone did ring, I just about killed myself getting to it. I had left it on the kitchen table and was soaping up in the shower when it rang. Wet with shampoo still in my hair, I barreled through the house. Rounding the corner into my kitchen, my wet feet slipped on the floor, and I ended up on my bare ass. Despite my bruised derriere, I reached up and grabbed my phone off the table.

"Cassi?" I asked expectantly, but my hopes were dashed when a male voice replied.

"Kye, is that you. About time you answered." It was Jeremiah, and I bit my lip at the resentment it wasn't Cassi.

"Hey Jeremiah. Sorry, I was in the shower, which I need to get back to." I tried not to let my disappointment seep into my voice, but I don't think I succeeded.

"Sorry, of course. How are you doing?"

Silence hung in the air as I fought to respond. My boss was never one for melodrama. To be frank, he really had no skills for situations like this.

So, I went with my best option. I lied. "I'm doing fine. I miss having a hot Fallen to fool around with, but I will find another."

Jeremiah drew a deep breath. I assumed he was trying to figure out how to be sympathetic. "Well, sex isn't everything," he replied, then he grunted, and I was sure Jean slugged him for being an idiot.

"I mean," he groaned. I could hear Jean's voice in the background coaching Jeremiah. "I mean, have faith. Things will work out."

I suppressed a laugh. "Thanks. And tell Jean to take it easier on you. Anything else you wanted to talk about?"

"Yes, Carl wants you to have lunch with him."

"Just to confirm, he wants to have lunch with me, not he wants to have me for lunch?" I joked. Truth be told, it wasn't entirely a joke. With Death, you had to be careful with wording.

"Yes, lunch *with* him."

"Since he's buying, I accept. I need to finish my shower first and will head on over." I omitted the part about trying to get off the floor with an aching ass.

"Yes," Jeremiah replied and hung up. He's still working on his phone etiquette.

I hobbled back to the shower, finished, and got dressed. Then, I walked out of my house and straight into Death's office. He must know it irritated the crap out of me, but I forced a smile.

He was Death after all.

"Kye, just in time for lunch. I was just setting the table." With a sweep of his arm, a table appeared. It was a small affair, just large enough for two. Fine china, crystal, and a single candle adorn the table. A smaller table off to the side held several bottles of wine. I caught the name on one of the wine labels. That pinot currently goes for a little under ten thousand dollars. I should know. I just sold a similar bottle.

"Please sit, food and drink first. Work later." Carl pulled my chair out, and I sat.

At this point, I'm either here as his date, which was weird in so many different ways, or this is my last meal. Either way, I decided to enjoy the food. The salad was amazing, and the steak melted in my mouth. The meat was cooked to a perfect medium. Carl had his rare, but I like mine cooked a little more. Don't judge.

Throughout the meal, we talked about politics, sports, and women. I was surprised to find he was a Packers fan. I am also, along with the Saints and the Rams. So, the Rams left Los Angeles, everyone needed to get over it. I had, but I still suspected Satan had something to do with the move.

We plowed through two bottles of wine before we finished the last course. When it came to wine, I don't usually register a buzz until the third bottle.

Carl put his fork down. "Dessert?"

I shook my head. "Not yet, at least. Still full, and that last bottle of wine looks very tempting," I said and meant it. Based upon the shape of the bottle, it was from Julius Caesar's private collection.

Carl chuckled and opened the bottle. After pouring a generous amount into my glass, he settled into his chair. I've had a few meals with Death, but this was the first time I really felt relaxed around him. It might be a fatal mistake, but I didn't care at that point.

"You look troubled," Death stated.

"Well, I may have just lost Cassi," I retorted.

"No. There's something else. Something you're not telling me."

I sighed. "There's the possibility I had a premonition," I said, trying to be casual, but then my voice cracked. "At least, that's what Kitten said it was."

Death frowned. "I need the details," he commanded.

After I related every detail of the premonition, Death blew out a breath and sat back in his chair. After several minutes of silence, my nerves were frayed.

I jerked when he finally broke the quiet. "And you're sure it was an angel?" When I nodded, he continued. "And you didn't recognize him?"

"His face was familiar, but I can't remember where I know him from."

Carl nodded. "That just confirms that we made the right choice."

I gave Death a quizzical look but remained quiet.

"Do you know why I asked you to lunch?"

"I'm hoping it was because you wanted lunch with someone that could appreciate fine food and provide interesting conversation," I said, then took a breath. "But I suspect it is because you are no longer in need of my services."

Carl eyed me. The slight upturn of his lips meant either I was right, or I had surprised him. "So, you think I'm about to kill you?"

"You are Death, after all. Isn't that your specialty?"

Carl laughed. "Well, when you put it that way, yes, it is. But no, I'm not going to kill you. In fact, I'm trying to keep you from being killed. And based upon your *premonition*, maybe others."

"Okay, more power for Kitten and me?" I asked.

"Sorry, no. Kitten has more than enough power." He paused to take a sip of his wine. "You've been an arbiter for over a hundred years. Your reputation is known throughout Heaven and Hell. Best of all, you've killed quite a few who have tried to take you down. Which means...you're up for a promotion."

I tried to play it cool but instead knocked my plate to the floor, and it shattered. With a wave of his hand, the plate repaired itself then disappeared. "Promotion? Do you mean like management? Supervising others? I don't want to question your choice, but I'm not any better at employee reviews than Jeremiah."

Believe it or not, Jeremiah does do yearly employee reviews. But I haven't quite got the hang of them. Last year, for the question "What is your best asset?" I replied, "My Mr. Willie." It was a toss-up between that or "my tight-white ass."

Jeremiah didn't take my response kindly, and I expected him to lecture me like any good boss. Instead, he literally knocked me into the following week. Still not sure how he did it, but it was a cool, if not painful, trick.

Carl shook his head. "No, no staff for you. At least, not yet. For now, I'm reassigning you to, uh, let's say, a different division."

I took a breath and slowly released it. Great, I was going to be a desk jockey in some celestial courtroom. But since I wanted to live, I smiled. "And how does promoting me keep me alive?"

"My two colleagues and I have set up a simple structure that prevents us from spending all of our time wiping out each other's staff. This promotion will make it extremely difficult for anyone to kill you and not face severe consequences."

I was intrigued and excited. Anything that would keep me alive was always a good thing. "And what's so special about this promotion?"

"You'll find out soon enough."

"Okay, when do I start?

Carl stood. "In a little while, but first I need you to represent me at a meeting, then I'll send the location of where to meet your new boss. For this meeting, a very powerful person has made an interesting proposal. I will leave it up to you to accept or decline."

I was a bit puckered. Leaving the final decision to me was a little like saying, "Get it right, or you're my plaything." I've seen the results of others that worked for Death who had been in the same situation. Note that I said 'worked'.

"I'll do my best. Now, where am I headed?"

Carl flicked his hand, and I disappeared.

Have I mentioned how much I hate being tossed around like a doll?

# Chapter Fifty

I appeared in a storage room and am immediately bombarded by falling rolls of toilet paper coming off a shelf.

"Nice!" I growled, sure Death did that on purpose.

I opened the door and stumbled past rolls of TP into a hallway. I wasn't sure where I was, but I heard voices and followed the sounds down a hallway. There was something strangely familiar about this hallway, and I put my hand on Kitten just in case. The voices led me to another door with a cross on it, and I released Kitten.

Oh, crap. I knew where I was and now recognized one of the male voices on the other side of the door. I smiled as it was my favorite Angel, Reverend Jim.

The irony of an angel that was also a reverend was not lost on me.

Overall, he's a great guy and one of the best angels I know. He personifies what Christianity was supposed to be about. He fought so hard to help mortals understand that there was good in the world and living a moral life was the best way. He always made time for anyone who wanted to talk, and he gave away just about everything he earned. The one thing we have in common was he also took the occasional bribe. The problem was, he gave his bribes to the poor.

Okay, so I was a bit of a jerk compared to him, but I work for Death. It's expected.

Knowing that Reverend Jim was involved in the 'Proposal', as Death put it, gave me an idea of what I was in for. Jim was known for running interference with the magical groups that inhabited earth. If a magical being, such as a wizard or a warlock, ran afoul of an angel, Jim was usually called in to rectify the situation.

I opened it just in time to hear Reverend Jim say, "I know, but rules are rules."

With a subject like 'Rules', I had to join the fun. I'm notoriously against rules, even rules against rules, if there was such a thing. I do make the exception for any rule that I create. "Maybe it's time we get rid of those rules."

Jim looked up and sighed when he saw me, then a smile appeared. He surprised me as he walked over and shook my hand. "I don't think that's our call, Kye."

My surprise continued as he winked at me. What was going on with this angel? First, he shook my hand then winked at me. I didn't think angels could get dementia, but I should probably ask.

My thoughts were interrupted when a warlock jumped into our conversation. "Then why don't you ask?"

The warlock was sporting a slight grin. I wasn't sure why, but I already liked the guy. Hopefully, I won't have to kill him anytime soon. A quick check and I found he was above average on the power scale for a warlock. But the woman standing off to the side was a different story. She looked to be in her seventies and was off-the-scale powerful. Plus, the look she gave me just about made me leave the room and head to detention.

I was about to reply but realized Death might be watching. "Well, my boss, uh, is a great guy." I looked around, waiting to see if he appeared. "However, he can be a little sensitive at times, and I'm not on the best of terms right now."

The man chuckled. "So, your boss is ticked at you, and you're afraid he would hand your tail to you if you asked."

I looked him dead in the eyes. "Yes, I am literally afraid he will slice me up and hand me my 'tail' as you put it."

"And I thought I had a tough boss," the man muttered under his breath. The older woman's head snapped in his direction, and he took a sudden interest in a nearby hymnal.

I suppressed a chuckle. With the withering look he received, I made a mental note to never get on this woman's bad side.

The woman then turned her stare to Jim. When she nodded toward me, Jim got the hint. "Oh, sorry, where are my manners? Let me introduce Kye Dodson. He works for Death."

Jim continued. "Kye. This is Jason, his son John, his daughter Kira, and this is Mistress Nelson, Head Mistress of the Warlocks."

"Death, as in *the* Death?" Kira exclaimed.

"Yep, the one and only," I replied proudly.

"Talk about a dead-end job," John quipped, then looked around with a red face. "Sorry."

Jason, Kira, and I broke out in laughter, but John received a stern stare from Mistress Nelson and then Jim. But as Jim looked away, I could see a bit of a grin on his face.

I got a good chuckle out of that one and shook John's hand. "While that's an old joke, it's probably the first time I've heard it from someone that is still living. It's also Death's favorite joke. Although only when he tells it."

"With any luck, he won't get the chance to tell it to me for a long time," Jason said, chuckling, then stared at me. I began to feel a little uncomfortable until he finally spoke. "I've seen you before."

Well, that's a bombshell. Usually, when a mortal sees me, even a warlock, it means they're dead or about to be.

"Where?" I asked. I'm glad Death sent me here. This was turning out to be most interesting.

Jason tapped his chin. "New Orleans, in a warehouse district. You and someone else were chasing something that definitely wasn't human."

I relaxed, and so did the reverend. No one was dying this instant. "Yes, a little late-night hunting. We noticed you were doing the same."

"Something like that, but we need to get back to why we are here," Jason said. "Rita needs to be part of this deal. And I want your word, reverend, that all will receive only the best in Heaven."

I'm not sure who Rita is and don't really care if she is part of the deal. But I am interested to see how far I can take this. "And what if we don't want to deal?"

"I think you do. The fact that someone was willing to kill over a bottle of bourbon means there is a desire to deal. Also, the fact that someone, maybe even one of your bosses, negotiated a lifetime ban down to five-hundred years means there is a lot of interest," Jason paused. "Although, I still have to wonder why the magical block on the bourbon worked. It seems to me there are some immensely powerful players involved. One of them must have the power to bypass a warlock's spell."

Well, fiery balls of poo, he's pretty good. I was about to have a little more fun when Jim cut me off. "Kye, let's not get into that right now. Jason, as for your proposal, for those I represent, I agree. Kye?"

"I also agree...with one stipulation."

"And?" Mistress Nelson asked. The look I received told me I was nearing a line I shouldn't cross. Catholic nuns had nothing on this woman. I would love to see Death and this warlock debate. I wasn't sure I would bet on Death.

Carl never said I couldn't benefit from the proposal, so I gave it a shot. "I'm dealing with an issue that I believe you may be able to help me with. I'll accept your terms if you agree to help me with my issue."

Reverend Jim eyed me but said nothing.

"And what's the issue?" Jason asked.

"I'm not really sure yet, but something is building. It may be a year or two, but I'm pretty sure I'm going to need a warlock's help."

"One of Death's, uh, employees, needing the help of a warlock. That can't be good, but I accept," Jason agreed. "Mistress Nelson?"

"In that case, the terms are that Jason, and his team, will be available to help deal with your issue. No one else. If that works for you, we have a deal."

Jason's good, Mistress Nelson was better. "Agreed."

"You have Tess?" Reverend Jim asked, and Jason handed him Tess's box.

My senses told me there was a corrupted human spirit in the box. This kept getting more and more interesting. I looked around for some popcorn to munch on.

The reverend took the box and put his hand on top of it. The box began to grow brighter and brighter until it disappeared, replaced with a small, glowing cloud. He removed his hands, and the cloud floated in the air and began a slow spin. The spin became faster as the cloud grew brighter. With a flash, the cloud disappeared. A woman now stood in her place. I had to assume this is Tess. She's attractive and a bit sultry, and in any other situation, I might have tried to hit on her. By the way, Jason stared at her, it's clear he loved her. The look in her eyes told me it was mutual.

Tess looked herself over and smiled. "That's much better, thank you, Reverend Jim."

She turned and called John and Kira to her.

"Mom, I don't want you to go," Kira sobbed.

"Mom, please stay. At least a little while," John begged.

Tess pulled them close, and they both leaned into her. "It feels so good to hold you two again. You have grown up so much. I am so proud of you and how you have taken care of your father while I was away." Tess kissed both.

"But I have to go. What you see here won't last long. Just know that I will be watching from Heaven and will be there when you need me."

Tears were flowing from everyone in the room. Even I had a tear running down my face. Like I said, I'm a sucker for sad stories. I pulled a tissue from my pocket and blew my nose.

"Okay, let me say goodbye to your dad," Tess said as she released the two.

Tess walked to Jason, and the two embraced. I don't know their history, but I am assuming she was his wife at some point. Jason pulled back, reached down with his hand placing his fingers on her chin, and raised her lips to his as he leaned in close. He's pretty good, and I noted the move for later use.

Jason broke the kiss. "What am I supposed to do without you?"

"The same thing you have been doing. Raise our family and survive. I don't know what will happen with Catie, but you need to find someone to love. Promise me you will find happiness."

"I don't think being a warlock and finding happiness is in the cards for me," Jason replied. When Tess raised an eyebrow, "But I promise, I will try."

"Good, I will be watching and will know if you break your promise," Tess said, then released him. She took a deep breath and turned to Mistress Nelson. "I will entrust my family's safety in your hands. After what I have done for the warlock nation, I think I am owed."

"We will do our best. We owe you much more," Mistress Nelson replied, then hugged Tess.

Tess turned to Reverend Jim. "I am ready."

Reverend Jim held out his hand, a white glow now emanating from him. "Tess, we welcome you to Heaven. For your efforts, you will be among the honored in our midst. Go now, rest, and find peace."

Tess began to glow, matching the reverend's glow. Her clothes turned white, and then she smiled at Jason as she faded away. Jason stood with his arms around Kira and John. All in tears.

Silence hung in the air. I rarely got to see this part. Most souls go through the celestial courts, so I rarely see souls ascend to Heaven. I have seen a few souls damned to Hell. It's brutal to watch, probably more brutal if you were the soul. I now steadfastly avoid such situations if I can.

"Right," I said, with a tear running down my face. "I must go..." I begin and but am interrupted when Carl sends the location for where I am being reassigned to. I wanted to scream, "You have to be kidding me?" but I caught myself and tried to continue, "Justin, it may be a while before I need your help but do know that I will be in touch eventually."

"Uh, Kale, it's Jason, not Justin."

I heard Jason speaking, but my mind was preoccupied with the implications of the meeting location with my new boss.

It's in Reverend Jim's office.

"Hmm, that's not good," I said, pondering the ramifications. Slowly, I turned my attention back to the warlocks. "Sorry about that, *Jason*."

The more I thought of it, the more I believed this might not be a bad idea. This could be fun. I now officially reported to an angel. I grinned as I saluted my new boss, then disappeared with a bright, grayish flash. I realized too late that I should have spread my wings to add to the moment.

I landed in the Reverend's office, and a surge of power flowed over me. I had no idea of what happened until I caught sight of myself in a mirror. My eyes were no longer gray. They're off-white. On a hunch, I unfurled my wings. They were now pure white, but the tips still had stripes of red, dark gray and ended with black tips.

Staring at myself in the mirror, I smiled. I was now a full-fledge Heaven's angel. If Heaven was ready for me, I wasn't sure, but I was ready for a little heavenly fun.

There was definitely an upside to this. The rules about Cassi and I not cohabitating no longer applied.

Cassi, I'm coming. Start ordering replacement furniture now.

## ABOUT THE AUTHOR

Stone Keye lives in south Louisiana with his family and a menagerie of animals. He has spent his adult life in various roles in IT and continues to look for his next challenge. Meanwhile he enjoys spending time with his family, working his dogs and horses, and working on his house.